Praise for

'Paula Hawkins does it again! *Into the Water* is a moody and chilling thriller that will have you madly turning the pages. A gripping, compulsive read!'

SHARI LAPENA,
author of *The Couple Next Door*

'Paula Hawkins effortlessly follows the success of *The Girl on the Train* with this immersive novel . . . Told from multiple points of view, this is clever and twisty fiction with a ghostly edge.'

RED

'Hawkins should be congratulated, both for daring to try something new, and for doing it well.'

DAILY TELEGRAPH

'*Into the Water* is superb. Sinister layers, complex characters and a plot that'll keep you guessing.'

ALI LAND,
author of *Good Me, Bad Me*

'Fans of *The Girl on the Train* rejoice: *Into the Water* is even better. A brilliantly plotted and fast-paced juggernaut of a read that hurtles to a heart-stopping conclusion.'

GOOD HOUSEKEEPING (Book of the Month)

'Wondering if *Into the Water* could be as good as
The Girl on the Train? It's better. A triumph.'

CLARE MACKINTOSH,
author of *I Let You Go*

'A twisting whodunnit that leaves you both gratified
and surprised . . . Not just a brilliant thriller but also
a furious feminist howl.'

STYLIST

'*Into the Water* is dark, brooding and
mesmerising, and had me completely entranced.
It's a triumph of a novel.'

COLETTE MCBETH,
author of *The Life I Left Behind*

'A brooding and complex read that deserves
to make a splash in its own right.'

SUNDAY MIRROR

'The breathtaking follow-up to
The Girl on the Train, with Paula Hawkins at her best . . .
confident, ambitious and intriguing.'

SUNDAY EXPRESS

Praise for THE GIRL ON THE TRAIN

'My vote for unreliable narrator of the year.'
THE TIMES

'Really great suspense novel. Kept me up most of the night.
The alcoholic narrator is dead perfect.'
STEPHEN KING

'The thriller scene will have to up its game
if it's to match Hawkins.'
OBSERVER

'Gripping, enthralling –
a top-notch thriller and a compulsive read.'

**S J WATSON,
author of *Before I Go To Sleep***

'Nothing short of sensational.'
DAILY MAIL

'Alfred Hitchcock for a new generation and a new era.'

**TERRY HAYES,
author of *I Am Pilgrim***

'A cleverly crafted piece of modern suburban noir.'
INDEPENDENT ON SUNDAY

'It sucked up my entire afternoon.
I simply could not put it down.'

TESS GERRITSEN

Into the Water

Paula Hawkins

BLACK SWAN

TRANSWORLD PUBLISHERS
61–63 Uxbridge Road, London W5 5SA
www.penguin.co.uk

Transworld is part of the Penguin Random House group of companies
whose addresses can be found at global.penguinrandomhouse.com

Penguin
Random House
UK

First published in Great Britain in 2017 by Doubleday
an imprint of Transworld Publishers
Black Swan edition published 2018

Copyright © Paula Hawkins 2017

Paula Hawkins has asserted her right under the Copyright,
Designs and Patents Act 1988 to be identified as the author of this work.

This book is a work of fiction and any resemblance to actual persons,
living or dead, is purely coincidental.

Extract from 'The Numbers Game', *Dear Boy* © Emily Berry,
reprinted by permission of Faber & Faber.
Lyrics from 'Down By The Water' by PJ Harvey reproduced by kind
permission of Hot Head Music Ltd. All rights reserved.
Extract from *Hallucinations* © Oliver Sacks 2012, reproduced by
permission of Pan Macmillan via PLSclear.

Every effort has been made to obtain the necessary permissions with
reference to copyright material, both illustrative and quoted. We
apologize for any omissions in this respect and will be pleased to make
the appropriate acknowledgements in any future edition.

A CIP catalogue record for this book
is available from the British Library.

ISBN
9781784162245 (B format)
9781784163402 (A format)

Typeset in 11/14.5pt Giovanni Book by Falcon Oast Graphic Art Ltd.
Printed and bound by Clays Ltd, Elcograf S.p.A.

Penguin Random House is committed to a sustainable
future for our business, our readers and our planet. This book
is made from Forest Stewardship Council® certified paper.

MIX
Paper from
responsible sources
FSC® C018179

5 7 9 10 8 6 4

I was very young when I was cracked open.

Some things you should let go of
Others you shouldn't
Views differ as to which

'The Numbers Game', Emily Berry

We now know that memories are not fixed or
frozen, like Proust's jars of preserves in a
larder, but are transformed, disassembled,
reassembled, and recategorized with every act
of recollection.

Hallucinations, Oliver Sacks

The People of Beckford

Nel Abbott – *whose sudden death is where it all begins . . .*

Jules Abbott – Nel's estranged sister, forced to return to Beckford

Lena Abbott – Nel's teenage daughter, suddenly in the care of her aunt

Sean Townsend – Detective Inspector

Helen Townsend – Sean's wife, school headmistress

Patrick Townsend – Sean's father

Katie Whittaker – *Lena's best friend, drowned 2015*

Louise Whittaker – Katie's mother

Alec Whittaker – Katie's father

Josh Whittaker – Katie's brother

Mark Henderson – Katie and Lena's teacher

Erin Morgan – Detective Sergeant, new to Beckford

Nickie Sage – psychic and/or fraudster

And not forgetting:

Libby Seeton – *drowned 1679*

Anne Ward – *drowned 1920*

Lauren Slater – *drowned 1983*

And all the others who swam with their sisters . . .

The Drowning Pool

Libby

'Again! Again!'

The men bind her again. Different this time: left thumb to right toe, right thumb to left. The rope around her waist. This time, they carry her into the water.

'Please,' she starts to beg, because she's not sure that she can face it, the blackness and the cold. She wants to go back to a home that no longer exists, to a time when she and her aunt sat in front of the fire and told stories to one another. She wants to be in her bed in their cottage, she wants to be little again, to breathe in woodsmoke and rose and the sweet warmth of her aunt's skin.

'Please.'

She sinks. By the time they drag her out the second time, her lips are the blue of a bruise, and her breath is gone for good.

2015

Jules

THERE WAS SOMETHING you wanted to tell me, wasn't there? What was it you were trying to say? I feel like I drifted out of this conversation a long time ago. I stopped concentrating, I was thinking about something else, getting on with things, I wasn't listening, and I lost the thread of it. Well, you've got my attention now. Only I can't help thinking I've missed out on some of the more salient points.

When they came to tell me, I was angry. Relieved first, because when two police officers turn up on your doorstep just as you're looking for your train ticket, about to run out of the door to work, you fear the worst. I feared for the people I care about – my friends, my ex, the people I work with. But it wasn't about them, they said, it was about you. So I was relieved, just for a moment, and then they told me what had happened, what you'd done, they told me that you'd been in the water and then I was furious. Furious and afraid.

I was thinking about what I was going to say to you when I got there, how I knew you'd done this to spite me, to upset me, to frighten me, to disrupt my life. To get my attention, to drag me back to where you wanted me. And there you go, Nel, you've succeeded: here I am in the place I never wanted to come back to, to look after your daughter, to sort out your bloody mess.

MONDAY, 10 AUGUST

Josh

SOMETHING WOKE ME UP. I got out of bed to go to the toilet and I noticed Mum and Dad's door was open, and when I looked I could see that Mum wasn't in bed. Dad was snoring as usual. The clock radio said it was 4:08. I thought she must be downstairs. She has trouble sleeping. They both do now, but he takes pills which are so strong you could stand right by the bed and yell into his ear and he wouldn't wake up.

I went downstairs really quietly because usually what happens is she turns on the TV and watches those really boring adverts about machines that help you lose weight or clean the floor or chop vegetables in lots of different ways and then she falls asleep. But the TV wasn't on and she wasn't on the sofa, so I knew she must have gone out.

She's done it a few times – that I know of, at least. I can't keep track of where everyone is all the time. The first time, she told me she'd just gone out for a walk to clear her head, but there was another morning when I woke up and she was gone and when I looked out of the window I could see that her car wasn't parked out front where it usually is.

I think she probably goes to walk by the river or to visit Katie's grave. I do that sometimes, though not in the middle of the night. I'd be scared to go in the dark, plus it would make me feel weird because it's what Katie did herself: she got up in the middle of the night and went to the river and didn't come back. I understand why Mum does it though: it's the closest she can get to Katie now, other than maybe sitting in her room, which is something else I know she does sometimes. Katie's room is next to mine and I can hear Mum crying.

I sat down on the sofa to wait for her, but I must have fallen asleep, because when I heard the door go it was light outside and when I looked at the clock on the mantelpiece it was quarter past seven. I heard Mum closing the door behind her and then run straight up the stairs.

I followed her up. I stood outside the bedroom and watched through the crack in the door. She was on her knees next to the bed, over on Dad's side, and she was red in the face, like she'd been running. She was breathing hard and saying, 'Alec, wake up. Wake up,' and she was shaking him. 'Nel Abbott is dead,' she said. 'They found her in the water. She jumped.'

I don't remember saying anything but I must have made a noise because she looked up at me and scrambled to her feet.

'Oh, Josh,' she said, coming towards me, 'oh, Josh.'

There were tears running down her face and she hugged me hard. When I pulled away from her she was still crying, but she was smiling, too. 'Oh, darling,' she said.

Dad sat up in bed. He was rubbing his eyes. It takes him ages to wake up properly.

'I don't understand. When . . . do you mean last night? How do you know?'

'I went out to get milk,' she said. 'Everyone was talking about it . . . in the shop. They found her this morning.' She sat down on the bed and started crying again. Dad gave her a hug but he was watching me and he had an odd look on his face.

'Where did you go?' I asked her. 'Where have you been?'

'To the shops, Josh. I just said.'

You're lying, I wanted to say. *You've been gone hours, you didn't just go to get milk.* I wanted to say that, but I couldn't, because my parents were sitting on the bed looking at each other, and they looked happy.

TUESDAY, 11 AUGUST

Jules

I REMEMBER. ON the back seat of the camper van, pillows piled up in the centre to mark the border between your territory and mine, driving to Beckford for the summer, you fidgety and excited – you couldn't wait to get there – me green with carsickness, trying not to throw up.

It wasn't just that I remembered, I felt it. I felt that same sickness this afternoon, hunched up over the steering wheel like an old woman, driving fast and badly, swinging into the middle of the road on the corners, hitting the brake too sharply, over-correcting at the sight of oncoming cars. I had that thing, that feeling I get when I see a white van barrelling towards me along one of those narrow lanes and I think, *I'm going to swerve, I'm going to do it, I'm going to swing right into its path*, not because I want to but because I have to. As though at the last moment I'll lose all free will. It's like the feeling you get when you stand on the edge of a cliff, or on the edge of the train platform, and you feel yourself impelled by some invisible hand. And what if? What if I just took a step forward? What if I just turned the wheel?

(You and me not so different, after all.)

What struck me is how well I remembered. Too well. Why is it that I can recall so perfectly the things that happened to me when I was eight years old, and yet trying to remember whether or not I spoke to my colleagues about rescheduling a client assessment for next week is impossible? The things I want to remember I can't, and the things I try so hard to forget just keep coming. The nearer I got to Beckford, the more undeniable it became, the past shooting out at me like sparrows from the hedgerow, startling and inescapable.

All that lushness, that unbelievable green, the bright, acid yellow of the gorse on the hill, it burned into my brain and brought with it a newsreel of memories: Dad carrying me, squealing and squirming with delight, into the water when I was four or five years old; you jumping from the rocks into the river, climbing higher and higher each time. Picnics on the sandy bank by the pool, the taste of sunscreen on my tongue; catching fat brown fish in the sluggish, muddy water downstream from the Mill. You coming home with blood streaming down your leg after you misjudged one of those jumps, biting down on a tea towel while Dad cleaned the cut because you weren't going to cry. Not in front of me. Mum, wearing a light-blue sundress, barefoot in the kitchen making porridge for breakfast, the soles of her feet a dark, rusty brown. Dad sitting on the river bank, sketching. Later, when we were older, you in denim shorts with a bikini top under your T-shirt, sneaking out late to meet a boy. Not just any boy, *the* boy. Mum, thinner and frailer, sleeping in the armchair in the living room; Dad disappearing on long walks with the vicar's plump, pale, sun-hatted wife. I remember a game of football. Hot sun on the water, all eyes on me; blinking back tears, blood on my thigh, laughter ringing in my ears. I can still hear it. And underneath it all, the sound of rushing water.

I was so deep into that water that I didn't realize I'd arrived. I was there, in the heart of the town; it came on me suddenly as though I'd closed my eyes and been spirited to the place, and before I knew it I was driving slowly through narrow lanes lined with four-by-fours, a blur of rose stone at the edge of my vision, towards the church, towards the old bridge, careful now. I kept my eyes on the tarmac in front of me and tried not to look at the trees, at the river. Tried not to see, but couldn't help it.

I pulled over to the side of the road and turned off the engine. I looked up. There were the trees and the stone steps, green with moss and treacherous after the rain. My entire body goose-fleshed. I remembered this: freezing rain beating the tarmac, flashing blue lights vying with lightning to illuminate the river and the sky, clouds of breath in front of panicked faces, and a little boy, ghost-white and shaking, led up the steps to the road by a policewoman. She was clutching his hand and her eyes were wide and wild, her head twisting this way and that as she called out to someone. I can still feel what I felt that night, the terror and the fascination. I can still hear your words in my head: *What would it be like? Can you imagine? To watch your mother die?*

I looked away. I started the car and pulled back on to the road, drove over the bridge where the lane twists around. I watched for the turning – the first on the left? No, not that one, the second one. There it was, that old brown hulk of stone, the Mill House. A prickle over my skin, cold and damp, my heart beating dangerously fast, I steered the car through the open gate and into the driveway.

There was a man standing there, looking at his phone. A policeman in uniform. He stepped smartly towards the car and I wound down the window.

'I'm Jules,' I said. 'Jules Abbott? I'm . . . her sister.'

'Oh.' He looked embarrassed. 'Yes. Right. Of course. Look,' he glanced back at the house, 'there's no one here at the moment. The girl . . . your niece . . . she's out. I'm not exactly sure where . . .' He pulled the radio from his belt.

I opened the door and stepped out. 'All right if I go into the house?' I asked. I was looking up at the open window, what used to be your old room. I could see you there still, sitting on the window sill, feet dangling out. Dizzying.

The policeman looked uncertain. He turned away from me and said something quietly into his radio before turning back. 'Yes, it's all right. You can go in.'

I was blind walking up the steps, but I heard the water and I smelled the earth, the earth in the shadow of the house, underneath the trees, in the places untouched by sunlight, the acrid stink of rotting leaves, and the smell transported me back in time.

I pushed the front door open, half expecting to hear my mother's voice calling out from the kitchen. Without thinking, I knew that I'd have to shift the door with my hip, at the point where it sticks against the floor. I stepped into the hallway and closed the door behind me, my eyes struggling to focus in the gloom; I shivered at the sudden cold.

In the kitchen, an oak table was pushed up under the window. The same one? It looked similar, but it couldn't be, the place had changed hands too many times between then and now. I could find out for sure if I crawled underneath to search for the marks you and I left there, but just the thought of that made my pulse quicken.

I remember the way it got the sun in the morning, and how if you sat on the left-hand side, facing the Aga, you got a view of the old bridge, perfectly framed. So beautiful, everyone remarked upon the view, but they didn't really see. They never opened the window and leaned out, they never looked down at the wheel, rotting where it stood, they never looked past the sunlight playing on the water's surface, they never saw what the water really was, greenish-black and filled with living things and dying things.

Out of the kitchen, into the hall, past the stairs, deeper into the house. I came across it so suddenly it threw me, beside the enormous windows giving out on to the river – *into* the river, almost, as though if you opened them, water would pour in over the wide wooden window seat running along beneath.

I remember. All those summers, Mum and I sitting on that window seat propped up on pillows, feet up, toes almost touching, books on our knees. A plate of snacks somewhere, although she never touched them.

I couldn't look at it; it made me heartsick and desperate, seeing it again like that.

The plasterwork had been stripped back, exposing bare brick beneath, and the decor was all you: oriental carpets on the floor, heavy ebony furniture, big sofas and leather armchairs, and too many candles. And everywhere, the evidence of your obsessions: huge framed prints, Millais's *Ophelia*, beautiful and serene, eyes and mouth open, flowers clutched in her hand. Blake's *Triple Hecate*, Goya's *Witches' Sabbath*, his *Drowning Dog*. I hate that one most of all, the poor beast fighting to keep his head above a rising tide.

I could hear a phone ringing, and it seemed to come from beneath the house. I followed the sound through the living room and down some steps – I think there used to be a store room there, filled with junk. It flooded one year and everything was left coated in silt, as though the house were becoming part of the riverbed.

I stepped into what had become your studio. It was filled with camera equipment, screens, standard lamps and light boxes, a printer, papers and books and files piled up on the floor, filing cabinets ranged against the wall. And pictures, of course. Your photographs, covering every inch of the plaster. To the untrained eye, it might seem you were a fan of bridges: the Golden Gate, the Nanjing Yangtze River Bridge, the Prince Edward Viaduct. But look again. It's not about the bridges, it's not some love of these masterworks of engineering. Look again and you see it's not just bridges, it's Beachy Head, Aokigahara Forest, Preikestolen. The places where hopeless people go to end it all, cathedrals of despair.

Opposite the entrance, images of the Drowning Pool. Over and over and over, from every conceivable angle, every vantage point: pale and icy in winter, the cliff black and stark, or sparkling in the summer, an oasis, lush and green, or dull flinty-grey with storm clouds overhead, over and over and over. The images blurred into one; a dizzying assault on the eye. I felt as though I were *there*, in that place, as though I were standing at the top of the cliff looking down into the water, feeling that terrible thrill, the temptation of oblivion.

Nickie

SOME OF THEM went into the water willingly and some didn't, and if you asked Nickie – not that anyone would, because no one ever did – Nel Abbott went in fighting. But no one was going to ask her and no one was going to listen to her, so there really wasn't any point in her saying anything. Especially not to the police. Even if she hadn't had her troubles with them in the past, she couldn't speak to them about this. Too risky.

Nickie had a flat above the grocery shop, just one room really, with a galley kitchen and a bathroom so tiny it barely warranted the name. Not much to speak of, not much to show for a whole life, but she had a comfortable armchair by the window which looked out on the town, and that's where she sat and ate and even slept sometimes, because she hardly slept at all these days so there didn't seem much point going to bed.

She sat and watched all the comings and goings, and if she didn't see, she *felt*. Even before the lights had started flashing blue over on the bridge, she'd felt something. She didn't know it was Nel Abbott, not at first. People

17

think the sight's crystal clear, but it isn't as simple as all that. All she knew was that someone had gone swimming again. With the light off, she sat and watched: a man with his dogs came running up the stairs, then a car arrived; not a proper cop car, just a normal one, dark blue. Detective Inspector Sean Townsend, she thought, and she was right. He and the man with the dogs went back down the steps and then the whole cavalry came, with flashing lights but no sirens. No point. No hurry.

When the sun had come up yesterday she'd gone down for milk and the paper and everyone was talking, everyone was saying, another one, second this year, but when they said who it was, when they said it was Nel Abbott, Nickie knew the second wasn't like the first.

She had half a mind to go over to Sean Townsend and tell him then and there. But as nice and polite a young man as he was, he was still a copper, and his father's son, and he couldn't be trusted. Nickie wouldn't have considered it at all if she hadn't had a bit of a soft spot for Sean. He'd been through tragedy himself and God knows what after that, and he'd been kind to her – he'd been the only one to be kind to her, at the time of her own arrest.

Second arrest, if she was honest. It was a while back, six or seven years ago. She'd all but given up on the business after her first fraud conviction, she kept herself to just a few regulars and the witching lot who came by every now and then to pay their respects to Libby and May and all the women of the water. She did a bit of tarot reading, a couple of seances over the summer; occasionally she was asked to contact a relative, or one of the swimmers. But she hadn't been soliciting any business, not for a good long while.

But then they cut her benefits for the second time, so Nickie came out of semi-retirement. With the help of one of the lads who volunteered at the library, she set up a website offering readings at £15 for half an hour. Comparatively good value, too – that Susie Morgan from the TV, who was about as psychic as Nickie's arse, charged £29.99 for twenty minutes, and for that you didn't even get to speak to her, just to one of her 'psychic team'.

She'd only had the site up a few weeks when she found herself reported to the police by a trading standards officer for 'failing to provide the requisite disclaimers under Consumer Protection Regulations'. Consumer Protection Regulations! Nickie said she hadn't known that she needed to provide disclaimers; the police told her the law had changed. How, she'd asked, was she supposed to know that? And that caused much hilarity, of course. Thought you'd have seen it coming! Is it only the future you can look into, then? Not the past?

Only Detective Inspector Townsend – a mere constable back then – hadn't laughed. He'd been kind, had explained that it was all to do with new EU rules. EU rules! Consumer Protection! Time was, the likes of Nickie were prosecuted (*per*secuted) under the Witchcraft Act and the Fraudulent Mediums Act. Now they fell foul of European bureaucrats. How are the mighty fallen.

So Nickie shut down the website, swore off technology and went back to the old ways, but hardly anyone came these days.

The fact that it was Nel in the water had given her a bit of a turn, she had to admit. She felt bad. Not *guilty* as such, because it wasn't Nickie's fault. Still, she wondered whether she'd said too much, given too much away. But she couldn't be blamed for starting all this. Nel Abbott was already playing with fire – she was obsessed with the river and its secrets, and that kind of obsession never ends well. No, Nickie never told Nel to go looking for trouble, she only pointed her in the right direction. And it wasn't as though she didn't warn her, was it? The problem was, nobody listened. Nickie said there were men in that town who would damn you as soon as look at you, always had been. People turned a blind eye, though, didn't they? No one liked to think about the fact that the water in that river was infected with the blood and bile of persecuted women, unhappy women; they drank it every day.

Jules

You NEVER CHANGED. I should have known that. I *did*
know that. You loved the Mill House and the water and
you were obsessed with those women, what they did
and who they left behind. And now this. Honestly, Nel.
Did you really take it that far?

Upstairs, I hesitated outside the master bedroom.
My fingers on the door handle, I took a deep breath. I
knew what they had told me but I also knew you, and
I couldn't believe them. I felt sure that when I opened
the door, there you would be, tall and thin and not at
all pleased to see me.

The room was empty. It had the feeling of a place
just vacated, as though you'd just slipped out and run
downstairs to make a cup of coffee. As though you'd
be back any minute. I could still smell your perfume in
the air, something rich and sweet and old-fashioned,
like one of the ones Mum used to wear, Opium or
Yvresse.

'Nel?' I said your name softly, as if to conjure you up,
like a devil. Silence answered me.

21

Further down the hall was 'my room' – the one I used to sleep in: the smallest in the house, as befits the youngest. It looked even smaller than I remembered, darker, sadder. It was empty save for a single, unmade bed and it smelled of damp, like the earth. I never slept well in this room, I was never at ease. Not all that surprising, given how you liked to terrify me. Sitting on the other side of the wall, scratching at the plaster with your fingernails, painting symbols on the back of the door in blood-red nail polish, writing the names of dead women in the condensation on the window. And then there were all those stories you told, of witches dragged to the water, or desperate women flinging themselves from the cliffs to the rocks below, of a terrified little boy who hid in the wood and watched his mother jump to her death.

I don't *remember* that. Of course I don't. When I examine my memory of watching the little boy, it makes no sense: it is as disjointed as a dream. You whispering in my ear – that didn't happen on some freezing night at the water. We were never here in winter anyway, there were no freezing nights at the water. I never saw a frightened child on the bridge in the middle of the night – what would I, a tiny child myself, have been doing there? No, it was a story you told, how the boy crouched amongst the trees and looked up and saw her, her face as pale as her nightdress in the moonlight, how he looked up and saw her flinging herself, arms spread like wings, into the silent air, how the cry on her lips died as she hit the black water.

I don't even know whether there really *was* a boy who

saw his mother die, or whether you made the whole thing up.

I left my old room and turned to yours, the place which used to be yours, the place which, by the look of it, is now your daughter's. A chaotic mess of clothes and books, a damp towel lying on the floor, dirty mugs on the bedside table, a fug of stale smoke in the air and the cloying smell of rotting lilies, wilting in a vase next to the window.

Without thinking, I began to tidy up. I straightened the bedding and hung the towel on the rail in the en suite. I was on my knees, retrieving a dirty plate from under the bed, when I heard your voice, a dagger in my chest.

'What the fuck do you think you're doing?'

Jules

I SCRABBLED TO my feet, a triumphant smile on my lips, because I knew it – I knew they were wrong, I knew you weren't really gone. And there you stood in the doorway, telling me to get the FUCK out of your room. Sixteen, seventeen years old, hand around my wrist, painted nails digging into my flesh. *I said get OUT, Julia. Fat cow.*

The smile died, because of course it wasn't you at all, it was your daughter, who looks almost exactly like you did when you were a teenager. She stood in the doorway, hand on hip. 'What are you doing?' she asked again.

'I'm sorry,' I said. 'I'm Jules. We haven't met, but I'm your aunt.'

'I didn't ask who you were,' she said, looking at me as though I were stupid, 'I asked what you were doing. What are you looking for?' Her eyes slid away from my face and she glanced over towards the bathroom door. Before I could answer she said, 'The police are downstairs,' and she stalked off down the corridor, long legs, lazy gait, flip-flops slapping on the tiled floor.

I hurried after her.

'Lena,' I said, putting my hand on her arm. She yanked it away as though scalded, spinning round to glare at me. 'I'm sorry.'

She dipped her eyes, her fingers massaging the place where I'd touched her. Her nails bore traces of old blue polish, her fingertips looked as though they belonged to a corpse. She nodded, not meeting my eye. 'The police need to talk to you,' she said.

She's not what I expected. I suppose I imagined a child, distraught, desperate for comfort. But she isn't, of course, she's not a child, she's fifteen and almost grown, and as for seeking comfort – she didn't seem to need it at all, or at least, not from me. She is your daughter, after all.

The detectives were waiting in the kitchen, standing by the table, looking out towards the bridge. A tall man with a dusting of salt-and-pepper stubble on his face and a woman at his side, about a foot shorter than him.

The man stepped forward, his hand outstretched, pale-grey eyes intent on my face. 'Detective Inspector Sean Townsend,' he said. As he reached out, I noticed he had a slight tremor. His skin felt cold and papery against mine, as though it belonged to a much older man. 'I'm very sorry for your loss.'

So strange, hearing those words. They said them yesterday, when they came to tell me. I'd almost said them myself to Lena, but now it felt different. Your *loss*. I wanted to tell them, she isn't lost. She can't be. You don't know Nel, you don't know what she's like.

Detective Townsend was watching my face, waiting

for me to say something. He towered over me, thin and sharp-looking, as though if you got too close to him you might cut yourself. I was still looking at him when I realized that the woman was watching me, her face a study in sympathy.

'Detective Sergeant Erin Morgan,' she said. 'I'm very sorry.' She had olive skin, dark eyes, blue-black hair the colour of a crow's wing. She wore it scraped back from her face, but curls had escaped at her temple and behind her ears, giving her a look of dishevelment.

'DS Morgan will be your liaison with the police,' Detective Townsend said. 'She'll keep you informed about where we are in the investigation.'

'There's an investigation?' I asked dumbly.

The woman nodded and smiled and motioned for me to sit down at the kitchen table, which I did. The detectives sat opposite me. DI Townsend cast his eyes down and rubbed his right palm across his left wrist in quick, jerky motions: one, two, three.

DS Morgan was speaking to me, her calm and reassuring tone at odds with the words coming out of her mouth. 'Your sister's body was seen in the river by a man who was out walking his dogs early yesterday morning,' she said. A London accent, her voice soft as smoke. 'Preliminary evidence suggests she'd been in the water just a few hours.' She glanced at the DI and back at me. 'She was fully clothed, and her injuries were consistent with a fall from the cliff above the pool.'

'You think she *fell*?' I asked. I looked from the police detectives to Lena, who had followed me downstairs and was on the other side of the kitchen, leaning against the counter. Barefoot in black leggings, a grey vest stretched over sharp clavicles and tiny buds of breasts, she was ignoring us, as if this were normal, banal. As though it were an everyday occurrence. She clutched her phone in her right hand, scrolling down with her thumb, her left arm wrapped around her narrow body, her upper arm roughly the width of my wrist. A wide, sullen mouth, dark brows, dirty blonde hair falling into her face.

She must have felt me watching, because she raised her eyes to me and widened them for just a moment, so that I looked away. She spoke. '*You* don't think she fell, do you?' she said, her lip curling. 'You know better than that.'

Lena

THEY WERE ALL just staring at me and I wanted to yell at them, to tell them to get out of our house. *My* house. It is my house, it's ours, it'll never be hers. *Aunt Julia.* I found her in my room, going through my things before she's even met me. Then she tried to be nice and told me she was sorry, like I'm supposed to believe she even gives a shit.

I haven't slept for two days and I don't want to talk to her or to anyone else. And I don't want her help or her fucking condolences, and I don't want to listen to lame theories about what happened to my mum from people who *didn't even know her.*

I was trying to keep my mouth shut, but when they said how she probably fell I just got angry, because of course she didn't. She didn't. They don't understand. This wasn't some random accident, *she did this.* I mean, it's not like it matters now, I suppose, but I feel like everyone should at least admit the truth.

I told them: 'She didn't fall. She jumped.'

The woman detective started asking stupid questions

about why would I say that and was she depressed and had she ever tried it before, and all the time Aunt Julia was just staring at me with her sad brown eyes like I was some sort of freak.

I told them: 'You know she was obsessed with the pool, with everything that happened there, with everyone who died there. You know that. Even *she* knows that,' I said, looking at Julia.

She opened her mouth and closed it again, like a fish. Part of me wanted to tell them everything, part of me wanted to spell it out for them, but what would even be the point? I don't think they're capable of understanding.

Sean – *Detective Townsend*, as I'm supposed to call him when it's official business – started asking Julia questions: when did she speak to my mother last? What was her state of mind then? Was there anything bothering her? And Aunt Julia sat there and lied.

'I've not spoken to her in years,' she said, her face going bright red as she said it. 'We were estranged.'

She could see me looking and she knew I knew she was full of shit and she just went redder and redder, then she tried to turn the attention away from herself by speaking to me. 'Why, Lena, why would you say that she jumped?'

I looked at her for a long time before I answered. I wanted her to know that I saw through her. 'I'm surprised you ask me that,' I said. 'Wasn't it you who told her she had a death wish?'

She started shaking her head and saying, 'No, no, I didn't, not like that . . .' *Liar.*

The other detective – the woman – started talking

about how they had 'no evidence at this time to indicate that this was a deliberate act', and about how they hadn't found a note.

I had to laugh then. 'You think she'd leave a *note*? My mother wouldn't leave a fucking note. That would be, like, so prosaic.'

Julia nodded. 'That is . . . it's true. I can see Nel wanting everyone to wonder . . . She loved a mystery. And she would have loved to be the centre of one.'

I wanted to slap her then. *Stupid bitch*, I wanted to say, *this is your fault, too.*

The woman detective started fussing around, pouring glasses of water for everyone and trying to press one into my hand, and I just couldn't take it any longer. I knew I was going to start crying and I wasn't going to do it in front of them.

I went to my room and locked the door and cried there instead. I wrapped myself in a scarf and cried as quietly as I could. I've been trying not to give in to it, the urge to let myself go and fall apart, because I feel like once it starts it's never going to stop.

I've been trying not to let the words come, but they go round and round in my head: *I'm sorry I'm sorry I'm sorry, it was my fault.* I kept staring at my bedroom door and going over and over that moment on Sunday night when Mum came in to say goodnight. She said, 'No matter what, you know how much I love you, Lena, don't you?' I rolled over and put my headphones in, but I knew she was standing there, I could feel her standing and watching me, it's like I could feel her sadness and I was glad because I felt she deserved it. I would do anything, anything, to be able to get up and hug her and tell her I love her, too, and it wasn't her fault at all, I should never have said it was all her fault. If she was guilty of something, then so was I.

Mark

IT WAS THE HOTTEST day of the year so far and since the Drowning Pool was off limits, for obvious reasons, Mark went upriver to swim. There was a stretch in front of the Wards' cottage where the river widened, the water running quick and cool across rust-coloured pebbles at the edge, but in the centre it was deep, cold enough to snatch your breath from your lungs and make your skin burn, the kind of cold that made you laugh out loud with the shock of it.

And he did, he laughed out loud – it was the first time he'd felt like laughing in months. It was the first time he'd been in the water in months, too. The river for him had gone from a source of pleasure to a place of horror, but today it switched back again. Today it felt right. He had known from the moment he woke up, lighter, clearer of head, looser of limb, that today was a good day for a swim. Yesterday, they found Nel Abbott dead in the water. Today was a good day. He felt not so much that a burden had lifted but as though a vice – one which had been pressing against his temples, threatening his sanity, threatening his life – had at last been loosened.

A policewoman had come to the house, a very young detective constable with a sweet, slightly girlish quality to her that made him want to tell her things he really shouldn't. Callie Something, her name was. He invited her in and he told the truth. He said that he'd seen Nel Abbott leaving the pub on Sunday evening. He didn't mention that he'd gone there with the express intention of bumping into her, that wasn't important. He said that they'd spoken, but only briefly, because Nel had been in a hurry.

'What did you talk about?' the DC asked him.

'Her daughter, Lena, she's one of my pupils. I had a bit of trouble with her last term – discipline issues, that sort of thing. She's going to be in my English class again in September – it's an important year, her GCSE year – so I wanted to make sure that we weren't going to have any further problems.'

True enough.

'She said she didn't have time, that she had other things to do.'

True, too, though not the *whole truth*. Not *nothing but*.

'She didn't have time to discuss her daughter's problems at school?' the detective asked.

Mark shrugged and gave her a rueful smile. 'Some parents get more involved than others,' he said.

'When she left the pub, where did she go? Was she in her car?'

Mark shook his head. 'No, I think she was heading home. She was walking in that direction.'

The DC nodded. 'You didn't see her again after that?' she asked, and Mark shook his head.

So, some of it was true, some of it was a lie, but in any case the detective seemed satisfied; she left him a card with a number to call and said he should get in touch if he had anything to add.

'I'll do that,' he said, and he smiled his winning smile and she flinched. He wondered if he'd overdone it.

He ducked under the water now, diving down towards the riverbed, driving his fingers into the soft, silty mud. He curled his body into a tight ball and then with one explosive burst of power pushed himself back to the surface, gulping air into his lungs.

He'd miss the river, but he was ready to go now. He'd have to start looking for a new job, perhaps up in Scotland, or perhaps even further afield: France, or Italy, somewhere nobody knew where he had come from, or what had happened on the way. He dreamed of a clean slate, a blank sheet, an unblemished history.

As he struck out for the bank he felt the vice tighten a little once more. He wasn't out of the woods yet. Not yet. There was still the matter of the girl, she could still cause problems, although since she'd been quiet this long, it didn't seem likely that she'd break her silence now. You could say what you liked about Lena Abbott, but she was loyal; she kept her word. And perhaps now, freed from the toxic influence of her mother, she might even turn into a decent person.

He sat on the bank for a while, his head bowed, listening to the river's song, feeling the sun on his shoulders. His exhilaration evaporated along with the water on his back but left in its place something else, not hope exactly, but a quiet premonition that hope might at least be possible.

He heard a noise and looked up. Someone was coming. He recognized the shape of her, the agonizing slowness of her walk, and his heart beat harder in his chest. Louise.

Louise

THERE WAS A man sitting on the bank. She thought at first that he was naked, but when he stood she could see that he was wearing swimming trunks, short and tight and fitted. She felt herself noticing him, noticing his flesh, and she blushed. It was Mr Henderson.

By the time she reached him, he had wrapped a towel around his waist and pulled a T-shirt over his head. He walked towards her with his hand outstretched.

'Mrs Whittaker, how are you?'

'Louise,' she said. 'Please.'

He ducked his head, half smiled. 'Louise. How are you?'

She tried to smile back. 'You know.' He didn't know. No one knew. 'They tell you – *they*, listen to me! The *grief counsellors* tell you that you will have good days and bad, and you just have to deal with it.'

Mark nodded, but his eyes slid from hers and she saw colour rise to his cheeks. He was embarrassed.

Everyone was embarrassed. She had never realized before her life was torn apart how awkward grief was, how *inconvenient* for everyone with whom the mourner came into contact. At first, it was acknowledged and re-spected and deferred to. But after a while it got in the way – of conversation, of laughter, of normal life. Every-one wanted to put it behind them, to get on with things, and there you were, in the way, blocking the path, drag-ging the body of your dead child behind you.

'How's the water?' she asked, and his colour deep-ened. The water, the water, the water – no way to get away from it in this town. 'Cold,' she said, 'I imagine.'

He shook his head like a wet dog. *'Brrr!'* he said and laughed self-consciously.

In between them stood an elephant and she felt she ought to point it out.

'You heard about Lena's mother?' As if he wouldn't have. As if anyone could live in this town and not know.

'Yes. Terrible. God, it's terrible. Such a shock.' He fell silent, and when Louise did not respond, he kept talk-ing. 'Um . . . I mean, I know you and she . . .' He tailed off, looking over his shoulder at his car. He was desper-ate to get away, poor thing.

'Didn't exactly see eye to eye?' Louise offered. She toyed with the chain around her neck, pulling the charm, a bluebird, back and forth. 'No, we didn't. Even so . . .'

Even so was the best she could do. *Didn't see eye to eye* was a ludicrous understatement, but there was no need to spell it out. Mr Henderson knew about the bad blood, and she was damned if she was going to stand by the river and pretend she was unhappy that Nel Abbott had met her end in it. She couldn't, she didn't want to.

She knew when she listened to the grief counsellors

that they were talking nonsense and she would never, ever have another good day for the rest of her life, and yet there had been times over the past twenty-four hours or so when she had found it hard to keep the triumph from her face.

'I suppose, in a horrible way,' Mr Henderson was saying, 'it's oddly fitting, isn't it? The way she went . . .'

Louise nodded grimly. 'Perhaps it's what she would have wanted. Perhaps it's what she *did* want.'

Mark frowned. 'You think she . . . You think it was deliberate?'

Louise shook her head. 'I've really no idea.'

'No. No. Of course not.' He paused. 'At least . . . at least now, what she was writing won't be published, will it? The book she was working on about the pool – it wasn't finished, was it? So it can't be published . . .'

Louise skewered him with a look. 'You think so? I would have thought the manner of her death would make it all the more publishable. A woman writing a book about the people who died in the Drowning Pool becomes one of the drowned herself? I'd say someone would want to publish it.'

Mark looked horrified. 'But Lena . . . surely Lena . . . she wouldn't want that . . .'

Louise shrugged. 'Who knows?' she said. 'I assume she'll be the one receiving the royalties.' She sighed. 'I need to be getting back, Mr Henderson.' She patted him on the arm and he covered her hand with his own.

'I'm so very sorry, Mrs Whittaker,' he said, and she was touched to see that there were tears in the poor man's eyes.

'Louise,' she said. 'Call me Louise. And I know. I know you are.'

Louise started on her way home. It took her hours, this walk up and down the river path – even longer in this heat – but she could find no other way to fill her days. Not that there weren't things to do. There were estate agents to contact, schools to research. A bed that needed stripping and a wardrobe full of clothes that needed to be packed away. A child that needed parenting. Tomorrow, perhaps. Tomorrow she would do those things, but today she walked by the river and thought of her daughter.

Today she did as she did every day, she searched her useless memory for signs she must have missed, red flags she must have breezed blithely past. She searched for scraps, for hints of misery in her child's happy life. Because the truth is, they never worried about Katie. Katie was bright, capable, poised, with a will of steel. She swanned into adolescence as if it were a trifle, she took it in her stride: if anything, Louise felt sad sometimes that Katie hardly seemed to need her parents at all. Nothing fazed her – not her schoolwork, not the cloying attention of her needy best friend, not even her swift, almost shocking blossoming into adult beauty. Louise could remember acutely the sharp, affronted shame she had felt when she noticed men looking at *her* body when she was a teenager, but Katie showed none of that. Different times, Louise told herself, girls are different now.

Louise and her husband, Alec, didn't worry about

Katie, they worried about Josh. Always sensitive, always an anxious child, something had changed this year, something was bothering him; he'd become more withdrawn, more introverted, seemingly by the day. They worried about bullying, about his slipping grades, about the dark shadows under his eyes in the morning.

The truth is – the truth *must be* – that while they were watching their son, waiting for him to fall, their daughter tripped instead, and they didn't notice, they weren't there to catch her. The guilt felt like a stone in Louise's throat, she kept expecting it to choke her, but it didn't, it wouldn't, and so she had to go on breathing; breathing and remembering.

The night before, Katie was quiet. It was just the three of them for dinner because Josh was staying over at his friend Hugo's house. It wasn't usually allowed on school nights, but they'd made an exception because they were worried about him. They took the opportunity to talk to Katie about it. Had she noticed, they asked, how anxious Josh seemed of late?

'He's probably worrying about going to the big school next year,' she said, but she didn't look at her parents when she spoke, she kept her eyes on her plate, and her voice wavered ever so slightly.

'He'll be all right though,' Alec was saying. 'Half his class will be there. And you'll be there.'

Louise remembered her daughter's hand clenching a little tighter around her glass of water when Alec said this. She remembered her swallowing hard, closing her eyes for just a second.

They did the washing-up together, Louise washing

and Katie drying, because the dishwasher was broken. Louise remembered saying that it was all right, that she could do it herself if Katie had homework, and that Katie had said, 'It's all done.' Louise remembered that every time Katie took a dish from her to dry, she let her fingers brush against her mother's for just a moment longer than she needed to.

Except now Louise couldn't be sure whether she remembered those things at all. Did Katie lower her eyes, look down at her plate? Did she really grip her glass more tightly, or let her touch linger? It was impossible to tell now, all her recollections seemed open to doubt, to misinterpretation. She wasn't sure if this was down to the shock of realizing that all she had known was certain was not so sure at all, or whether her mind had been permanently fogged by the drugs she'd swallowed in the days and weeks after Katie died. Louise had gobbled pills upon pills, each handful offering hours of blank relief, only to be plunged freshly back into her nightmare on waking. After a while she came to grasp that the horror of rediscovering her daughter's absence, over and over again, was not worth the hours of oblivion.

Of this, she felt she could be sure: when Katie said goodnight, she smiled and kissed her mother the way she always did. She hugged her, no closer or longer than usual, and said, 'Sleep tight.'

And how could she have done that, knowing what she was going to do?

In front of Louise, the path blurred, her tears obscuring her vision, so she didn't notice the tape until she was upon it. *Police Line. Do Not Cross.* She was already halfway up the hill and was approaching the ridge; she had to take a sharp detour to the left so as not to disturb the last ground that Nel Abbott ever stood on.

She lumbered over the crest and down the side of the hill, her feet aching and her hair plastered to her scalp with sweat, down to the welcome shade where the path passed through a thicket of trees at the edge of the pool. A mile or so further along the path, she reached the bridge and climbed the steps to the road. A group of young girls was approaching from her left and she looked, as she always did, for her daughter amongst them, searching for her bright-chestnut head, listening for the rumble of her laugh. Louise's heart broke again.

She watched the girls, their arms draped around one another's shoulders as they clung to each other, an entwined mass of downy flesh, and at their centre, Louise realized, was Lena Abbott. Lena, so solitary these past few months, was having her moment of celebrity. She too would be gawped at and pitied and, before too long, shunned.

Louise turned away from the girls and started up the hill towards home. She hunched her shoulders and dropped her chin and hoped that she could shuffle off unnoticed, because looking at Lena Abbott was a terrible thing, it conjured terrible images in Louise's mind. But the girl had spotted her and cried out, 'Louise! Mrs Whittaker! Please wait.'

Louise tried to walk faster, but her legs were heavy and her heart was as deflated as an old balloon, and Lena was young and strong.

'Mrs Whittaker, I want to talk to you.'

'Not now, Lena. I'm sorry.'

Lena put her hand on Louise's arm, but Louise pulled away, she couldn't look at her. 'I'm very sorry. I can't talk to you now.'

Louise had become a monster, an empty creature who would not comfort a motherless child, who – worse, so much worse – could not look at that child without thinking, *Why not you? Why weren't you in the water, Lena? Why wasn't it you? Why my Katie? Kind and gentle and generous and hard-working and driven – better than you in every possible way. She should never have gone in. It should have been you.*

The Drowning Pool, Danielle Abbott (unpublished)

Prologue

WHEN I WAS *seventeen, I saved my sister from drowning.*

But that, believe it or not, is not where all this started.

There are people who are drawn to water, who retain some vestigial, primal sense of where it flows. I believe that I am one of them. I am most alive when I am near the water, when I am near this water. This is the place where I learned to swim, the place where I learned to inhabit nature and my body in the most joyous and pleasurable way.

Since I moved to Beckford in 2008, I have swum in the river almost every day, in winter and in summer, sometimes with my daughter and sometimes alone, and I have become fascinated by the idea that this place, my place of ecstasy, could be for others a place of dread and terror.

When I was seventeen, I saved my sister from drowning, but I had become obsessed with the Beckford pool long before that. My parents were storytellers, my mother especially; it was from her mouth that I first heard Libby's tragic story, of the shocking slaughter at the Wards' cottage, the terrible tale of the boy who watched his mother jump. I made her tell me, again and again. I remember my father's dismay ('These stories aren't really for children') and my mother's resistance ('Of course they are! They're history').

She sowed a seed in me, and long before my sister went into the water, long before I picked up a camera or set pen to paper, I spent hours daydreaming and imagining what it must have been like, what it must have felt like, how cold the water must have been for Libby that day.

As an adult, the mystery that has consumed me is, of course, that of my own family. It shouldn't be a mystery, but it is, because despite my efforts to build bridges, my sister has not spoken to me for many years. In the well of her silence, I have tried to imagine what drew her to the river in the dead of night, and even I, with my singular imagination, have failed. Because my sister was never the dramatic one, never the one for a bold gesture. She could be sly, cunning, as vengeful as the water itself, but I am still at a loss. I wonder if I always will be.

I decided, while in the process of trying to understand myself and my family and the stories we tell each other, that I would try to make sense of all the Beckford stories, that I would write down all the last moments, as I imagined them, in the lives of the women who went to the Beckford Drowning Pool.

Its name carries weight; and yet, what is it? A bend in the river, that's all. A meander. You'll find it if you follow the river in all its twists and turns, swelling and flooding, giving life and taking it, too. The river is by turns cold and clean, stagnant and polluted; it snakes through forest and cuts like steel through the soft Cheviot Hills, and then, just north of Beckford, it slows. It rests, just for a while, at the Drowning Pool.

This is an idyllic spot: oaks shade the path, beech and plane trees dot the hillsides, and there's a sloping sandy bank on the south side. A place to paddle, to take the kids; the perfect picnic spot for a sunny day.

But appearances are deceptive, for this is a deathly place. The water, dark and glassy, hides what lies beneath: weeds to entangle you, to drag you down, jagged rocks to slice through flesh. Above looms the grey slate cliff: a dare, a provocation.

This is the place that, over centuries, has claimed the lives of Libby Seeton, Mary Marsh, Anne Ward, Ginny Thomas, Lauren Slater, Katie Whittaker, and more – countless others, nameless and faceless. I wanted to ask why, and how, and what their lives and deaths tell us about ourselves. There are those who would rather not ask those questions, who would rather hush, suppress, silence. But I have never been one for quiet.

In this work, this memoir of my life and the Beckford pool, I wanted to start not with drowning, but with swimming. Because that is where it begins: with the swimming of witches – the ordeal by water. There, at my pool, that peaceful beauty spot not a mile from where I sit right now, was where they brought them and bound them and threw them into the river, to sink or to swim.

Some say the women left something of themselves in the water, some say it retains some of their power, for ever since then it has drawn to its shores the unlucky, the desperate, the unhappy, the lost. They come here to swim with their sisters.

Erin

It's a fucking weird place, Beckford. It's beautiful, quite breathtaking in parts, but it's strange. It feels like a place apart, disconnected from everything that surrounds it. Of course, it is miles from anywhere – you have to drive for hours to get anywhere civilized. That's if you consider Newcastle civilized, which I'm not sure I do. Beckford is a strange place, full of odd people, with a downright bizarre history. And all through the middle of it there's this river, and that's the weirdest thing of all – it seems like whichever way you turn, in whatever direction you go, somehow you always end up back at the river.

There's something a bit off about the DI, too. He's a local boy, so I suppose it's to be expected. I thought it the first time I laid eyes on him, yesterday morning when they pulled Nel Abbott's body out of the water. He was standing on the river bank, hands on hips, head bent. He was speaking to someone – the medical examiner, it turned out – but from a distance it looked as though he was praying. That's what I thought of – a priest. A tall, thin man in dark clothes, the black water as a backdrop, the slate cliff behind him, and at his feet a woman, pale and serene.

Not serene, of course, dead. But her face wasn't contorted, it wasn't ruined. If you didn't look at the rest of her, the broken limbs or the twist of her spine, you'd think she'd drowned.

I introduced myself and thought straight away there was something strange about him – his watery eyes, a slight tremor in his hands, which he tried to suppress by rubbing them together, palm against wrist – it made me think of my dad on those mornings-after-the-night-before when you needed to keep your voice and your head down.

Keeping my head down seemed like a good idea in any case. I'd been up north less than three weeks, after a hasty transfer from London thanks to an ill-advised relationship with a colleague. Honestly, all I wanted to do was work my cases and forget the whole mess. I was fully anticipating being thrown the boring stuff at first, so I was surprised when they wanted me on a suspicious death. A woman, her body spotted in a river by a man out walking his dogs. She was fully clothed, so she hadn't been swimming. The chief inspector set me straight. 'It'll almost certainly be a jumper,' he told me. 'She's in the Beckford Drowning Pool.'

It was one of the first things I asked DI Townsend. 'Did she jump, do you think?'

He looked at me for a moment, he *considered* me. Then he pointed to the clifftop. 'Let's go up there,' he said, 'find the scientific officer and see if they've discovered anything – evidence of a struggle, blood, a weapon. Her phone would be a good start, because she's not got it on her.'

'Right you are.' As I walked away, I glanced at the woman and thought how sad she looked, how plain and unadorned.

'Her name is Danielle Abbott,' Townsend said, his voice slightly raised. 'She lives locally. She's a writer and photographer, quite successful. She has a daughter, fifteen years old. So no, in answer to your question, I don't think it's likely that she jumped.'

We went up to the cliff together. You follow the path from the little beach along the side of the pool until it veers right, through a clump of trees, then it's a steep climb up the hill to the top of the ridge. The path was muddy in places – I could see where boots had slipped and skidded, erasing the traces of footprints laid before. At the top, the path turns sharply left and, emerging from the trees, leads right to the edge of a cliff. My stomach lurched.

'Jesus.'

Townsend glanced back over his shoulder. He looked almost amused. 'Scared of heights?'

'Perfectly reasonable fear of putting a foot wrong and falling to my death,' I said. 'You'd think they'd put a barrier up or something, wouldn't you? Not exactly safe, is it?'

The DI didn't answer, just continued on, walking purposefully towards the cliff edge. I followed, pressing myself against the gorse bushes to avoid looking over the sheer face to the water below.

The science officer – pale-faced and hairy, as they always seem to be – had little in the way of good news.

'No blood, no weapon, no obvious sign of a struggle,' he said with a shrug. 'Not even much in the way of fresh litter. Her camera's damaged though. And there's no SD card.'

'Her camera?'

Hairy turned to me. 'Would you believe it? She set up a motion-activated camera as part of this project she was working on.'

'Why?'

He shrugged. 'To film people up here . . . to see what they get up to? You get some weirdos hanging around sometimes, you know, because of the whole history of the place. Or maybe she wanted to catch a jumper in the act . . .' He grimaced.

'*Christ*. And someone's damaged her camera? Well, that's . . . inconvenient.'

He nodded.

Townsend sighed, folding his arms across his chest. 'Indeed. Although it doesn't necessarily mean anything. Her equipment's been vandalized before. Her project had its detractors locally. In fact,' he took a couple of steps closer to the edge of the cliff and I felt my head swim, 'I'm not even sure she replaced the camera after the last time.' He peered over the edge. 'There is another one, isn't there? Fixed somewhere below. Anything on that?'

'Yeah, it looks intact. We're going to bring it in, but . . .'

'It won't show anything.'

Hairy shrugged again. 'Might show her going in, but it won't tell us what happened up here.'

More than twenty-four hours had passed since then, and we seemed no closer to finding out what really had happened up there. Nel Abbott's phone hadn't shown up, which was odd, although perhaps not quite odd enough. If she'd jumped, there was a chance she might have disposed of it first. If she'd fallen, it might still be in the water somewhere, it might have sunk down into the mud or been washed away. If she was pushed, of course, whoever pushed her might have taken it off her first, but given the lack of any sign of a struggle up on the cliff, it didn't seem likely that someone had wrested it away from her.

I got lost on the way back from taking Jules (*NOT Julia*, apparently) to do the ID at the hospital. I dropped her back at the Mill House and I thought I was heading back towards the station when I found that I wasn't: after I crossed the bridge I'd somehow swung round and found myself back at the river again. Like I said, whichever way you turn. In any case, I had my phone out, trying to figure out where I was supposed to be going, when I spotted a group of girls walking over the bridge. Lena, a head taller than the others, broke away from them.

I abandoned the car and went after her. There was something I wanted to ask her, something her aunt had mentioned, but before I could reach her she'd started arguing with someone – a woman, perhaps in her forties. I saw Lena grab her arm, the woman pulling away and raising her hands to her face, as though afraid of being struck. Then they separated abruptly, Lena going left and the woman straight on up the hill. I followed Lena. She refused to tell me what it was all about. She insisted there was nothing wrong, that it hadn't been an argument at all, that it was none of my business anyway. A bravado performance, but her face was streaked with tears. I offered to see her home, but she told me to fuck off.

So I did. I drove back to the station and gave Townsend the low-down on Jules Abbott's formal identification of the body.

In keeping with the general theme, the ID was weird. 'She didn't cry,' I told the boss, and he made a kind of dipping motion with his head as though to say, *Well, that's normal.* 'It wasn't normal,' I insisted. 'This wasn't normal shock. It was really odd.'

He shifted in his seat. He was sitting behind a desk in a tiny office at the back of the station, and he seemed altogether too big for the room, as though if he stood up he might hit his head on the ceiling. 'Odd how?'

'It's hard to explain, but she seemed to be talking without making any sound. And I don't mean that kind of noiseless sobbing either. It was strange. Her lips were moving as though she was saying something . . . and not just saying something, but talking to someone. Having a conversation.'

'But you couldn't actually hear anything?'

'Nothing.'

He glanced at the laptop screen in front of him and then back at me. 'And that was it? Did she say anything to you? Anything else, anything useful?'

'She asked about a bracelet. Apparently Nel had a bracelet that belonged to their mother, which she wore all the time. Or at least, she wore it all the time when Jules last saw Nel, which was years ago.'

Townsend nodded, scratching at his wrist.

'There's no sign of one in her belongings, I checked. She was wearing a ring – no other jewellery.'

He fell silent for so long that I thought maybe the conversation was over. I was just about to leave the room when suddenly he said, 'You should ask Lena about that.'

'I was planning to,' I told him, 'only she wasn't all that interested in talking to me.' I filled him in on the encounter at the bridge.

'This woman,' he said. 'Describe her.'

So I did: early forties, slightly on the heavy side, dark hair, wearing a long red cardigan despite the heat.

Townsend studied me for a long time.

'Doesn't ring any bells then?' I asked.

'Oh yes,' he said, looking at me as though I was a particularly simple child. 'It's Louise Whittaker.'

'And she is?'

He frowned. 'Have you not seen any background on this?'

'I haven't, actually,' I said. I felt like pointing out that filling me in on any relevant background might be considered to be his job, since he was the local.

He sighed and began tapping at the keys of his computer. 'You should be up to speed with all this. You should have been given the files.' He smacked a particularly vicious return, as though he was banging keys on a typewriter rather than an expensive-looking Mac-Book. 'And you should also read through Nel Abbott's manuscript.' He looked up at me and frowned. 'The project she was working on? It was going to be a sort of coffee-table book, I think. Pictures and stories about Beckford.'

'A local history?'

He exhaled sharply. 'Of sorts. Nel Abbott's interpretation of events. Of selected events. Her . . . *spin* on things. As I mentioned, not something that many of the locals were keen on. We have copies, in any case, of what she'd written so far. One of the DCs will get you one. Ask Callie Buchan – you'll find her out front. The point is that one of the cases she wrote about was that of Katie Whittaker, who took her own life in June. Katie was a close friend of Lena Abbott's and Louise, her mother, was once friendly with Nel. They fell out, apparently over the focus of Nel's work, and then when Katie died . . .'

'Louise blamed her,' I said. 'She holds her responsible.'

He nodded. 'Yes, she does.'

'So I should go and talk to her then, this Louise?'

'No,' he replied. His eyes remained on the screen. 'I'll do it. I know her. I was the DI on the investigation into her daughter's death.'

He fell into another long silence. He hadn't dismissed me, so eventually I spoke. 'Was there ever any suspicion that there was anyone else involved in Katie's death?'

He shook his head. 'None. There didn't appear to be a clear reason, but as you well know there often isn't. Not one that makes sense to those left behind, in any case. But she did leave a note saying goodbye.' He passed his hand over his eyes. 'It was just a tragedy.'

'So two women have died in that river this year?' I said. 'Two women who knew each other, who were connected . . .' The DI said nothing, he didn't look at me, I wasn't even sure he was listening. 'How many have died there? I mean, in total?'

'Since when?' he asked, shaking his head again. 'How far back would you like to go?'

Like I said, fucking weird.

Jules

I'VE ALWAYS BEEN a little bit afraid of you. You knew that, you enjoyed my fear, enjoyed the power it gave you over me. So I think, despite the circumstances, you would have enjoyed this afternoon.

They asked me to do the identification – Lena volunteered, but they told her no, so I had to say yes. There was no one else. And although I didn't want to see you, I knew that I had to, because seeing you would be better than imagining you; the horrors conjured up by the mind are always so much worse than what *is*. And I needed to see you, because we both know that I wouldn't believe it, wouldn't be able to believe that you were gone, until I did.

You lay on a gurney in the middle of a cold room, a pale-green sheet covering your body. There was a young man there, dressed in scrubs, who nodded at me and at the detective, and she nodded back. As he reached out his hand to pull back the sheet I held my breath. I can't remember feeling that afraid since I was a child.

I was waiting for you to jump out at me.

You didn't. You were still and beautiful. There was always so much in your face – so much expression, joy or venom – and it was all still there, the traces of it; you were still you, still perfect, and then it struck me: you jumped.

You jumped?

You *jumped*?

That word, which felt wrong in my mouth. You wouldn't jump. You never would, that's not the way to do it. *You* told me that. The cliff's not high enough, you said. It's only fifty-five metres from the clifftop to the surface of the water – people can survive the fall. So, you said, if you mean it, if you really mean it, you need to make sure. Go in head first. If you mean it, you don't jump, you dive.

And unless you mean it, you said, why do it? Don't be a tourist. No one likes a tourist.

People can survive the fall, but that doesn't mean they will. Here you are, after all, and you didn't dive. You went in feet first and here you are: your legs are broken, your back is broken, you are broken. What does that mean, Nel? Does it mean that you lost your nerve? (Not like you at all.) Could you not bear it, the idea of going in head first, ruining your beautiful face? (You always were very vain.) It doesn't make sense to me. It's not like you to do what you said you wouldn't, to go against yourself.

(Lena said there's no mystery here, but what does she know?)

I took your hand and it felt alien in mine, not just because it was so cold, but because I didn't recognize the shape of it, the feel. When did I last hold your hand? Perhaps you reached for mine at Mum's funeral? I remember turning away from you, turning to Dad. I remember the look on your face. (What did you expect?) My heart turned wooden in my chest, its beat slowed to a mournful drum.

Someone spoke. 'Sorry, but you're not supposed to touch her.'

The light buzzed above my head, illuminating your skin, pale and grey against the steel beneath you. I placed my thumb upon your forehead, ran my finger along the side of your face.

'Please, don't touch her.' DS Morgan was standing just behind me. I could hear her breathing, slowly and evenly, above the sound of the buzzing lights.

'Where are her things?' I asked. 'The clothes she was wearing, her jewellery?'

'They'll be returned to you,' DS Morgan said, 'after Forensics have checked them over.'

'Was there a bracelet?' I asked her.

She shook her head. 'I don't know, but whatever she was wearing, it'll be returned to you.'

'There should be a bracelet,' I said quietly, looking down at Nel. 'A silver bracelet with a clasp made of onyx. It belonged to Mum, it was engraved with her initials. SJA. Sarah Jane. She wore it all the time. Mum did. And then you did.' The detective was staring at me. 'I mean, she did. I mean Nel did.'

I returned my gaze to you, to your slender wrist, to the place where the onyx clasp would have rested on blue veins. I wanted to touch you again, to feel your skin. I felt sure I could wake you up. I whispered your name and waited for you to quiver, for your eyes to flick open and follow me around the room. I thought perhaps that I should kiss you, if like Sleeping Beauty that might do the trick, and that made me smile because you'd hate that idea. You were never the princess, you were never the passive beauty waiting for a prince, you were something else. You sided with darkness, with the wicked stepmother, the bad fairy, the witch.

I felt the detective's eyes on me and I pursed my lips to suppress the smile. My eyes were dry and my throat empty, and when I whispered to you there seemed to be no sound at all.

'What did you want to tell me?'

Lena

IT SHOULD HAVE been me. I am her next of kin, her family. The person who loved her. It should have been me, but they wouldn't allow me to go. I was left alone, with nothing to do but sit in an empty house and smoke until I ran out of cigarettes. I went to the village shop to get some – the fat woman in there sometimes asks for ID but I knew she wouldn't today. I was just leaving when I saw those bitches from school – Tanya and Ellie and all that lot – coming down the road towards me.

I felt like I was going to be sick, I just put my head down and turned away and started walking as fast as I could, but they saw me, they called out and they all started running to catch up with me. I didn't know what they were going to do. Actually when they caught up they all started hugging me and saying how sorry they were and Ellie actually had the gall to cry some fucking fake tears. I let them hang all over me, let them put their arms around me and smooth back my hair. It actually felt good to be touched.

We walked over the bridge – they were talking about

going up to the Wards' cottage to take some pills and go swimming – 'It would be like a wake, kind of a cele- bration,' Tanya said. Fucking idiot. Did she honestly think I felt like getting monged and swimming in that water today? I was trying to think of what to say but then I saw Louise and it was like serendipity and I could just walk away from them without saying anything and there was nothing they could do.

At first I thought she hadn't heard me but when I caught up with her I could see she was crying and she didn't want to be near me. I grabbed hold of her. I don't know why, but I just wanted her to not walk away, to not leave me there with those vulture bitches watch- ing and pretending to be sad and all the while enjoying the fucking drama. She was trying to pull away, prising my fingers away one at a time, and she was saying, 'I'm sorry, Lena, I can't talk to you now. I can't talk to you.'

I wanted to say something to her, like: *You lost your daughter and I lost my mother. Doesn't that make us even? Can't you just forgive me now?*

I didn't, though, and then that clueless policewoman came along and tried to make out we were arguing, so I told her where to go, and I walked home alone.

I thought Julia would be back by the time I came home. How long would it take, really, to go to the morgue and watch them pull the sheet back and say, yes, that's her? It's not as though Julia would have wanted to sit with her, to hold her hand, to comfort her, like I would have done.

It should have been me, but they wouldn't let me go.

I lay on my bed in silence. I can't even listen to music

because I feel everything has this other meaning that I didn't see before and it hurts too fucking much to face it now. I don't want to cry all the time, it makes my chest hurt and my throat hurt, and the worst thing is that no one comes to help me. There's no one left to help me. So I lay on the bed and chain-smoked until I heard the front door go.

She didn't call out to me or anything like that, but I heard her in the kitchen, opening and closing cupboards, rattling pots and pans. I waited for her to come to me, but eventually I just got bored and I was feeling sick from smoking so much and was really, really hungry, so I went downstairs.

She was standing at the stove stirring something and when she turned round and saw me there she jumped. But it wasn't like how usually someone gives you a fright and then you laugh; the fear stayed in her face.

'Lena,' she said. 'Are you all right?'

'Did you see her?' I asked.

She nodded and looked at the floor. 'She looked . . . like herself.'

'That's good,' I said. 'I'm glad. I don't like to think of her . . .'

'No. No. And she wasn't. Broken.' She turned back to the hob. 'Do you like spaghetti bolognese?' she asked. 'I'm making . . . that's what I'm making.'

I do like it, but I didn't want to tell her that, so I didn't reply. Instead I asked her, 'Why did you lie to the police?'

She turned round sharply, the wooden spoon in her hand spraying red sauce on the floor.

'What do you mean, Lena? I didn't lie—'

'Yes, you did. You told them that you never speak to my mother, that you haven't had any contact in years—'

'We haven't.' Her face and neck were bright red, her mouth turned down like a clown's, and I saw it, the ugliness that Mum talked about. 'I haven't had any *meaningful* contact with Nel since—'

'She phoned you all the time.'

'Not *all the time*. Occasionally. And in any case, we didn't talk.'

'Yes, she told me that you refused to speak to her, no matter how hard she tried.'

'It's a bit more complicated than that, Lena.'

'How is it complicated?' I snapped. 'How?' She looked away from me. 'This is your fault, you know.'

She put the spoon down and took a couple of steps towards me, her hands on her hips, her expression all concerned, like a teacher who's about to tell you how *disappointed* they are with your attitude in class.

'What do you mean?' she asked. 'What's my fault?'

'She tried to contact you, she wanted to talk to you, she needed—'

'She didn't need me. Nel never needed me.'

'She was unhappy!' I said. 'Don't you even fucking care?'

She took a step back. She wiped her face as though I'd spat at her. 'Why was she unhappy? I don't . . . She never said she was unhappy. She never told me she was unhappy.'

'And what would you have done if she had? Nothing! You'd have done nothing, just like you always have

63

done. Just like when your mother died and you were horrible to her, or when she invited you to come here when we moved, or when she asked you to come that time for my birthday and you didn't even reply! You just ignored her, like she didn't exist. Even though you knew she didn't have anyone else, even though—'

'She had you,' Julia said. 'And I never suspected she was unhappy, I—'

'Well, she was. She didn't even swim any more.'

Julia stood very still, turning her head towards the window as though she were listening for something. 'What?' she asked, but she wasn't looking at me. It was like she was looking at someone else, or at her reflection. 'What did you say?'

'She stopped swimming. All my life I can remember her going to a pool or to the river, every single day, it was her thing, she was a swimmer. Every single day, even in winter here when it's fucking freezing and you have to break the ice on the surface. And then she stopped. Just like that. That's how unhappy she was.'

She didn't say anything for a bit, she just stood there, staring out of the window, as if she were looking for someone. 'Do you know . . . Lena, do you think she had upset someone? Or that someone was bothering her, or . . .?'

I shook my head. 'No. She would've told me.' She would have warned me.

'Would she?' Julia asked. 'Because, you know, Nel . . . your mum . . . she had a way about her, didn't she? I mean, she knew how to get under people's skin, how to piss them off—'

'No, she didn't!' I snapped, although it was true that sometimes she did, but only stupid people, only people who didn't understand her. 'You didn't know her at all, *you* didn't understand her. You're just a jealous bitch – you were back when you were young and you are now. Jesus. There's no point even talking to you.'

I left the house even though I was starving. Better to starve than to sit and eat with her, it would feel like a betrayal. I kept thinking about Mum sitting there, talking into the phone, and the silence on the other end. Cold bitch. I got annoyed with her about it once, said, Why don't you just give it a rest? Forget about her? She obviously wants nothing to do with us. Mum said, She's my sister, she's my only family. I said, What about me, I'm family. She laughed then and said, You're not family. You're *more* than family. You're part of me.

Part of me is gone, and I wasn't even allowed to see her. I wasn't allowed to squeeze her hand or kiss her goodbye or tell her how sorry I am.

Jules

I DIDN'T FOLLOW. I didn't actually *want* to catch up with Lena. I didn't know what I wanted. So I just stood there, on the front steps, my hands rubbing against my upper arms, my eyes gradually growing accustomed to the gathering dusk.

I knew what I didn't want: I didn't want to confront her, didn't want to hear any more. *My fault?* How could this be my fault? If you were unhappy, you never told me. If you had told me that, I would have listened. In my head, you laughed. OK, but if you'd told me you'd stopped swimming, Nel, then I would have known something was wrong. Swimming was essential to your sanity, that's what you told me; without it, you fell apart. Nothing kept you out of the water, just like nothing could draw me into it.

Except that something did. Something must have done.

I felt suddenly ravenous, had a violent urge to be sated, somehow. I went back inside and served myself a bowl of bolognese, and then another, and a third.

I ate and ate and then, disgusted with myself, I went upstairs.

On my knees in the bathroom, I left the light off. A habit long abandoned but so old it felt almost like comfort, I hunched over in the dark, the blood vessels in my face strained to bursting point, my eyes streaming as I purged. When I felt there was nothing left, I stood and flushed, then splashed water on my face, avoiding my own gaze in the mirror only to have it fall on the reflection of the bathtub behind me.

I have not sat immersed in water for more than twenty years. For weeks after my near-drowning, I found it difficult to wash properly at all. When I began to smell, my mother had to force me under the shower head and hold me there.

I closed my eyes and splashed my face again. I heard a car slowing in the lane outside, my heart rate rising as it did, and then falling once more as the car sped off. 'No one is coming,' I said out loud. 'There's nothing to be afraid of.'

Lena hadn't returned, yet I had no idea where to look for her in this town, at once familiar and foreign. I went to bed but didn't sleep. Each time I closed my eyes I saw your face, blue and pale, your lips lavender, and in my imagination they drew back over your gums and even though your mouth was full of blood, you smiled.

'*Stop it, Nel.*' I was speaking out loud again, like a madwoman. '*Just stop it.*'

I listened for your reply and all I got was silence; silence broken by the sound of the water, the noise of the house moving, shifting and creaking as the river pushed past. In the dark, I fumbled for my phone on the bedside table and dialled into my voicemail. *You have no new messages*, the electronic voice told me, *and seven saved messages.*

The most recent one came last Tuesday, less than a week before you died, at one thirty in the morning.

Julia, it's me. I need you to call me back. Please, Julia. It's important. I need you to call me, as soon as you can, all right? I . . . uh . . . it's important. OK. Bye.

I pressed 1 to repeat the message, again and again. I listened to your voice, not just the huskiness, the faint but irritating mid-Atlanticism of the pronunciation, I listened to *you*. What were you trying to tell me?

You left the message in the middle of the night and I picked it up in the early hours of the morning, rolling over in bed to see the tell-tale white flash on my phone. I listened to your first three words, *Julia, it's me*, and hung up. I was tired and I was feeling low and I didn't want to hear your voice. I listened to the rest of it later. I didn't find it strange and I didn't find it particularly intriguing. It's the sort of thing you do: leave cryptic messages in order to pique my interest. You've been doing it for years, and then when you call again, a month or two later, I realize that there was no crisis, no mystery, no big event. You were just trying to get my attention. It was a game.

Wasn't it?

I listened to the message, over and over, and now that I was hearing it properly I couldn't believe I hadn't noticed before the slight breathlessness of your delivery, the uncharacteristic softness of your speech, hesitant, faltering.

You were afraid.

What were you afraid of? *Who* were you afraid of? The people in this village, the ones who stop and stare but offer no condolences, the ones who bring no food, send no flowers? It doesn't seem, Nel, that you are much missed. Or maybe you were afraid of your strange, cold, angry daughter, who doesn't weep for you, who insists that you killed yourself, without evidence, without reason.

I got out of bed and crept next door to your bedroom. I felt suddenly childlike. I used to do this – creep next door – when my parents slept here, when I was afraid at night, when I'd had nightmares after listening to one of your stories. I pushed the door open and slipped inside.

The room felt stuffy, warm, and the sight of your unmade bed brought me suddenly to tears.

I perched on the edge of it, picked up your pillow, crisp slate-grey linen with blood-red edging, and held it against me. I had the clearest memory of the two of us coming in here on Mum's birthday. We'd made breakfast for her, she was ill then and we were making an effort, trying to get along. Those truces never lasted long: you tired of having me around, I never failed to lose your attention. I'd drift back to Mum's side and you would watch through narrowed eyes, contemptuous and hurt at the same time.

I didn't understand you, but if you were strange to me then, you are utterly alien now. Now I'm sitting here in your home, amongst your things, and it is the house that is familiar, not you. I haven't known you since we were teenagers, since you were seventeen and I thirteen.

Since that night when, like an axe swung down on to a piece of wood, circumstance cleaved us, leaving a fissure wide and deep.

But it wasn't until six years later that you lowered that axe again and split us for good. It was at the wake. Our mother just buried, you and me smoking in the garden on a freezing November night. I was struck dumb with grief, but you'd been self-medicating since breakfast and you wanted to talk. You were telling me about a trip you were going to take, to Norway, to the Pulpit Rock, a six-hundred-metre cliff above a fjord. I was trying not to listen, because I knew what it was and I didn't want to hear about it. Someone – a friend of our father's – called out to us, 'You girls all right out there?' His words were slightly slurred. 'Drowning your sorrows?'

'Drowning, drowning, drowning . . .' you repeated. You were drunk too. You looked at me from under hooded eyelids, a strange light in your eyes. 'Ju-ulia,' you said, slowly dragging out my name, 'do you ever think about it?'

You put your hand on my arm and I pulled it away. 'Think about what?' I was getting to my feet, I didn't want to be with you any longer, I wanted to be alone.

'That night. Do you . . . have you ever talked to anyone about it?'

I took a step away from you but you grabbed my hand and squeezed it hard. 'Come on, Julia . . . Tell me honestly. Wasn't there some part of you that liked it?'

After that, I stopped speaking to you. That, according to your daughter, was *me* being horrible to *you*. We tell our stories differently, don't we, you and I?

I stopped talking to you, but that didn't stop you from calling. You left strange little messages, telling me about your work or your daughter, an award you had won, an accolade received. You never said where you were or who you were with, although sometimes I heard noises in the background, music or traffic, sometimes voices. Sometimes I deleted the messages and sometimes I saved them. Sometimes I listened to them over and over, so many times that even years later I could remember your exact words.

Sometimes you were cryptic, other times angry; you repeated old insults, you dredged up long-submerged disagreements, railed against old slurs. The death wish! Once, in the heat of the moment, tired of your morbid obsessions, I'd accused you of having a death wish, and oh, how you harped on about that!

Sometimes you were maudlin, talking about our mother, our childhood, happiness had and lost. Other times you were up, happy, hyper. *Come to the Mill House!* you entreated me. *Please come! You'll love it. Please, Julia, it's time we put all that stuff behind us. Don't be stubborn. It's time.* And then I'd be furious – *It's time!* Why should *you* get to choose when to call time on the trouble be-tween us?

All I wanted was to be left alone, to forget Beckford, to forget you. I built a life for myself – smaller than yours, of course, how could it not be? But mine. Good friends, relationships, a tiny flat in a lovely suburb of north London. A job in social work which gave me purpose; a job which consumed me and fulfilled me, despite its low pay and long hours.

I wanted to be left alone, but you wouldn't have it. Sometimes twice a year and sometimes twice a month, you called: disrupting, destabilizing, unsettling me. Just like you'd always done – it was a grown-up version of all the games you used to play. And all the time I waited, I waited for the one call I might actually respond to, the one where you would explain how it was that you behaved the way you did when we were young, how you could have hurt me, stood by while I was being hurt. Part of me wanted to have a conversation with you, but not before you told me that you were sorry, not before you begged for my forgiveness. But your apology never came, and I'm still waiting.

I pulled open the top drawer of the bedside table. There were postcards, blank ones – pictures of places you'd been, perhaps – condoms, lubricant, an old-fashioned silver cigarette lighter with the initials *LS* engraved on the side. *LS*. A lover? I looked around the room again and it struck me that there were no pictures of men in this house. Not up here, not downstairs. Even the paintings are almost all of women. And when you left your messages you talked of your work and the house and Lena, but you never mentioned a man. Men never seemed that important to you.

There was one though, wasn't there? A long time ago, there was a boy who was important to you. When you were a teenager, you used to sneak out of the house at night, you'd climb out of the laundry window, drop down on to the river bank and creep around the house, up to your ankles in mud. You'd scramble up the bank and on to the lane, and he'd be waiting for you. Robbie.

Thinking of Robbie, of you and Robbie, was like going over the humpback bridge at speed: dizzying. Robbie was tall, broad and blond, his lip curled into a perpetual sneer. He had a way of looking at a girl that turned her inside out. Robbie Cannon. The alpha, the top dog, always smelling of Lynx and sex, brutish and mean. You loved him, you said, although it never looked much like love to me. You and he were either all over each other or throwing insults at each other, never anything in between. There was never any peace. I don't remember a lot of laughter. But I did have the clearest memory of you both lying on the bank at the pool, limbs entangled, feet in the water, him rolling over you, pushing your shoulders down into the sand.

Something about that image jarred, made me feel something I hadn't felt in a while. Shame. The dirty, secret shame of the voyeur, tinged with something else, something I couldn't quite put my finger on and didn't want to. I tried to turn away from it but I remembered: that wasn't the only time I'd watched him with you.

I felt suddenly uncomfortable so I got up from your bed and paced around the room, looking at the photos. Pictures everywhere. Of course. Framed pictures of you on the chest of drawers, tanned and smiling, in Tokyo and Buenos Aires, on skiing holidays and on beaches, with your daughter in your arms. On the walls, framed prints of magazine covers you shot, a story on the front page of the *New York Times*, the awards you received. Here it is: all the evidence of your success, the proof that you outdid me in everything. Work, beauty, children, life. And now you've outdone me again. Even in this, you win.

One picture stopped me in my tracks. It was a photo of you and Lena – not a baby any longer, a little girl, maybe five or six years old, or maybe older, I can never tell children's ages. She's smiling, showing tiny white teeth, and there's something strange about it, something that made my hair stand up on end; something about her eyes, the set of her face, gives her the look of a predator.

I could feel a pulse in my neck, an old fear rising. I lay back down on the bed and tried not to listen to the water, but even with the windows shut, at the top of the house, the sound was inescapable. I could feel it pushing against the walls, seeping into the cracks of the brickwork, rising. I could taste it, muddy and dirty in my mouth, and my skin felt damp.

Somewhere in the house, I could hear someone laughing, and it sounded just like you.

AUGUST 1993

Jules

MUM BOUGHT ME a new swimming costume, an old-fashioned one in blue-and-white gingham with 'support'. It was supposed to have a kind of 1950s look to it, the sort of thing Marilyn might have worn. Fat and pale, I was no Norma Jean, but I put it on anyway because she'd gone to a lot of trouble to find it. It wasn't easy finding swimwear for someone like me.

I put on a pair of blue shorts and an extra-large white T-shirt over the top. When Nel came down for lunch in her denim cut-offs and a halter-neck bikini, she took one look at me and said, 'Are you coming to the river this afternoon?' in a tone which made it obvious that she didn't want me to, and then she caught Mum's eye and said, 'I'm not looking after her, OK? I'm going there to meet my friends.'

Mum said, 'Be nice, Nel.'

Mum was in remission then, so frail a stiff breeze might knock her over, her olive skin yellowed, like old paper, and Nel and I were under strict instructions from our father to Get Along.

Part of Getting Along meant Joining In and so yes, I was going to the river. Everyone went to the river. It was all there was to do, really. Beckford wasn't like the beach, there was no funfair, no games arcade, not so much as a mini-golf course. There was the water: that was it.

A few weeks into the summer, once routines were established, once everyone had figured out where they belonged and who they belonged with, once outsiders and locals had mingled, friendships and enmities established, people started hanging out in groups along the river bank. The younger kids tended to swim south of the Mill House, where the water moved slowly and there were fish to catch. The bad kids hung out at the Wards' cottage, where they took drugs and had sex, played with Ouija boards and tried to conjure up angry spirits. (Nel told me that if you looked hard enough, you could still find traces of Robert Ward's blood on the walls.) But the biggest crowd gathered at the Drowning Pool. The boys jumped off the rocks and the girls sunbathed, music played and barbecues were lit. Someone always brought beer.

I would have preferred to stay at home, indoors, out of the sun. I'd have preferred to lie on my bed and read, or play cards with Mum, but I didn't want her to worry about me, she had more important things to worry about. I wanted to show her I could be sociable, I could make friends. I could Join In.

I knew Nel wouldn't want me to go. As far as she was

concerned, the more time I spent inside, the better, and the less likely it would be that her friends would see me – the blob, the embarrassment: *Julia*, fat, ugly and uncool. She squirmed in my company, always walking a few paces ahead or lagging ten behind; her discomfort around me was obvious enough to attract attention. Once, when the two of us left the village shop together, I heard one of the local boys talking. 'She *must* be adopted. There's no way that fat bitch is Nel Abbott's real sister.' They laughed, and I looked to her for comfort, but all I saw was shame.

That day, I walked to the river alone. I carried a bag containing a towel and a book, a can of Diet Coke and two Snickers, in case I got hungry between lunch and dinner. My stomach ached and my back hurt. I wanted to turn back, to return to the privacy of my small, cool, dark room, where I could be alone. Unseen.

Nel's friends arrived soon after I did; they colonized the beach, the little crescent of sandy bank on the nearside of the pool. It was the nicest place to sit, sloping down so that you could lie with your toes in the water. There were three girls – two locals and a girl called Jenny who came from Edinburgh and had gorgeous ivory skin and dark hair in a blunt-cut bob. Although she was Scottish she spoke the Queen's English and the boys were desperately trying to get off with her because rumour had it she was still a virgin.

All the boys except Robbie, of course, who only had eyes for Nel. They'd met two years before, when he was seventeen and she was fifteen, and they were a regular summer thing now, even though they were allowed to see other people the rest of the year because it wasn't realistic to expect him to be faithful when she wasn't around. Robbie was six foot one, he was handsome and popular, he played a lot of rugby, his family had money.

When Nel had been with Robbie, she sometimes came back with bruises on her wrists or the top of her arms. When I asked her how that happened, she laughed and said, 'How do you think?' Robbie gave me a weird feeling in my stomach and I couldn't help but stare at him whenever he was around. I tried not to, but I kept looking at him. He'd noticed it now and he'd started to stare back. He and Nel made jokes about it, and sometimes he'd look at me and lick his lips and laugh.

The boys were there too, but they were over on the other side, swimming, climbing up the bank, shoving each other off the rocks, laughing and swearing and calling each other gay. That's the way it always seemed to be: the girls would sit and wait and the boys would mess around until they got bored and then they'd come over and do things to the girls, which the girls sometimes resisted and sometimes didn't. All the girls except Nel, who wasn't afraid of diving into the water and getting her hair wet, who relished the rough and tumble of their games, who managed to walk the tightrope between being one of the boys and the ultimate object of their desire.

I didn't sit with Nel's friends, of course. I laid out my towel under the trees and sat down alone. There was another group of younger girls, around my age, sitting a little way off and one of them was a girl I recognized from summers past. She smiled at me and I smiled back. I gave her a little wave, but she looked away.

It was hot. I longed, then, to go into the water. I could imagine exactly what it would feel like on my skin, smooth and clean, I could imagine the squelch of warm mud between my toes, I could see the warm orange light on my eyelids as I lay back to float. I took my T-shirt off, but that didn't make me any cooler. I noticed that Jenny was watching me and she wrinkled her nose and then looked down at the ground because she knew that I'd clocked the disgust on her face.

I turned away from them all, lay on my right-hand side and opened my book. I was reading *The Secret History*. I longed for a group of friends like that, tightly knit and closed off and brilliant. I wanted someone to follow, someone who would protect me, someone remarkable for her brain, not her long legs. Though I knew that if there were people like that round here or at my school in London, they wouldn't want to be friends with me. I wasn't stupid, but I didn't shine.

Nel shone.

She came down to the river sometime in mid afternoon. I heard her calling out to her friends, and the boys calling back to her from the top of the cliff where they were sitting, legs dangling over the edge, smoking cigarettes. I looked over my shoulder, watching as she stripped off and waded slowly into the water, splashing it up against her body, enjoying the attention.

The boys were coming down off the clifftop now, through the wood. I rolled on to my stomach, keeping my head down, eyes fixed firmly on the page, the words a blur. I wished I hadn't come, wished I could slink away unnoticed, but there was nothing I could do unnoticed, literally nothing. My shapeless white bulk didn't slink anywhere.

The boys had a football, and they started to have a kickabout. I could hear them calling for passes, the ball slapping against the surface of the water, shrieks of laughter from the girls as they got splashed. Then I felt it, a stinging smack against my thigh as the ball hit me. They were all laughing. Robbie held his hand up and ran towards me to get the ball.

'Sorry, sorry,' he was saying, a wide grin on his face. 'Sorry, Julia, didn't mean to hit you.' He picked up the ball and I saw him looking at me, at the red, muddy mark on my flesh, pale and marbled like cold animal fat. Someone said something about a big target, yeah, you couldn't hit a barn door but you can't miss that arse.

I went back to my book. The ball hit a tree just a few feet away from me, and someone called out, 'Sorry.' I ignored them. It happened again, and then again. I rolled over; they were aiming at me. Target practice. The girls were doubled up, helpless with laughter, Nel's shrieks of mirth loudest of all.

I sat up, tried to brazen it out. 'Yeah, *OK*. Very funny. You can stop now. Come on! Stop it,' I called out, but another one was taking aim. The ball came towards me. I lifted my arm to protect my face and the ball slapped against my flesh, a hard, stinging blow. Tears pricking the backs of my eyes, I scrabbled to my feet. The other girls, the younger ones, were watching too. One of them had her hand over her mouth.

'Stop it!' she shouted out. 'You've hurt her. She's bleeding.'

I looked down. There was blood on my leg, trickling down the inside of my thigh towards my knee. It wasn't that, I knew right away, they hadn't hurt me. The stomach cramps, the backache – and I'd been feeling more miserable than usual all week. I was bleeding properly, heavily, not just spotting – my shorts were soaked through. And they were looking at me, all of them, staring at me. The girls weren't laughing any longer, they glanced at each other open-mouthed, halfway between horror and amusement. I caught Nel's eye and she looked away, I could almost feel her cringing. She was mortified. She was ashamed of me. I pulled my T-shirt on as quickly as I could, wrapped my towel around my waist and hobbled awkwardly away, back along the path. I could hear the boys starting to laugh again as I left.

That night, I went into the water. It was later – much, much later – and I'd been drinking, my first ever experience of alcohol. Other things had happened, too. Robbie came to find me, he sought me out, he apologized for the way he and his friends had behaved. He told me how sorry he was, he put his arm around my shoulders, he told me I needn't feel ashamed.

But I went to the Drowning Pool anyway, and Nel dragged me out. She pulled me to the bank and hauled me to my feet. She slapped my face hard. 'You bitch, you stupid fat bitch, what have you done? What are you trying to do?'

2015

WEDNESDAY, 12 AUGUST

Patrick

THE WARDS' COTTAGE hadn't belonged to the Wards in almost a hundred years, and it didn't belong to Patrick either – it didn't really seem to belong to anyone any more. Patrick supposed that it probably belonged to the local council, though no one had ever laid claim to it. But in any case, Patrick had a key, so that made him feel proprietorial. He paid the small electric and water bills, and he'd fitted the lock himself some years back after the old door had been smashed down by yobs. Now only he and his son, Sean, had keys, and Patrick saw to it that the place was kept clean and tidy.

Only sometimes the door was left unlocked and, if he was perfectly honest, Patrick could no longer be certain he had locked it. He'd begun to feel, more and more over the past year, moments of confusion which filled him with a dread so cold he refused to face it.

Sometimes he lost words or names and it took him a long time to find them again. Old memories resurfaced to breach the peace of his thoughts, and these were fiercely colourful, disturbingly loud. Around the edges of his vision, shadows moved.

Patrick headed upriver every day, it was part of his routine: up early, walk the three miles along the river to the cottage, sometimes he'd fish for an hour or two. He did that less these days. It wasn't just that he was tired, or that his legs ached, it was the will that was lacking. He didn't derive pleasure from the things he'd once enjoyed. He still liked to check up on things though, and when his legs were feeling good he could still manage the walk there and back in a couple of hours. This morning, however, he'd woken with his left calf swollen and painful, the dull throb in his vein persistent as a ticking clock. So he decided to take the car.

He hauled himself out of bed, showered, dressed, and then remembered with a snap of irritation that his car was still at the garage – he'd clean forgotten to pick it up the previous afternoon. Muttering to himself, he hobbled across the courtyard to ask his daughter-in-law if he could borrow hers.

Sean's wife, Helen, was in the kitchen, mopping the floor. In term time, she'd be gone by now – she was head teacher at the school and made a point of being in her office by seven thirty every morning. But even in the school holidays, she wasn't one for a lie-in. It wasn't in her nature to be idle.

'Up and about early,' Patrick said as he entered the kitchen, and she smiled. With lines crinkling around her eyes and streaks of grey in her short brown hair, Helen looked older than her thirty-six years. Older, Patrick thought, and more tired than she should be.

'Couldn't sleep,' she said.

'Oh, sorry, love.'

She shrugged. 'What can you do?' She put the mop into the bucket and propped it upright against the wall. 'Can I make you some coffee, Dad?' That's what she called him now. It had felt strange at first, but now he liked it; it warmed him, the affection in her voice as she sounded the word. He said he'd take some coffee in a flask, explaining that he wanted to go upriver. 'You won't be anywhere near the pool, will you? Only I think . . .'

He shook his head. 'No. Of course not.' He paused. 'How's Sean getting on with all that?'

She shrugged again. 'You know. He doesn't really say.'

Sean and Helen lived in the home that Patrick had once shared with his wife. After she died, Sean and Patrick had lived there together. Much later, after Sean's marriage, they converted the old barn just across the courtyard and Patrick moved out. Sean protested, saying he and Helen should be the ones to move, but Patrick wouldn't hear of it. He wanted them there, he liked the sense of continuity, the sense of the three of them being their own little community, part of the town and yet apart from it.

When he reached the cottage, Patrick saw right away that someone had been there. The curtains were drawn and the front door was slightly ajar. Inside, he found the bed unmade. Wine-stained glasses stood empty on the floor and a condom floated in the toilet bowl. There were cigarette butts in an ashtray, roll-ups. He picked one up and sniffed it, searching for the scent of marijuana, but smelling only cold ash. There were other things there, too, bits of clothing and assorted junk – an odd blue sock, a string of beads. He gathered everything up and shoved it into a plastic bag. He stripped the sheets from the bed, washed the glasses in the sink, threw the cigarette butts into the dustbin and carefully locked the door behind him. He carried everything out to the car, dumping the sheets on the back seat, the rubbish in the boot and the assorted debris in the glove compartment.

He locked the car and walked to the river's edge, lighting a cigarette on the way. His leg ached and his chest tightened as he inhaled, the hot smoke hitting the back of his throat. He coughed, imagining he could feel the acrid scrape against tired and blackened lungs. He felt suddenly very sad. These moods took him from time to time, seized him with such a force that he found himself wishing it was all over. All of it. He looked at the water and sniffed. He'd never be one of those who gave in to the temptation to submit, to submerge themselves, to make it all go away, but he was honest enough to admit that sometimes even he could see the appeal of oblivion.

By the time he got back to the house it was mid morning, the sun high in the sky. Patrick spotted the tabby, the stray that Helen had been feeding, moving lazily across the courtyard, heading for the rosemary bush in the bed outside the kitchen window. Patrick

THURSDAY, 13 AUGUST

Erin

MY SHITTY NEIGHBOURS in my shitty short-let flat in Newcastle were having the mother of all arguments at four o'clock this morning, so I decided to get up and go for a run. I was all dressed and ready and then I thought, why run here when I could run there? So I drove to Beckford, parked outside the church and headed off up the river path.

It was hard going, at first. Once you pass the pool you've got to get up that hill and then back down the slope on the other side, but after that the terrain becomes much flatter and it's a dream run. Cool before the summer sun hits, quiet, picturesque and cyclist-free, a far cry from my London run along Regent's Canal, dodging bikes and tourists all the way.

A few miles up the river, the valley widens out, the green hillside opposite, speckled with sheep, rolling gently away. I ran along flat, pebbled ground, barren save for patches of coarse grass and the ubiquitous gorse. I ran hard, head down, until a mile or so further up I reached a little cottage set back slightly from the river's edge, backed by a stand of birch trees.

I slowed to a jog to catch my breath, making my way towards the building to look around. It was a lonely place, seemingly unoccupied but not abandoned. There were curtains, partly drawn, and the windows were clean. I peered inside to see a tiny living room, furnished with two green armchairs and a little table between them. I tried the door but it was locked, so I sat down on the front step in the shade and took a swig from my bottle of water. Stretching my legs out in front of me, flexing my ankles, I waited for my breathing and my heart rate to slow. On the base of the door frame I noticed someone had scratched a message – *Mad Annie was here* – with a little skull drawn alongside it.

There were crows arguing in the trees behind me, but apart from that and the occasional bleating of sheep, the valley was quiet, and perfectly unspoiled. I think of myself as a city girl through and through, but this place – weird as it is – gets under your skin.

DI Townsend called the briefing just after nine. There weren't many of us there – a couple of uniforms who'd been helping out with house-to-house, the youngish detective constable, Callie, Hairy the science guy and me. Townsend had been in with the coroner for the post-mortem – he gave us the low-down, most of which was to be expected. Nel died due to injuries sustained in the fall. There was no water in her lungs – she didn't drown, it was already over by the time she hit the water. She had no injuries that could not be explained by the fall – no scratches or bruises which seemed out of place or which might suggest that someone else had been involved. She also had a fair amount of alcohol in her blood – three or four glasses' worth.

Callie gave us the low-down on the house-to-house – not that there was much to tell. We know that Nel was at the pub briefly on the Sunday evening, and that she left around seven. We know that she was at the Mill House until at least ten thirty, which was when Lena went to bed. No one reported seeing her after that. No one has reported seeing her in any altercations recently either, although it is widely agreed that she wasn't much liked. The locals didn't like her attitude, the sense of entitlement of an outsider coming to their town and purporting to tell their story. Where exactly did she get off?

Hairy has been going through Nel's email account – she'd set up an account dedicated to her project and invited people to send in their stories. Mostly, she'd just received abuse. 'Though I wouldn't say it's much worse than a lot of women get on the internet in the normal course of things,' he said, giving me an apologetic shrug, as though he was responsible for every idiot misogynist in cyberspace. 'We'll follow up, of course, but . . .'

The rest of Hairy's testimony was actually pretty interesting. It demonstrated that Jules Abbott was a liar, for starters: Nel's phone was still AWOL, but her phone records showed that although she didn't use her mobile much, she had made *eleven* calls to her sister's phone over the past three months. Most of the calls lasted less than a minute, sometimes two or three; none of them was particularly long, but they weren't hang-ups either.

He'd managed to establish the time of death, too. The camera down on the rocks – the one that wasn't damaged – had picked something up. Nothing graphic, nothing telling, just a sudden blur of movement in the darkness, followed by a spray of water. Two thirty-one a.m., the camera told us, was the moment Nel went in.

But he saved the best for last. 'We got a print off the case of the other camera, the damaged one,' he said. 'It doesn't match anyone on file, but we could ask the locals to start coming in, to rule themselves out?'

Townsend nodded slowly.

'I know that camera was vandalized before,' Hairy continued with a shrug, 'so it won't necessarily give us anything conclusive, but . . .'

'Even so. Let's see what we find. I'll leave that with you,' Townsend said, looking at me. 'I'll have a word with Julia Abbott about those phone calls.' He got to his feet, folding his arms across his chest, his chin down. 'You should all be aware,' he said, his voice low, apologetic almost, 'I've had Division on the phone just this morning.' He sighed deeply, and the rest of us exchanged glances. We knew what was coming. 'Given the results of the PM and the lack of any physical evidence of any sort of altercation up on that cliff, we are under pressure not to *waste resources*' – he put little air quotes around the words – 'on a suicide or accidental death. So. I know there is still work to be done, but we need to work quickly and efficiently. We aren't going to be given a great deal of time on this.'

It didn't exactly come as a shock. I thought about the conversation I'd had with the DCI on the day I got the assignment – *almost certainly a jumper*. Jumping all round, from cliffs to conclusions. Hardly surprising, given the history of the place.

But still. I didn't like it. I didn't like that there were two women in the water in the space of just a few months, and that they knew each other. They were connected, by place and by people. They were connected by Lena: best friend of one, daughter of the other. The last person to see her mother alive, and the first to insist that this – not just her mother's death, but the mystery surrounding it – was *what she wanted*. Such an odd thing for a child to suggest.

I said as much to the DI on our way out of the station. He looked at me balefully. 'God only knows what's going through that girl's head,' he said. 'She'll be trying to make sense of it. She—' He stopped. There was a woman walking towards us – shuffling more than walking, really – muttering to herself as she did. She was wearing a black coat, despite the heat, her grey hair was streaked with purple, and she had dark polish on her nails. She looked like an elderly goth.

'Morning, Nickie,' Townsend said.

The woman glanced up at him and then at me, eyes narrowing beneath beetling brows.

'Hmph,' she muttered, presumably by way of greeting. 'Getting anywhere, are you?'

'Getting anywhere with what, Nickie?'

'Finding out who did it!' she spluttered. 'Finding out who pushed her.'

'Who *pushed* her?' I repeated. 'You're referring to Danielle Abbott? Do you have information which might be useful to us, Mrs . . . er . . . ?'

She glowered at me and then turned back to Townsend. 'Who's this when she's at home?' she asked, jabbing a thumb in my direction.

'This is Detective Sergeant Morgan,' he said evenly. 'Do you have something you'd like to tell us, Nickie? About the other night?'

She harrumphed again. 'I didn't see anything,' she grumbled, 'and even if I did, it's not as if the likes of you would listen, is it?'

She continued her shuffle past us, down the sun-bright road, muttering as she went.

'What was that about, do you think?' I asked the DI. 'Is she someone we ought to speak to officially?'

'I wouldn't take Nickie Sage too seriously,' he replied with a shake of the head. 'She's not exactly reliable.'

'Oh?'

'She's says she's a "psychic", that she speaks to the dead. We've had some trouble with her before, fraud and so on. She also claims she's descended from a woman who was killed here by witch hunters,' he added drily. 'She's mad as a hatter.'

Jules

I WAS IN the kitchen when the doorbell rang. I glanced out of the window and saw the detective, Townsend, standing on the front steps, looking up at the windows. Lena got to the door before I did. She opened up for him and said, 'Hi, Sean.'

Townsend stepped into the house, brushing past her skinny body as he did, noticing (he must have noticed) her denim cut-offs, the Rolling Stones T-shirt with the tongue sticking out. He held out his hand to me and I took it. His palm was dry but his skin had an unhealthy sheen to it and there were greyish circles under his eyes. Lena watched him from beneath lowered lids. She raised her fingers to her mouth and chewed on a nail.

I showed him into the kitchen and Lena followed. The detective and I sat down at the table, while Lena leaned against the counter. She crossed one ankle over the other, then shifted her body and crossed them again.

Townsend didn't look. He coughed, rubbed one hand

against his wrist. 'The post-mortem has been completed,' he said in a soft voice. He glanced at Lena and back at me. 'Nel was killed by the impact. There's no indication that anyone else was involved. There was some alcohol in her blood.' His voice grew softer still. 'Enough to impair her judgement. To make her unsteady on her feet.'

Lena made a noise, a long, shuddering sigh. The detective was looking at his hands, now folded in front of him on the table.

'But . . . Nel was sure-footed as a goat up on that cliff,' I said. 'And she could handle more than a few glasses of wine. Nel could handle a bottle . . .'

He nodded. 'Perhaps,' he said. 'But at night, up there . . .'

'It wasn't an accident,' Lena said sharply.

'She *didn't jump*,' I snapped back.

Lena squinted at me, lip curled. 'What would *you* know?' she asked. She turned to look at the detective. 'Did you know that she lied to you? She lied about not being in contact with my mother. Mum tried to call her, like, I don't even know how many times. She never answered, she never called back, she never—' She stopped, looking back at me. 'She's just . . . why are you even here? I don't want you here.' She stalked out of the room, slamming the kitchen door behind her. A few moments later, her bedroom door slammed too.

DI Townsend and I sat in silence. I waited for him to ask me about the phone calls, but he said nothing; his eyes were shuttered, his face expressionless.

'Does it not strike you as odd,' I said at last, 'how convinced she is that Nel did this deliberately?'

He turned to me, his head cocked to one side slightly. Still he said nothing.

'Do you not have any suspects in this investigation? I mean . . . it just doesn't seem to me that anyone here cares that she's dead.'

'But you do?' he said evenly.

'What sort of a question is that?' I could feel my face growing hot. I knew what was coming.

'Ms Abbott,' he said. 'Julia.'

'Jules. It's Jules.' I was stalling, delaying the inevitable.

'Jules.' He cleared his throat. 'As Lena just mentioned, although you told us that you hadn't had any contact with your sister in years, Nel's mobile phone records reveal that in the past three months alone, she made eleven calls to your phone.' My face hot with shame, I looked away. '*Eleven* calls. Why lie to us?'

(*She's always lying*, you muttered darkly. *Always lying. Always telling tales.*)

'I didn't *lie*,' I said. 'I never spoke to her. It's like Lena said: she left messages, I didn't respond. So I didn't lie,' I repeated. I sounded weak, wheedling, even to myself. 'Look, you can't ask me to explain this to you, because there is no way of doing so to an outsider. Nel and I had problems going back years – but that doesn't have anything to do with this.'

'How can you know?' Townsend asked. 'If you didn't speak to her, how do you know what it had to do with?'

'I just . . . Here,' I said, holding out my mobile phone.

'Take it. Listen for yourself.' My hands were trembling and, as he reached for the phone, so were his. He listened to your final message.

'Why would you not call her back?' he said, something akin to disappointment on his face. 'She sounded upset, wouldn't you say?'

'No, I . . . I don't know. She sounded like Nel. Sometimes she was happy, sometimes she was sad, sometimes she was angry, more than once she was drunk . . . it didn't *mean anything*. You don't know her.'

'The other calls she made,' he demanded, a harder edge to his voice now. 'Do you still have the messages?'

I didn't, not all of them, but he listened to the ones I had, his hand gripping my phone so tightly his knuckles whitened. When he finished, he handed the phone back to me.

'Don't erase those. We may need to listen to them again.' He pushed his chair back and got to his feet, and I followed him out into the hall.

At the door, he turned to face me. 'I have to say,' he said, 'I find it odd that you didn't answer her. That you didn't try to find out why she needed to speak to you so urgently.'

'I thought she just wanted attention,' I said quietly and he turned away.

It was only after he had closed the door behind him that I remembered. I ran out after him.

'Detective Townsend,' I called out, 'there was a bracelet. My mother's bracelet. Nel always wore it. Have you found it?'

He shook his head, turning again to look at me.

'We've found nothing, no. Lena told DS Morgan that while Nel did wear it often, it wasn't something she had on every day. Although,' he went on, dipping his head, 'I suppose you couldn't have known that.' With a glance up at the house, he climbed into his car and backed slowly out of the driveway.

Jules

So somehow, this has ended up being my fault. You really are something, Nel. You are gone, possibly killed, and everyone is pointing the finger at me. I wasn't even here! I felt petulant, reduced to my teenage self. I wanted to scream at them, *How is this my fault?*

After the detective left, I stomped back into the house, catching sight of myself in the hallway mirror as I did, and I was surprised to see you looking back at me (older, not so pretty, but still you). Something snagged in my chest. I went into the kitchen and cried. If I failed you, I need to know how. I may not have loved you, but I can't have you abandoned like this, dismissed. I want to know if someone hurt you and why; I want them to pay. I want to lay all this to rest so that maybe you can stop whispering in my ear about how you *didn't jump, didn't jump, didn't jump.* I believe you, all right? And (*whisper it*), I want to know that I am safe. I want to know that no one is coming for me. I want to know that the child I am to take under my wing is just that – a blameless child – not something else. Not something dangerous.

I kept seeing the way Lena looked at DI Townsend, the tone of her voice when she called him by his first name (his first name?), the way he looked at her. I wondered whether what she'd told them about the bracelet was true. It rang false, to me, because you'd been so quick to claim it, to make it yours. It was possible, I supposed, that you only insisted on taking it because you knew how much I wanted it. When you found it amongst Mum's things and slipped it on to your wrist, I complained to Dad (yes, telling tales again). I asked, Why should *she* have it? *Why not?* you replied. *I'm the eldest.* And when he was gone, you smiled as you admired it on your wrist. *It suits me*, you said. *Don't you think it suits me?* Pinching a layer of fat on my forearm. *I doubt it would fit around your chubby little arm.*

I wiped my eyes. You stung me like that often; cruelty always was your strong suit. Some jibes – about my size, about how slow I was, how dull – I shrugged off. Others – *Come on, Julia, tell me honestly. Wasn't there some part of you that liked it?* – were barbs embedded deep in my flesh, irrecoverable unless I wanted to tear open fresh wounds. That last one, slurred into my ear on the day we buried our mother – oh, I could happily have strangled you with my bare hands for those words. And if you did that to *me*, if you were capable of making me feel like that, who else did you make murderous?

Down in the bowels of the house, in your study, I began to sift through your papers. I started with the mundane stuff. From the wooden filing cabinets against the wall I retrieved files containing medical records for you and Lena, a birth certificate for Lena, with no father named. I'd known that would be the case, of course; this was one of your mysteries, one of your secrets held tight to your chest. But for even Lena not to know? (I had to wonder, unkindly, whether you genuinely didn't know either.)

There were school reports, from the Park Slope Montessori in Brooklyn, and from the local primary and secondary here in Beckford. The deeds to the house, a life-insurance policy (Lena the beneficiary), bank statements, investment accounts. All the ordinary debris of a relatively well-ordered life, with no secrets to spill, no hidden truths to tell.

In the lower drawers were your files relating to 'the project': boxes filled with rough prints of pictures, pages of notes, some typed, some in your own spidery hand, in blue and green ink, words crossed out and capitalized and underlined, like the ravings of a conspiracy theorist. A madwoman. Unlike the other files, the administrative ones, none of it was in order, everything was a mess, all jumbled up. As though someone had been through the files, looking for something. My skin prickled, my mouth was dry. *The police have been through them, of course*. They had your computer, but they'd still want to see this. Maybe they've been looking for a note.

I flicked through the first box of pictures. They were mostly of the pool, the rocks, the little sandy beach. On some, you'd marked things on the borders, codes I couldn't decipher. There were photos of Beckford, too: its streets and houses, the pretty stone ones and uglier new ones. One of these was pictured over and over, a plain Edwardian semi with dirty curtains, half drawn. There were photos of the town centre, the bridge, the pub, the church, the graveyard. Libby Seeton's grave.

Poor Libby. You were obsessed with her when you were a child. I hated the story, sad and cruel as it was, but you wanted to hear it, over and over again. You wanted to hear how Libby, still a child, was brought to the water, accused of witchcraft. *Why?* I'd ask, and our mother would say, Because she and her aunt knew about herbs and plants. They knew how to make medicine. That seemed a stupid reason, but adult stories were full of stupid cruelties: little children turned away at the school gates because their skin was the wrong colour; people beaten or killed for worshipping the wrong god. Later you told me that it wasn't about making medicine, it was because Libby seduced (you explained the word) an older man and enticed him to leave his wife and child. That didn't diminish her in your eyes; it was a sign of her power.

When you were little, six or seven, you insisted on wearing one of Mum's old skirts to the pool; it trailed in the dirt although you'd pulled it up under your chin. You climbed up the rocks and flung yourself into the water while I played on the beach. You were Libby: *Look, Mum! Look! Do you think I'll sink or swim?*

I can see you doing it, the excitement on your face. I can feel my mother's soft hand in mine, warm sand between my toes as we watched you. That doesn't make any sense: if you were six or seven, then I was two or three – there's no way I could remember that, could I?

I thought about the lighter that I found in your

The Drowning Pool

Libby, 1679

YESTERDAY THEY SAID *tomorrow, so that's today now. She knows it won't be long. They'll come to take her to the water, to swim her. She wants it to come, wills it to come, it can't come soon enough. She's tired of feeling so dirty, of the itch on her skin. Knows it won't really help with the sores, putrid now and smelling bad. She needs elderberry, or marigold maybe, she's not sure what would be best, or whether it's too late to do anything at all. Aunt May would know, but she's gone now, swung from a gibbet these eight months past.*

Libby likes the water, loves the river though she's afraid of the deep. It'll be cold enough to freeze her now, but at least it'll take the insects from her skin. They shaved her when they first arrested her, but the hair's grown back a bit now, and there are things crawling everywhere, burrowing into her, she feels them in her ears, at the corners of her eyes and in between her legs. She scratches until she bleeds. It'll be good to have all that washed away, the smell of the blood, of herself.

They come in the morning. Two men, young, rough-handed, rough-mouthed, she's felt their fists before. No more though, they're careful about that, because they heard what the man said, the one who saw her in the forest, her legs spread and the Devil between them. They laugh and slap, but they're afraid of her, too, and in any case, she's not much to look at these days.

She wonders, will he be there to watch her, and what will he think? He thought her beautiful once, but now her teeth are rotting, and her skin is mottled blue and purple as though she were half dead already.

They take her to Beckford, where the river turns sharp around the cliff and then runs slow, slow and deep. This is where she'll swim.

It is autumn, a cold wind blowing, but the sun is bright and so she feels ashamed, stripped there in the bright light before all the men and women of the village. She thinks she can hear them gasp, in horror or surprise, at what's become of lovely Libby Seeton.

She's bound with ropes thick and rough enough to bring bright, fresh blood to her wrists. Just her arms. Legs left free. Then they tie a rope around her waist, so that should she sink, they can bring her back again.

When they take her to the river's edge, she turns and looks for him. The children scream then, thinking she's turning the curse on them, and the men push her into the water. The cold takes all of her breath. One of the men has a pole and he shoves it at her back, pressing her on and on and on until she cannot stand. She slips down, into the water.

She sinks.

The cold is so shocking that she forgets where she is. She opens her mouth to gasp and sucks in black water, she starts to choke, she struggles, she kicks with her legs, but she's disoriented, no longer feels the riverbed beneath her feet.

The rope pulls hard at her, biting into her waist, ripping her skin.

When they drag her to the bank, she is crying.

'Again!'

Someone is calling for a second ordeal.

'She sank!' a woman's voice cries. 'She's no witch, she's just a child.'

'Again! Again!'

The men bind her again for the second ordeal. Different this time: left thumb to right toe, right thumb to left. The rope around her waist. This time, they carry her into the water.

'Please,' she starts to beg, because she's not sure that she can face it again, the blackness and the cold. She wants to go back to a home that no longer exists, to a time when she and her aunt sat in front of the fire and told stories to one another. She wants to be in her bed in their cottage, she wants to be little again, to breathe in woodsmoke and rose and the sweet warmth of her aunt's skin.

'Please.'

She sinks. By the time they drag her out the second time, her lips are the blue of a bruise, and her breath is gone for good.

MONDAY, 17 AUGUST

Nickie

NICKIE SAT IN her chair by the window, watching the sun rise and burn the morning mist off the hills. She'd hardly slept at all, what with this heat and her sister prattling in her ear all night long. Nickie didn't like the heat. She was a creature built for cold weather: her father's family came from the Hebrides. Viking stock. On her mother's side they came from the east of Scotland, driven down south hundreds of years ago by witch hunters. The folk around Beckford might not believe it, they might scoff and scorn, but Nickie knew she was descended from the witches. She could draw a direct line all the way back, from Sage to Seeton.

Showered and fed and dressed in respectful black, Nickie went first to the pool. A long, slow shuffle along the path. She was grateful for the shade offered by oak and beech. Even so, sweat prickled in her eyes, it collected at the base of her spine. When she reached the little beach on the south side, she took off her sandals and went in up to her ankles. She reached down and scooped up handfuls of water, splashing it over her face and her neck and her upper arms. Time was, she would have climbed up to the clifftop to pay her respects to those who had fallen and those who had jumped and those who were pushed, but her legs just weren't up to it any longer, so whatever she had to say to the swimmers, she would have to say it from down here.

Nickie had been standing on pretty much exactly this spot the first time she ever laid eyes on Nel Abbott. It was a couple of years back and she'd been doing just this – having a bit of a paddle, cooling off – when she'd spotted a woman up on the cliff. She watched her walk back and forth, once and then twice, and by the third time there was a tingle over Nickie's palms. Something wicked, she thought. She watched the woman crouch down, lower herself to her knees and then, like a snake slithering on its belly, manoeuvre herself to the very edge of the cliff, her arms dangling over the edge. Heart in mouth, Nickie cried out, 'Oi!' The woman looked down, and, to Nickie's surprise, she smiled and waved.

Nickie saw her around quite a bit after that. She was at the pool a lot, taking pictures, making sketches, writing things down. Up there at all times of night and day, in all weathers. From her window, Nickie had watched Nel walk through the village towards the pool in the dead of night, in a snow storm, or when bitter rain lashed down hard enough to strip skin from flesh.

Sometimes, Nickie would pass her on the path and Nel wouldn't flinch, she didn't even notice she had company, so absorbed was she by the task at hand. Nickie liked that, she admired the focus of the woman, the way her work consumed her. She liked Nel's devotion to the river, too. Time was, Nickie liked a dip in the water of a warm summer's morning, although those days were behind her now. But Nel! She swam at dawn and dusk, in winter as in summer. Though now she thought of it, Nickie hadn't seen her swim in the river for some time, not for a couple of weeks. Longer, maybe? She tried to remember the last time she'd actually seen her in the water, but she couldn't, thanks to her sister chattering in her ear again, clouding her mind's eye.

She did wish she'd shut up.

Everyone thought Nickie was the black sheep of the family, but really that was her sister, Jean. Throughout childhood, everyone said Jeannie was the good girl, did as she was told, and then she turns seventeen and what do you know, she joins the police. The police! Their father was a miner, for Christ's sake. It was a betrayal, that's what her mother said, a betrayal of the whole family, the whole community. Her parents stopped talking to Jean then and Nickie was supposed to cut her off cold, too. Only she couldn't, could she? Jeannie was her little sister.

Bloody big mouth on her, that was her trouble – didn't know when to keep it shut. After she quit the police and before she left Beckford, Jean told Nickie a story to make her hair stand on end, and ever since Nickie had been biting her tongue and spitting in the dirt, murmuring her invocations to protect herself, every time Patrick Townsend crossed her path.

So far, it had worked. She was protected. Not Jeannie,

though. After that business with Patrick and his wife and all the trouble that followed, Jeannie moved to Edinburgh and married a useless man and together they set about spending the next fifteen years drinking themselves to death. But Nickie still saw her now and again, she still spoke to her. More often, recently. Jeannie had become garrulous again. Noisy, troublesome. Insistent.

She'd been chattering more than ever the past few nights, since Nel Abbott went in. Jeannie would have liked Nel, would have seen something of herself in her. Nickie liked her, too, liked their conversations, liked the fact that Nel *listened* when Nickie talked. She listened to her stories, but she didn't heed her warnings, did she? Just like Jeannie, Nel was another one who didn't know when to keep her mouth shut.

The thing is, sometimes, say after a heavy rain, the river rises. Unruly, it sucks back the earth and turns it over and reveals something lost: the bones of a lamb, a child's wellington boot, a gold watch encased in silt, a pair of spectacles on a silver chain. A bracelet with a broken clasp. A knife, a fishing hook, a sinker. Tin cans and supermarket trolleys. Debris. Things with significance and things without. And that's all fine, that's the way of things, the way of the river. The river can go back over the past and bring it all up and spit it out on the banks in full view of everyone, but people can't. Women can't. When you start asking questions and putting up little advertisements in shops and pubs, when you start taking pictures and talking to newspapers and asking questions about witches and women and lost souls, you're not asking questions, you're asking for trouble.

Nickie should know.

By the time she'd dried her feet and put her sandals back on and walked, oh-so-slowly, back along the path and up the steps and over the bridge, it was after ten, it was almost time. She went to the shop and bought herself a can of Coca-Cola and sat down on the bench across the way from the churchyard. She wasn't going to go in – church was no place for her – but she wanted to watch them. She wanted to watch the mourners and the rubberneckers and the bald-faced hypocrites.

She settled herself down and closed her eyes – just for a moment, she thought – but when she opened them again it had started. She watched the young policewoman, the new one, strutting about, twisting her head round like a meerkat. She was a watcher, too. Nickie saw the folk from the pub, the landlord and his wife and the young girl who worked behind the bar, a couple of teachers from the school, the fat dowdy one and the handsome one, sunglasses covering his eyes. She saw the Whittakers, all three of them, misery rising off them like steam from a pot, the father all hunched up with grief, the boy terrified of his own shadow, only the mother with her head up. A gaggle of young girls honking like geese, with a man following behind, a face from the past, an ugly face. Nickie knew him but couldn't place him, couldn't fix him in her mind. She was distracted by the dark-blue car swinging into the car park, by the prickle on her skin, the sensation of cool air on the back of her neck. She saw the woman first, Helen Townsend, plain as a brown bird, emerging from the back seat of the car. Her husband climbed out of the driver's seat and from the passenger's side came the old man, Patrick, straight-backed as a sergeant major. Patrick Townsend: family man, pillar of the community, ex-copper. Scum. Nickie spat on the ground and said her invocation. She felt the old man turn his gaze towards her and Jeannie whispered, *Look away, Nic.*

Nickie counted them in and she counted them out again half an hour later. There was some sort of kerfuffle at the door, people bumping into each other, pushing past each other, and then something happened between the handsome teacher and Lena Abbott, a word exchanged sharply. Nickie watched and she could tell the policewoman was watching, too, Sean Townsend stalking around head and shoulders above the rest. Keeping order. Something got missed though, didn't it? Like one of those con tricks, when you take your eye off the ball for a second and the whole game changes.

Helen

HELEN SAT AT the kitchen table and cried noiselessly, her shoulders jerking, hands clasped in her lap. Sean misread the situation completely.

'You don't have to go,' he said, placing a hand gingerly on her shoulder. 'There's no reason for you to go.'

'She does have to go,' Patrick said. 'Helen does, and you do – we all do. We are part of this community.'

Helen nodded, wiping away tears with the heels of her hands. 'Of course I'll come,' she said, clearing her throat. 'Of course I will.'

She wasn't upset about the funeral. She was upset because Patrick had drowned the tabby in the river that morning. It was pregnant, he told her, and they couldn't afford to let the place get overrun with cats. They'd become a nuisance. He was right, of course, but that didn't help. The tabby, wild as she was, had begun to feel like a pet to Helen. She liked watching her pad across the courtyard every morning, sniffing around the front door for a treat, lazily swatting at the bees buzzing around the rosemary. The thought of it made her well up again.

After Sean went upstairs, she said, 'You didn't have to

drown her. I could have taken her to the vet, they could have put her to sleep.'

Patrick shook his head. 'No need,' he said gruffly. 'It's the best way. It was over very quickly.'

But Helen had seen the deep scratches on his forearms attesting to how strongly the cat had fought. *Good*, she thought. *I hope she bloody hurt you*. Then she felt bad, because of course he hadn't done it to be cruel. 'I'll need to do something about those,' she said, indicating the marks on his arms.

He shook his head. 'It's all right.'

'It's not all right, you could get an infection. And you're going to get blood on your shirt.'

She sat him down at the kitchen table, cleaned his scratches and rubbed antiseptic into the wounds, then taped up the worst cuts with Elastoplast. He watched her face all the while, and she imagined he must have felt a bit remorseful because when she was finished he kissed her hand and said, 'Good girl. You're a good girl.'

She got to her feet and moved away from him, stood at the kitchen sink with her hands on the counter and looked at the sun-drenched cobbles. She bit her lip.

Patrick sighed, lowering his voice to a murmur. 'Look, love, I know this is difficult for you. I know that. But we need to go as a family, don't we? We need to support Sean. This is not about grieving for her. This is about us putting all that business behind us.'

Helen couldn't tell whether it was the words he spoke or his breath on the back of her neck, but her hair stood up on end. 'Patrick,' she said, turning to look at him. '*Dad*. I need to talk to you about the car, about . . .'

Sean was coming down the stairs loudly, two at a time. 'About what?'

'Never mind,' she said, and he frowned. She shook her head. 'It doesn't matter.'

She went upstairs and washed her face and put on the dark-grey trouser suit usually reserved for attending the school board. She ran a comb through her hair, trying not to meet her own eye in the mirror. She didn't want to admit, even to herself, that she was afraid; she didn't want to face what she was afraid of. She'd found some things in the glove box of her car, things she couldn't explain, and she wasn't sure she wanted the explanation. She'd taken everything and hidden it – stupidly, childishly – under her bed.

'Are you ready?' Sean was calling to her from downstairs. She took a deep breath, forcing herself to look at her own reflection, at her pale, clean face, her eyes clear as grey glass.

'I'm ready,' she said, to herself.

Helen sat in the back seat of Sean's car, Patrick riding up front next to his son. Nobody spoke, but she could tell by the way her husband kept touching his palm to his wrist that he was anxious. He would be hurting, of course. All this – these deaths in the river – raised painful memories for him and his father.

As they crossed the first bridge, Helen glanced down at the greenish water and tried not to think of her, held down, fighting for her life. The cat. She was thinking of the cat.

Josh

I HAD A fight with Mum before we left for the funeral. I came downstairs and she was there in the hallway, putting on lipstick in the mirror. She was wearing a red top. I said, You can't wear that to a funeral, it's disrespectful. She just kind of gave a funny laugh and went into the kitchen and carried on as though I hadn't said anything at all. I wasn't about to give up on it though, because we don't need any more attention drawn to us. The police are bound to be there – the police always show up at the funerals of people who die in suspicious ways. It's bad enough that I've already lied to them, and that Mum did too – what are they going to think when they see her turning up dressed like she's going to a party?

I followed her into the kitchen. She asked me if I wanted some tea, and I said no. I said I didn't think she should be going to the funeral at all, and she said, why on earth not? You didn't even like her, I said. Everyone knows you didn't like her. She gave me this annoying smile and said, oh they do, do they? I said, I'm going because I'm Lena's friend, and she said, no you're not.

Dad came downstairs and said, don't say that, Lou. Of course he is. He said something to her, really quietly so I couldn't hear, and she nodded and went upstairs.

Dad made me some tea, which I didn't want, but I drank it anyway.

'Will the police be there, do you think?' I asked him, even though I knew the answer.

'I expect so. Mr Townsend knew Nel, didn't he? And, well – I imagine a number of people from the village will want to pay their respects, whether they knew her or not. I know . . . I know it's complicated with us, but I think it's right that we try to pull together, don't you?' I didn't say anything. 'And you'll want to see Lena, won't you, to tell her how sorry you are. Imagine how poor Lena must be feeling.' I still didn't say anything. He reached out to ruffle my hair but I ducked away from him.

'Dad,' I said, 'you know how the police asked about Sunday night, about where we were and all that?'

He nodded, but as he did I saw him look over my head to check Mum wasn't listening. 'You said you didn't hear anything unusual, didn't you?' he asked. I nodded. 'You told the truth.'

I wasn't sure whether he said, *You told the truth?*, like a question, or *You told the truth*, like it was an instruction.

I wanted to say something, I wanted to say it out loud. I wanted to say, *What if? What if she did something bad?*, just so Dad could tell me how ridiculous I was being, so he could shout at me and say, *How could you even think that?*

I said, 'Mum went to the shops.'

He looked at me like I was thick. 'Yes, I know. She went to the shops that morning to get milk. Josh . . . Oh! There you go,' he said, looking over my shoulder. 'There she is now. That's better, isn't it?'

She'd changed her red shirt to a black one.

It was better, but I was still scared of what was going to happen. I was scared that she'd say something, or that she'd laugh in the middle of the service or something. She had a look at that moment that was really bugging me, not like she was happy or anything, it was more like . . . like the look she gives Dad when she wins an argument, like when she says, *I told you it would have been quicker to take the A68*. It was like she'd been proved right about something and she couldn't get that winning look off her face.

When we got to the church there were already a lot of people milling around – that made me feel a bit better. I saw Mr Townsend and I think he saw me, but he didn't come over and say anything. He was just standing there, looking around, and then he stopped and watched as Lena and her aunt walked over the bridge. Lena looked really grown up, different to how she normally is. Still pretty. As she walked past us she saw me and she gave me a sad smile. I wanted to go over and give her a hug, but Mum was holding on to my hand really tightly so I couldn't pull away.

I needn't have worried about Mum laughing. When we got into the church she started crying, sobbing so loudly that other people turned around and looked. I wasn't sure whether that made things better or worse.

Lena

THIS MORNING, I felt happy. I was lying in bed, covers thrown back. I could feel the heat of the day building and I knew it was going to be beautiful, and I could hear Mum singing. Then I woke up.

On the back of my bedroom door hung the dress I was planning to wear. It's Mum's, from Lanvin. She'd never in a million years let me wear it, but today I didn't think she'd mind. It hadn't been dry-cleaned since she wore it last, so it still smelled of her. When I put it on it was like having her skin against mine.

I washed and dried my hair, then tied it back. I usually wear it down, but Mum liked it up. *Totes sophis*, she'd say in the way she did when she wanted me to roll my eyes at her. I wanted to go into her room to look for her bracelet – I knew it would be in there somewhere – but I couldn't do it.

I haven't been able to bring myself to go into her room since she died. The last time I was in there was last Sunday afternoon. I was bored and feeling sad about Katie, so I went into her room to look for some weed.

I couldn't find any in the bedside table so I started looking through her coat pockets in the wardrobe, because sometimes she keeps stuff in there. I wasn't expecting her home. When Mum caught me, she didn't look pissed off, she just looked sort of sad.

'You can't tell me off,' I said. 'I'm looking for shit in *your room*. So you can't get pissed off with me. That would make you a total hypocrite.'

'No,' she said, 'that would make me a grown-up.'

'Same thing,' I said, and she laughed.

'Yeah, maybe, but the fact is that I'm allowed to smoke weed and drink alcohol and you are not. Why are you looking to get wasted in the middle of a Sunday afternoon anyway? On your own? Kind of sad, isn't it?' Then she went on, 'Why don't you go for a swim or something? Call a friend?'

I lost it with her, because it sounded like she was saying the kind of thing that Tanya and Ellie and all those bitches say about me – that I'm sad, that I'm a loser, that I've got no friends now the only person who ever liked me topped herself. I started yelling, 'What fucking friend? I don't have any, don't you remember? Don't you remember what happened to my best friend?'

She went really quiet and held her hands up, the way she does – did – when she doesn't want a fight. But I didn't back off, I just wouldn't back off. I was yelling about how she was never around, how she just left me alone all the time, how she was so distant it seemed like she didn't even want me around at all. She was shaking her head, saying, 'That isn't true, that isn't true.' She said, 'I'm sorry if I've been distracted, but there are some things going on that I can't explain. There's something I need to do, and I can't explain how difficult it is.'

I was cold with her. 'You don't need to *do* anything, Mum. I swear you promised me you'd keep your mouth shut. So you don't have to do anything. Jesus, haven't you done enough already?'

'Lenie,' she was saying, 'Lenie, please. You don't know *everything*. I'm the parent here, you have to trust me.'

I said some shitty things then, about how she'd never been much of a parent, what kind of parent has dope lying around the house and brings men home at night so that I can hear? I told her that if it had been the other way round, if it had been me who'd been in trouble like Katie was, Louise would have known what to do, she'd have been the parent and she'd have done something and she'd have helped. And it was all bullshit, of course, because I was the one who didn't want Mum to say anything, and she pointed that out and then she said that in any case she had tried to help. And then I just started screaming at her, telling her everything was her fault, that if she went and blabbed to anyone I would leave and never speak to her again. I said it over and over, *You've done enough damage.* The last thing I ever said to her was that it was her fault Katie was dead.

Jules

IT WAS HOT, the day of your funeral, heat shimmering
over the water, the light too bright, the air too close,
heavy with moisture. Lena and I walked to the church.
She started out a few paces in front of me and the distance between us stretched; I'm no good in heels, she is
a natural. She looked very elegant, very beautiful, much
older than her fifteen years, in a black crêpe dress with
a keyhole on the bodice. We walked in silence, the river
snaking muddily past us, sullen and quiet. The warm
air smelled of decay.

I felt afraid, as we turned the corner on the approach
to the bridge, of who might be at the church. I was
afraid that no one would turn up at all and that Lena
and I would be forced to sit alone with nothing but you
between us.

I kept my head down, I watched the road, I concen-
trated on putting one foot in front of the other, trying
not to stumble on the uneven tarmac. My shirt (black
and synthetic with a pussy bow at the throat, wrong for
the weather) clung to my lower back. My eyes began to

water. *No matter*, I thought, *if my mascara runs. People will think I've been crying.*

Lena still hasn't cried. Or at least she hasn't cried in front of me. Sometimes I think I hear her sobbing in the night, but she comes to breakfast clear-eyed and insouciant. She slips in and out of the house without a word. I hear her talking in a low voice in her room, but she ignores me, she shrinks from me when I approach, she snarls at my questions, she shuns my attention. She wants nothing to do with me. (I remember you coming into my room after Mum died, you wanted to talk, I sent you away. Is this the same? Is she doing the same thing? I can't tell.)

As we approached the churchyard I noticed a woman sitting on a bench by the side of the road, who smiled at me with rotted teeth. I thought I could hear someone laughing, but it was just you, in my head.

Some of the women you wrote about are buried in that churchyard, some of your *troublesome* women. Were all of you troublesome? Libby was, of course. At fourteen years of age she seduced a thirty-four-year-old man, enticed him away from his loving wife and infant child. Aided by her aunt, the hag May Seeton, and the numerous devils that they conjured, Libby cajoled poor blameless Matthew into any number of unnatural acts. Troublesome indeed. Mary Marsh was said to have performed abortions. Anne Ward was a killer. But what about you, Nel? What had you done? Who were you troubling?

Libby is buried in the churchyard. You knew where she lay, her and the others, you showed me the stones, scraped away the moss so that we could read the words. You kept some of it – the moss, I mean – and you snuck into my room and put some under my pillow, then you told me that Libby had left it there. At night she walked the river bank, you told me; if you listened hard enough, you could hear her calling for her aunt, for May, to come and rescue her. But May never comes: she can't. She isn't in the graveyard. After they extracted her confession they hanged her in the town square; her body is buried in the woods outside the churchyard walls, nails driven through her legs so that she'll never rise again.

At the crest of the bridge, Lena turned, just for a second, to look at me. Her expression – impatience, perhaps just a hint of pity – was so like yours that I shivered. I clenched my fists together and bit my lip: I cannot be afraid of her! She's just a child.

My feet hurt. I could feel the prickle of sweat at my hairline, I wanted to rip the fabric of my shirt, I wanted to rip my skin. I could see a small crowd gathered in the car park in front of the church, they were turning now, turning towards us, watching our approach. I thought about how it would feel to pitch myself over the stone walls: terrifying, yes, but only for a short while. I could slip down into the mud and let the water close over my head; it would be such a relief to feel cold, to be unseen.

Inside, Lena and I sat side by side (a foot apart) in the front pew. The church was full. Somewhere behind us, a woman sobbed, on and on, as though her heart were broken. The vicar talked about your life, he listed your achievements, he spoke of your devotion to your daughter. I was mentioned in passing. I was the one who had given him the information, so I suppose I couldn't complain that his speech felt perfunctory. I could have said something myself, perhaps I should have done, but I couldn't think how I could talk about you without betraying something – you, or myself, or the truth.

The service finished abruptly, and before I knew it Lena was getting to her feet. I followed her along the aisle, the heat of attention turned towards us somehow threatening, not heartening. I tried not to see the faces around me, but I couldn't help myself: the crying woman, her face crumpled and red, Sean Townsend, his eyes meeting mine, a young man with head bowed, a teenager laughing behind his fist. A violent man. I stopped suddenly, and the woman behind me stepped on my heel. 'Sorry, sorry,' she muttered, manoeuvring past. I didn't move, didn't breathe, couldn't swallow, my insides turning to liquid. It was him.

Older, yes, uglier, gone to seed, but unmistakable. A violent man. I waited for him to turn his eyes to me. I thought that if he did, one of two things would happen: I would cry or I would lunge at him. I waited, but he wasn't looking at me. He was looking at Lena, watching her intently. My liquid insides turned to ice.

I followed blindly, pushing people out of my way. He stood to one side, his eyes still trained on Lena. He was watching her take off her shoes. Men watch girls who look like Lena in all sorts of ways: desire, hunger, distaste. I couldn't see his eyes, but I didn't need to. I knew what was in them.

I started towards him, a noise rising in my throat. People were looking at me, with pity or confusion,

I didn't care. I needed to get to him . . . And then he turned abruptly and walked away. He walked quickly down the pathway and out into the car park, and I stood, breath suddenly rushing to my lungs, adrenaline making my head swim. He climbed into a large green car, and was gone.

'Jules? Are you all right?' DS Morgan appeared at my side and placed a hand on my arm.

'Did you see that man?' I asked her. 'Did you see him?'

'Which man?' she said, looking around her. 'Who?'

'He's a violent man,' I said.

She looked alarmed. 'Where, Jules? Did someone do something . . . say something to you?'

'No, I . . . no.'

'Which man, Jules? Who are you talking about?'

My tongue was tied in reeds and my mouth was full of mud. I wanted to tell her, I wanted to say, *I remember him. I know what he's capable of.*

'Who did you see?' she asked me.

'Robbie,' I said his name at last. 'Robbie Cannon.'

AUGUST 1993

Jules

I'D FORGOTTEN. BEFORE the football game, something else happened. I was sitting on my towel, reading my book, no one else yet around, and then you came. You and Robbie. You didn't see me under the trees, you ran into the water with him after you, and you swam and splashed and kissed. He took your hand and pulled you to the water's edge, he lay on top of you, pushed your shoulders down, arched his back and looked up. And saw me, watching. And smiled.

Later that afternoon, I returned to the house alone. I took off the gingham bathing suit and the blue shorts and left them soaking in cold water in the sink. I ran myself a bath and climbed in and sank down and thought, *I will never be rid of it, all this awful flesh.*

A big girl. A bruiser. Legs to kickstart a 747. She could play front row for England.

Too big for the spaces I inhabited, always overflowing. I took up too much room. I sank down into the bath and the water rose. Eureka.

Back in my room, I climbed under the bedcovers and lay there, suffocating with misery, self-pity mingled with guilt, because my mother lay in bed in the very next room and she was dying of breast cancer and all I could think about was how much I didn't want to go on, didn't want to live like this.

I fell asleep.

My father woke me. He had to take my mother to the hospital for more tests, and they were going to stay the night in town because it would be an early start. There was some supper in the oven, he said, I was to help myself.

Nel was at home, I knew, because I could hear her music in the room next door. After a while, the music stopped, and then I could hear voices, low and then louder, and other noises too, moaning, grunting, a sharp intake of breath. I got out of bed, got dressed and went out into the corridor. The light was on, the door to Nel's room slightly ajar. It was darker in there, but I could hear her, she was saying something, she was saying his name.

Barely daring to breathe, I took a step closer. Through the crack in the door I could make out their shapes moving in the darkness. I couldn't bring myself to look away, I watched until I heard him make a loud, animal noise. Then he started laughing and I knew that they were finished.

Downstairs, all the lights were on. I walked around turning them off, then wandered into the kitchen and opened the fridge. I stared at its contents and out of the corner of my eye noticed a bottle of vodka, opened, half full, on the counter. I copied what I'd seen Nel do: I poured myself half a glass of orange juice and topped it up with vodka, and then, steeling myself for the nasty, bitter alcoholic taste I'd experienced from trying wine and beer, I took a sip, and found that it was sweet, not bitter at all.

I finished the drink and poured another. I enjoyed the physical sensation, the warmth spreading from my stomach into my chest, my blood heating up, my whole body loosening, that afternoon's misery ebbing away.

I went into the living room and looked out at the river, a slick black snake running underneath the house. It was surprising to me, how suddenly I could see what I hadn't before – that the problem of me was not insurmountable at all. I had a sudden moment of clarity: I didn't have to be fixed, I could be fluid. Like the river. Perhaps it wouldn't be so difficult, after all. Wasn't it possible, to starve myself, to move more (in secret, when no one was watching)? To be transformed, caterpillar into butterfly, to become a different person, unrecognizable, so that the ugly, bleeding girl would be forgotten? I would be made new.

I went back to the kitchen to get some more to drink.

I heard footsteps upstairs, padding along the landing and then coming down the stairs. I slipped back into the living room, turned off the lamp and crouched in the darkness on the window seat, my feet pulled up beneath me.

I saw him go into the kitchen, heard him opening the fridge – no, the freezer, I could hear him cracking ice out of the trays. I heard the glug of liquid and then

I saw him as he walked past. And then he stopped. And took a step back.

'Julia? Is that you?'

I didn't say anything, didn't breathe. I didn't want to see anyone – I certainly didn't want to see him – but he was fumbling for the light switch, and then the lights came on and there he stood, in boxer shorts and nothing else, his skin a deep tan, his shoulders wide, body tapering to a tight waist, the fuzz on his stomach leading down into his shorts. He smiled at me.

'Are you OK?' he asked. As he stepped closer I could see that his eyes looked a little glazed, his grin stupider, lazier than usual. 'Why are you sitting here in the dark?' He caught sight of my glass and the smile grew wider. 'I thought the vodka was looking low . . .' He walked over to me and clinked his glass against mine, then sat down at my side, his thigh pressed against my foot. I moved away, put my feet on the floor and started to get up, but he put his hand on my arm.

'Hey, wait,' he said. 'Don't run off. I want to talk to you. I wanted to apologize for this afternoon.'

'That's OK,' I said. I could feel my face reddening. I didn't look at him.

'No, I'm sorry. Those guys were being dickheads. I'm really sorry, OK?'

I nodded.

'It's nothing to be ashamed of.'

I cringed, my whole body burned with the shame of it. Some small, stupid part of me had hoped they hadn't seen, hadn't realized what it was.

He squeezed my arm, narrowing his eyes as he looked

at me. 'You've got a pretty face, Julia, you know that?'
He laughed. 'I mean it, you have.' He released my arm,
slung his own around my shoulders.

'Where's Nel?' I asked.

'Sleeping,' he said. He sipped his drink and smacked
his lips. 'Think I wore her out.' He pulled my body closer
to his. 'Have you ever kissed a guy before, Julia?' he
asked me. 'Do you want to kiss me?' He turned my face
to his and put his lips against mine, I felt his tongue,
hot and slimy, pushing into my mouth. I thought I
might gag, but I let him do it, just to see what it was like.
When I pulled away, he smiled at me. 'You like that?' he
asked, hot breath, stale smoke and alcohol in my face.
He kissed me again and I kissed him back, trying to
feel whatever it was I was supposed to be feeling. His
hand slid into the waistband of my pyjama bottoms.
I wriggled away, mortified, as I felt his fingers pushing
against the fat of my belly, into my knickers.

'No!' I thought I'd cried out, but it was more like a
whisper.

'It's OK,' he said. 'Don't worry. I don't mind a bit of
blood.'

He got angry with me afterwards because I wouldn't
stop crying.

'Oh, come on, it didn't hurt that much! Don't cry.
Come on, Julia, stop crying. Didn't you think it was
nice? It was good, how it felt, wasn't it? You were wet
enough. Come on, Julia. Have another drink. There you
go. Have a sip. Jesus Christ, stop crying! Fuck's sake. I
thought you'd be grateful.'

2015

Sean

I DROVE HELEN and my father home, but when we got to the front door I was reluctant to cross the threshold. Occasionally strange thoughts take hold of me and I struggle to shake them off. I stood outside the house, my wife and father inside, looking back at me expectantly. I told them to eat without me. I said I needed to go back to the station.

I am a coward. I owe my father more than this. I should be with him today, today of all days. Helen will help him, of course, but even she cannot understand how he will be feeling, the depth of his suffering. And yet I couldn't sit with him, I couldn't meet his eye. Somehow, he and I can never look each other in the eye when our minds are on my mother.

I took the car and drove, not to the station but back to the churchyard. My mother was cremated; she isn't here. My father took her ashes to a 'special place'. He never told me where exactly, although he did promise that one day he'd take me. We never went. I used to ask about it, but it always upset him, so after a while I let it be.

The church and graveyard were deserted, no one in sight except for old Nickie Sage, hobbling slowly around outside. I left the car, taking the path around the stone wall towards the trees behind the church. When I reached Nickie, she was standing with one hand on the wall, breath whistling in her chest. She turned suddenly. Her face was a florid pink and she was sweating profusely.

'What do you want?' she wheezed. 'Why are you following me?'

I smiled. 'I'm not *following* you. I spotted you from my car and I just thought I'd come over and say hello. Are you all right?'

'I'm fine, I'm fine.' She didn't look fine. She leaned against the wall and looked up at the sky. 'There'll be a storm later.'

I nodded. 'Smells like it.'

She jerked her head back. 'That all done, then? Nel Abbott? Closing the file? Consigning her to history?'

'The case isn't closed,' I said.

'Not yet. Will be soon, though, won't it?' She muttered something else under her breath.

'What was that?'

'It's all sewn up, isn't it?' She turned to face me full on and prodded me in the chest with a fat forefinger. 'You know, don't you, that this wasn't like the last one? This wasn't like Katie Whittaker. This was like your mother.'

I took a step backwards. 'What is that supposed to

mean?' I asked her. 'If you know something, you should tell me. Do you? Do you know something about Nel Abbott's death?'

She turned away, muttering again, her words indistinguishable.

My breath quickened, my body flushed with heat. 'Don't mention my mother to me like that. Today of all days. Christ! What sort of person does that?'

She waved a hand at me. 'Oh, you don't listen, you lot never listen,' she said, and tottered off down the path, still talking as she went, every now and again reaching out to the stone wall to steady herself.

I was angry with her, but more than that, I felt blindsided, wounded almost. We'd known each other for years and I'd never been anything but polite to her. She was misguided, sure, but I didn't think of her as a bad person, and I certainly never thought of her as cruel.

I trudged back towards the car before changing my mind and veering off to the village shop. I bought a bottle of Talisker – my father likes it, though he doesn't drink a great deal. I thought we could share a glass together later, to make up for before, for my leaving like that. I tried to picture it, the two of us sitting at the kitchen table, the bottle between us, raising a glass. I wondered what – who – we would raise it to? The mere imagining of it made me fearful, and my hand started to shake. I opened the bottle.

The smell of the whisky and the heat of the alcohol in my chest brought to mind childhood fevers, fraught dreams, waking with my mother sitting on the edge of my bed, pushing damp hair from my forehead, rubbing

Vicks into my chest. There have been times in my life when I have barely thought of her at all, but lately she has been in my thoughts more and more – and more than ever over the past few days. Her face comes to me; sometimes she is smiling, sometimes not. Sometimes she reaches for me.

The summer storm started without me noticing. Perhaps I dropped off. I only know that when I came to, the road ahead looked like a river and thunder seemed to shake the car. I turned the key in the ignition, but then it struck me that the whisky bottle in my lap was only two-thirds full, so I switched the engine off again. Under the drum of thunderous rain I could hear my breathing, and just for a moment I thought I could hear someone else's breath too. I was struck by the ridiculous notion that if I turned around, there would be someone there, on the back seat of the car. For a moment I was so sure of this that I was too afraid to move.

I decided a walk in the rain would sober me up. I opened the car door, checking the back seat, despite myself, and stepped out. I was instantly soaked through and blinded by water. A fork of lightning split the air and in that second I saw Julia, drenched, half walking, half running towards the bridge. I slid back into the car and flashed the lights on and off. She stopped. I flashed the lights again and, tentatively, she made her way towards me. She stopped a few metres away. I wound down the window and called out to her.

She opened the door and got in. She was still wearing her funeral clothes, though they were sodden now and clinging to her small frame. She'd changed her shoes, though. I noticed that her tights had laddered – I could see a small circle of pale flesh on her knee. It seemed shocking because whenever I've seen her before, her body has always been covered – long sleeves and high collars, no skin on show. Unreachable.

'What are you doing out here?' I asked. She glanced down at the whisky in my lap, but made no comment. Instead, she reached over, pulled my face to hers and kissed me. It was strange, heady. I could taste blood on her tongue and for a second I succumbed, before pulling violently away from her.

'I'm sorry,' she said, wiping her lips, her eyes cast down. 'I'm so sorry. I've no idea why I did that.'

'No,' I said. 'Neither do I.' Incongruously, we both started to laugh, nervously at first and then wholeheartedly, as though the kiss were the most hilarious joke in the world. When we stopped, we were both wiping tears from our faces.

'What are you doing out here, Julia?'

'Jules,' she said. 'I was looking for Lena. I'm not sure where she is . . .' She looked different to me, no longer closed off. 'I'm frightened,' she said, and she laughed again, as though embarrassed now. 'I'm really frightened.'

'Frightened of what?'

She cleared her throat and pushed her wet hair back from her face.

'What are you afraid of?'

She took a deep breath. 'I don't . . . This sounds strange, I know, but there was a man at the funeral, a man I recognized. He used to be Nel's boyfriend.'

'Oh?'

'I mean . . . not recently. Forever ago. When we were teenagers. I've no idea if she'd seen him more recently than that.' There were two high spots of colour in her cheeks. 'She never mentioned him in any of her phone messages. But he was there at the funeral, and I think . . . I can't explain why, but I think he might have done something to her.'

'Done something? You're saying you think he might have been involved in her death?'

She looked at me imploringly. 'I can't say that, of course, but you need to look into him, you need to find out where he was when she died.'

My scalp shrivelled, adrenaline cutting through the alcohol. 'What's this man's name? Who are you talking about?'

'Robbie Cannon.'

I drew a blank for a moment, but then it came to me. 'Cannon? Local guy? The family had car dealerships, a lot of money. That one?'

'Yes. That one. You know him?'

'I don't know him, but I remember him.'

'You remember . . . ?'

'From school. He was in the year above. Good at sport. Did well with girls. Not very bright.'

Her head bent so that her chin almost touched her chest, Jules said, 'I didn't know you were at school here.'

'Yes,' I said. 'I've always lived here. You wouldn't re-member me, but I remember you. You and your sister, of course.'

'Oh,' she said, and her face closed, like a shutter

slamming shut. She put her hand on the door handle, as though making to leave.

'Hang on,' I said. 'What makes you think Cannon did something to your sister? Did he say something, do something? Was he violent towards her?'

Jules shook her head and looked away. 'I just know that he's dangerous. He's not a good person. And I saw him . . . looking at Lena.'

'Looking at her?'

'Yes, *looking*.' She turned her head and met my eye at last. 'I didn't like the way he looked at her.'

'OK,' I said. 'I'll, uh . . . I'll see what I can find out.'

'Thank you.'

She made to open the car door again, but I put my hand on her arm. 'I'll drive you back,' I said.

Again, a glance at the bottle, but no word. 'OK.'

It took just a couple of minutes to get back to the Mill House and neither of us spoke until Jules had opened the car door. I shouldn't have said anything, but I wanted to tell her.

'You're very like her, you know.'

She looked shocked and gave a startled, hiccupping laugh.

'I'm nothing at all like her.' She brushed a tear from her cheek. 'I'm the anti-Nel.'

'I don't think so,' I said, but she was already gone.

I don't remember driving home.

The Drowning Pool

Lauren, 1983

FOR LAUREN'S THIRTY-SECOND birthday, in a week's time, they would go to Craster. Just her and Sean, because Patrick would be working. 'It's my favourite place in all the world,' she told her son. 'There's a castle, and a beautiful beach, and sometimes you can see seals on the rocks. And after we've been to the beach and the castle, we'll go to the smokehouse and eat kippers on brown bread. Heaven.'

Sean wrinkled his nose. 'I think I'd rather go to London,' he announced, 'to see the Tower. And have ice creams.'

His mother laughed and said, 'OK then, perhaps we could do that instead.'

In the end, they didn't do either.

It was November, the days short and bitter, and Lauren was distracted. She was aware that she was acting differently, but couldn't seem to stop. She found herself sitting at the breakfast table with her family and all of a sudden her skin would flush, her face would burn, and she would have to turn away to hide it. She turned away when her husband came to kiss her, too – the movement of her head was almost involuntary, beyond her control, so that his lips brushed her cheek, or the corner of her mouth.

Three days before her birthday, there was a storm. It built all day, a vicious wind ripping down the valley, white horses riding the breadth of the pool. At night, the storm broke, the river pushing at its banks, trees felled along its length. The rain came down in sheets, the whole world underwater.

Lauren's husband and son slept like babies, but Lauren was awake. In the study downstairs, she sat at her husband's desk, a bottle of his favoured Scotch at her elbow. She drank a glass and tore a sheet of paper from a notebook. She drank another glass, and another, and the page remained blank. She couldn't even decide on a form of address – 'dear' seemed dismissive and 'dearest' a lie. With the bottle almost empty and the page still unmarked, she walked out into the storm.

Her blood thick with drink and grief and anger, she made her way to the pool. The village was empty, hatches battened down. Unseen and undisturbed, she clambered and slipped through mud to the cliff. She waited. She waited for someone to come, she prayed that the man she had fallen in love with might miraculously somehow know, might somehow sense her despair and come to save her from herself. But the voice she heard, calling her name in panicked desperation, was not the one she wanted to hear.

And so boldly she stepped up to the precipice and, eyes wide open, pitched herself forward.

There was no way she could have seen him, no way she could have known that her boy was down there, behind the treeline.

No way she could have known that he had been woken

by his father's shouts and the sound of the front door slamming, that he had got up and run downstairs and out into the storm, his feet bare and his skinny limbs covered only by the thinnest cotton.

Sean saw his father climbing into the car and screamed for his mother. Patrick turned, yelling at his son to go back into the house. He ran towards him, grabbing him roughly by the arm and yanking him off his feet, and tried to force him back into the house. But the boy begged, 'Please, please, don't leave me here.'

Patrick relented. He gathered the boy up and carried him to the car, securing him in the back seat, where Sean cowered, terrified and uncomprehending. He squeezed his eyes tightly shut. They drove to the river. His father parked the car up on the bridge and said to him, 'Wait. Wait here.' But it was dark and the rain on the roof of the car sounded like bullets and Sean couldn't escape the feeling that there was someone else in the car with him, he could hear their ragged breathing. So he got out and ran, tripping down the stone steps and falling in the mud on the path, blundering in the darkness and the rain towards the pool.

There was a story, later, at school, that he saw it – he was the boy who watched his mother jump to her death. It wasn't true. He didn't see anything. When he got to the pool, his father was already in the water, swimming out. He didn't know what to do, so he went back and sat under the trees, his back to a stout trunk so that no one could sneak up on him.

It seemed as though he was there for a very long time. Thinking back, he wondered if he might even have fallen asleep, although with the darkness and the noise and the fear, that didn't seem terribly likely. What he could remember was a woman coming – Jeannie, from the police station. She had a blanket and a torch and she took him back up to the bridge and gave him sweet tea to drink, and they waited there for his father.

Later, Jeannie drove him to her house and made him cheese on toast.

But there was no way Lauren could have known any of that.

Erin

LEAVING THE FUNERAL, I noticed how many people who had attended the service made their way over to say a few words to Sean Townsend's father, a man I had been introduced to, incredibly briefly, as Patrick Townsend. There was much shaking of hands and doffing of caps, and all the while he stood there like a major general on parade, back straight and lip stiff.

'Miserable bugger, isn't he?' I said to the uniform standing next to me. The PC turned and looked at me like I had just crawled out from under a rock.

'Show some respect,' he hissed, and turned his back on me.

'Excuse me?' I said, talking to the scruff of his neck.

'He's a highly decorated officer,' the PC said. 'And a widower. His wife died here, in this river.' He turned again to face me and without a hint of deference to my position he sniffed, 'So you ought to show some respect.'

I felt like a fucking idiot. But really, how was I supposed to know that the Sean in Nel Abbott's story was the Sean in the police station? I didn't know his parents' names. Fuck's sake. Nobody told me, and when I read through Nel Abbott's work it wasn't like I was paying *that* much attention to the details of a suicide that took place more than three decades ago. It didn't seem overly pressing, under the circumstances.

Seriously: how is anyone supposed to keep track of all the bodies around here? It's like *Midsomer Murders*, only with accidents and suicides and grotesque historical misogynistic drownings instead of people falling into the slurry or bashing each other over the head.

I drove back to the city after work – some of the others were going to the pub, but thanks to the Patrick Townsend faux pas I was wearing my outsider status a little more heavily than before. In any event, this case is over, isn't it? No point hanging around.

I felt relieved, the way you do when you finally figure out what movie you've seen an actor in before, when something hazy that's been bothering you suddenly snaps into focus. The DI's strangeness – the watery eyes, the shaky hands, his disconnectedness – it all makes sense now. It makes sense if you know his history. His family has suffered almost exactly what Jules and Lena are suffering now – the same horror, the same shock. The same wondering why.

I reread Nel Abbott's section on Lauren Townsend. It doesn't tell much of a story. She was an unhappy wife, in love with another man. It talks of her distraction, her absence – maybe she was depressed? In the end, who knows? It's not like this stuff is gospel, it's just Nel Abbott's version of history. It must take a strange sense of entitlement, I would have thought, to take someone else's tragedy like that and write it as though it belonged to you.

Rereading it, the thing I don't understand is how Sean could have stayed here. Even if he didn't see her fall, he was *there*. What the fuck does that do to you? Still. He would have been small, I suppose. Six or seven? Kids can block it out, trauma like that. But the father? He walks by the river every day, I've seen him. Imagine that. Imagine walking past the place where you lost someone, every single day. I can't credit it, couldn't do it. But then I suppose I've never really lost anyone. How would I know what that kind of grief feels like?

PART TWO

TUESDAY, 18 AUGUST

Louise

LOUISE'S GRIEF WAS like the river: constant and ever-changing. It rippled, flooded, ebbed and flowed, some days cold and dark and deep, some days swift and blinding. Her guilt was liquid, too, it seeped through cracks when she tried to dam it out. She had good days and bad.

Yesterday, she had gone to the church to watch them put Nel in the ground. In reality – and she ought to have known this – they didn't. Still, she got to watch her be taken away to burn, so that was what passed for a good day. Even the outpouring of emotion – she had sobbed throughout the service, despite herself – was cathartic.

But today was going to be a bitch. She felt it when she woke, not a presence but an absence. The elation she'd felt at first, her vengeful satisfaction, was already waning. And now, with Nel burned to ashes, Louise was left with nothing. Nothing. At no one's door could she lay her pain and suffering, because Nel was gone.

And she worried that in the end the only place she had to bring her torment was home.

Home to her husband and son. So. Today was going to be a bitch, but that bitch had to be faced, stared down. She had made up her mind; it was time to move on. They needed to go before it was too late.

Louise and her husband, Alec, had been arguing about this – the sort of low-level, quiet arguments they had these days – for weeks. Alec felt it would be better to move before the new school term started. They should let Josh start the new school year in a completely new place, he argued, where no one knew who he was. Where he wouldn't be confronted with his sister's absence every day.

'So he'll never have to talk about her?' Louise asked.

'He'll talk about her with *us*,' Alec replied.

They'd been standing in the kitchen, their voices strained and hushed. 'We need to sell this house and start over,' Alec said. 'I know,' he said, raising his hands as Louise began to protest. 'I know this is her home.' He faltered then, placing his big hands, mottled with sun damage, on the counter. He hung on as if for dear life. 'We have to make some kind of new start, Lou, for Josh. If it were just you and me . . .'

If it were just them, she thought, they'd follow Katie into the water and be done with it. Wouldn't they? She wasn't sure Alec would. She used to think that only parents can understand the sort of love that swallows you up, but now she wondered whether it was only mothers who did. Alec felt the grief, of course, but she wasn't sure he felt the despair. Or the hatred.

So the fault lines were already beginning to show in a marriage she'd thought unshakable. But of course she'd known nothing before. Now, it was obvious: no marriage could survive this loss. It would always sit between them – that neither of them had been able to stop her. Worse, that neither of them had suspected a thing. That the two of them had gone to bed and fallen asleep and discovered her empty bed in the morning and had not for a single second imagined she'd be in the river.

There was no hope for Louise, and little, she thought, for Alec, but Josh was different. Josh would miss his sister every day for the rest of his life, but he could be happy: he would. He would carry her with him, but he would also work, travel, fall in love, live. And the best chance he had was to be away from here, away from Beckford, away from the river. Louise knew that her husband was right about that.

Somewhere inside, she'd known this already, she'd just been reluctant to face it. But yesterday, watching her son after the funeral, she had been gripped by terror. His pinched, anxious face. How easily he startled, flinching at loud noises, cowering like a frightened dog in a crowd. The way he constantly turned his gaze to her, as though he was retreating back into early childhood, no longer an independent twelve-year-old, but a frightened, needy little boy. They had to get him away from here.

And yet. This was where Katie had taken her first steps, spoken her first words, played hide and seek, cartwheeled around the garden, fought with her little brother, soothed him afterwards, laughed and sung and cried and cursed and bled and hugged her mum every day when she got home from school.

But Louise had made up her mind. Like her daughter, she was determined, although the effort was immense. Just to get up from the kitchen table, walk to the bottom of the stairs and then climb them, to place her hand on the door handle, to push down, to enter her room for the last time. Because that's what it felt like. This was the last time it would be *her* room. After today, it would be something else.

Louise's heart was a block of wood; it didn't beat, it only pained her, scraping against soft tissue, tearing through vein and muscle, flooding her chest with blood.

Good days and bad.

She couldn't leave the room like this. Hard as it was to think about packing up Katie's things, putting away her clothes, taking her pictures down from the walls, tidying her away, hiding her from view, it was worse to think of strangers in here. It was worse to imagine what they would touch, how they would look for clues, how they would marvel at how normal everything looked, how normal Katie had looked. *Her?* Surely not? Surely *she* can't be the one who drowned?

So Louise would do it: she would clear the school things from the desk and pick up the pen that once rested in her daughter's fist. She would fold up the soft grey T-shirt that Katie slept in, she would make her bed. She would take the blue earrings that Katie's favourite aunt had given her for her fourteenth birthday and tidy them away into her jewellery box. She would take the big, black suitcase from the top of the cupboard in the hallway, she would fill it with Katie's clothes.

She would.

She was standing in the middle of the room, thinking all this, when she heard a noise behind her, and she turned to see Josh standing in the doorway, watching her.

'Mum?' He was white as a ghost, his voice caught in his throat. 'What are you doing?'

'Nothing, darling, I'm just . . .' She took a step towards him, but he stepped back.

'Are you . . . are you going to clear her room now?'

Louise nodded. 'I'm going to make a start,' she said.

'What will you do with her things?' he asked, his voice rising even higher. He sounded strangled. 'Will you give them away?'

'No, darling.' She went to him and reached out to smooth his soft hair from his forehead. 'We'll keep everything. We won't give anything away.'

He looked worried. 'But shouldn't you wait for Dad? Shouldn't he be here? You shouldn't be doing this by yourself.'

Louise smiled at him. 'I'm just going to make a start,' she said, as brightly as she could. 'I actually thought you'd gone round to Hugo's this morning, so . . .' Hugo was Josh's friend, possibly his only true friend. (Every day Louise thanked the Lord for the existence of Hugo and Hugo's family, who took Josh in whenever he needed an escape.)

'I did, but I forgot my phone, so I came back for it.' He held it up for her to see.

'OK,' she said. 'Good boy. Are you staying there for lunch?'

He nodded, and he tried to smile, and then he was gone. She waited until she heard the front door slam before she sat down on the bed and allowed herself to cry properly.

On the bedside table there was an old hair tie, stretched and worn down almost to a thread, long strands of Katie's glorious dark hair still entwined in it. Louise picked it up and turned it over in her hands, lacing it between her fingers. She held it against her face. She got to her feet and walked over to the dressing table, opened the heart-shaped pewter jewellery box and placed the hair tie inside. It would remain there along with her bracelets and earrings – nothing would be thrown away, everything would remain. Not here, but somewhere; it would travel with them. No part of Katie, nothing she had touched, would languish on a dusty charity-shop shelf.

Around Louise's neck hung the necklace which Katie had been wearing when she died, a silver chain with a little bluebird. It bothered Louise that she'd chosen that particular piece of jewellery. Louise hadn't thought it a favourite. Not like the white-gold earrings which Louise and Alec had given her on her thirteenth birthday, which she'd adored, not like the woven friendship bracelet ('brotherhood bracelet') which Josh bought for her (with his own money!) on their last holiday to Greece. Louise couldn't fathom why Katie had chosen that – a present from Lena, to whom she'd no longer seemed particularly close, the bird engraved (most un-Lena-like) *with love*.

She'd worn no other jewellery. Jeans, a jacket, far too warm for the summer evening, its pockets filled with stones. Her backpack similarly laden. When they found her, she was surrounded by flowers, some of them still clutched in her fist. Like Ophelia. Like the picture on Nel Abbott's wall.

People said it was tenuous at best, ridiculous and cruel at worst, to lay the blame at Nel Abbott's door for what happened to Katie. Just because Nel wrote about the pool, talked about the pool, took pictures there, conducted interviews, published articles in the local press, spoke once to a BBC radio programme about it, just because she said the words 'suicide spot', just because she talked about her beloved 'swimmers' as glorious, romantic heroines, as women of courage meeting easeful death in their chosen place of beauty, *she* could not be held responsible.

But Katie didn't hang herself from the back of her bedroom door, she didn't cut her wrists or take a handful of pills. She chose the pool. What was truly ridiculous was to ignore that, to ignore the context, to ignore how suggestible some people can be – sensitive people, young people. Teenagers – good, intelligent, kind children – become intoxicated with ideas. Louise didn't understand why Katie did what she did, she never would, but she knew that her act hadn't happened in isolation.

The grief counsellor she had seen for just two sessions told her that she shouldn't seek to know why. That she wouldn't ever be able to answer that question, that no one could; that in many cases where someone takes their own life, there isn't one reason why, life just isn't that simple. Louise, despairing, had pointed out that Katie had no history of depression, she wasn't being bullied (they talked to the school, they went through her email, her Facebook, they found nothing but love). She was pretty, she was doing well in school, she had ambition, drive. She wasn't unhappy. Wild-eyed sometimes, excitable often. Moody. *Fifteen*. Most of all, she wasn't secretive. If she had been in trouble, she would have told her mother. She told her mother everything, she always had. 'She didn't keep things from me,' Louise said to the counsellor, and she watched his eyes slide from her face.

'That's what all parents think,' he said quietly, 'and I'm afraid all parents are wrong.'

Louise didn't see the counsellor again after that, but the damage had been done. A fissure had opened and guilt seeped through, a trickle at first and then a flood. She didn't know her daughter. That was why the necklace bothered her so much, not just because it came from Lena, but because it became a symbol for everything she didn't know about her daughter's life. The more she thought about that, the more she blamed herself: for being too busy, for focusing too much on Josh, for failing so completely to protect her child.

The tide of guilt rose and rose and there was only one way to keep her head above it, to keep from drowning, and that was to find a reason, to point to it, to say, *There. That was it.* Her daughter made a senseless choice, but pockets filled with stones and hands grasping flowers: the choice had context. The context was provided by Nel Abbott.

Louise

Louise placed the black suitcase on the bed, opened the wardrobe and began to slip Katie's clothes off their hangers: her bright T-shirts, her summer dresses, the shocking-pink hoodie she wore all last winter. Her vision blurred and she tried to think of something to stop the tears coming, she tried to find some image on which to fix her mind's eye, and so she thought of Nel's body, broken in the water, and she took what comfort she could from that.

Sean

I WAS ROUSED by the sound of a woman calling out, a desperate, faraway sound. I thought I must have dreamed it, but then I was jolted awake by banging, loud and close and intrusive and real. There was someone at the front door.

I dressed quickly and ran downstairs, glancing at the clock in the kitchen as I passed. It was only just after midnight – I couldn't have been sleeping for more than half an hour. The hammering at the door persisted and I could hear a woman calling my name, a voice I knew but for a moment couldn't place. I opened the door.

'Do you see this?' Louise Whittaker was shouting at me, red-faced and furious. 'I told you, Sean! I told you there was something going on!' The *this* to which she referred was an orange plastic vial, the sort you get prescription drugs in, and on the side there was a label, with a name. Danielle Abbott. 'I told you!' she said again, and then she burst into tears. I ushered her inside – too late. Before I closed the kitchen door I saw a light go on in the upstairs bedroom of my father's house.

Sean

It took quite a while to understand what Louise was telling me. She was hysterical, her sentences running into each other and making no sense. I had to tease the information out of her gradually, one gulping, breathless, furious phrase at a time. They had decided at last to put the house on the market. Before viewings could start, she needed to clear out Katie's bedroom. She wasn't having strangers tramping through there, touching her things. She had made a start on it that afternoon. While she was packing away Katie's clothes she had found the orange vial. She'd been removing a coat from a hanger, the green one, one of Katie's favourites. She'd heard a rattling noise. She'd slipped her hand into the pocket and discovered the bottle of pills. She was shocked, even more so when she saw that the name on the bottle was Nel's. She had never heard of the drug – Rimato – before, but she looked it up on the internet and discovered that it was a kind of diet pill. *The pills are not legally available in the UK. Studies in the United States have linked their use to depression and suicidal thoughts.*

'You missed it!' she cried. 'You told me she had nothing in her blood. You said Nel Abbott had nothing to do with it. But here,' she banged her fist on the table, making the vial jump into the air, 'see! She was supplying my daughter with drugs, with *dangerous* drugs. And you let her get away with it.'

It was strange, but all the time she was saying this, attacking me, I felt relieved. Because now there was a reason. If Nel had supplied Katie with drugs, then we could point to that, and say, Look, there, that's why it happened. That's why a brilliant, happy young girl lost her life. That's why *two* women lost their lives.

It was comforting, but it was also a lie. I knew it was a lie. 'Her blood tests were negative, Louise,' I said. 'I don't know how long this . . . this Rimato? I've no idea how long it stays in the system. We've no idea if this even *is* Rimato, but . . .' I got to my feet, fetched a plastic sandwich bag from the kitchen drawer and held it out to Louise. She picked the vial up from the table and dropped it into the bag. I sealed it up. 'We can find out.'

'And then we'll know,' she said, gulping for air again.

The truth was, we wouldn't know. Even if there were traces of a drug in her system, even if there was something that had been missed, it wouldn't tell us anything definitive.

'I know it's too late,' Louise was saying, 'but I want this to be known. I want everyone to know what Nel Abbott did – Christ, she might have given pills to other girls . . . You need to speak to your wife about this – as head teacher, she should know someone's selling this shit in her school. You need to search the lockers, you need—'

'Louise,' I sat down at her side, 'slow down. Of course we'll take this seriously – we will – but we have no way of knowing how this bottle came into Katie's possession. It's possible that Nel Abbott purchased the pills for her own use . . .'

'And what? What are you saying? That Katie *stole* them? How dare you even suggest that, Sean! You knew her—'

The kitchen door rattled – it sticks, especially after

rain – and flew open. It was Helen, looking dishevelled in tracksuit bottoms and a T-shirt, her hair uncombed. 'What's going on? Louise, what's happened?'

Louise shook her head, but said nothing. She covered her face with her hands.

I got to my feet and spoke to Helen. 'You should go on up to bed,' I said, keeping my voice low. 'There's nothing to worry about.'

'But—'

'I just need to chat to Louise for a bit. It's all right. You go on upstairs.'

'All right,' she said warily, glancing down at the woman sobbing quietly at our kitchen table. 'If you're sure . . .'

'I am.'

Helen slipped quietly out of the kitchen, closing the door behind her as she left. Louise wiped her eyes. She was looking at me oddly, wondering, I suppose, where Helen had been. I could have explained: she doesn't sleep well, my father's an insomniac too, sometimes they sit up together, do crosswords, listen to the radio. I could have explained, but the prospect felt tiring all of a sudden, so instead I said, 'I don't think Katie stole anything, Louise. Of course I don't. But she might have . . . I don't know, picked them up absent-mindedly. She might have been curious. You say they were in a coat pocket? Perhaps she picked them up and then forgot about them.'

'My daughter didn't take things from other people's homes,' Louise replied sourly, and I nodded. No point arguing this one.

'I'll look into it, first thing tomorrow. I'll have these sent to the labs, and we'll look at Katie's blood tests again. If I missed something, Louise . . .'

She shook her head. 'I know it doesn't change anything. I know it won't bring her back,' she said quietly. 'It would just help me. To understand.'

'I see that. Of course I do. Would you like me to drive you home?' I asked her. 'I can bring your car over in the morning.'

She shook her head again and gave me a shaky smile. 'I'm OK,' she said. 'Thank you.'

The echo of her thanks – unwarranted, undeserved – rang out in the silence after she'd gone. I felt wretched, and was grateful for the sound of Helen's footsteps on the stairs, grateful that I wouldn't have to be alone.

'What's going on?' she asked me as she entered the kitchen. She looked pale and very tired, with circles like bruises under her eyes. She sat down at the table and reached for my hand. 'What was Louise doing here?'

'She found something,' I said. 'Something which she thinks might have some bearing on what happened to Katie.'

'Oh, God, Sean. What?'

I puffed out my cheeks. 'I shouldn't . . . probably shouldn't discuss it in detail just yet.' She nodded and squeezed my hand. 'Tell me, when was the last time you confiscated drugs at school?'

She frowned. 'Well, that little toerag, Watson – Iain – had some marijuana taken off him at the end of term, but before that . . . oh, not for a while. Not for a long while. Back in March, I think, that business with Liam Markham.'

'That was pills, wasn't it?'

'Yes, ecstasy – or something purporting to be ecstasy, in any case, and Rohypnol. He was excluded.'

I vaguely remembered the incident, though it's not the sort of thing I involve myself in. 'There's been nothing since? You haven't come across any diet pills, have you?'

She raised an eyebrow. 'No. Nothing illegal, in any case. Some of the girls take those blue ones – what do they call them? Alli, I think. It's available over the counter, although I don't think it's supposed to be sold to minors.' She wrinkled her nose. 'It makes them horribly flatulent, but apparently that's an acceptable price to pay for a thigh gap.'

'To pay for a what?'

Helen rolled her eyes at me. 'A thigh gap! They all want legs so skinny they don't meet at the top. Honestly, Sean, sometimes I think you live on a different planet.' She squeezed my hand again. 'Sometimes I wish I lived there with you.'

We went up to bed together for the first time in a long time, but I couldn't touch her. Not after what I'd done.

WEDNESDAY, 19 AUGUST

Erin

IT TOOK HAIRY the science guy about five minutes to find the email receipt for the diet pills in Nel Abbott's spam folder. As far as he could tell, she only bought the pills on one occasion, unless of course she had another email account which was no longer in use.

'Odd, isn't it?' commented one of the uniforms, one of the older guys whose name I haven't bothered to learn. 'She was such a thin woman. Wouldn't have thought she needed them. The sister, she was the fat one.'

'Jules?' I said. 'She isn't fat.'

'Oh, aye, not now, but you should have seen her back in the day.' He started laughing. 'She was a heifer.'

Fucking charming.

Since Sean told me about the pills, I've been swotting up on Katie Whittaker. It was pretty clear cut, although the question of *why* loomed large – as is so often the case. Her parents didn't suspect anything was up. Her teachers said that perhaps she'd been a little distracted, maybe a bit more reserved than usual, but there were no red flags. Her bloodwork was clean. She'd no history of self-harm.

The only thing – and it wasn't much of a thing – was an alleged falling-out with her best friend, Lena Abbott. A couple of Katie's school friends claimed that Lena and Katie had had a disagreement about something. Louise, Katie's mother, said they'd been seeing less of each other, but she didn't think there had been an argument. If there had been, she said, Katie would have mentioned it. They'd had fights in the past – teenage girls will do that – and Katie had always been upfront about it with her mum. And in the past, they'd always kissed and made up. After one fight, Lena had felt bad enough to give Katie a necklace.

These school friends though – Tanya Something and Ellie Something Else – said that something big was up, though they couldn't say what. All they knew was that a month or so before Katie died, she and Lena had what they called a 'vicious argument' that ended in them being physically separated by a teacher. Lena hotly denied it, claiming Tanya and Ellie had it in for her, that they were just trying to get her into trouble. Certainly Louise had never heard of this row, and the teacher involved – Mark Henderson – claimed it wasn't really an argument at all. They were play-fighting, he said. Messing about. It got very noisy and he told them to quieten down. And that was it.

I skimmed over that when I was reading Katie's file, but I kept coming back to it. Something felt off. Do teenage girls play-fight? It seems like something teenage boys would be more likely to do. Perhaps I've internalized more sexism than I care to admit. But I was just looking at pictures of those girls – pretty, poised, Katie in particular very well groomed – and they didn't look much like play-fighters to me.

When I parked the car outside the Mill House, I heard a noise and glanced up. Lena was leaning out of one of the upstairs windows, a cigarette in her hand.

'Hello, Lena,' I called out. She didn't say anything, but, very deliberately, took aim and flicked the cigarette butt in my direction. Then she withdrew, slamming the window shut. I don't buy the play-fighting thing at all: I imagine that when Lena Abbott fights, she fights for real.

Jules let me in, glancing nervously over my shoulder as she did so.

'Everything all right?' I asked her. She looked awful: haggard, grey, eyes bleary, hair unwashed.

'I can't sleep,' she said softly. 'I just don't seem to be able to get to sleep.'

She shuffled through to the kitchen, flicked the kettle on and slumped down at the table. She reminded me of my sister three weeks after she gave birth to her twins – barely enough strength to hold her head up.

'Perhaps you ought to get the doctor to prescribe you something,' I suggested, but she shook her head.

'I don't want to sleep too deeply,' she said, her eyes widening, giving her a manic cast. 'I need to be alert.'

I could have said that I'd seen greater alertness from coma patients, but I didn't.

'This Robbie Cannon you were asking about,' I said. She twitched, and chewed on a nail. 'We had a little look into him. You're right about him being violent – he's got a couple of domestic-violence convictions, amongst other things. But he wasn't involved in your sister's death. I went over to Gateshead – that's where he lives – and had a little chat with him. He was in Manchester visiting his son the night Nel died. He says he hasn't seen her in years, but when he read about her death in the local paper he decided he would come up here to pay his respects. He seemed pretty gobsmacked that we were asking him about it at all.'

'Did he . . .' Her voice was little more than a whisper. 'Did he mention me? Or Lena?'

'No. He didn't. Why do you ask? Has he been here?' I thought of the tentative way in which she'd opened the front door, the way she'd looked over my shoulder as though watching out for someone.

'No. I mean, I don't think so. I don't know.'

I managed to get nothing more out of her on the subject. It was clear that she was frightened of him for some reason, but she wouldn't say why. It was unsatisfactory, but I left it at that, as I had another awkward subject to raise.

'This is a bit difficult,' I said to her. 'I'm afraid we need to search the house again.'

She stared at me, horrified. 'Why? Have you found something? What's happened?'

I explained about the pills.

'Oh, God.' She squeezed her eyes shut and hung her head. It might have been exhaustion dulling her re-action, but she didn't seem shocked.

'She purchased them in November of last year, on

the eighteenth, from an American website. We can't find a record of any other purchases, but we need to make sure—'

'All right,' she said. 'Of course.' She rubbed her eyes with the tips of her fingers.

'A couple of uniforms will come round this afternoon. Is that OK?'

She shrugged. 'Well, if you have to, but I . . . what date did you say she bought them?'

'The eighteenth of November,' I said, checking my note. 'Why?'

'It's just . . . that's the anniversary. Of our mother's death. It seems . . . oh, I don't know.' She frowned. 'It just seems odd, because Nel usually called me on the eighteenth, and last year was notable because she didn't. It turned out she was in hospital, for an emergency appendectomy. I suppose I'm just surprised she would have been spending her time buying diet pills when she was in hospital for emergency surgery. You're sure it was the eighteenth?'

Back at the station, I checked with Hairy. I was right about the date.

'She could have bought them on her mobile,' Callie suggested. 'It is really boring in hospital.'

But Hairy shook his head. 'No, I've checked the IP address – whoever made the purchase did so at four seventeen p.m. and they did so from a computer using the Mill House router. So it had to be someone in or near the house. Do you know what time she went into hospital?'

I didn't, but it wasn't difficult to find out. Nel Abbott

was admitted in the small hours of 18 November for an emergency appendectomy, just like her sister said. She remained in hospital all that day, and they kept her in overnight, too.

Nel couldn't have bought the pills. They were purchased by someone else, using her card, in her home.

'Lena,' I said to Sean. 'It's got to be Lena.'

He nodded, grim-faced. 'We're going to need to talk to her.'

'You want to do it now?' I asked him and he nodded again.

'No time like the present,' he said. 'No time like immediately after the child has lost her mother. Christ, this is a mess.'

And it was about to get messier. We were on our way out of the office when we were waylaid by an overexcited Callie.

'The prints!' she said breathlessly. 'They've got a match. Well, not quite a match, because there's no match to anyone who's come forward, only—'

'Only what?' the DI snapped.

'Some bright spark decided to take a look at the print on the pill bottle and compare it to the print on the camera – you know, the damaged one?'

'Yes, we remember the damaged camera,' Sean replied.

'OK, well, they match. And before you say it, it's not Nel Abbott's print, and it's not Katie Whittaker's. Someone else handled both those objects.'

'Louise,' Sean said. 'It has to be. Louise Whittaker.'

Mark

MARK WAS ZIPPING up his suitcase when the detective arrived. A different detective this time, another woman, a bit older and not so pretty.

'DS Erin Morgan,' she said, shaking his hand. 'I was wondering if I could have a word.'

He didn't invite her in. The house was a mess and he wasn't in the mood to be accommodating.

'I'm packing to go on holiday,' he said. 'I'm driving to Edinburgh this evening to pick up my fiancée. We're going to Spain for a few days.'

'It won't take long,' DS Morgan said, her gaze slipping over his shoulder and into the house.

He pulled the front door to. They spoke on the front step.

He assumed it would be about Nel Abbott again. He was, after all, one of the last people to see her alive. He'd seen her outside the pub, they'd spoken briefly, he'd watched her head off towards the Mill House. He was prepared for that conversation. He wasn't prepared for this one.

Mark

'I know you've already been over this, but there are a few things we need to clarify,' the woman said, 'about events leading up to the death of Katie Whittaker.'

Mark felt his pulse quicken. 'What, er . . . what about it?'

'I understand that you had cause to intervene in an argument between Lena Abbott and Katie, about a month before Katie died?'

Mark's throat felt very dry. He struggled to swallow. 'It wasn't an argument,' he said. He held up his hand to shield his eyes from the sun. 'Why . . . sorry, why is this coming up again? Katie's death was ruled a suicide, I thought—'

'Yes,' the detective interrupted, 'yes it was, and that hasn't changed. However, we've come to understand that there might have been, er, *circumstances* surrounding Katie's death which we didn't know about before and which may require further investigation.'

Mark turned abruptly, pushing the front door open so hard it rebounded on to him as he stepped into the hallway. The vice was tightening on his skull, his heart was pounding, he had to get out of the sun.

'Mr Henderson? Are you all right?'

'I'm fine.' His eyes adjusting to the darkness of the hallway, he turned back once more to look at her. 'Fine. A bit of a headache, that's all. The glare, it's just—'

'Why don't we get you a glass of water?' DS Morgan suggested with a smile.

'No,' he replied, realizing even as he spoke how sullen he sounded. 'No, I'm fine.'

There was a silence. 'The argument, Mr Henderson? Between Lena and Katie?'

Mark shook his head. 'It wasn't an argument . . . I told the police this at the time. I didn't have to *separate* them. Not . . . at least, not in the way that was suggested. Katie and Lena were very close, they could be excitable and voluble, the way many girls of that age – children of that age – can be.'

The detective, still standing in the sunshine on the front step, was now a faceless outline, a shadow. He preferred her that way.

'Some of Katie's teachers reported that she seemed distracted, perhaps a bit more reserved than usual, in the weeks running up to her death. Is that your recollection?'

'No,' Mark said. He blinked slowly. 'No. I don't believe so. I don't believe that she had changed. I didn't notice anything different. I didn't see it coming. We – none of us – saw this coming.'

His voice was low and strained and the detective noticed. 'I'm sorry to bring all this up again,' she said. 'I understand how terrible—'

'I don't imagine that you do, actually. I saw that girl every day. She was young and bright and . . . She was one of my best students. We were all very . . . fond of her.' He stumbled over *fond*.

'I'm very sorry, I really am. But the thing is that some new facts have come to light, and we have to look into them.'

Mark nodded, struggling to hear her over the pounding of blood in his ears; his entire body felt very cold, as though someone had poured petrol all over him.

'Mr Henderson, we have been led to understand that Katie may have been taking a drug, something called Rimato. Have you heard of it?'

Mark peered at her. Now he did want to see her eyes, he wanted to read her expression. 'No . . . I . . . I thought they said that she hadn't taken anything? That was what the police said at the time. Rimato? What is that? Is that . . . recreational?'

Morgan shook her head. 'It's a diet pill,' she said.

'Katie wasn't overweight,' he said, realizing how stupid that sounded even as he said it. 'They talk about it all the time, though, don't they? Teenage girls. About their weight. And not just teenagers, either. Grown women, too. My fiancée never shuts up about it.'

True, though not the *whole truth*. Because his fiancée was no longer his fiancée, she no longer moaned to him about her weight, nor was she waiting for him to pick her up to accompany him to Málaga. In her last email, sent some months ago now, she'd wished misery on him, told him she'd never forgive him for the way he'd treated her.

But what had he done that was so terrible? If he'd been a truly awful man, a cold, cruel, unfeeling man, he'd have strung her along for appearances' sake. It would have been in his interests, after all. But he *wasn't* a bad man. It was just that when he loved, he loved completely – and what on earth was wrong with that?

After the detective left, he walked around the house, opening drawers, thumbing through the pages of books, looking. Looking for something he knew very well he wouldn't find. The night after Midsummer, angry and frightened, he'd built a fire in the back garden and had piled on to it cards and letters, a book. Other gifts. If he looked out of the back window now, he could still see it, a little patch of scorched earth where he had eradicated every trace of her.

As he pulled open the desk drawer in his living room, he knew exactly what he'd see, because this wasn't the first time he'd done it. He'd searched and searched for something he'd missed, sometimes in fear and often in grief. But he'd been thorough that first night.

There were pictures, he knew, in the head's office at school. A file. Closed now, but still kept. He had a key to the admin block and he knew exactly where to look. And he wanted something, he *needed* something to take with him. This wasn't a triviality, it was essential, he felt, because the future was suddenly so uncertain. He had an inkling that when he turned the key in the back door, locking up the house, he might never do that again. Perhaps he wouldn't come back. Perhaps it was time to disappear, to start over.

He drove to the school, parking in the empty car park. Sometimes Helen Townsend worked there during the school holidays, but there was no sign of her car today. He was alone. He let himself into the building and headed up past the staff room to Helen's office. Her door was closed, but when he tried the handle, he found it unlocked.

He pushed the door open, breathing in the nasty chemical whiff of carpet cleaner. He crossed the room to the filing cabinet and pulled open the top drawer. It had been emptied, and the drawer below was locked. He realized with an acute sense of disappointment that someone had rearranged everything, that in fact he didn't know exactly where to look, that perhaps this had been a wasted journey. He darted out to the hallway to check that he was still alone – he was, his red Vauxhall still the only vehicle in the car park – and went back to the head's office. Taking care not to disturb anything, he opened Helen's desk drawers one by one, looking for the keys to the filing cabinet. He didn't find them, but he did find something else: a trinket he couldn't imagine Helen wearing. Something which struck him as vaguely familiar. A silver bracelet with an onyx clasp, and an engraving reading *SJA*.

He sat and stared at it for a long time. He couldn't for the life of him think what it meant, the fact that it was *here*. It meant nothing. It couldn't mean anything. Mark replaced the bracelet in the desk, abandoned his search and returned to his car. He had the key in the ignition when it struck him exactly when he'd seen that bracelet last. He'd seen it on Nel, outside the pub. They'd spoken briefly. He'd watched her head off to-wards the Mill House. But before that, before she had left him, she had been fidgeting with something on her wrist as they spoke, and there, it was there. He retraced his steps, went back to Helen's office and opened the drawer, took the bracelet and put it into his pocket. He knew as he was doing it that if someone asked him why, he wouldn't be able to explain himself.

It was, he thought, as though he were in deep water, as though he were reaching for something, anything, to save himself. It was as though he had reached for a lifebuoy and instead found weeds, and grabbed hold of them anyway.

Erin

THE BOY – JOSH – was standing outside the house when we arrived, like a little soldier on guard, pale and watchful. He greeted the DI politely, looking more suspiciously at me. He was holding a Swiss army knife in his hands, his fingers working nervously around the blade as he opened and closed it.

'Is your mum in, Josh?' Sean asked him, and he nodded.

'Why do you want to talk to us again?' he asked, his voice rising with a sharp squeak. He cleared his throat.

'We just need to check a couple of things,' Sean said. 'It's nothing to worry about.'

'She was in bed,' Josh announced, his eyes flicking from Sean's face to mine. 'That night. Mum was asleep. We were all asleep.'

'What night?' I asked. 'What night was that, Josh?'

He blushed and looked down at his hands and fiddled with his knife. A little boy who hadn't learned yet how to lie.

His mother opened the door behind him. She looked

from me to Sean and sighed, rubbing her fingers over her brows. Her face was the colour of weak tea and when she turned to talk to her son I noticed that her back was hunched, like an old woman. She beckoned him to her, speaking quietly.

'But what if they want to talk to me too?' I heard him asking.

She placed her hands firmly on his shoulders. 'They won't, darling,' she said. 'Off you go.'

Josh closed his knife and slipped it into his jeans pocket, his eyes on mine as he did. I smiled and he turned away, walking quickly down the path, glancing back just once as his mother was pulling the door closed behind us.

I followed Louise and Sean into a big, bright living room leading out into one of those boxy, modern conservatories which seem to make the house bleed seamlessly into the garden. Outside, I could see a wooden hutch on the lawn and bantams, pretty black and white and golden hens, scratching around for food. Louise indicated for us to sit on the sofa. She lowered herself into the armchair opposite, slowly and carefully, like someone recovering from an injury, afraid of inflicting more damage.

'So,' she said, raising her chin slightly as she looked at Sean. 'What have you got to tell me?'

He explained that the new blood tests gave the same results as the original ones: there were no traces of drugs in Katie's system.

Louise listened, shaking her head in clear disbelief. 'But you don't know, do you, how long that sort of drug stays in the system? Or how long it takes for the effects to manifest, or to wear off? You can't dismiss this, Sean—'

'We're dismissing nothing, Louise,' he said evenly. 'All I'm telling you is what we have found.'

'Surely . . . well, surely supplying illegal drugs to someone – to a child – is an offence, in any case? I know . . .' She grazed her teeth over her lower lip. 'I know it's too late to *punish* her, but it should be made known, don't you think? What she did?'

Sean said nothing. I cleared my throat and Louise glared at me as I began to speak.

'From what we've discovered, Mrs Whittaker, regarding the timing of the purchase of the pills, Nel could not have purchased them. Although her credit card was used, it—'

'What are you suggesting?' Her voice rose angrily. 'Now you're saying Katie stole her credit card?'

'No, no,' I said. 'We're not saying anything of the sort . . .'

Her face changed as realization dawned on her. 'Lena,' she said, leaning back in her chair, her mouth fixed in grim resignation. 'Lena did it.'

We didn't know that for sure either, Sean explained, though we would certainly be questioning her about it. In fact, she was due to visit the station that afternoon. He asked Louise whether she'd found anything else of concern amongst Katie's possessions. Louise dismissed the question bluntly. 'This is it,' she said, leaning forward. 'Can't you see that? You combine the pills and this place and the fact that Katie spent so much time round at the Abbotts', surrounded by all those pictures and those stories, and . . .' She tailed off. Even she didn't seem entirely convinced by the story she was telling. Because even if she was right, and even if those pills had made her daughter depressed, none of it changed the fact that she hadn't noticed.

I didn't say that, of course, because what I had to ask was difficult enough. Louise was hauling herself to her feet, assuming our meeting to be over, expecting us to leave, and I had to stop her.

'There's something else we need to ask you about,' I said.

'Yes?' She remained standing, her arms crossed over her chest.

'We wondered if you would be prepared to let us take your fingerprints—'

She interrupted before I could explain. 'What for? Why?'

Sean shifted uneasily in his chair. 'Louise, we have a matching print from the pill bottle you gave me and from one of Nel Abbott's cameras, and we need to establish why. That's all.'

Louise sat back down. 'Well, they're probably Nel's,' she said. 'Wouldn't you imagine?'

'They're not Nel's,' I replied. 'We've checked. They're not your daughter's either.'

She flinched at that. 'Of course they're not Katie's. What would Katie be doing with the camera?' She pursed her lips, raising her hand to the chain around her neck, running the little bluebird back and forth. She sighed heavily. 'Well, they're mine, of course,' she said. 'They're mine.'

It happened three days after her daughter died, she told us. 'I went to Nel Abbott's house. I was . . . well, I doubt you can imagine the state I was in, but you can try. I beat on her front door, but she wouldn't come out. I wouldn't give up, I just stayed there, pounding on the door and calling out for her, and eventually,' she said, sweeping a strand of hair from her face, 'Lena opened the door. She was crying, sobbing, practically hysterical. It was quite a scene.' She tried and failed to smile. 'I said some things to her – cruel things, I suppose, in retrospect, but . . .'

'What sort of things?' I asked.

'I . . . I don't really remember the details.' Her composure was starting to slip, her breath shortening, her hands gripping the sides of her armchair, the effort turning the olive skin over her knuckles to yellow. 'Nel must have heard me. She came outside and told me to leave them alone. She said' – Louise gave a yelping laugh – 'she said that she was *sorry for my loss*. She was sorry for my loss, but it had nothing to do with her, nothing to do with her daughter. Lena was on the ground, I remember that, she was making a noise like . . . like an animal. A wounded animal.' She paused to catch her breath before continuing. 'We argued, Nel and I. It was rather violent.' She half smiled at Sean. 'You're surprised? You've not heard this before? I thought Nel would have told you about it – or Lena, at least. Yes, I . . . well, I didn't hit her, but I lunged at her, and she held me off. I demanded to see the footage from her camera. I wanted . . . I didn't want to see it, but I wanted more than anything for her not to have . . . I couldn't bear . . .'

Louise broke down.

Watching someone in the throes of raw grief is a terrible thing; the act of watching feels violent, intrusive, a violation. Yet we do it, we have to do it, all the time, you just have to learn to cope with it whatever way you can. Sean coped by bowing his head and remaining very still; I coped with distraction: I watched the chickens scratching around on the lawn outside the window. I looked at the bookshelves, my eyes passing over worthy contemporary novels and military-history books; I took in the framed pictures above the fireplace. The wedding photo and the family shot and the photograph of a baby. Just one, a little boy in blue. Where was Katie's picture? I tried to imagine what it would feel like to take the framed picture of your child down from its place of pride and put it in a drawer. When I looked over at Sean, I saw that his head was no longer bent, he was glowering at me. I realized that there was a tapping sound in the room and that it was coming from me, the sound of my pen knocking against my notepad. I wasn't doing it deliberately. I was shaking all over.

After what seemed like a very long time, Louise spoke again. 'I couldn't bear for *Nel* to be the last one to see my child. She told me there was no footage, that the camera wasn't working, that even if it had been, it was up on the cliff, so it wouldn't have . . . wouldn't have captured her.' She heaved a huge sigh, a shudder working itself through her entire body, from her shoulders to her knees. 'I didn't believe her. I couldn't risk it. What if there was something on camera and she used it? What if she showed my girl to the world, alone and frightened

and . . .' She stopped and took a deep breath. 'I told her
. . . Lena must have told you all this? I told her that I
wouldn't rest until I saw her pay for what she'd done.
Then I left. I went to the cliff and tried to open the
camera to get the SD card out of it, but I couldn't. I tried
to break it free from its mount, I ripped my fingernail
out doing so.' She held up her left hand – the nail of her
forefinger was stunted and buckled. 'I kicked it a few
times, I smashed at it with a stone. Then I went home.'

Erin

JOSH WAS SITTING on the pavement opposite the house as we left. He watched us walking towards the car, crossing the road quickly once we'd got fifty yards or so down the street and disappearing into the house. The DI, in his own world, didn't seem to notice.

'She *wouldn't rest until she saw Nel pay*?' I repeated when we reached the car. 'Does that not sound like a threat to you?'

Sean regarded me with his familiar, blank expression, his irritating look of not-really-there-ness. He said nothing.

'I mean, doesn't it seem odd that Lena wouldn't even mention that to us? And Josh? That business about them all being asleep? It was such an obvious lie . . .'

He nodded curtly. 'Yes. It seemed so. But I wouldn't set too much store by the tales of grieving children,' he said quietly. 'There's no telling what he's feeling, or imagining, or what he thinks he should or shouldn't be saying. He knows that we know that his mother bore a grudge against Nel Abbott, and I imagine he's afraid that she's going to be blamed, that she's going to be taken away from him. You have to think about how much he's already lost.' He paused. 'As for Lena, if she truly was as hysterical as Louise suggests, she may not even remember the incident clearly, she may remember very little other than her own distress.'

For my part, I was finding it difficult to marry Louise's description of Lena that day – a howling, wounded beast – with the usually self-contained and occasionally venomous girl we had encountered. It seemed bizarre to me that her reaction to her friend's death would be so extreme, so visceral, when her reaction to her mother's was so *restrained*. Was it possible that Lena had been so affected by Louise's grief, by Louise's conviction that Nel was to blame for Katie's death – that she had come to believe it herself? A prickle ran over my skin. It didn't seem likely, but what if, like Louise, Lena blamed her mother for Katie's death? And what if she decided to do something about that?

Lena

WHY DO ADULTS always ask the wrong questions? The pills. That's what they're all on about now. Those stupid fucking diet pills – I'd forgotten I even bought them, it was so long ago. And now they've decided that THE PILLS ARE THE ANSWER TO EVERYTHING and so I had to go to the police station – with Julia, who is my *appropriate adult*. That made me laugh. She's, like, the least appropriate adult possible for this particular situation.

They took me into a room at the back of the police station which was not like what you see on television, it was just an office. We all sat around a table and that woman – DS Morgan – asked the questions. Mostly. Sean asked some too, but mostly it was her.

I told the truth. I bought the pills on Mum's card because Katie asked me to, and neither of us had any clue that they were bad for you. Or I didn't, in any case, and if Katie did she never said anything to me about it.

'You don't seem particularly concerned,' DS Morgan said, 'that they might have contributed to Katie's negative state of mind at the end of her life?'

I nearly bit through my tongue. 'No,' I told her, 'I'm not concerned about that. Katie didn't do what she did because of any pills.'

'So why did she?'

I should have known she'd seize on that, so I kept talking. 'She didn't even take that many. A few, probably not more than four or five. Count the pills,' I said to Sean. 'I'm pretty sure the order was for thirty-five. Count them.'

'We will,' he said. Then he asked, 'Did you supply pills to anyone else?' I shook my head, but he wouldn't leave it at that. 'This is important, Lena.'

'I know it is,' I told him. 'That was the only time I bought them. I was doing a favour for a friend. That was all it was. Honestly.'

He leaned back in his chair. 'All right,' he said. 'The thing I'm struggling to understand is why Katie would want to take pills like that at all.' He looked at me, and then at Julia, as though she might know the answer. 'It's not as though she was overweight.'

'Well, she wasn't thin,' I said, and Julia made a strange noise, like a cross between a snort and a laugh, and when I looked at her she was looking back at me like she *hated* me.

'Did people say that to her?' DS Morgan asked me. 'At school? Were there comments made about her weight?'

'Jesus!' I was finding it so hard not to lose my temper. 'No. Katie wasn't being bullied. You know what? She used to call me skinny bitch all the time. She used to laugh at me, because, you know . . .' I got embarrassed because Sean was looking right at me, but I'd started so I had to finish, 'Because I've got no boobs. So she called me skinny bitch and sometimes I replied with fat cow, and *neither of us meant it.*'

They didn't get it. They never do. And the problem was, I couldn't explain it all properly. Sometimes, I didn't even understand myself, because although she wasn't thin, it really didn't bother her. She never talked about it the way the others did. I've never had to try, but Amy and Ellie and Tanya did. Always low-carbing or fasting or purging or whatever-the-fuck. But Katie didn't care, she *liked* having tits. She liked the way her body looked, or at least she always used to. And then – I honestly don't know what it was – some stupid comment on Insta or a dumb remark from some Cro-Magnon at school and she got weird about it. That was when she asked me for the pills. But by the time I'd got them, she seemed to be over it – and she said they didn't work anyway.

I thought the interview was over. I thought I'd made my point, and then DS Morgan went off on a completely different tangent, asking me about the day Louise came round just after Katie died. I was like, yes, *of course* I remember that day. It was one of the worst days of my life. I still get upset just thinking about it.

'I've never seen anything like that,' I told them, 'like the way Louise was that day.'

She nodded, then she asked – all earnest, all concerned, 'When Louise said to your mother that "she wouldn't rest until she saw Nel pay", how did you take that? What did you think she meant by that?'

I lost it then. 'She didn't mean *anything*, you fucking moron.'

'Lena.' Sean was glaring at me. 'Language, please.'

'Well, I'm sorry, but for God's sake! Louise's daughter had just died, she didn't even know what she saying. She was *crazy*.'

I was ready to leave, but Sean asked me to stay. 'I don't have to though, do I? I'm not under arrest, am I?'

'No, Lena, of course you're not,' he said.

I spoke to him, because he understood. 'Look, Louise wasn't serious. She was totally hysterical. Off her head. You remember, don't you? What she was like? I mean, of course she was saying all sorts of things, we all were, I think we all went a bit mad after Katie died. But – for God's sake – Louise didn't hurt Mum. Honestly, I think if she'd had a gun or a knife that day, maybe she would have. But she didn't.'

I wanted to tell the whole truth. I really did. Not to the woman detective, not even to Julia, really, but I wanted to tell Sean. But I couldn't. It would have been a betrayal, and after everything I'd done, I couldn't betray Katie now. So I said all I could. 'Louise didn't do anything to my mother, OK? She didn't. Mum made her own choice.'

I got up to go, but DS Morgan wasn't done yet. She was looking at me, this strange expression on her face, like she didn't believe a word I'd been saying, and then she said, 'You know what strikes me as odd, Lena? You don't seem remotely curious as to why Katie did what she did, and why your mother did what *she* did. When someone dies like this, the question everyone asks is *why.* Why would they do that? Why would they take their own lives when they have so much to live for? But not you. And the only reason – *the only reason* – I can think of for that, is because you already know.'

Sean took me by the arm and led me from the room before I could say anything.

Lena

JULIA WANTED TO drive me home, but I told her I felt like a walk. It wasn't true, but a) I didn't want to be in the car alone with her, and b) I saw Josh, on his bike, across the road, going round and round in circles, and I knew he was waiting for me.

"Sup, Josh?' I said when he came riding over. When he was about nine or ten, he started saying "Sup?' to people instead of hello, and Katie and I never let him forget it. Usually he laughs, but this time he didn't. He looked frightened. 'What's wrong, Josh? What's happened?'

'What were they asking you about?' he said in this little whispery voice.

'It's nothing, don't worry. They found some pills that Katie took and they think that they – the pills, I mean – might have something to do with . . . what happened. They're wrong, obviously. Don't worry.' I gave him a little hug and he pulled away, which he never does. Usually he'll use any excuse to have a cuddle or hold my hand.

'Did they ask you about Mum?' he said.

'No. Well, yeah, I suppose. A little. Why?'

'I don't know,' he said, but he wouldn't look at me.

'Why, Josh?'

'I think we should tell,' he said.

I could feel the first spots of warm rain on my arms and I looked up at the sky. It was deathly dark, a storm coming over. 'No, Josh,' I said. 'No. We're not going to tell.'

'Lena, we have to.'

'No!' I said again, and I grabbed his arm more tightly than I meant to and he yelped like a puppy when you step on its tail. 'We made a promise. *You* made a promise.' He shook his head and so I dug my nails into his arm.

He started to cry. 'But what good does it do now?'

I let go of his arm and put my hands on his shoulders. I forced him to look at me. 'A promise is a promise, Josh. I mean it. You do not tell anyone.'

He was right, in a way, we weren't doing any good. There was no good to be done. But still, I couldn't betray her. And if they knew about Katie, they'd ask questions about what happened afterwards, and I didn't want anyone to know about what we did, Mum and I. What we did, and what we didn't do.

I didn't want to leave Josh like that, and I didn't want to go home anyway, so I put my arm around him and gave him a comforting squeeze, and then I took his hand. 'Come on,' I said to him. 'Come with me. I know something we can do, something that'll make us feel better.' He turned bright red and I started laughing.

'Not *that*, you dirty boy!' He laughed too then, and wiped the tears from his face.

We walked in silence towards the southern end of town, Josh pushing his bike along beside me. There was no one about, the rain was coming down harder and harder and I could feel Josh sneaking the occasional glance across at me because my T-shirt was now totally see-through and I wasn't wearing a bra. I crossed my arms over my chest and he blushed again. I smiled, but I didn't say anything. In fact, we didn't talk at all until we got to Mark's road, and then Josh said, 'What are we doing here?' I just grinned at him.

When we were outside Mark's door he asked again, 'Lena, what are we doing here?' He looked frightened again, but excited too, and I could feel all the adrenaline rushing up inside of me, making me feel dizzy and sick.

'This,' I said. I picked up a stone from under the hedge and chucked it as hard as I could against the big window at the front of his house, and it went straight through, just making a small hole.

'Lena!' Josh yelled, anxiously looking around to see if anyone was watching. They weren't. I grinned at him and picked up another stone and did it again, and this time it shattered the window and the whole pane came crashing down. 'Come on,' I said to him, and I handed him a stone, and together we went round the whole house. It was like we were high on hatred – we were laughing and shouting and calling that piece of shit every name we could think of.

The Drowning Pool

Katie, 2015

ON THE WAY to the river, she stopped from time to time to pick up a stone, or a piece of brick, which she put into her backpack. It was cold, not yet light, though if she'd turned back to look in the direction of the sea, she would have seen a hint of grey on the horizon. She did not turn back, not once.

She walked quickly at first, down the hill towards the centre of town, putting some distance between herself and her home. She didn't head straight to the river; she wanted, one last time, to walk through the place she grew up in, past the primary school (not daring to look at it in case flashbacks to her childhood stopped her in her tracks), past the village shop, still shuttered to the night, past the green where her father had tried and failed to teach her to play cricket. She walked past the houses of her friends.

There was a particular house to visit on Seward Road, but she couldn't quite bring herself to walk along it, so instead she chose another, and her pace slowed as her burden became heavier, as the road climbed back towards the old town, the streets narrowing between stone houses clad with climbing roses.

She continued on her way, north past the church until the road took a sharp turn to the right. She crossed the river, stopping for a moment on the humpbacked bridge. She looked down into the water, oily and slick, moving quickly over stones. She could see, or perhaps only imagine, the dark outline of the old mill, its hulking, rotting wheel still, unturned for half a century. She thought about the girl sleeping inside and laid her hands, bluish-white with cold, on the side of the bridge to stop them from trembling.

She descended a steep flight of stone steps from the road to the river-bank path. On this track she could walk all the way to Scotland if she wanted to. She'd done it before, a year ago, last summer. Six of them, carrying tents and sleeping bags, they did it in three days. They camped next to the river at night, drank illicit wine in the moonlight, telling the stories of the river, of Libby and Anne and all the rest. She couldn't possibly have imagined back then that one day she would walk where they had walked, that her fate and theirs were intertwined.

On the half-mile from the bridge to the Drowning Pool, she walked slower still, the pack heavy on her back, hard shapes digging into her spine. She cried a little. Try as she might, she could not stop herself from thinking about her mother, and that was the worst, the very worst thing.

As she passed under the canopy of beech trees at the riverside, it was so dark she could barely see a foot in front of her, and there was comfort in that. She thought that perhaps she would sit down for a while, take off her pack and rest, but she knew that she couldn't, because if she did, the sun would *come up, and it would be too late, and nothing would have changed, and there would be another day on which she would have to get up before dawn and leave the house sleeping. So, one foot in front of the other.*

One foot in front of the other, until she reached the treeline, one foot in front of the other, off the path, a little stumble down the bank, and then, one foot in front of the other, into the water.

Jules

You were making up stories. Rewriting history, retelling it with your own slant, your own version of the truth.

(The hubris, Nel. The fucking *hubris*.)

You don't know what happened to Libby Seeton and you certainly don't know what was going through Katie's head when she died. Your notes make that clear:

> *On the night of Midsummer's Day, Katie Whittaker went into the Drowning Pool. Her footsteps were found on the beach at its southern edge. She wore a green cotton dress and a simple chain around her neck, a bluebird charm engraved 'with love'. On her back, she carried a pack filled with bricks and stones. Tests carried out after her death revealed she was sober and clean.*
>
> *Katie had no history of mental illness or self-harm. She was a good student, pretty and popular. The police found no evidence of bullying, either IRL or on social media.*
>
> *Katie came from a good home, a good family. Katie was loved.*

I was sitting cross-legged on the floor in your study, leafing through your papers in the late-afternoon gloom, looking for answers. Looking for *something*. In amongst the notes – which were disorganized and in disarray, barely legible scribbles in the margins, words underlined in red or crossed out in black – there were pictures, too. In a cheap Manila folder I found print-outs on low-grade photography paper: Katie with Lena, two little girls grinning at the camera, not pouting, not posing, throwbacks to some distant, innocent, pre-Snapchat era. Flowers and tributes left at the edge of the pool, teddy bears, trinkets. Footprints in the sand at the edge of the pool. Not hers, I presume. Not Katie's *actual* prints, surely? No, they must have been your version, a reconstruction. You followed in her footsteps, didn't you? You walked where she walked, you couldn't resist feeling what it felt like.

That was always a thing with you. When you were younger, you were fascinated by the physical act, the bones of it, the viscera. You asked questions: would it hurt? For how long? What did it feel like, to hit water from a height? Would you feel yourself break? You thought less, I think, about the rest of it: about what it took to get someone to the top of the cliff, or to the edge of the beach, and to propel them to keep moving.

At the back of the folder was an envelope with your name scrawled on the front. Inside was a note on lined paper, written in a shaky hand:

I meant what I said when I saw you yesterday. I do not want my daughter's tragedy to become part of your

*macabre 'project'. It's not just that I find it repulsive
that you would gain financially from it. I have told you
time and time again that I believe what you are doing
to be DEEPLY IRRESPONSIBLE and Katie's death is
PROOF OF THAT. If you had an ounce of compassion
you would stop what you are doing now, accept that what
you write and print and say and do has consequences. I
don't expect you to listen to me – you've shown no sign
of doing so in the past. But if you continue down this
path, I've no doubt that someday someone will make
you listen.*

It wasn't signed, but it was obvious it came from
Katie's mother. She warned you – and not just this once
either. In the police station, I'd listened to the detective
ask Lena about an incident just after Katie died, about
how she threatened you and told you she would make
you pay. Is that what you wanted to tell me? Were you
afraid of her? Did you think she was coming for you?

The idea of her, a wild-eyed woman, mad with grief,
hunting you down – it was horrifying, it frightened me.
I no longer wanted to be here, amongst your things. I
raised myself to my feet, and as I did, the house seemed
to shift, to tilt like a boat. I could feel the river pushing
against the wheel, urging it to turn, water seeping into
cracks widened by accomplice weed.

I rested one hand on the filing cabinet and walked
up the stairs into the living room, silence buzzing in
my ears. I stood for a moment, my eyes adjusting to
the brighter light, and for a second I felt sure that I saw
someone, there on the window seat, in the spot where

I used to sit. Just for a moment, and then she was gone, but my heart bludgeoned my ribs and my scalp prickled. Someone was here, or someone had been here. Or someone was coming.

My breath quick and shallow, I half ran to the front door, which was bolted, just as I'd left it. But in the kitchen there was a strange smell – something different, sweet, like perfume – and the kitchen window was wide open. I didn't remember opening it.

I went over to the freezer and did something I almost never do – I poured myself a drink: cold, viscous vodka. I filled a glass and drank it quickly; it burned all the way down my throat and into my belly. Then I poured myself another.

My head swam and I leaned against the kitchen table for support. I was keeping an eye out, I suppose, for Lena. She'd disappeared again, refusing to be given a lift home. Part of me was grateful – I hadn't wanted to share a space with her. I told myself it was because I was angry with her – supplying diet pills to another girl, body-shaming her – but really I was afraid about what the woman detective said. That Lena isn't curious because Lena already knows. I couldn't stop seeing her face, that photo upstairs with her sharp teeth and her predatory smile. What does Lena know?

I went back to the study and sat down on the floor again, gathered up the notes I'd pulled out and began to rearrange them, trying to establish some sort of order. Trying to get a sense of your narrative. When I came to the picture of Katie and Lena, I stopped. There was a smudge of ink on its surface, just beneath Lena's chin.

I turned the picture over in my hands. On the reverse you had written a single line. I read it aloud: *Sometimes troublesome women take care of themselves.*

The room darkened. I looked up and a cry caught in my throat. I hadn't heard her, hadn't heard the front door go or her footsteps crossing the living room, she was just there all of a sudden, standing in the doorway, blocking the light, and from where I was sitting, the shadow profile was Nel's. Then the shadow stepped further into the room and I saw Lena, a smear of dirt on her face, her hands filthy, her hair tangled and wild.

'Who are you talking to?' she asked. She was hopping from one foot to the other, she looked hyper, manic.

'I wasn't talking, I was—'

'Yes, you were,' she giggled. 'I heard you. Who were you—' She broke off then, and the curl of her lip disappeared as she noticed the picture. 'What are you doing with that?'

'I was just reading . . . I wanted—' I didn't have time to get the words out of my mouth before she was upon me, towering over me, and I cowered. She lunged at me and grabbed the picture from my hands.

'What are you doing with this?' She was trembling, her teeth gritted together, red-faced with rage. I scrabbled to my feet. 'This has nothing to do with you!' She turned away from me, placed Katie's picture on the desk and smoothed it over with her palm. 'What right do you have to do this?' she asked, turning back to face me, her voice quavering. 'To go through her stuff, to touch her things? Who gave you permission to do this?'

She took a step towards me, kicking over the glass of

vodka as she did so. It flew up and smashed against the wall. She dropped to her knees and began gathering up the notes I'd been sorting through. 'You shouldn't be touching this!' She was almost spitting with rage. 'This has nothing to do with you!'

'Lena,' I said, 'don't.'

She drew back sharply with a little gasp of pain. She'd put her hand on a piece of glass, it was bleeding. She grabbed a sheaf of the papers and clutched them to her chest.

'Come here,' I said, trying to take the papers from her. 'You're bleeding.'

'Get away from me!' She piled the papers on to the desk. My eye was drawn to the smear of blood across the top sheet and the words printed below it: *Prologue*, in heavy type, and below that: *When I was seventeen, I saved my sister from drowning.*

I felt hysterical laughter rise in me; it burst out of me so loudly that Lena jumped. She stared at me in amazement. I laughed harder, at the furious look on her beautiful face, at the blood dripping from her fingers to the floor. I laughed until the tears came to my eyes, until everything blurred, as though I were submerged.

AUGUST 1993

Jules

ROBBIE LEFT ME on the window seat. I drank the rest of the vodka. I'd never been drunk before, I didn't realize how quickly the twist comes, the slide from elation to despair, from up to down. Hope seemed suddenly lost, the world bleak. I wasn't thinking straight, but it felt as though my train of thought made sense. The river is the way out. Follow the river.

I've no idea what I wanted when I stumbled off the lane, down the bank, on to the river path. I was walking blindly; the night seemed blacker than ever, moonless, silent. Even the river was quiet, a slick, frictionless, reptilian thing, sliding along beside me. I wasn't afraid. What did I feel? Humiliated, ashamed. Guilty. I looked at him, I watched him, watched him with you, and he saw me.

It's a couple of miles from the Mill House to the pool, it must have taken me a while. I wasn't quick at the best of times, but in the dark, in that state, I'd have been slower still. So you didn't follow, I suppose. But eventually you came.

I was in the water by then. I remember the cold around my ankles, and then my knees, and then sinking softly into blackness. The cold was gone, my whole body burning, up to my neck now, no way out, and no one could see me. I was hidden, I was disappearing, not taking up too much space, taking up no space at all.

The heat buzzed through me, it dissipated and the cold returned, not on my skin but in my flesh, in my bones, heavy, like lead. I was tired, it seemed a very long way back to the bank, I wasn't sure I could make it back. I kicked out, and down, but I couldn't reach the bottom and so I thought that perhaps I would just float for a while, untroubled, unseen.

I drifted. Water covered my face and something brushed against me, soft, like a woman's hair. There was a crushing sensation in my chest and I gasped, gulping water. Somewhere in the distance, I heard a woman scream. *Libby*, you said, *you can hear her, sometimes at night you can hear her beg*. I struggled, but something squeezed my ribs; I felt her hand in my hair, sudden and sharp, and she pulled me deeper. Only witches float.

It wasn't Libby, of course, it was you, shouting at me. Your hand on my head, holding me down. I was fighting to get away from you. Holding me down, or dragging me out? You grabbed at my clothes, clawed at my skin, gave me scratches on my neck and arms to match the ones Robbie had left on my legs.

Eventually, we were on the bank, me on my knees,

gasping for breath, and you standing above me, shouting at me. 'You stupid fat bitch, what were you doing? What the fuck are you trying to do?' You fell to your knees then and put your arms around me, then you smelled the alcohol on me and started yelling again. 'You're *thirteen*, Julia! You can't drink, you can't . . . What were you doing?' Your bony fingers dug into the flesh of my arms, you shook me hard. 'Why are you doing this? Why? To spite me, is that it? To make Mum and Dad angry with me? Jesus, Julia, what have I ever done to you?'

You took me home, dragged me upstairs and ran a bath. I didn't want to get in, but you manhandled me, wrestling me out of my clothes and into the hot water. Despite the heat, I could not stop shivering. I would not lie down. I sat, hunched over, the roll of my belly tight and uncomfortable, while you scooped hot water over my skin with your hands. 'Jesus, Julia. You're a little girl. You shouldn't be . . . you shouldn't have . . .' You didn't seem to have the words. You wiped my face with a cloth. You smiled. You were trying to be kind. 'It's OK. It's OK, Julia. It's OK. I'm sorry I yelled at you. And I'm sorry he hurt you, I am. But what did you expect, Julia? What did you honestly expect?'

I let you bathe me, your hands so much softer than they had been in the pool. I wondered how you could be so calm about it now, I thought you'd have been angrier. Not just with me, but on my behalf. I supposed I must have been overreacting, or that you just didn't want to think about it.

You made me swear that I wouldn't tell our parents

about what happened. 'Promise me, Julia. You won't tell them, you won't tell anyone about this. OK? Not ever. We can't talk about it, all right? Because . . . Because we'll all get into trouble. OK? Just don't talk about it. If we don't talk about it, it's like it didn't happen. Nothing happened, OK? Nothing happened. Promise me. Promise me, Julia, you'll never speak about it again.'

I kept my promise. You didn't.

2015

Helen

ON HER WAY to the supermarket, Helen passed Josh Whittaker on his bike. He was drenched through and had mud on his clothes; she slowed the car and wound down her window.

'Are you all right?' she called out and he waved and bared his teeth at her – an awkward attempt at a smile, she supposed. She drove on slowly, watching him in the rear-view mirror. He was dawdling, turning the handle-bars this way and that, and every now and again standing up on his pedals to check over his shoulder.

He'd always been an odd little character, and the recent tragedy had exacerbated things. Patrick had taken him fishing a couple of times after Katie died – as a favour to Louise and Alec, to give them some time to themselves. They'd been at the river for hours and hours and, Patrick said, the boy barely spoke a word.

'They should get him away from here,' Patrick said to her. 'They should leave.'

'You didn't,' she replied softly, and he nodded.

'That's different,' he said. 'I had to stay. I had work to do.'

After he retired, he stayed for them – for her and for Sean. Not *for* them, but to be close to them, because they were all he had: them, the house, the river. But time was running out. No one said anything, because that's just the sort of family they were, but Patrick wasn't well.

Helen heard him coughing in the night, on and on and on, she saw in the mornings how it pained him to move. The worst thing of all was that she knew it wasn't solely physical. He had been so sharp all his life and now he had become forgetful, confused sometimes. He would take her car and forget where he'd left it, or sometimes return it to her filled with junk, as he had the other day. Rubbish he'd found? Trinkets he'd taken? Trophies? She didn't ask, didn't want to know. She was afraid for him.

She was afraid for herself, too, if she was completely honest. She'd been all over the place lately, distracted, unreasonable. Sometimes she thought she was going mad. Losing her grip.

It wasn't like her. Helen was practical, rational, decisive. She considered her options carefully, and then she acted. Left-brained, her father-in-law called her. But lately, she had not been herself. The events of the past year had unsettled her, thrown her off course. Now she found herself questioning the things about her life she'd thought were least open to interrogation: her marriage, their family life, even her competence in her job.

It started with Sean. First with her suspicions and then – via Patrick – the awful confirmation. Last autumn she had discovered that her husband – her solid, steadfast, resolutely moral husband – was not at all what she thought him to be. She'd found herself quite lost. Her rationale, her decisiveness, deserted her. What was she to do? Leave? Abandon her home and her responsibilities? Should she issue an ultimatum? Cry, cajole? Should she punish him? And if so, how? Cut holes in the fabric of his favourite shirts, break his fishing rods in half, burn his books in the courtyard?

All of these things seemed impractical or foolhardy or simply ridiculous, so she turned to Patrick for advice. He persuaded her to stay. He assured her that Sean had seen sense, that he deeply regretted his infidelity and that he would work to earn her forgiveness. 'In the meantime,' he said, 'he would understand – we both would – if you would like to take the spare room here? It might do you good to have some time to yourself – and I'm certain it would benefit him to get even a small taste of what he stands to lose.' Almost a year later, she still slept in her father-in-law's house most nights.

Sean's *mistake*, as it came to be known, was just the start of it. After she moved into Patrick's home, Helen found herself afflicted by terrible insomnia: a debilitating, anxiety-inducing, waking hell. Which, she discovered, her father-in-law shared. He couldn't sleep either – he'd been that way for years, so he said. So they were sleepless together. They stayed up together – reading, doing crosswords, sitting in companionable silence.

Occasionally, if Patrick had a nip of whisky, he liked

to talk. About his life as a detective, about how the town used to be. Sometimes he told her things which disturbed her. Stories of the river, old rumours, nasty tales long buried and now dug up and revived, spread as truth by Nel Abbott. Stories about their family, hurtful things. Lies, libellous falsehoods, surely? Patrick said it wouldn't come to libel, wouldn't come to law courts. 'Her lies won't ever see the light of day. I'll see to that,' he told her.

Only that wasn't the problem. The problem, Patrick said, was the damage she'd already done – to Sean, to the family. 'Do you honestly think he'd have behaved the way he has if it hadn't been for her, filling his head with these stories, making him doubt who he is, where he comes from? He's changed, hasn't he, love? And it's her that's done that.' Helen worried that Patrick was right and that things would never go back to the way they'd been, but he assured her they would. He'd see to that, too. He'd squeeze her hand and thank her for listening and kiss her forehead and say, 'You're such a good girl.'

Things got better, for a while. And then they got worse. For just when Helen found herself able to sleep for more than a couple of hours at a time, just when she caught herself smiling at her husband in the old way, just when she felt the family moving back towards its old, comfortable equilibrium, Katie Whittaker died.

Katie Whittaker, a star of the school, a diligent and polite student, an untroubled child – it was shocking, inexplicable. And it was her fault. She had failed Katie Whittaker. They all had: her parents, her teachers, this whole community. They hadn't noticed that happy Katie needed help, that she wasn't happy at all. While Helen was laid low by her domestic problems, befuddled by insomnia and plagued with self-doubt, one of her charges had fallen.

By the time Helen arrived at the supermarket, the rain had stopped. The sun was out and steam rose from the tarmac, bringing with it the smell of the earth. Helen scrabbled around in her handbag for her list: she was to buy a joint of beef for dinner, vegetables, pulses. They needed olive oil and coffee and capsules for the washing machine.

Standing in the canned-goods aisle, looking for the brand of chopped tomatoes she considered most flavoursome, she noticed a woman approach and realized with horror that it was Louise.

Walking slowly towards her, her expression vacant, Louise was pushing a giant, near-empty shopping trolley. Helen panicked and fled, abandoning her own trolley and scurrying to the car park, where she hid in her car until she saw Louise's own vehicle swing past and out into the road.

She felt stupid and ashamed – she knew that this wasn't like her. A year ago, she wouldn't have behaved in such a disgraceful way. She would have spoken to Louise, squeezed her hand and asked after her husband and son. She would have behaved honourably.

Helen was not herself. How else could she explain the things she'd thought of late, the way she had acted? All this guilt, this doubt, it was corrosive. It was changing her, twisting her. She was not the woman she used to

Sean

FOR SEVERAL DAYS after my mother died, I didn't speak. Not a single word. So my father tells me in any case. I don't remember much about that time, although I do remember the way Dad shocked me out of my silence, which was by holding my left hand over a flame until I cried out. It was cruel, but it was effective. And afterwards, he let me keep the cigarette lighter. (I kept it for many years, I used to carry it around with me. I recently lost it, I don't recall where.)

Grief, shock, it affects people in strange ways. I've seen people react to bad news with laughter, with seeming indifference, with anger, with fear. Jules's kiss in the car after the funeral, that wasn't about lust, it was about grief, about wanting to feel something – anything – other than sadness. My mutism when I was a child was probably the result of the shock, the trauma. Losing a sister may not be the same as losing a parent, but I know that Josh Whittaker was close to his sister, so I am loath to judge him, to read too much into what he says and does and the way he behaves.

Erin called me to say there had been a disturbance at a house on the south-eastern fringes of town – a neighbour had called, saying she'd arrived home to see the windows of the house in question broken and a young boy on a bike leaving the scene. The house belonged to one of the teachers at the local school, while the boy – dark-haired, wearing a yellow T-shirt and riding a red bike – I was fairly certain was Josh.

He was easy to find. He was sitting on the bridge wall, the bike leaned up against it, his clothes soaked through and his legs streaked with mud. He didn't run when he saw me. If anything, he seemed relieved when he greeted me, polite as ever. 'Good afternoon, Mr Townsend.'

I asked him if he was OK. 'You'll catch cold,' I said, indicating his wet clothes, and he half smiled.

'I'm all right,' he said.

'Josh,' I said, 'were you riding your bike over on Seward Road this afternoon?' He nodded. 'You didn't happen to go past Mr Henderson's house, did you?'

He chewed on his bottom lip, soft brown eyes widening to saucers. 'Don't tell my mum, Mr Townsend. Please don't tell my mum. She's got enough on her plate.' A lump formed in my throat, and I had to fight back tears. He's such a small boy, and so vulnerable-looking. I kneeled down at his side.

'Josh! What on earth were you doing? Was there anyone else there with you? Some older boys, maybe?' I asked hopefully.

He shook his head, but didn't look at me. 'It was just me.'

'Really? Are you sure?' He looked away. 'Because I saw you talking to Lena outside the station earlier. This wouldn't have anything to do with her, would it?'

'No!' he cried, his voice a painful, humiliating squeak. 'No. It was me. Just me. I threw rocks at his windows. At that . . . *bastard*'s windows.' 'Bastard' was enunciated carefully, as though he were trying out the word for the first time.

'Why on earth would you do that?'

He met my eye then, his lower lip trembling. 'Because he deserved it,' he said. 'Because I hate him.'

He started to cry.

'Come on,' I said, picking up his bike, 'I'll drive you home.' But he grabbed hold of the handlebars.

'No!' he sobbed. 'You can't. I don't want Mum to hear about this. Or Dad. They can't hear this, they can't . . .'

'Josh,' I crouched down again, resting my hand on the saddle of his bike. 'It's all right. It's not that bad. We'll sort it out. Honestly. It's not the end of the world.'

At that, he began to howl. 'You don't understand. Mum will never forgive me . . .'

'Of course she will!' I suppressed an urge to laugh. 'She'll be a bit cross, I'm sure, but you haven't done anything *terrible*, you didn't hurt anyone . . .'

His shoulders shook. 'Mr Townsend, you don't understand. You don't understand what I've done.'

In the end, I took him back to the station. I wasn't sure what else to do, he wouldn't let me drive him home and I couldn't leave him by the side of the road in that state. I installed him in the back office and made him a cup of tea, then got Callie to run out and buy some biscuits.

'You can't interview him, Sir,' Callie said, alarmed. 'Not without an appropriate adult.'

'I'm not *interviewing* him,' I replied tetchily. 'He's frightened and he doesn't want to go home yet.'

The words triggered a memory: *He's frightened and he doesn't want to go home.* I was younger than Josh, just six years old, and a policewoman was holding my hand. I never know which of my memories are real – I've heard so many stories about that time, from so many different sources, that it's difficult to distinguish memory from myth. But in this one I was shivering and afraid, and there was a policewoman at my side, stout and comforting, holding me against her hip protectively while men talked above my head. 'He's frightened and he doesn't want to go home,' she said.

'Could you take him to your place, Jeannie?' my father said. 'Could you take him with you?' That was it. Jeannie. WPC Sage.

My phone ringing brought me back to myself.

'Sir?' It was Erin. 'The neighbour on the other side saw a girl running off in the opposite direction. A teenager, long blonde hair, denim shorts and white T-shirt.'

'Lena. Of course.'

'Yeah, sounds like it. You want me to go and pick her up?'

'Leave her for today,' I said. 'She's had enough. Have you managed to get hold of the owner – of Henderson?'

'Not yet. I've been calling, but it's going straight to voicemail. When I spoke to him earlier he said something about a fiancée in Edinburgh, but I don't have a number for her. They may even be on the plane already.'

I took the cup of tea in to Josh. 'Look,' I said to him, 'we need to get in touch with your parents. I just need to let them know that you're here, and you're OK, all right? I don't have to give them any details, not right now, I'll just tell them that you're upset and that I've brought you here to have a chat. That sound OK?' He nodded. 'And then you can tell me what it is that you're upset about, and we'll take it from there.' He nodded again. 'But at some point, you are going to have to explain the business about the house.'

Josh sipped his tea, hiccupping occasionally, not quite recovered from his earlier emotional outburst. His hands were wrapped tightly around the mug, and his mouth worked as he tried to find whatever words he wanted to say to me.

Eventually, he looked up at me. 'Whatever I do,' he said, 'someone is going to be upset with me.' Then he shook his head. 'No, actually, that's not right. If I do the right thing, everyone is going to be upset with me, and if I do the wrong thing, they won't. It shouldn't be like that, should it?'

'No,' I said, 'it shouldn't. And I'm not sure you're correct about that. I can't think of a situation in which doing the right thing will make everyone upset with you. One or two people, maybe, but surely if it's the right thing, some of us will see it that way? And be grateful to you?'

He chewed his lip again. 'The problem,' he said, his

voice trembling again, 'is that the damage is already done. I'm too late. It's too late to do the right thing now.'

He cried again, but not like before. He wasn't wailing or panicking, this time he cried like someone who has lost everything, lost all hope. He was in despair, and I couldn't bear it.

'Josh, I must get your parents here, I must,' I said, but he clung to my arm.

'Please, Mr Townsend. Please.'

'I want to help you, Josh. I really do. Please tell me what it is that's upsetting you so much.'

(I remembered sitting in a warm kitchen, not my own, eating cheese on toast. Jeannie was there, she sat at my side. *Won't you tell me what happened, darling? Please tell me.* I said nothing. Not a word. Not a single word.)

Josh, though, was ready to speak. He wiped his eyes and blew his nose. He coughed and sat up straight in his chair. 'It's about Mr Henderson,' he said. 'About Mr Henderson and Katie.'

THURSDAY, 20 AUGUST

Lena

IT STARTED AS a joke. The thing with Mr Henderson. A game. We'd played it before, with Mr Friar, the biology teacher, and with Mr Mackintosh, the swimming coach. You just had to get them to blush. We took turns trying. One of us would go, and if they didn't succeed then it was the other person's turn. You could do whatever you liked, and you could do it whenever you liked, the only rule was that the other person had to be present, because otherwise it wasn't verifiable. We never included anyone else, it was our thing, mine and Katie's – I don't actually remember whose idea it was.

With Friar, I went first and it took about thirty seconds. I went up to his desk and I smiled at him and bit my lip when he was explaining something about homeostasis and I leaned forward so that my shirt gaped open a bit and bingo. With Mackintosh, it took a bit more work because he was used to seeing us in our swimming costumes so it wasn't like he was going to go mad over a bit of skin. But Katie got there in the end, by acting sweet and shy and just a little bit embarrassed when she talked to him about the kung-fu films we knew he liked.

With Mr Henderson, though, it was another story. Katie went first, because she'd won the round with Mr Mac. She waited until after class, and while I was packing away my books really slowly, she went up to his desk and perched on the edge of it. She smiled at him, leaning forward a bit, and began to speak, but he pushed his chair back suddenly and got to his feet, taking a step backwards. She carried on, but half-heartedly, and as we were leaving he gave us a look like he was *furious*. When I tried, he yawned. I did my best, standing close to him and smiling and touching my hair and my neck and nibbling my lower lip, and he *yawned*, really obviously. Like I was boring him.

I couldn't get that out of my head, the way he'd looked at me like I was nothing, like I wasn't interesting in the slightest. I didn't want to play any more. Not with him, it wasn't fun. He just acted like a dick. Katie said, 'Do you think so?' and I said I did, and she said, all right then. And that was that.

I didn't find out that she'd broken the rules until much later, months later. I had no idea, so when Josh came to see me on Valentine's Day with the most hilarious story I'd ever heard I messaged her with a little heart picture. *Heard about your bae*, I wrote. *KW & MH 4eva*. I got a text message about five seconds later saying DELETE THAT. NOT JOKING. DELETE. I texted back, WTF? And she texted again. DELETE NOW OR I SWEAR

TO GOD I WILL NEVER TALK TO YOU AGAIN. *Jesus*, I thought. *Chill*.

The next morning in class, she ignored me. Didn't even say hello. On our way out, I grabbed her arm.

'Katie? What is going on?' She virtually shoved me into the loos. 'What the fuck?' I said. 'What was that about?'

'Nothing,' she hissed at me. 'I just thought it was *lame*, all right?' She gave me this look, one I'd been getting from her more and more, like she was a grown-up and I was a child. 'What made you do that anyway?'

We were standing at the far end of the bathroom, under the window. 'Josh came round to see me,' I told her. 'He said he saw you and Mr Henderson holding hands in the car park . . .' I started laughing.

Katie didn't laugh. She turned away from me and stood in front of the basin, looking at her reflection. '*What?*' She pulled a mascara out of her bag. 'What *exactly* did he say?' Her voice sounded strange, not angry, not upset, it was like she was frightened.

'He said he'd been waiting for you after school and he'd seen you with Henderson and you were holding hands . . .' I started laughing again. 'Jesus, it's not a big drama. He was just making up stories because he wanted an excuse to come and see me. It was Valentine's Day, so . . .'

Katie squeezed her eyes shut. 'God! You're such a fucking narcissist,' she said quietly. 'You really do think everything is about you.'

I felt like I'd been slapped. 'What . . . ?' I didn't even know how to respond, it was so unlike her. I was still trying to think of what to say when she dropped the mascara into the basin, gripped its edge and began to cry.

'Katie . . .' I put my hand on her shoulder and she sobbed harder. I put my arms around her. 'Oh, God, what's wrong? What's happened?'

'Haven't you noticed,' she sniffed, 'that things have been different? Haven't you noticed, Lenie?'

Of course I had. She'd been different, distant, for a while. She was busy all the time. She had homework, so we couldn't hang out after school, or she was going shopping with her mum, so she couldn't come to the cinema, or she had to babysit Josh, so she couldn't come over that night. She'd been different in other ways, too. Quieter at school. She didn't smoke any more. She'd started dieting. She seemed to drift out of conversations, like she was bored by what I was saying, like she had better things to think about.

Of course I'd noticed. I was hurt. But I wasn't going to *say* anything. Showing someone you're hurt is the worst thing you can do, isn't it? I didn't want to look weak, or needy, because no one wants to be around someone like that. 'I thought . . . I don't know, K, I thought you were just *bored* with me or something.' She cried even harder then, and I hugged her.

'I'm not,' she said. 'I'm not bored with you. But I couldn't tell you, I couldn't tell anyone—' She broke off suddenly and pulled herself out of my arms. She walked to the other end of the room and sank to her knees, then crawled towards me, checking under each stall.

'Katie? What *are* you doing?'

It took until then for it to hit me. That's how clueless I was. 'Oh my *God*,' I said, as she got back to her feet. 'Are you . . . are you actually saying . . .' I lowered my voice to a whisper, 'there's something going on?' She said nothing but looked me dead in the eye and I knew that it was true. 'Fuck. Fuck! You can't be . . . That is insane. You can't. You *can't*, Katie. You have to stop this . . . before anything *happens*.'

She looked at me like I was a bit dim, like she felt sorry for me. 'Lena, it's already happened.' She half smiled, wiping the tears from her face. 'It's been *happening* since November.'

I didn't tell the police any of that. It wasn't any of their business.

They came to the house in the evening, when Julia and I were in the kitchen eating dinner. Correction: I was eating dinner. She was just pushing her food around her plate like she always does. Mum told me Julia doesn't like to eat in front of other people – it's a hangover from when she was fat. Neither of us were talking – we hadn't said anything to each other since I came home yesterday and found her with Mum's things – so it was a relief when the doorbell went.

When I saw that it was Sean and Detective Sergeant Morgan – *Erin*, as I'm supposed to call her now we're all spending so much time together – I thought it must be about the broken windows, although I did think that both of them coming seemed like overkill. I held my hands up to it right away.

'I'll pay for the damage,' I said. 'I can afford it now, can't I?' Julia pursed her lips like she thought I was a disappointment to her. She got up and started clearing away the dishes, even though she hadn't eaten a thing.

Sean took her chair and pulled it round so that he was sitting next to me. 'We'll get to that later,' he said, a sad and serious expression on his face. 'But first we need to talk to you about Mark Henderson.'

I went cold, my stomach flipping over like when you know something really bad is about to happen. They knew. I felt devastated and relieved at the same time, but I tried my best to keep my face totally blank and innocent. 'Yeah,' I said. 'I know. I smashed up his house.'

'Why did you smash up his house?' Erin asked.

'Because I was bored. Because he's a dick. Because—'

'That's enough, Lena!' Sean interrupted. 'Stop messing about.' He looked properly pissed off. 'You know that's not what we're talking about, don't you?' I didn't say a word, I just looked out of the window. 'We've been talking to Josh Whittaker,' he said, and my stomach flipped again. I suppose I'd known all along that Josh wouldn't be able to keep quiet about this for ever, but I'd hoped that smashing up Henderson's house might satisfy him, for a little while at least. 'Lena? Are you listening to me?' Sean was leaning forward in his chair. I noticed that his hands were shaking a bit. 'Josh has made a very serious allegation about Mark Henderson. He's told us that Mark Henderson was engaged in a relationship – a sexual relationship – with Katie Whittaker in the months before she died.'

'Bullshit!' I said, and I tried to laugh. 'That's total

bullshit.' Everyone was staring at me and it was impossible to keep my face from going red. 'It's bullshit,' I said again.

'Why would he invent a story like that, Lena?' Sean asked me. 'Why would Katie's little brother come up with a story like that?'

'I don't know,' I said. 'I don't know. But it's not true.' I was staring at the table and trying to think of a reason, but my face just kept getting hotter and hotter.

'Lena,' Erin said, 'you're obviously not telling the truth. What's less clear is why on earth you would lie about something like this. Why would you try to protect a man who has taken advantage of your friend like that?'

'Oh, for *fuck*'s sake—'

'What?' she asked, getting right up in my face. 'For fuck's sake what?' There was something about her, about how close she got to me and the expression on her face, that made me want to slap her.

'He didn't *take advantage* of her. She wasn't a child!'

She looked really pleased with herself then, and I wanted to slap her even more, and she just kept talking. 'If he didn't take advantage of her, why do you hate him so much? Were you jealous?'

'I think that's enough,' Julia said, but no one listened to her.

Erin just kept talking, kept going on and on at me. 'Did you want him for yourself, was that it? Were you pissed off, because you thought you were the prettier one, you thought you should get all the attention?'

I just lost it then. I knew that if she didn't shut up I

was going to hit her, so I said it. 'I hated him, you stupid bitch. I hated him because he took her from me.'

Everyone went quiet for a bit. Then Sean said, 'He took her from you? How did he do that, Lena?'

I couldn't help it. I was just so fucking tired, and it was obvious that they were going to find out now anyway, now that Josh had gone and opened his big mouth. But most of all, I was just too tired to lie any more. So I sat there in our kitchen and I betrayed her.

I'd promised her. After we argued, after she swore to me that they'd split up and she wasn't seeing him any longer, she made me swear: that no matter what happened, *no matter what*, I would never tell anyone about them. We went to the pool together for the first time in ages. We sat under the trees where no one could see us and she cried and held my hand. 'I know you think it's wrong,' she said, 'that I shouldn't have been with him. I get that. But I loved him, Lenie. I still do. He was *everything* to me. I can't have him hurt, I just can't. I couldn't bear it. Please don't do anything that would hurt him. Please, Lenie, keep this secret for me. It's not about him, I know you hate him. Do it for me.'

And I tried. I really did. Even when my mum came to my room and told me that they'd found her in the water, even when Louise came to the house half mad with grief, even when that piece of shit gave a statement to the local papers about what a great student she was, how much she was loved and admired by students and teachers alike. Even when he came up to me at my mother's funeral and offered his condolences, I bit my fucking tongue.

But I'd been biting and biting and biting for months now and if I didn't stop I was going to bite clean through. I was going to choke on it.

So I told them. Yes, Katie and Mark Henderson had a relationship. It started in the autumn. It ended in March or April. It started up again, in late May, I thought, but not for long. She ended the relationship. No, I didn't have proof.

'They were really careful,' I told them. 'No emails, no texts, no Messenger, nothing electronic. It was a rule with them. They were strict about it.'

'They were, or he was?' Erin asked.

I glared at her. 'Well, I never discussed it with *him*, did I? That's what she told me. It was their rule.'

'When did you first find out about this, Lena?' Erin asked. 'You need to go right back to the beginning.'

'No, actually, I don't think she does,' Julia said suddenly. She was standing over by the door; I'd forgotten she was even in the room. 'I think Lena is very tired and should be left alone for now. We can come by and do this at the police station tomorrow, or you can come back here, but that's enough for today.'

I actually wanted to *hug* her; for the first time since I'd met her, I felt like Julia was on my side. Erin was about to protest, but Sean said, 'Yes, you're right,' and he got up and they all marched out of the kitchen and into the hallway. I followed them. When they were at the door, I said to them, 'Do you realize what this will do to her mum and dad? When they find out?'

Erin turned round to face me. 'Well, at least they'll have a reason why,' she said.

'No, they won't. They won't have a *reason*,' I said. 'There was no reason to do what she did. Look, you're proving it right now. By being here, you're proving that she did it for nothing.'

'What do you mean, Lena?' They were all stood there, staring at me, expectant.

'She didn't do it because he broke her heart or because she felt guilty or anything like that. She did it to protect him. She thought that someone had found out. She thought he was going to be reported and that he'd be in the papers. She thought there would be a trial, and he would be convicted, and he would go to prison as a sex offender. She thought he'd be beaten, or raped, or whatever it is that happens to men like that inside. So she decided to get rid of the evidence,' I said. I was starting to cry by then and Julia stepped out in front of me and put her arms around me; she was going, 'Shhh, Lena, it's all right, shhh.'

But it wasn't all right. 'That's what she was doing,' I said. 'Don't you understand? She was getting rid of the evidence.'

FRIDAY, 21 AUGUST

Erin

THE COTTAGE BY the river, the one I saw when I went running, is to be my new home. In the short term, at least. Just until we sort out this business with Henderson. It was Sean who suggested it. He overheard me telling Callie, the DC, that I'd almost run the car off the road this morning I'd been so knackered, and he said, 'Well, we can't have that. You should stay in town. You could use the Wards' cottage. It's just upriver and it's empty. It's not luxurious, but it won't cost you anything. I'll get you the keys this afternoon.'

As he left, Callie grinned at me. 'The Wards' cottage, eh? Watch out for mad Annie.'

'I'm sorry?'

'That place by the river that Patrick Townsend uses as his fishing cabin – it's known as the Wards' cottage. As in Anne Ward? She's one of *the women*. They say,' she said, lowering her voice to a whisper, 'that if you look hard enough you can still see *the blood on the walls*.' I

227

must have looked nonplussed – I had no idea what she was talking about – because she smiled and said, 'It's just a story, one of the old ones. One of those ancient Beckford stories.' I wasn't paying a lot of attention to century-old Beckford stories – I had fresher ones to concern myself with.

Henderson hadn't been answering his phone, and we'd taken the decision to leave him alone until his return. If the Katie Whittaker story was true, and if he got wind that we knew about it, he might not come back at all.

In the meantime, Sean had asked me to question his wife, who, as head teacher at the school, is Henderson's boss. 'I'm certain she never had the faintest suspicion about Mark Henderson,' he said. 'I believe she thinks rather highly of him, but someone needs to talk to her and it obviously can't be me.' He told me she'd be at the school, and that she'd be expecting me.

If she was expecting me, she certainly didn't act like it. I found her in her office on her hands and knees, her cheek pressed to the grey carpet as she craned her head to look under a bookcase. I coughed politely and she jerked her head up, alarmed.

'Mrs Townsend?' I said. 'I'm DS Morgan. Erin.'

'Oh,' she said. 'Yes.' She blushed, putting a hand to her neck. 'Lost an earring,' she said.

'Both, by the looks of it,' I said.

She made an odd sort of huffing noise and indicated that I should sit. She tugged at the hem of her blouse and smoothed her grey trousers before sitting herself. If I'd been asked to picture the DI's wife, I'd have imagined someone quite different. Attractive, well dressed, probably sporty – a marathon runner, a triathlete. Helen wore clothes more suited to a woman twenty years her senior. She was pale, and her limbs soft, like someone who rarely went out or saw the sun.

'You wanted to speak to me about Mark Henderson,' she said, frowning slightly at a pile of papers in front of her. No small talk, then, no preamble – straight down to business. Perhaps that's what the DI likes about her.

'Yes,' I said. 'You've heard the allegations made by Josh Whittaker and Lena Abbott, I take it?'

She nodded, her thin lips disappearing as she pressed them together. 'My husband told me yesterday. It was, I can assure you, the first I'd heard of such a thing.' I opened my mouth to say something, but she continued. 'I recruited Mark Henderson two years ago. He came with excellent references and his results so far have been encouraging.' She shuffled the pages in front of her. 'I have specifics if you need them?' I shook my head, and again, she started speaking before I could ask the next question. 'Katie Whittaker was conscientious and hard-working. I have her grades here. There was, admittedly, some slippage last spring, but it was short term, she'd improved again by the time . . . by the time she . . .' she passed a hand over her eyes, 'by the summer.' She sank a little into her chair.

'So you had no suspicions, there were no rumours . . . ?'

She cocked her head to one side. 'Oh, I didn't say anything about rumours. Detective . . . er. . . Morgan. The rumours that fly around the average secondary school would make your hair curl. I'm sure,' she said, a twitch around her mouth, 'that if you put your mind to it, you might be able to imagine the sort of things they say and write and tweet about me and Ms Mitchell, the PE teacher.' She paused. 'Have you met Mark Henderson?'

'I have.'

'So you understand, then. He's young. Good-looking. The girls – it is always the girls – say all sorts of things about him. All sorts. But you have to learn to cut through the noise. And I believed I had done that. I still believe I'd done that.' Again, I wanted to speak, and again, she pressed ahead. 'I have to tell you,' she said, raising her voice, 'that I am deeply suspicious about these allegations. *Deeply* suspicious, because of their source and because of the timing.'

'I—'

'I understand that the allegation came first from Josh Whittaker, but I'd be surprised if Lena Abbott isn't behind all this – Josh dotes on her. If Lena decided that she wanted to deflect attention away from her own wrongdoing – purchasing illegal drugs for her friend, for example – I'm sure she could have persuaded Josh to come up with this story.'

'Mrs Townsend—'

'Another thing I should mention,' she continued, permitting no interruption, 'is that there was some history between Lena Abbott and Mark Henderson.'

'History?'

'A couple of things. First, that her behaviour could at times be inappropriate.'

'In what way?'

'She flirts. Not just with Mark either. It seems she's been taught that it's the best way to get what she wants. Many of the girls do it, but in Lena's case Mark seemed to feel that it went too far. She made remarks, touched him . . .'

'Touched him?'

'On the arm – nothing outrageous. She stood too close, as the song goes. I had to speak to her about it.' She seemed to flinch slightly at the memory. 'She was reprimanded, though of course she didn't take it seriously. I think she said something along the lines of *He wishes*.' I laughed at that, and she frowned at me. 'It really isn't a laughing matter, Detective. These things can be terribly damaging.'

'Yes, of course. I know. I'm sorry.'

'Yes. Well.' She pursed her lips again, every inch the schoolmarm. 'Her mother didn't take it seriously, either. Which is hardly surprising.' She coloured, an angry flush of red appearing at her neck, her voice rising. 'Hardly surprising at all. All that flirting, the endless batting of lashes and tossing of hair, that insistent, tiresome expression of sexual availability – where do you imagine Lena learned that?' She took a deep breath and exhaled, pushing her hair from her eyes. 'The second thing,' she said, calmer now, more measured, 'was an incident in the spring. Not flirting this time, but aggression. Mark had to send Lena out of his class because she was being aggressive and quite abusive, using foul language during a discussion about a text they were studying.' She glanced down at her notes. '*Lolita*, I believe it was.' She raised an eyebrow.

'Well, that's . . . *interesting*,' I said.

'Quite. It might even suggest where she got the idea for these accusations,' Helen said, which wasn't what I'd been thinking at all.

In the evening, I drove out to my temporary cottage. It looked much lonelier with dusk looming, the bright birches behind it now ghostly, the chuckle of the river not so much cheerful as menacing. The banks of the river and the hillside opposite were deserted. No one to hear you scream. When I'd come past on my run I'd seen a peaceful idyll. Now I was thinking more along the lines of the desolate cabin of a hundred horror films.

I unlocked the door and took a quick look around, trying, as I did, not to look for *blood on the walls*. But the place was tidy, with the astringent smell of some sort of citrusy cleaning product, the fireplace swept, a pile of chopped wood neatly arranged at its side. There wasn't much to it, it was more of a cabin than a cottage really: just two rooms – a living room with a galley kitchen leading off it, and a bedroom with a small double bed, a pile of clean sheets and a blanket folded on the mattress, with a small en-suite.

I opened the windows and the door to get rid of the artificial lemon smell, opened one of the beers I'd bought at the Co-op on the way down, and sat on the front step, watching the bracken on the hill opposite turn bronze to gold with the sinking sun. As the shadows lengthened, I felt solitude morph into loneliness, and I reached for my phone, not certain who I was going to call. Then I realized – *of course* – no signal. I hauled myself to my feet and wandered about, waving the phone in the air – nothing, nothing, nothing, until I walked right down to the river's edge where a couple of bars appeared. I stood there a while, the water just about lapping my toes, watching the black river run past, quick and shallow. I kept thinking I could hear someone laughing, but it was just the water, sliding nimbly over the rocks.

I took ages to fall asleep and when I woke suddenly, feverishly hot, it was to inky darkness, the kind of deep black that makes it impossible to see your hand in front of your face. Something had woken me, I felt sure: a sound? Yes, a cough.

I reached for my phone, knocking it off the little bedside table, the clatter as it fell to the floor startlingly loud in the silence. I scrabbled around for it, gripped suddenly by fear, sure that if I turned on the light it would reveal someone standing there in the room. In the trees behind the cottage I could hear an owl hooting, and then again: someone coughing. My heart was beating too fast, I was stupidly afraid to pull back the curtain above my bed, just in case there was a face on the other side of the glass, looking back at me.

Whose face was I expecting? Anne Ward's? Her husband's? *Ridiculous*. Muttering reassurances to myself, I turned on the light and flung back the curtains. Nothing and no one. Obviously. I slipped out of bed, pulled on tracksuit bottoms and a sweatshirt and went through to the kitchen. I considered making a cup of tea, but thought better of it when I discovered a half-empty bottle of Talisker in the kitchen cupboard. I poured myself a couple of fingers' worth and drank it quickly. I slipped on my trainers, put my phone in my pocket, grabbed a torch from the counter and unlocked the front door.

The batteries in the torch must have been low. The beam was weak, reaching no more than six or seven feet in front of me. Beyond that was perfect obscurity. I angled the torch downwards to light up the ground in front of my feet, and walked out into the night.

The grass was heavy with dew. Within a few steps my trainers and tracksuit bottoms were soaked through. I walked slowly all the way around the cottage, watching the torchlight dancing off the silvery bark of the beech trees, a cohort of pale ghosts. The air felt soft and cool, and there was a kiss of rain in the breeze. I heard the owl again, and the low chatter of the river, and the rhythmic croak of a toad. I finished my circuit of the cottage and started walking towards the river bank. Then the croaking suddenly stopped, and again, I heard that coughing sound. It wasn't nearby at all, it was coming from the hillside, somewhere across the river, and it didn't sound so much like a cough this time either. More of a bleat. A sheep.

Feeling somewhat sheepish myself, I went back into the cottage, poured myself another shot of whisky and grabbed Nel Abbott's manuscript from my bag. I curled up in the armchair in the living room and began to read.

The Drowning Pool

Anne Ward, 1920

IT WAS ALREADY in the house. It was there. There was nothing to fear outside, the danger was within. It was waiting, it had been waiting there all along, ever since the day he came home.

In the end, though, for Anne, it wasn't the fear, it was the guilt. It was the knowledge, cold and hard as a pebble picked from the stream, of what she'd wished for, the dream she had allowed herself at night when the real nightmare of her life became too much. The nightmare was him, lying beside her in bed, or sitting by the fire with his boots on, glass in hand. The nightmare was when she caught him watching her, and saw the disgust in his face, as though she were physically repugnant. It wasn't just her, she knew that. It was all women, all children, old men, every man who hadn't joined the fight. Still, it hurt to see, to feel – stronger and more clearly than anything she'd ever felt in her life – how much he hated her.

She couldn't say she didn't deserve it though, could she?

The nightmare was real, it was living in her house, but

it was the dream that haunted her, that she allowed herself to long for. In the dream, she was alone in the house; it was the summer of 1915 and he'd only just gone away. In the dream, it would be evening, the light just dipping over the hillside across the river, darkness gathering in the corners of the house, and there'd be a knock at the door. There would be a man waiting, uniformed, and he'd hand her a telegram, and she'd know then that her husband was never coming back. When she daydreamed about it, she didn't really mind how it happened. She didn't care if he'd died a hero, saving a friend, or as a coward fleeing the enemy. She didn't care, so long as he was dead.

It would have been easier for her. That was the truth of it, wasn't it? So why shouldn't he hate her? If he'd died out there, she would have mourned him, people would have felt sorry for her, her mam, her friends, his brothers (were there any left). They would have helped out, rallied round, and she would have got through it. She'd have grieved for him, for a long time, but it would have come to an end. She would be nineteen, twenty, twenty-one, and she'd have a life ahead of her.

He was right to hate her. Three years, close to three years he was out there, drowning in shit and the blood of men whose cigarettes he'd lit, and now she wished he'd never come back; she cursed the day the telegram didn't come.

She had loved him since she was fifteen years old, couldn't remember what life felt like before he came along. He'd been eighteen when the war started and nineteen when he went, and he came back older every time, not by months, but by years, decades, centuries.

The first time, he'd still been himself, though. He'd cried

in the night, shaken like a man with a fever. He told her he couldn't go back, he was too afraid. The night before he was due to return, she found him by the river and dragged him home. (She should never have done that. She should have let him go then.) It had been selfish of her to stop him. Now look what she had wrought.

The second time he came home, he didn't cry. He was silent, shuttered, barely looked at her, except slyly, side-on from under hooded lids, and never when they were in bed. He turned her over and didn't stop even when she begged, even when she bled. He hated her then, hated her already; she didn't see it at first, but when she told him how sad she felt about how they were treating those girls up in prison, about the conscientious objectors and all that, he slapped her face and spat at her and called her a traitorous fucking whore.

The third time he came home, he wasn't there at all.

And she knew that he'd never come back now. There was nothing left of the man he had once been. And she couldn't leave, she couldn't go and fall in love with someone else because he was all there ever was for her, and now he was gone . . . Gone, but he still sat by the fire with his boots on, and drank and drank, and looked at her as if she was the enemy, and she wished he was dead.

What sort of life is that?

Anne wished there could have been some other way. She wished she'd known the secrets that the other women knew, but Libby Seeton was long dead now and she had taken them with her. Anne knew some things, of course, most of the women from the village did. They knew which mushrooms to pick and which to leave, they were warned about the beautiful lady, belladonna, told never, ever to touch it. She knew where it grew in the woods, but she knew what it did, too, and she didn't want him to go like that.

He was afraid all the time. She could see it, could read it on him whenever she sneaked a glance: his eyes always on the door, the way he looked out at dusk, trying to see beyond the treeline. He was afraid and he was waiting for something to come. And all the time, he was looking in the wrong place, because the enemy wasn't out there, it had already come inside, into his home. It sat at his hearth.

She didn't want him to feel afraid. She didn't want him to see the shadow fall across him, so she waited until he was sleeping, slumped over in his chair with his boots on, the bottle empty at his side. She was quiet and she was quick. She put the blade against the back of his neck and drove it in hard so that he barely woke, and he was gone for good.

Better that way.

There was a hell of a mess though, of course there was, so afterwards she went to the river to wash her hands.

SUNDAY, 23 AUGUST

Patrick

THE DREAM PATRICK had of his wife was always the same. It was night, and she was in the water. He left Sean on the bank and dived in, he swam and swam, but somehow as soon as he was close enough to reach out for her, she drifted further away and he had to swim again. In the dream, the pool was wider than in real life. It wasn't a pool, it was a lake, it was an ocean. He seemed to swim for ever, and only when he was so exhausted that he was sure he'd go under himself did he eventually manage to grab hold of her, to pull her towards him. As he did, her body rotated slowly in the water, her face turned towards his, and through her broken, bloodied mouth she laughed. It was always the same, only last night, when the body rolled in the water towards him, the face was Helen's.

He woke with a terrible fright, his heart pounding fit to burst. He sat up in bed with his palm flat against his chest, not wanting to acknowledge his own fear, or how it was mixed with a deep sense of shame. He pulled back his curtains and waited for the sky to lighten, black to grey, before going next door to Helen's room. He entered quietly, gently lifting the stool from beside the dressing table and placing it at her bedside. He sat. Her face was turned away from him, just as it had been in the dream, and he fought the urge to put his arm on her shoulder, to shake her awake, to make sure that her mouth was not full of blood and broken teeth.

When she finally stirred, rolling over slowly, she started when she saw him, jerking her head violently backwards and banging it on the wall behind her as she did.

'Patrick! What's wrong? Is it Sean?'

He shook his head. 'No. Nothing's wrong.'

'Then . . .'

'Did I . . . did I leave some things in your car?' he asked her. 'The other day? I took some rubbish from the cottage and I meant to throw it away, but then the cat . . . I was distracted, and I believe I left it there. Did I?'

She swallowed and nodded, her eyes black, the pupils squeezing the irises to pale-grey slivers. 'Yes, I . . . From the cottage? You took those things from the cottage?' She frowned, as if she was trying to figure something out.

'Yes. From the cottage. What did you do with them? What did you do with the bag?'

She sat up. 'I threw it away,' she said. 'It was rubbish, wasn't it? It looked like rubbish.'

'Yes. Just rubbish.'

Her eyes darted away and then returned to his. 'Dad,

do you think it had started up again?' She sighed. 'Him and her. Do you think . . . ?'

Patrick leaned forward and smoothed the hair back from her forehead. 'Well, I'm not sure. Maybe. I think maybe it had. But it's over now, isn't it?' He tried to get to his feet, but he found that his legs were weak and he had to haul himself up with one hand on the bedside table. He could feel her watching him and he felt ashamed. 'Would you like some tea?' he asked her.

'I'll make it,' she said, pushing back the covers.

'No, no. Stay where you are. I'll do it.' At the door, he turned back to her. 'You got rid of it? That rubbish?' he said again. Helen nodded. Slowly, his limbs wooden and his chest tight, he made his way down the stairs and into the kitchen. He filled the kettle and sat at the table, his heart heavy in his chest. He had never known Helen to lie to him before, but he'd been fairly certain, back there, that she had.

Perhaps he should have been angry with her, but mostly he was angry with Sean, because it was his mistake that had led them here. Helen shouldn't even be in this house! She should be at home, in her husband's bed. And he should not have been placed in this position, the ignominious position of cleaning up his son's mess. The indelicate position of sleeping in the room next door to his daughter-in-law. The skin on his forearm itched beneath his bandage and he scratched at it absent-mindedly.

And yet, if he was honest, and he always tried to be, who was he to criticize his son? He remembered what it was to be a young man, rendered helpless by biology.

He had chosen badly for himself and he still felt the shame of it. He chose a beauty, a weak, selfish beauty, a woman who lacked self-control in almost every regard. An insatiable woman. She had set herself on a self-destructive path and the only thing that surprised him now, when he thought about it, was that it took as long as it did. Patrick knew what Lauren had never understood – just how many times she had come perilously close to losing her life.

He heard footfall on the stairs and turned. Helen stood in the doorway, still in her pyjamas, her feet bare.

'Dad? Are you all right?' He got to his feet, prepared to make the tea, but she put her hand on his shoulder. 'Sit down. I'll do it.'

He'd chosen badly once, but not the second time. Because Helen, the daughter of a colleague, quiet and plain and hard-working, was *his* choice. He saw at once that she would be steady and loving and faithful. Sean had to be persuaded. He had fallen in love with a woman he'd met as a trainee, but Patrick knew that wouldn't last, and when it went on longer than it should have, he put an end to it. Now he watched Helen and knew that he had chosen well for his son: Helen was straightforward, modest, intelligent – wholly uninterested in the kind of celebrity trivia and gossip that seemed to consume most women. She didn't waste time with television or novels, she worked hard and didn't complain. She was easy company, quick to smile.

'Here you go.' She was smiling at him now as she handed him his tea. 'Oh,' she inhaled sharply through her teeth, 'that doesn't look good.' She was looking at his arm, where he'd scratched it and torn away the bandage. The skin underneath was red and swollen, the wound dark. She fetched warm water, soap, antiseptic, fresh bandages. She cleaned the wound and bound his arm again, and when she was finished he leaned forward and kissed her mouth.

'Dad,' she said, and pushed him gently away.

'I'm sorry,' he said. 'I'm sorry.' And the shame returned, overwhelming now, and the anger, too.

Women brought him low. Lauren first and then Jeannie, and on and on. But not Helen. Surely not Helen? And yet she'd lied to him that morning. He'd seen it in her face, her candid face, unused to deception, and he'd shuddered. He thought again of the dream, Lauren turning in the water, history repeating itself, only the women getting worse.

Nickie

JEANNIE SAID IT was about time someone did something about all this.

'Easy for you to say,' Nickie retorted. 'And you've changed your tune, haven't you? Used to be that I was supposed to keep my mouth shut, for my own protection. Now you're telling me to throw caution to the wind?' Jeannie was silent on that point. 'Well, in any case, I've tried. You know I've tried. I've been pointing in the right direction. I left the sister a message, didn't I? Not my fault if no one listens to me. Oh, too subtle, am I? Too subtle! You want me to go around shooting my mouth off? Look where talking got you!' They'd been arguing about it all night. 'It isn't my fault! You can't say it's my fault. I never meant to get Nel Abbott into any trouble. I told her what I knew, that's all. Like you'd been telling me to. I can't win with you, I really can't. I don't know why I even bother.'

Jeannie was getting on her nerves. She just *would not* shut up. And the worst of it, well, not the worst of it, the worst of it was getting no bloody sleep at all, but the second worst of it was that she was probably right. Nickie had known it all along, from that first morning, sitting at her window, when she felt it. Another one. Another swimmer. She'd thought it then; she'd even thought about talking to Sean Townsend. But she'd done well to hold her tongue there: she'd seen how he reacted when she mentioned his mother, that snarl of anger, the kindly mask slipping. He was his father's son, after all.

'So who, then? Who, old girl? Who am I supposed to talk to? Not the policewoman. Don't even suggest it. They're all the same! She'll go straight to her boss, won't she?' Not the policewoman, so who? Nel's sister? Nothing about the sister inspired Nickie with confidence. The girl, though, she was different. *She's just a child*, Jeannie said, but Nickie replied, 'So what? She's got more get-up-and-go in her little finger than half the people in this town.'

Yes, she would talk to the girl. She just wasn't sure what she was going to say yet.

Nickie still had Nel's pages. The ones they'd worked on together. She could show the girl that. They were typed, not handwritten, but surely Lena would recognize her mother's words, her tone? Of course, they didn't spell things out the way Nickie had thought they ought to. It was part of the reason they'd fallen out. Artistic differences. Nel had gone off in a huff and said that if Nickie couldn't tell the truth then they were wasting their time, but really what did she know about the truth? They were all just telling stories.

Are you still here? Jeannie asked. *I thought you were going to talk to the girl*, and Nickie replied, 'All right. Keep your hair on. I will. I'll do it later. I'll do it when I'm ready.'

Sometimes she wished Jeannie would shut up and sometimes she wished more than anything that she were here, in the room, sitting by the window with her, watching. They should have grown old together, getting on each other's nerves properly, instead of bickering over the airwaves like they had to now.

Nickie wished that when she pictured Jeannie, she didn't see her the way she was the last time she came to this flat. It had been just a couple of days before Jeannie had left Beckford for good, and she was pale with shock and shaking with fear. She had come to tell Nickie that Patrick Townsend had been to see her. He'd told her that if she kept on talking like she had been, if she kept on asking questions, if she continued to try to *ruin his reputation*, he would see to it that she was hurt. 'Not by me,' he said, 'I wouldn't bloody touch you. I'll get someone else to do the dirty work. And not just the one fella either. I'll make sure there's a few, and that each of them takes his turn. You know I know people, don't you, Jean? You don't doubt that I know people who would do things like that, do you, girl?'

Jeannie had stood right there in that room and made Nickie promise, made her swear she'd leave it alone. 'There isn't anything we can do now. I should never have said anything to you.'

'But . . . the boy,' Nickie said. 'What about the boy?'

Jeannie wiped the tears from her eyes. 'I know. I know. It makes me sick to think of it, but we'll just have to leave him there. You have to be quiet, say nothing.

Because Patrick will do for me, Nicks, and he'll do for you, too. He's not messing around.'

Jeannie left a couple of days later; she never came back.

Jules

TELL ME HONESTLY. Wasn't there some part of you that liked it?

I woke with your voice in my head. It was mid afternoon. I can't sleep at night, this house rocks like a boat and the sound of the water is deafening. In the day, it's not so bad somehow. At any rate, I must have fallen asleep because I woke with your voice in my head, asking:

Wasn't there some part of you that liked it? Liked or enjoyed? Or was it *wanted*? I can't remember now. I only remember taking my hand from yours and raising it to hit you, and the look on your face, uncomprehending.

I dragged myself across the hall to the bathroom and turned on the shower. I was too exhausted to undress, so I just sat there, while the room got steamier and steamier. Then I turned off the water and went to the sink and splashed my face. When I looked up I saw, appearing in the condensation, two letters traced on the surface of the mirror, an 'L' and an 'S'. I got such a fright that I cried out.

I heard Lena's door open and then she was pounding on the bathroom door. 'What? What's happening? Julia?'

I opened the door to her, furious. 'What are you doing?' I demanded. 'What are you trying to do to me?' I pointed back at the mirror.

'What?' She looked annoyed. '*What?*'

'You know very well, Lena. I don't know what you think you're trying to do, but—'

She turned her back on me and started to walk away. 'Christ, you're such a *freak.*'

I stood there staring at the letters for a while. I wasn't imagining things, they were definitely there: LS. It was the sort of thing you used to do all the time: leave me ghostly messages on the mirror or draw tiny pentagrams in red nail polish on the back of my door. You left things to scare me. You loved to freak me out and you must have told her that. You must have, and now she was doing it, too.

Why LS? Why Libby Seeton? Why fixate on her? Libby was an innocent, a young woman dragged to the water by men who hated women, who heaped blame on them for things that they themselves had done. But Lena thought you went there of your own volition, so why Libby? Why LS?

Wrapped in a towel, I padded across the hallway and into your bedroom. It seemed undisturbed, but there was a smell in the air, something sweet – not your perfume, another. Something cloying, heavy with the scent of overblown roses. The drawer next to your bed was closed and when I pulled it open everything was as it had been, with one exception. The lighter, the one on which you'd had Libby's initials engraved, was gone. Someone had been in the room. Someone had taken it.

I went back to the bathroom and splashed my face again and rubbed the letters from the mirror, and as I did I saw you standing behind me, that exact same look on your face, uncomprehending. I whirled around and Lena raised her hands as though in self-defence. 'Jesus, Julia, chill. What is going on with you?'

I shook my head. 'I just . . . I just . . .'

'You just what?' She rolled her eyes.

'I need some air.'

But on the front step I almost cried out again, because there were women – two of them – at the gate, dressed in black and bent over, entangled in some way. One of them looked up at me. It was Louise Whittaker, the mother of the girl who had died. She dragged herself away from the other woman, speaking angrily as she did.

'Leave me! Leave me alone! Don't you come near me!'

The other one waved a hand at her – or at me, I couldn't be sure. Then she turned and slowly hobbled off along the lane.

'Bloody nutcase,' Louise spat as she approached the house. 'She's a menace, that Sage woman. Don't engage with her, I'm telling you. Don't let her through your door. She's a liar and a con artist, all she wants is money.' She paused to catch her breath, frowning at me. 'Well. You look about as awful as I feel.' I opened my mouth and shut it again. 'Is your niece at home?'

I showed her into the house. 'I'll just get her for you,'

I said, but Louise was already at the foot of the staircase, calling Lena's name. Then she went into the kitchen and sat down at the table to wait.

After a moment, Lena appeared. Her typical expression, that combination of haughtiness and boredom so reminiscent of you, was gone. She greeted Louise meekly, although I'm not even sure if Louise noticed because her eye was trained elsewhere, on the river outside or some place beyond.

Lena sat down at the table, raising her hands to wind her hair into a knot at the nape of her neck. She lifted her chin slightly, as though she were preparing herself for something, an interview. An interrogation. I may as well have been invisible for all the attention they paid me, but I remained in the room. I stood by the counter, not relaxed but on the balls of my feet, in case I needed to intervene.

Louise blinked, slowly, and her gaze finally came to rest on Lena, who held it for a second before looking down at the table.

'I'm sorry, Mrs Whittaker. I'm really sorry.'

Louise said nothing. Tears coursed down the lines of her face, in runnels carved from months of unrelenting grief.

'I'm so sorry,' Lena repeated. She was crying too now, letting her hair down again, twisting it through her fingers like a little girl.

'I wonder if you'll ever know,' Louise said at last, 'how it feels to realize that you didn't know your own child.' She took a deep, shuddering breath. 'I have all her things. Her clothes, her books, her music. The pictures she treasured. I know her friends, and the people she admired, I know what she loved. But that wasn't her. Because I didn't know *who* she loved. She had a life – *a whole life* – that I didn't know about. The most important part of her, I didn't know.' Lena tried to speak, but Louise went on. 'The thing is, Lena, that you could have helped me. You could have told me about it. You could have told me when you first found out. You could have come to me and told me that my daughter had got herself caught up in something, something she couldn't control, something you knew, *you must have known*, would end up being harmful to her.'

'But I couldn't . . . I couldn't . . .' Again, Lena tried to say something, and again, Louise wouldn't let her.

'Even if you were blind enough or stupid enough or careless enough not to see how much trouble she was in, you could still have helped *me*. You could have come to me, after she died, and said, this isn't something you did, or didn't do. This isn't your fault, this isn't your husband's fault. You could have stopped us from driving ourselves mad. But you didn't. You chose not to. All that time, you said nothing. All this time, you . . . And worse, even worse than that, you let him . . .' Her voice rose and then disappeared into the air, like smoke.

'Get away with it?' Lena finished the sentence. She was no longer crying, and although her voice rose, it was strong, not weak. 'Yes. I did, and it made me sick. It made me fucking *sick*, but I did it for her. Everything I have done, I did for Katie.'

'Don't you say her name to me,' Louise hissed. 'Don't you dare.'

'Katie, Katie, Katie!' Lena was half on her feet, leaning forward, her face inches from Louise's nose. 'Mrs Whittaker,' she collapsed back into her seat, 'I *loved* her. You know how much I loved her. I did what she wanted me to do. I did what she asked of me.'

'It wasn't your decision, Lena, to keep something as important as that from me, her mother—'

'No, it wasn't my decision, it was hers! I know you think you have the right to know everything, but you don't. She wasn't a child, she wasn't a little girl.'

'She was *my* little girl!' Louise's voice was a wail, an ululation. I realized I was gripping the counter, that I, too, was about to cry.

Lena spoke again, her voice softer now, supplicating. 'Katie made a choice. She made a decision and I honoured it.' More gently still, as though knowing she was moving on to dangerous ground, 'And I'm not the only one. Josh did, too.'

Louise drew back her hand and hit Lena once, very hard, across the face. The smack resounded, echoing off the walls. I leaped forward and grabbed Louise's arm. 'No!' I shouted. 'That's enough! That's enough!' I tried to pull her to her feet. 'You need to go.'

'Leave her!' Lena snapped. The left side of her face was an angry red, but her expression was calm. 'Stay out of it, Julia. She can hit me if she wants. She can scratch my eyes out, pull my hair. She can do whatever she wants to me. What does it matter now?'

Louise's mouth was open, I could smell her sour breath. I let go.

'Josh didn't say anything because of *you*,' she said,

wiping spittle from her lips. 'Because *you* told him not to say anything.'

'No, Mrs Whittaker.' Lena's tone was perfectly even as she placed the back of her right hand against her cheek to soothe it. 'That isn't true. Josh kept his mouth shut because of Katie. Because *she* asked him to. And then, later on, because he wanted to protect you and his dad. He thought that it would hurt you too much. To know that she'd been . . .' She shook her head. 'He's young, he thought—'

'Don't tell me what my son thought,' Louise said. 'What he was trying to do. Just don't.' She raised her hand to her throat; a reflex. No, not a reflex: she was gripping the bluebird that hung on her chain between thumb and forefinger. 'This,' she said, a hiss, not a word. 'It wasn't from you, was it?' Lena hesitated for a moment before shaking her head. 'It was from him. Wasn't it? He gave it to her.' Louise pushed her chair back, scraping its feet across the tiles. She pulled herself upright and with a vicious tug ripped the chain from her neck, slamming it down on the table in front of Lena. 'He gave that thing to her, and you let me hang it around my neck.'

Lena closed her eyes for a moment, shaking her head again. The meek, apologetic girl who'd crept into the kitchen a few minutes ago was gone and in her stead sat someone different, someone older, the adult to Louise's desperate, intemperate child. All at once I had the clearest memory of you, a little younger than Lena is now, one of the few memories I have of you sticking up for me. There was a teacher at my school who had accused me of taking something that didn't belong to me, and I remembered you admonishing her. You were clear-sighted and cool, and you didn't raise your voice when you told her how wrong she was to make accusations without evidence, and she was cowed by you. I remembered how proud I was of you then, and I had the same feeling here, the same sensation of heat in my chest.

Louise began to speak again, her voice very low. 'Explain this to me, then,' she said, sitting back down, 'since you know so much. Since you *understand* so much. If Katie loved that man, and if he loved her back, then why? Why did she do what she did? What did he do to her? To drive her to that?'

Lena turned her gaze to me. She looked afraid, I think, or maybe just resigned – I couldn't quite read her expression. She watched me for a second before closing her eyes, squeezing tears out of them. When she spoke again, her voice was higher, tighter than before.

'He didn't drive her to that. It wasn't him.' She sighed. 'Katie and I argued,' she said. 'I wanted her to stop it, to stop seeing him. I didn't think it was right. I thought she was going to get into trouble. I thought . . .' She shook her head. 'I just didn't want her to see him any more.'

A flash of understanding crossed Louise's face; she understood, in that moment, as did I.

'You threatened her,' I said. 'With exposure.'

'Yes,' Lena said, barely audible. 'I did.'

Louise left without a word. Lena sat motionless, staring at the river outside the window, not crying and not speaking. I had nothing to say to her, no way of reaching her. I recognized in her something I know I used to have too, something maybe everyone has at that age, some essential unknowability. I thought how odd it was that parents believe they know their children, *understand* their children. Do they not remember what it was like to be eighteen, or fifteen, or twelve? Perhaps having children makes you forget being one. I remember you at seventeen and me at thirteen, and I'm certain that our parents had no idea who we were.

'I lied to her.' Lena's voice broke my train of thought. She hadn't moved, she was still watching the water.

'Lied to who? To Katie?' She shook her head. 'To Louise? What did you lie about?'

'There's no point telling her the truth,' Lena said. 'Not now. She may as well blame me. At least I'm around. She needs somewhere to put all that hate.'

'What do you mean, Lena? What are you talking about?'

She turned her cold green eyes on mine, and she looked older than before. She looked the way you did the morning after you'd pulled me from the water. Changed, weary. 'I didn't threaten to tell anyone. I would never have done that to her. I loved her. None of you seem to get what that means, it's like you don't know what love is at all. I would have done anything for her.'

'So, if you didn't threaten her . . .'

I think I knew the answer before she said it. 'It was Mum,' she said.

Jules

THE ROOM FELT colder; if I believed in spirits I would have said that you'd joined us.

'We did argue, like I said. I didn't want her to see him any more. She said she didn't care what I thought, that it didn't matter. She said that I was immature, that I didn't understand what it was like to be in a real relationship. I called her a slut, she called me a virgin. It was that sort of fight. Stupid, horrible. When Katie left, I realized that Mum was in her room, right next door – I'd thought she was out. She'd overheard the whole thing. She told me she had to speak to Louise about it. I begged her not to, I told her it would ruin Katie's whole life. So then she said maybe the best thing was to talk to Helen Townsend, because after all Mark was the one doing something wrong, and Helen is his boss. She said maybe they could get him fired but keep Katie's name out of it. I told her that was stupid, and she knew it was. They wouldn't just be able to fire him, it would have to be done officially. The police would get involved. It would go to court. It would be made public. And even if Katie's name wasn't in the papers, her parents would find out, everyone at school would know . . . That stuff doesn't stay private.' She took a deep breath, exhaling slowly. 'I told Mum at the time, I said Katie would rather die than go through that.'

Lena leaned forward and opened the kitchen window, then fished around in the pocket of her hoodie and pulled out a pack of cigarettes. She lit one and blew smoke out into the air. 'I begged her. I mean it, I actually begged, and Mum told me that she'd have to think about it. She said that I had to convince Katie to stop seeing him, that it was an abuse of power and that it was totally wrong. She promised me that she wouldn't do anything without giving me time to persuade Katie.' She crushed her barely smoked cigarette on the window sill and flicked it towards the water.

'I believed her. I trusted her.' She turned to face me again. 'But then a couple of days later I saw Mum in the car park at school, talking to Mr Henderson. I don't know what they were talking about but it didn't look friendly, and I knew I had to say something to Katie, just in case, because she needed to know, she needed to be prepared . . .' Her voice cracked, and she swallowed. 'She died three days later.'

Lena sniffed, wiping her nose with the back of her hand. 'The thing is, when we talked about it afterwards, Mum swore she never even mentioned Katie to Mark Henderson. She said they were arguing about me, about problems I was having in class.'

'So . . . Lena, hang on, I don't understand. You're saying your mum *didn't* threaten them with exposure?'

'I couldn't understand it either. She swore she hadn't said anything, but she felt so *guilty*, I could see it. I knew that it was my fault, but she kept acting like it was hers. She stopped swimming in the river, and she became obsessed with *telling the truth*, she kept going on and on about it, how it was wrong to be afraid of facing the truth, of letting people know the truth, she just went on and on . . .'

(I wasn't sure if that was odd or perfectly consistent: you didn't tell the truth, you never did – the stories you'd been telling weren't *the* truth, they were *your* truth, your agenda. I should know. I've been on the dirty side of your truth most of my life.)

'But she didn't, did she? She never told anyone, or wrote about Mark Henderson, in her . . . *story* about Katie, there's no mention of him.'

Lena shook her head. 'No, because I wouldn't let her. We fought and fought and I kept telling her I would have loved to see that piece of shit go to prison, but it would have broken Katie's heart. And it would have meant that she did what she did for nothing.' She gulped. 'I mean, I *know*. I know what Katie did was stupid, fuck-ing *pointless*, but she died to protect him. And if we went to the police, that would mean her death meant noth-ing. But Mum just kept going on about the truth, how it was irresponsible to just let things go. She was . . . I don't know.' She looked up at me, her gaze as cool as the one with which she'd fixed Louise, and said, 'You would know all this, Julia, if you'd only spoken to her.'

'Lena, I'm sorry, I am sorry about that, but I still don't see why—'

'Do you know how I know my mother killed herself? Do you know how I know for sure?' I shook my head. 'Because on the day she died, we had a fight. It started over nothing, but it ended up being about Katie, like everything did. I was yelling at her and calling her a bad mother and saying that if she'd been a good parent she could have helped us, helped Katie, and then none of this would have happened. And she told me she *had* tried to help Katie, that she'd seen her walking home late one day, and had stopped to offer her a ride. She said Katie was all upset and wouldn't say why, and Mum said, *You don't have to go through this by yourself.* She said, *I can help you.* And, *Your mum and dad can help you, too.* When I asked her why she'd never told me about that before, she wouldn't say. I asked her when it happened and she said, Midsummer, June the twenty-first. Katie went to the pool that night. Without meaning to, it was Mum who tipped her over the edge. And so, like that, Katie tipped Mum over the edge, too.'

A wave of sadness hit me, a swell so forceful I thought it might knock me from my chair. Was that it, Nel? After all this, you *did* jump, and you did it because you felt guilty and you despaired. You despaired because you had no one to turn to – not your angry, grieving daughter and certainly not me, because you knew that if you called I wouldn't answer. Did you despair, Nel? Did you jump?

I could feel Lena watching me, and I knew that she could see my shame, could see that finally I got it, I understood that I, too, was to blame. But she didn't look triumphant, or satisfied, she just looked tired.

'I didn't tell the police any of this, because I didn't want anyone to know. I didn't want anyone to blame her – more than they already do, in any case. She didn't do it out of hate. And she suffered enough, didn't she? She suffered things she shouldn't have, because it wasn't her fault. It wasn't hers or mine.' She gave me a small, sad smile. 'It wasn't yours. It wasn't Louise's or Josh's. It wasn't our fault.'

I tried to embrace her, but she pushed me away. 'Don't,' she said. 'Please, I just . . .' She tailed off. Her chin lifted. 'I need to be by myself. Just for a bit. I'm going to go for a walk.'

I let her leave.

Nickie

NICKIE DID AS Jeannie told her to, she went to talk to Lena Abbott. The weather had cooled, a hint of autumn coming early, so she wrapped herself up in her black coat, stuffed the pages into the inside pocket and walked across to the Mill House. But when she got there, she found that there were other people around, and she was in no mood for a crowd. Especially not after what the Whittaker woman said, about how all she cared about was money and exploiting people's grief, which wasn't fair at all. That was never what she intended – if only people would listen. She stood outside the house a while, watching, but her legs ached and her head was full of noise and so she turned around and walked all the way back home again. Some days, she felt her age, and some days she felt her mother's.

She had no stomach for the day, for the fight ahead. Back in her room, she dozed in her chair, then woke and thought that maybe she had seen Lena heading for the pool, but it might have been a dream, or a premonition. Later, though, much later, in the dark, she was certain

262

that she saw the girl, moving like a ghost through the square, a ghost with purpose, fairly whipping along. Nickie could feel the split of the air as she passed, the energy buzzing off her, she could feel it all the way up there in her dark little room and it lifted her, stripped the years back. That was a girl on a mission. That girl had fire in her belly, she was a dangerous girl. The sort you don't mess with.

Seeing Lena like that reminded Nickie of herself way back when; it made her want to get up and dance, made her want to howl at the moon. Well, her dancing days might be over, but, pain or no pain, she decided she would make it to the river that night. She wanted to feel them up close, all those troublesome women, those troublesome girls, dangerous and vital. She wanted to feel their spirit, to bathe in it.

She took four aspirin and got hold of her cane, then made her way slowly and carefully down the stairs, out of the back door and into the alley behind the shops. She hobbled across the square towards the bridge.

It seemed to take a very long time; everything took so long these days. No one warned you about that when you were younger, no one told you how slow you would become, and how bored you would be by your slowness. She should have foreseen it, she supposed, and she laughed to herself in the dark.

Nickie could remember a time when she was fleet of foot, a whippet. Back then, when she was young, she and her sister ran races by the river, way upstream. They tore along, skirts tucked into their knickers, feeling every rock, every crevice in the hard ground through the soles of their flimsy plimsolls. Unstoppable, they were. Later, much later, older and a bit slower, they met in the same spot, upriver, and they walked together, sometimes for miles, often in silence.

It was on one of those walks that they spotted Lauren, sitting on the steps at Anne Ward's place, a cigarette in her hand and her head leaning back against the door. Jeannie called out to her, and when Lauren looked up, they saw that the side of her face had all the colours of the sunset. 'He's a devil, her old man,' Jeannie had said.

They say you speak of the Devil and then you feel the heat. As Nickie stood there, remembering her sister, her elbows propped on the cold stone of the bridge, chin resting on her hands, eyes cast down at the water, she felt him. She felt him before she saw him. She hadn't spoken his name, but maybe Jeannie's whispering had conjured him up, the small-town Satan. Nickie turned her head and there he was, walking towards her from the east side of the bridge, cane in one hand, cigarette in the other. Nickie spat on the ground like she always did, and said her invocation.

Usually she'd leave it at that, but this night – and who knows why, maybe she was feeling Lena's spirit, or Libby's, or Anne's, or Jeannie's – she called out. 'It won't be long now,' she said.

Patrick stopped. He looked up as though surprised to see her. 'What's that?' he snarled. 'What did you say?'

'I said, it won't be long now.'

Patrick took a step towards her and she felt the spirit again, angrily hot, surging up from her stomach to her chest and into her mouth. 'They've been talking to me lately.'

Patrick waved a hand at her in dismissal, said something she couldn't hear. He continued on his way, and still the spirit wouldn't be silenced. She called out, 'My sister! Your wife! Nel Abbott, too. All of them, they've all been talking to me. And she had your number, didn't she? Nel Abbott?'

'Shut up, you old fool,' Patrick spat. He made as if to come towards her, just a feint, and Nickie started. He laughed, turning away again. 'Next time you speak to her,' he called over his shoulder, 'do give your sister my best.'

Jules

I WAITED IN the kitchen for Lena to come home – I rang her phone, I left voicemail messages. I fretted hopelessly, and in my head you scolded me for not going after her, like you'd gone after me. You and I, we tell our stories differently. I know that, because I've read your words: *When I was seventeen, I saved my sister from drowning*. You were heroic, without context. You didn't write about how I got there, about the football game, or the blood, or Robbie.

Or the pool. *When I was seventeen, I saved my sister from drowning*, you say, but what a selective memory you have, Nel! I can still feel your hand on the back of my neck, I can still remember fighting against you, the agony of airless lungs, the cold panic when, even in my stupid, hopeless, drunken stupour, I knew I was going to drown. You held me there, Nel.

Not for long. You changed your mind. With your arm locked around my neck, you dragged me towards the bank, but I've always known that there was some part of you that wanted to leave me there.

You told me never to talk about it, you made me promise, *for Mum's sake*, and so I put it away. I suppose I always thought that one day, far into the future, when we were old and you were different, when you were sorry, we'd return to it. We'd talk about what happened, about what I did and what you did, about what you said and how we ended up hating each other. But you never said that you were sorry. And you never explained to me how it was that you could have treated me, your little sister, the way you did. You never changed, you just went and died, and I feel like my heart has been ripped out of my chest.

I want so desperately to see you again.

I waited for Lena until, defeated by exhaustion, I finally went to bed. I'd had so much trouble sleeping since I returned to this place and it was catching up with me. I collapsed, drifting in and out of dreams until I heard the door go downstairs, Lena's footsteps on the stairs. I heard her going into her room and turning her music on, loud enough for me to hear a woman singing.

> That blue-eyed girl
> said *'No more'*,
> and that blue-eyed girl
> became blue-eyed whore.

I slowly drifted back to sleep. When I woke again the music was still playing, the same song, louder now. I wanted it to stop, was desperate for it to stop, but I found I couldn't raise myself from the bed. I wondered whether I was awake at all, because if I was awake, what was this weight on my chest, crushing me? I couldn't breathe, couldn't move, but I heard the woman singing still.

Little fish, big fish, swimming in the water –
come back here man, gimme my daughter.

Suddenly, the weight lifted and I rose from the bed, furious. I stumbled into the hall and shouted for Lena to turn the music down. I lunged for her door handle and yanked the door open. The room was empty. Lights on, windows open, cigarette butts in the ashtray, a glass next to the empty bed. The music seemed to be getting louder and louder, my head pounded and my jaw ached, and I kept shouting even though there was no one there. I found the iPod dock and ripped it out of the wall, and at last, at last, all I could hear was the sound of my own breath and my own blood pulsing in my ears.

I returned to my room and phoned Lena again; when there was no answer, I tried Sean Townsend but the call went straight to voicemail. Downstairs, the front door was locked and all the lights were on. I went from room to room, turning them off one by one, stumbling as though drunk, as though drugged. I lay down on the window seat where I used to sit and read books with my mother, where twenty-two years ago your boyfriend raped me, and again I fell asleep.

I dreamed that the water was rising. I was upstairs in my parents' bedroom. I was lying on the bed with

Robbie at my side. Outside, rain thundered down, the river kept on rising, and somehow I knew that downstairs the house was flooding. Slowly at first, just a trickle of water seeping under the door, and then more quickly, the doors and windows bursting open, filthy water pouring into the house, lapping against the stairs. Somehow I could see the living room, submerged in murky green, the river reclaiming the house, the water reaching the neck of the *Drowning Dog*, only now he was no longer a painted animal, he was real. His eyes were white and wide with panic, and he was struggling for his life. I tried to get up, to go downstairs to save him, but Robbie wouldn't let me, he was pulling my hair.

I awoke with a start, panicked out of my nightmare. I checked my phone, it was after three in the morning. I could hear something, someone moving around the house. Lena was home. Thank God. I heard her coming down the stairs, her flip-flops slapping against stone. She stopped, framed in the doorway, the light behind her illuminating her silhouette.

She started to move towards me. She was saying something, but I couldn't hear her, and I saw that she wasn't wearing flip-flops at all, she was wearing the heels she wore to the funeral, and the same black dress, which was dripping wet. Her hair clung to her face, and her skin was grey, her lips blue. She was dead.

I woke up, gasping. My heart was hammering in my chest, the banquette beneath me was soaked with sweat. I sat up, confused, I looked at the paintings opposite me and they seemed to shift, and I thought, *I'm still asleep, I can't wake, I can't wake*. I pinched my skin as hard as I could, dug my nails into the flesh of my forearm and saw real marks, felt real pain. The house was dark and silent save for the river's quiet susurration. I called Lena's name.

I ran upstairs and along the corridor; Lena's door was ajar and the light was on. The room was exactly as I'd left it hours before, the water glass and the unmade bed and the ashtray untouched. Lena wasn't home. She hadn't been home. She was gone.

PART THREE

It wouldn't have made a difference though, would it? It wouldn't matter what he said, what he did, how he'd lived his life: they would crucify him anyway. It wouldn't matter to the newspapers, to the police, the school, the community, that he wasn't some deviant with a history of chasing after girls half his age. It wouldn't matter that he had fallen in love, and been fallen in love with. The mutuality of their feelings would be ignored – Katie's maturity, her seriousness, her intelligence, her *choice* – none of these things would matter. All they would see was his age, twenty-nine, and hers, fifteen, and they would rip his life apart.

He stood on the lawn, staring at the boarded-up windows, and he sobbed. If there had been anything left to smash, he would have broken it himself then. He stood on the lawn and he cursed her, cursed the day he'd first set eyes on her, so much more beautiful than her silly, self-assured friends. He cursed the day she'd walked slowly towards his desk, full hips swinging gently and a smile on her lips, and asked, 'Mr Henderson? Can I ask for your help with something?' The way she'd leaned towards him, close enough that he could smell her clean, unperfumed skin. He'd been startled at first, and angry, he'd thought she was toying with him. Teasing him. Hadn't she been the one who started all this? And why should it be him, then, left alone to suffer the consequences? He stood on the lawn, tears in his eyes, panic rising in his throat, and he hated Katie, and he hated himself, and he hated the stupid mess he'd got himself into, from which he now saw no escape.

What to do? Go into the house, pack the rest of his

things and leave? Run? His mind fogged: where to go, and how? Were they already watching? They must be. If he withdrew money, would they know? If he tried to leave the country again, would they be there? He imagined the scene, the passport official glancing at his photo and picking up a phone, uniformed men dragging him from a queue of holidaymakers, the curious looks on their faces. Would they know, when they saw him, what he was? No drug-dealer, no terrorist – no: he must be something else. Something worse. He looked at the blank and boarded windows, and imagined that they were inside, they were waiting for him there, they'd already been through his things, his books and his papers, they'd already turned the house upside down searching for evidence of what he had done.

And they would have found nothing. He felt the faintest gleam of hope. There was nothing to find. No love letters, no pictures on his laptop, no evidence at all that she had ever set foot in his house (the bedlinen long gone, the entire house cleaned, disinfected, scrubbed of every last trace of her). What evidence would they have, save for the fantasies of a vindictive teenage girl? A teenage girl who had tried herself to win his favour and been resoundingly knocked back. No one knew, no one really knew, what had passed between himself and Katie, and no one need know. Nel Abbott was ash, and her daughter's word worth just about as much.

He gritted his teeth and fished for his keys in his pocket, then walked around the house and opened the back door.

*

She came at him before he had time to turn on the light, barely flesh, nothing but a dark maw, teeth and nails. He batted her away, but she came again. What choice did he have? What choice did she leave him?

And now there was blood on the floor and he didn't have time to clean it up. It was getting light. He had to go.

Jules

IT CAME TO me, quite suddenly. An epiphany. One moment I was terrified and panicking, and the next I was not, because I knew. Not where Lena was, but *who* she was. And with that, I could start to look for her.

I was sitting in the kitchen, dazed, punch-drunk. The police had left, gone back to the river to continue the search. They told me to stay put, just in case. In case she came home. Keep calling, they said, keep your phone on. *OK, Julia? Keep your phone on*. They talked to me as though I were a child.

I couldn't blame them, I suppose, because they'd been sitting there asking me questions I couldn't answer. I knew when I had seen Lena last, but I couldn't say when she was last in the house. I didn't know what she'd been wearing when she left; I couldn't remember what she'd been wearing when I saw her last. I couldn't distinguish dream from reality: was the music real, or did I imagine that? Who locked the door, who turned on the lights? The detectives eyed me with suspicion and disappointment: why did I let her go, if she was so distressed after her confrontation with Louise Whittaker? How could I not have run after her, to comfort her? I saw the looks that passed between them, the unspoken judgement. What sort of guardian will this woman make?

You were in my head, too, admonishing me. *Why didn't you go after her, like I went after you? Why didn't you save her, like I saved you? When I was seventeen, I saved my sister from drowning.* When you were seventeen, Nel, you drove me into the water and held me down. (That old argument, back and forth – you say, I say, you say, I say. I was losing the stomach for it, I didn't want to have it any longer.)

And that was where it was. In the buzz of exhaustion, the sick thrill of fear, I saw something, caught sight of something. It was as though something moved, a shadow just out of my line of sight. *Was it really me,* you asked, *who drove you to the water?* Was it you, or was it Robbie? Or some combination of the two?

The floor seemed to tilt and I grabbed hold of the kitchen counter to steady myself. *Some combination of the two.* I felt breathless, my chest tight as though I were going to have a panic attack. I waited for the world to go white, but it didn't. I kept standing, I kept breathing. *Some combination.* I ran to the stairs, bolted up them and into your room, and there! That picture of you with Lena, when she's smiling her predator's smile – that isn't you. That isn't your smile. It's *his.* It's Robbie Cannon's. I can see it now, flashing up at me while he lies on top of your body and pushes your shoulders down into the sand. That's who she is, who Lena is. She's a combination of the two of you. Lena is yours, and she is his. Lena is Robbie Cannon's daughter.

Jules

I SAT DOWN on the bed, the photo frame in my hand. You and she smiled up at me, bringing bright hot tears to my eyes, and finally I cried for you as I should have done at your funeral. I thought of him that day, the way he'd looked at Lena – I'd misread that look completely. It wasn't predatory, it was *proprietary*. He wasn't looking at her as a girl to be seduced, to be possessed. She already belonged to him. So maybe he'd come for her, to take what was rightfully his?

He wasn't hard to find. His father used to have a string of flashy car dealerships all over the north-east. Cannon Cars, the company was called. That didn't exist any longer, it had gone bankrupt years ago, but there was a smaller, sadder, low-rent version in Gateshead. I found a badly designed website with a picture of him on its homepage, the photo taken some time ago, by the look of it. Less paunchy then, still a hint of the handsome, cruel boy in his face.

I didn't call the police, because I was sure they wouldn't listen to me. I just picked up the car keys and left. I was feeling almost pleased with myself as I drove out of Beckford – I'd figured it out, I was taking control. And the further I drove from the village, the stronger I felt, the fog of tiredness clearing, my limbs loosening. I felt hungry, savagely hungry, and I relished the sensation; I chewed the inside of my cheek and tasted iron. Some old part of me, some furious, fearless relic, had surfaced; I imagined myself lashing out at him, clawing at him. I pictured myself an Amazon, ripping him limb from limb.

The garage was in a rundown part of town, under the railway arches. An ominous place. By the time I arrived, I was no longer brave. My hands shook as I reached to change gear or flick the indicator switch, the taste in my mouth was bile, not blood. I was trying to focus on what I had to do – to find Lena, to make Lena safe – but all my energy was sapped by the effort it took to push back against memories I hadn't let surface for over half a lifetime, memories which rose now like driftwood out of water.

I parked across the road from the garage. There was a man standing outside, smoking a cigarette – a younger man, not Cannon. I got out of the car and on trembling legs crossed the road to talk to him.

'I was hoping to speak to Robert Cannon?' I said.

'That your motor, is it?' he said, indicating the car behind me. 'You can just bring it in . . .'

'No, it's not about that. I need to speak to . . . Is he here?'

'It's not about the motor? He's in the office,' he said,

jerking his head to indicate behind him. 'You can go on in if you want.'

I peered into the cavernous dark space and my stomach contracted. 'No,' I said as firmly as I could, 'I'd prefer to speak to him out here.'

He sucked his teeth and flicked his half-smoked cigarette into the street. 'Suit yourself,' he said, and strolled on inside.

I slipped my hand into my pocket and realized that my phone was in my handbag, which was still on the passenger seat. I turned to go back, knowing that if I did I wouldn't return, that if I made it to the safety of the driver's seat I would lose all courage completely, I would start the engine and drive away.

'Can I help you?' I froze. 'Did you want something, pet?'

I turned around, and there he was, uglier even than he had looked on the day of the funeral. His face had become heavy and hangdog, his nose purpled, mapped with blue veins which spread to his cheeks like an estuary. His gait was familiar, listing side to side like a ship as he approached. He peered at me. 'Do I know you?'

'You're Robert Cannon?' I asked.

'Yes,' he said. 'I'm Robbie.'

For a fraction of a second, I felt sorry for him. It was the way he said his name, still using the diminutive. Robbie is a child's name, the name of a little boy who runs around the back garden and climbs trees. It's not the name of some overweight loser, some bankrupt running a dodgy garage in a shitty part of town. He stepped towards me and I caught a whiff of him, body odour and booze, and any pity evaporated as my body remembered the feeling of his, crushing the breath out of me.

'Look, love, I'm very busy,' he said.

My hands clenched into fists. 'Is she here?' I asked.

'Is *who* here?' He frowned, then rolled his eyes, reaching into his jeans pocket for his cigarettes. 'Ah, fuck's sake, you're not a mate of Shelley's, are you? Because, as I told her old man, I haven't seen the slag in weeks, so if it's about that, you can just do one, all right?'

'Lena Abbott,' I said, my voice little more than a hiss. 'Is she here?'

He lit his cigarette. Behind his dull brown eyes, something sparked. 'You're looking for . . . who now? Nel Abbott's girl? Who are you?' He looked around him. 'Why d'you think Nel's girl would be here?'

He wasn't faking it. He was too stupid to fake it, I could see that. He didn't know where Lena was. He didn't know who she was. I turned to go. The longer I stayed, the more he'd wonder. The more I'd give away.

'Hang on,' he said, placing a hand on my shoulder, and I spun round, shoving him away from me.

'Easy!' he said, raising his hands, looking around as though for back-up. 'What's going on here? Are you . . . ?' He squinted at me. 'I saw you – you were at the funeral.' Finally, it dawned on him. '*Julia?*' His face broke into a smile. 'Julia! Bloody hell. I didn't recognize you before . . .' He took me in, head to toe. 'Julia. Why didn't you say something?'

He offered me a cup of tea. I started laughing and I couldn't stop, I laughed until tears streamed down my face while he stood there, half giggling along at first, until his uncertain mirth petered out and he stood, dull and uncomprehending, watching me.

'What's going on?' he asked, irritated.

I wiped my eyes with the back of my hand. 'Lena ran off,' I said. 'I've been looking for her everywhere, I thought maybe . . .'

'Well, she isn't *here*. Why on earth d'you think she'd be here? I don't even know the kid, first time I laid eyes on her was at the funeral. Gave me a bit of a turn, if I'm honest. She's so like Nel.' He rearranged his features into a facsimile of concern. 'I was sorry to hear about what happened. Really sorry, Julia.' He tried to touch me again, but I pulled away. He took a step closer to me. 'I just . . . I can't believe you're Julia! You look so different.' An ugly smile smeared across his face. 'Don't know how I could forget,' he said quietly, his voice low. 'I popped your cherry, didn't I, girl?' He laughed. 'Long time ago now.'

Popped your cherry. Pop! A joyful sound, of balloons and birthday parties. And cherries, sweet on the lips, delicious and sticky; these things were a million miles from his slimy tongue in my mouth and his dirty fingers pushing me open. I thought I would gag.

'No, Robbie,' I said, and I was surprised by how clear my voice sounded, how loud, how steady. 'You didn't pop my cherry. You raped me.'

The smile slipped from his ruined face. He cast a glance over his shoulder before stepping towards me again. My head swimming with adrenaline now, breath quickening, I clenched my fists and stood my ground.

'I what?' he hissed. 'I fucking *what*? I never . . . I didn't *rape* you.'

He whispered it, *rape*, as though afraid someone might hear us.

'I was thirteen years old,' I said. 'I told you to stop, I was crying my fucking eyes out, I . . .' I had to stop because I could feel the tears filling my throat, drowning my voice, and I didn't want to cry in front of the bastard now.

'You cried 'cos it was your first time,' he said, his voice low, wheedling, 'because it hurt a bit. You never said you didn't want to. You never said no.' Then, louder, definitive, 'You lying bitch, you never said no.' Now he started laughing. 'I could have whatever I wanted, don't you remember? I had half the girls in Beckford trailing after me with their knickers wet. I had your sister, who was the hottest girl around. You honestly think I needed to rape a fat cow like you?'

He believed it. I could see that he believed every word he said, and in that moment I was defeated. All this time, he'd never felt guilty. He'd never felt a second of remorse, because in his head what he'd done wasn't rape. All this time, and he still believed he'd been doing the fat girl a favour.

I walked away from him. Behind me, I could hear him coming after me, swearing under his breath. 'You always were a mad bitch, weren't you? You always were. Can't believe you coming in saying this kind of shit, saying—'

I stopped suddenly, a few feet from the car. *Wasn't there some part of you that liked it?* Something shifted. If

Robbie didn't think he'd raped me, how could you have done? What were you talking about, Nel? What were you asking me? Some part of me that liked *what*?

I turned around. Robbie was standing behind me, hands hanging at his sides like slabs of meat, his mouth open. 'Did she know?' I asked him.

'What?'

'Did Nel know?' I yelled at him.

His lip curled. 'Did Nel know what? That I fucked you? You're joking, aren't you? Imagine what she'd have said to that, if I told her I'd banged her little sister just after I was done banging her?' He laughed. 'I told her the first bit, how you tried it on, how you were drunk and sloppy and leaning all over me and looking up at me with your sad fat face and begging, *please*? Like a little dog, you were, always hanging around, always watching us whenever I was with her, spying on us, even when we were in bed you liked to watch, didn't you? Thought we didn't notice, didn't you?' He laughed again. 'We did. We use to joke about what a little perv you were, sad little fatso, never been touched, never been kissed, liked to watch her hot sister getting it.' He shook his head. '*Rape?* Don't make me laugh. You wanted some of what Nel was getting, you made that very fucking clear.'

I pictured myself, sitting under the trees, standing outside the bedroom, watching. He was right, I *did* watch them, but not with lust, not with envy, with a kind of horrible fascination. I watched the way a child does, because that was what I was. I was a little girl who didn't want to see what was being done to her sister (because that's what it looked like, it always looked as though something was being done to you), but who couldn't look away.

'I told her you tried it on with me and then you ran off crying when I knocked you back, and she ran off after you.'

There was a sudden tumbling of images in my head: the sound of your words, the heat of your anger, the pressure of your hands as you held me down in the water and then grabbed my hair and pulled me to the bank.

You bitch, you stupid fat bitch, what have you done? What are you trying to do?

Or was it, *You stupid bitch, what were you doing?*

And then it was, *I know he hurt you, but what did you expect?*

I made it to the car, fumbling for my keys with trembling hands. Robbie was still behind me, still talking. 'Yeah, run along then, you lying slag. You never thought that girl was here, did you? That was an excuse, wasn't it? You came to see me. Did you want another taste?' I could hear him laughing as he walked away, delivering his parting shot from across the street. 'No chance, pet, not this time. You might have lost a bit of weight, but you're still a fucking minger.'

I started the car, pulled away, stalled. Cursing, I started the engine again and lurched off down the road, putting my foot down, putting as much distance as possible between him and me and what had just happened, and knowing I should be worrying about Lena, but unable to think about that because all I could think was this: *You didn't know.*

You didn't know that he raped me.

When you said, *I'm sorry he hurt you*, you meant you were sorry I felt rejected. When you said, *What did you expect?* you meant that of course he would reject me, I was just a child. And when you asked me, *Wasn't there some part of you that liked it?* you weren't talking about sex, you were talking about the water.

The scales fell. I have been blind and blinkered. You didn't know.

I pulled the car over to the side of the road and started to sob, my whole body racked with the awful, horrible knowledge: you didn't know. All these years, Nel. All these years, I attributed to you the most vicious cruelty, and what had you done to deserve it? What did you do to deserve it? All those years, and I didn't listen, I never listened to you. And now it seemed impossible that I could not have seen, could not have understood that when you asked me, *Wasn't there some part of you that liked it?* you were talking about the river, about that night at the river. You wanted to know what it felt like to abandon yourself to the water.

I stopped crying. In my head, you muttered: *You don't have time for this, Julia*, and I smiled. 'I know,' I said out loud. 'I know.' I didn't care any longer what Robbie thought, I didn't care that he'd spent all his life telling himself he did nothing wrong; that's what men like him do. And what does it matter what he thought? He was nothing to me. What mattered was you, what you knew and didn't know, and that I'd been punishing you all your life for something you didn't do. And now I had no way to tell you I was sorry.

*

Back in Beckford, I stopped the car on the bridge, climbed down the mossy steps and walked along the river path. It was early afternoon, the air was cooling and the breeze was getting up. Not a perfect day for a swim, but I'd been waiting so long and I wanted to be there, with you. It was the only way now that I could get close to you, the only thing I had left.

I took off my shoes and stood in jeans and T-shirt on the bank. I started to walk forward, one foot after the other. I closed my eyes, gasping as my feet sank into the cool mud, but I didn't stop. I kept going, and when the water closed over my head, I realized through my terror that it did feel good. It did.

Mark

BLOOD SEEPED THROUGH the bandage wrapped around Mark's hand. He'd not done a very good job of patching it up and, try as he might, he couldn't stop himself from gripping the steering wheel too tightly. His jaw ached and a bright, startling pain pulsed behind his eyes. The vice was back again, clamped around his temples; he could feel the blood squeezing through the veins in his head, could almost hear his skull begin to crack. Twice he'd had to stop the car at the side of the road to throw up.

He had no idea where to run. He'd started off by driving north, back towards Edinburgh, but halfway there he changed his mind. Would they expect him to go that way? Would there be roadblocks at the entrance to the city, torchlight shone in his face, rough hands dragging him from the car, quiet voices telling him there's worse to come than this? Far worse. He turned back and took a different route. He couldn't think with his head splitting like this. He needed to stop, to breathe, to plan. He turned off the main road and drove towards the coast.

Everything he'd feared was coming to pass. He saw

his future unravelling before him and he played it over and over in his mind: the police at the door, the journalists screaming questions at him as he was dragged, head covered with a blanket, to a car. Windows repaired, just to be smashed again. Vile insults on the walls, excrement through the letter box. The trial. Oh, God, the trial. The look on his parents' faces as Lena levelled her accusations, the questions the court would ask: when and where and how many times? The shame. The conviction. Prison. Everything he'd warned Katie about, everything he'd told her he would face. He wouldn't survive it. He'd told her that he wouldn't survive it.

That Friday evening in June, he hadn't been expecting her. She was supposed to be going to a birthday party, something she couldn't get out of. He remembered opening the door, feeling the rush of pleasure he always got from looking at her, before he had time to process the look on her face. Anxious, suspicious. He'd been seen that afternoon, speaking to Nel Abbott in the school car park. What had they been talking about? Why was he speaking to Nel at all?

'I was *seen*? By whom?' He was amused, he thought she was jealous.

Katie turned away, rubbing her hand against the back of her neck, the way she did whenever she felt nervous or self-conscious. 'K? What's the matter?'

'She *knows*,' Katie said quietly, without looking at him, and the ground fell away, pitching him into nothingness. He grabbed hold of her arm, twisting her round to face him. 'I think Nel Abbott knows.'

And then it all came tumbling out, all the things she'd lied about, the things she'd been hiding from him. Lena had known for months, Katie's brother too.

'Jesus Christ! Jesus Christ, Katie, how could you not tell me? How could you . . . *Jesus!*' He'd never yelled at her before, he could see how frightened she was, how terrified and upset, and yet he couldn't stop himself. 'Do you understand what they'll do to me? Do you fucking understand what it is like to go to prison as a sex offender?'

'You're not!' she cried.

He grabbed her again (he felt hot, even now, with the shame of it). 'But I am! That's exactly what I am. That is what you've made me.'

He told her to leave, but she refused. She begged, pleaded. She swore to him that Lena would never talk. Lena would never say anything to anyone about it. *Lena loves me, she would never hurt me.* She'd persuaded Josh that it was over, that nothing had ever actually happened, that he had nothing to worry about, that if he did say something all it would do was break their parents' hearts. But Nel?

'I'm not even sure if she does know,' Katie told him. 'Lena said she *might* have overheard something . . .' She tailed off, and he could tell by the cut of her gaze that she was lying. He couldn't believe her, couldn't believe anything she said. This beautiful girl, who had entranced him, bewitched him, couldn't be trusted.

It was over, he told her, watching her face crumple, disentangling himself as she tried to wrap her arms around him, pushing her away, gently at first and then more firmly. 'No, listen, listen to me! I *cannot* see you any longer, not like this. Not ever, do you understand? It is over. It never happened. There is nothing between us – there was never anything between us.'

'Please don't say that, Mark, please.' She was sobbing so hard she could barely breathe, and his heart broke. 'Please don't say that. I love you . . .'

He felt himself weaken, he let her hold him, he let her kiss him, he felt his resolve subside. She pressed herself into him and he had a sudden, clear image of another pressing against him, and not just one but several: male bodies pressing against his beaten, broken, violated body; he saw this and pushed her violently away.

'No! No! Do you have any idea what you've done? You have *ruined* my life, do you understand that? When this gets out – when that bitch tells the police – and she *will* tell the police – my life will be over. Do you know what they do to men like me in prison? You know, don't you? Do you think I'll survive that? I won't. My life will be *over.*' He saw the fear and hurt in her face and still he said, 'And it will be down to you.'

When they pulled her body from the pool, Mark punished himself. For days, he could barely get out of bed, and yet he had to face the world, he had to go to school, to look at her empty chair, to face the grief of her friends and her parents and show none of his own. He, the one who loved her most, was not permitted to grieve for her the way she deserved. He wasn't permitted to grieve the way *he* deserved to, because although he punished himself for what he had said to her in anger, he knew that this wasn't really his fault. None of it was his fault – how could it be? Who could control the one they fell in love with?

Mark heard a thump and jumped, swerving out into the middle of the road, over-correcting back again and skidding on to the gravelled verge. He checked the rear-view mirror. He thought he'd hit something, but there was nothing there, nothing but empty tarmac. He took a deep breath and squeezed the wheel again, wincing as it pressed into the wound on his hand. He switched on the radio, turned it up as loud as it would go.

He still had no idea what he was going to do with Lena. His first idea had been to drive north to Edinburgh, dump the car in a car park and then get the ferry to the Continent. They'd find her soon enough. Well, they'd find her eventually. He might feel terrible, but he had to keep reminding himself that this was not his fault. *She* came at *him*, not the other way round. And when he tried to fight her off, *fend* her off, she just came at him again and again, shouting and clawing, talons drawn. He had fallen, sprawling on the kitchen floor, his carry-on bag skidding away from him across the tiles. And from it fell, as though directed by a deity with a sick sense of humour, the bracelet. The bracelet he'd been carrying around since he took it from Helen Townsend's desk, this thing which held a power he hadn't yet figured out how to wield, out it came, skittering across the floor between them.

Lena looked at it as though it were an alien thing. It might as well have been glowing green kryptonite from the expression on her face. And then confusion passed and she was upon him again, only this time she had the kitchen scissors in her hand and she was swinging hard at him, at his face, at his neck, swinging like she meant it. He raised his hands in self-defence and she sliced one of them open. It throbbed now, angrily, in time with his racing heartbeat.

Thump, thump, thump. He checked the rear-view again – no one behind him – and jammed his foot on the brake. There was a sickening, satisfying thud as her body slammed into metal, and all was quiet again.

He pulled the car over to the side of the road again, not to be sick this time, but to weep. For himself, for his ruined life. He cried racking sobs of frustration and despair, he beat his right hand against the steering wheel again and again and again, until it hurt as much as the left one.

Katie was fifteen years and two months old the first time they slept together. Another ten months and she would have been legal. They would have been untouchable – legally, in any case. He'd have had to walk away from the job and some people might still have thrown stones, they'd still have called him names, but he could have lived with that. They could have lived with it. Ten fucking months! They should have waited. He should have insisted they wait. Katie was the one in a hurry, Katie was the one who couldn't stay away, Katie was the one who forced the issue, who wanted to make him hers, undeniably. And now she was gone, and he was the one who was going to pay for it.

The unfairness of it rankled, it seared his flesh like acid, and the vice just kept squeezing, tighter and tighter, and he wished to God it would just crush him, split his head open, and like her, like Katie, he'd be done with it.

Lena

I WAS FRIGHTENED when I woke up, I didn't know where I was. I couldn't see a thing. It was totally dark. But I realized from the noise, the movement and the smell of petrol that I was in a car. My head was really sore and my mouth too, it was hot and stuffy and there was something digging into my back, something hard, like a metal bolt. I wiggled my hand round behind my back to try to grab it, but it was attached.

That was a shame, because what I really needed was a weapon.

I was frightened, but I knew I couldn't let my fear get the better of me. I needed to think clearly. Clearly and fast, because sooner or later the car was going to stop and then it was going to be him or me, and there was *no way* that he was going to do for Katie *and* Mum *and* me. No fucking way. I had to believe it, had to keep telling myself over and over: this was going to end with me alive and him dead.

Over the weeks since Katie died, I'd thought about a lot of ways to make Mark Henderson pay for what he'd done, but I never considered murder. I'd thought about other things: painting things on his walls, smashing his windows (been there, done that), calling his girlfriend to tell her everything Katie had told me: how many times, when, where. How he liked to call her 'teacher's pet'. I thought about getting some of the guys in the year above to kick the shit out of him. I thought about cutting off his dick and feeding it to him. But I didn't think about killing him. Not until today.

How did I end up here? I can't believe how stupid I was to let him get the upper hand. I should never have gone to his house, not without a clear plan, not without knowing exactly what I was going to do.

I didn't even think, I was just making it up as I went along. I knew that he was coming back from holiday – I'd heard Sean and Erin talking about it. And then, after everything Louise said, and after the conversation I had with Julia about how it wasn't my fault or Mum's, I just thought, you know what? It's time. I just wanted to stand in front of him and make him share a little in the blame. I wanted him to admit it, to admit what he'd done and that it was wrong. So I just went there, and I'd already smashed the window of the back door, so it was easy enough getting in.

The house smelled dirty, like he'd gone away without emptying the rubbish or something. For a while, I just stood in the kitchen and used the torch on my phone to look around, but then I decided I'd turn on the light, because you wouldn't be able to see it from the road and even if his neighbours saw it they'd just think he'd come home.

It smelled dirty because it was dirty. Disgusting, actually – washing-up in the sink and ready-meal cartons with bits of food still stuck in them, and all the surfaces coated in grease. And shitloads of empty red-wine bottles in the recycling bin. It's not how I expected it would be at all. From the way he was at school – always really neatly dressed and his fingernails clean, clipped close – I thought he'd be kind of anal.

I went through to the living room and scanned around using my phone again – I didn't turn the light on in there in case you could see it from the road. It was so ordinary. Cheap furniture, lots of books and CDs, no pictures on the walls. It was ordinary and dirty and sad.

Upstairs was a mess. The bedroom was rank. The bed was unmade, the wardrobes open, and it smelled bad – different to downstairs, it smelled sour and sweaty, like a sick animal. I closed the curtains and turned on the bedside light. It was even worse than downstairs, it looked like somewhere someone old would live – ugly yellow walls and brown curtains and clothes and papers on the floor. I opened a drawer and there were ear plugs and nail clippers inside. In the bottom drawer, there were condoms and lube and fluffy cuffs.

I felt sick. I sat down on the bed, and then I noticed that the sheet had pulled away from the mattress a bit in the opposite corner and I could see a brown stain underneath. I actually thought I was going to vomit. It was painful, physically painful, to think about Katie being here, with him, in this horrible room in this disgusting house. I was ready to leave. It was a stupid idea anyway, going there without a plan. I turned off the light and went back downstairs, and I was almost at the back door when I heard a noise from outside, footsteps coming up the path. And then the door swung open and there he was. He looked ugly, his face and eyes red, his mouth open. I just went for him. I wanted to scratch his eyes out of his ugly face, I wanted to hear him scream.

I don't know what happened then. He fell, I think, and I was on my knees, and something skittered across the floor towards me. A piece of metal, like a key. I reached for it, and found that it wasn't jagged, but smooth. A circle. A silver circle with a black onyx clasp. I turned it over in my hand. I could hear the kitchen clock ticking loudly, and the sound of Mark's breath. 'Lena,' he said, and I looked up and met his eye and I could see that he was afraid. I got to my feet. 'Lena,' he said again, and he stepped towards me. I could feel myself smiling, because out of the corner of my eye I'd spotted another silver thing, a sharp thing, and I knew exactly what I was going to do. I was going to take a breath and steady myself, and I was going to wait until he said my name one more time, and then I was going to take the scissors that were lying on the kitchen table and I was going to jam them into his fucking neck.

'Lena,' he said, and he reached for me, and everything happened really fast after that. I grabbed the scissors and I went for him, but he's taller than me and his arms were raised and I must have missed, mustn't I? Because he isn't dead, he's driving, and I'm stuck back here with a bump on my head.

I started yelling, stupidly, because, seriously, who was going to hear me? I could tell the car was moving fast, but I yelled anyway, *Let me out, let me out, you stupid bastard!* I banged my fists on the metal hood above me, screaming as loud as I could, and then suddenly, bang! The car stopped moving and I slammed into the edge of the car boot, and then I let myself cry.

It wasn't just the pain. For some reason I kept thinking about all those windows we broke, Josh and I, and about how much it would have upset Katie. She would hate this, all of it: she'd hate her brother having to tell the truth after months of lying, she'd hate me being hurt like this, but most of all she'd hate those broken windows, because they were the thing she dreaded. Broken windows and *paedo* scrawled on the walls and shit through the letter box and journalists on the pavement and people spitting, throwing punches.

I cried for the pain and I cried because I felt bad for Katie, for how this would have broken her heart. *But you know what, K?* I found myself whispering to Katie, like a madwoman, like Julia muttering to herself in the dark. *I'm sorry. I'm really sorry, because that isn't what he deserves. I can say this now, because you're gone and I'm lying in the boot of his car with my mouth bleeding and my head split open, I can say this categorically: Mark Henderson doesn't deserve to be hounded or beaten. He deserves worse. I know you loved him, but he didn't just ruin your life, he's ruined mine too. He killed my mother.*

Erin

I was in the back office with Sean when the call came in. A pale young woman with a stricken expression stuck her head around the door. 'There's another one, Sir. Someone spotted her from up on the ridge. Someone in the water, a young woman.' From the look on Sean's face, I thought he was going to heave.

'There can't be,' I said. 'There's uniforms all over the place, how can there be another one?'

By the time we got there, there was a crowd on the bridge, uniforms doing their best to keep them up there. Sean ran and I followed, we hammered along under the trees. I wanted to slow down, I wanted to stop. The last thing on earth I wanted to see was them pulling that girl out of the water.

It wasn't her, though, it was Jules. She was already on the bank when we got there. There was a weird sound in the air, like a magpie scolding. It took me a while to realize that it was coming from her, from Jules. The chattering of her teeth. Her entire body shook, her sodden clothes clung to her pitifully thin frame which folded in on itself like a collapsing deck chair. I called her name and she stared up at me, her bloodshot eyes looking straight through me, as though she couldn't focus, as though she didn't register who I was. Sean took off his jacket and put it around her shoulders.

She muttered, trance-like. She wouldn't say a word to us, she hardly seemed to notice we were there. She just sat, trembling, glowering at the black water, her lips working the way they did when she saw her sister on the slab, soundless but purposeful, as though she were having an argument with some unseen adversary.

The relief, such as it was, lasted barely a few minutes before the next crisis hit. The uniforms who'd gone to welcome Mark Henderson home from his holiday had found his house empty. And not just empty, bloody: there were signs of a struggle in the kitchen, blood smeared all over the floor and the door handles, and Henderson's car was nowhere to be found.

'Oh Christ,' Sean said. 'Lena.'

'No,' I cried, trying to convince myself as well as Sean. I was thinking about the conversation I'd had with Henderson, the morning before he left for his holiday. There was something about him, something weak. Something wounded. There is nothing more dangerous than a man like that. 'No. There were uniforms at the house, they were waiting for him, he couldn't have—'

But Sean was shaking his head. 'No, they weren't. They weren't there. There was a bad smash on the A68 last night and it was all hands on deck. A decision was taken to redeploy resources. There was no one at Henderson's house, not until this morning.'

'Fuck. *Fuck.*'

'Quite. He'll have come back and seen the windows all smashed up and jumped to the right conclusion. That Lena Abbott told us something.'

'And then what – he went to her house, and took her, and brought her back to his place?'

'How the hell should I know?' Sean snapped. 'This is our fault. We should have been watching the house, we should have been watching her . . . It's our fault she's gone.'

Jules

THE POLICEMAN – NOT one I'd met before – wanted to come into the house with me. He was young, twenty-five perhaps, although his hairless, cherubic face made him look even younger. As kind as he appeared, I insisted he leave. I didn't want to be alone with a man in the house, no matter how harmless he looked.

I went upstairs and ran myself a bath. Water, water, everywhere. I had no great desire to be immersed in water again, but I could think of no better way to drive the chill from my bones. I sat on the edge of the tub, biting my lip to stop my teeth from chattering, my phone in my hand. I kept ringing Lena's number, over and over, I kept hearing her cheery message, her voice full of a light I've never heard when she speaks to me.

When the bath was half full, I lowered myself in, my teeth gritted against panic, my heartbeat rising as my body sank. It's OK, it's OK, it's OK. You said that. That night, when we were in here together, when you poured hot water over my skin, when you soothed me. *It's OK*, you said. *It's OK, Julia. It's OK*. It wasn't, of course, but you didn't know that. All you thought had happened was that I'd had an awful day, been made fun of, humiliated, rejected by a boy I liked. And finally, in an act of extreme melodrama, I'd gone to the Drowning Pool and flung myself in.

You were angry because you thought I'd done it to hurt you, to get you into trouble. To make Mum love me more, even more than she already did. To make her reject you. Because it would have been your fault, wouldn't it? You had bullied me, and you were supposed to be keeping an eye on me, and this had happened on your watch.

I turned the tap with my toe and let my body slip down into the tub; my shoulders submerged, my neck, my head. I listened to the sounds of the house, distorted, muffled, made alien by the water. A sudden thump made me jerk upwards into the cold air. I listened. Nothing. I was imagining things.

But when I slipped back down I was sure I heard a creak on the stairs, footsteps, slow, and regular, along the corridor. I sat bolt upright, gripping the edge of the tub. Another creak. A door handle turning.

'Lena?' I called out, my voice sounding childish, reedy and thin. 'Lena, is that you?'

The answering silence rang in my ears, and in it I imagined I heard voices.

Your voice. Another of your phone calls, the first one. The first one after our fight at the wake, after the night when you asked that terrible question. It wasn't long after – a week, maybe two – when you rang late at night and left me a message. You were tearful, your words slurred, your voice barely audible. You told me you were going back to Beckford, you were going to see an old friend. You needed to talk to someone, and I was no use. I didn't think about it at the time, I didn't care.

Only now I understood, and I shivered despite the warmth of the water. All this time, I've been blaming you, but it should have been the other way around. You went back to see an old friend. You were looking for solace because I rejected you, because I wouldn't talk to you. And you went to *him*. I failed you, and I kept on failing you. I sat up again, my arms wrapped tightly around my knees, and the waves of grief just kept coming: I failed you, I hurt you, and the thing that kills me is that you never knew why. You spent your whole life trying to understand why I hated you so much, and all I had to do was tell you. All I had to do was answer when you called. And now it was too late.

There was another noise, louder – a creak, a scrape, I wasn't imagining it. There was someone in the house. I pulled myself out of the bath and dressed as quietly as I could. *It's Lena*, I told myself. *It is. It's Lena.* I crept through the upstairs rooms, but there was no one there, and from every mirror my terrified face mocked me. *It's not Lena. It's not Lena.*

It had to be, but where would she be? She'd be in the kitchen, she'd be hungry – I'd go downstairs and there she would be with her head stuck in the fridge. I tiptoed down the stairs, across the hall, past the living-room door. And there, out of the corner of my eye, I saw it. A shadow. A figure. Someone sitting on the window seat.

Erin

ANYTHING WAS POSSIBLE. When you hear hooves you look for horses but you can't *discount* zebras. Not out of hand. Which is why, while Sean took Callie to have a look at the scene at Henderson's place, I'd been dispatched to speak to Louise Whittaker about this 'confrontation' she'd had with Lena just before Lena disappeared.

When I got to the Whittakers' house, Josh answered the door, as he always seemed to do. And, as always seemed to be the case, he looked alarmed to see me. 'What's going on?' he asked. 'Have you found Lena?'

I shook my head. 'Not yet. But don't worry . . .'

He turned away from me, shoulders slumped. I followed him into the house. At the bottom of the stairs he turned back to face me. 'Is it because of Mum that she ran away?' he asked, his cheeks reddening a little.

'Why would you ask that, Josh?'

'Mum made her feel bad,' he replied sourly. 'Now that Lena's mum's not alive, she blames Lena for everything. It's stupid. It's as much my fault as hers, but she blames her for everything. And now Lena's gone,' he said, his voice rising. 'She's gone.'

'Who are you talking to, Josh?' Louise called from upstairs. Her son ignored her, so I responded. 'It's me, Mrs Whittaker. DS Morgan. Can I come up?'

Louise was wearing a grey tracksuit which had seen better days. Her hair was pulled back, her face wan. 'He's angry with me,' she said by way of greeting. 'He blames me for Lena's running off. He thinks it's my fault.' I followed her along the landing. 'He blames me, I blame Nel, I blame Lena, round and round and round we go.' I stopped in the bedroom doorway. The room was all but empty, bed stripped, wardrobe empty. The pale-lilac walls bore the scars of hastily removed Blu-Tack. Louise smiled wearily. 'You can come in. I'm almost done in here.' She kneeled down, returning to the task I must have interrupted, which was placing books into cardboard boxes. I squatted down at her side to help, but before I was able to pick up my first book, she placed her hand firmly on my arm. 'No, thank you. I'd rather do this myself.' I stood up. 'I don't mean to be rude,' she said, 'I just don't want other people to touch her things. It's silly, isn't it?' she said, looking up at me, eyes shining. 'But I only want *her* to have touched them. I want there to be something left of her, on the book jackets, on the bedclothes, on her hairbrush . . .' She stopped and took a deep breath. 'I don't seem to be making a lot of progress. Moving on, moving past things, moving at all . . .'

'I don't think anyone would expect you to,' I said softly. 'Not—'

'Not yet? Which implies that at some point I won't feel like this. But the thing people don't seem to realize is that I don't want to not feel like this. How can I not feel like this? My sadness feels right. It . . . weighs the right amount, crushes me just enough. My anger is clean, it bolsters me. Well . . .' She sighed. 'Only now my son thinks I'm responsible for Lena going missing. Sometimes I wonder if he thinks I pushed Nel Abbott off that cliff.' She sniffed. 'In any case, he holds me responsible for the fact that Lena was left like that. Motherless. Alone.'

I stood in the middle of the room, my arms carefully folded, trying not to touch anything. Like I was at a crime scene, like I didn't want to contaminate anything.

'She's motherless,' I said, 'but is she fatherless? Do you honestly believe that Lena has *no idea* who her father is? Do you know if she and Katie ever spoke about that?'

Louise shook her head. 'I'm pretty sure she doesn't know. That was what Nel always said. I thought it was odd. Like a lot of Nel's parenting choices, not just odd, but irresponsible – I mean, what if there was a genetic issue, an illness, something like that? It seemed unfair on Lena in any case, not to even give the child the option of getting to know her father. When pressed – and I did press her, back when she and I were on better terms – she said it was a one-night stand, someone she met when she first moved to New York. She claimed not to have known his last name. When I thought about that later on, I concluded it must have been a lie, because I'd seen a photograph of Nel moving into her first flat in Brooklyn, her T-shirt stretched tight over her already pregnant belly.'

Louise stopped stacking books. She shook her head

again. 'So, in that sense, Josh is right. She *is* alone. There's no other family apart from the aunt. Or none that I ever heard of. And as for boyfriends . . .' She gave a rueful smile. 'Nel once told me that she only ever slept with married men, because they were discreet and undemanding and they let her get on with her life. Her affairs were private. I've no doubt there were men, but she didn't make that sort of thing public. Whenever you saw her, she was alone. Alone or with her daughter.' She gave a little sigh. 'The only man I think I've ever seen Lena be even vaguely affectionate to is Sean.' She coloured slightly as she said his name, turning her head away from me, as though she'd said something she shouldn't have.

'Sean Townsend? Really?' She didn't reply. 'Louise?' She got to her feet to fetch another pile of books from the shelf. 'Louise, what are you saying? That there's something . . . *untoward* between Sean and Lena?'

'God, no!' She gave a brittle laugh. 'Not Lena.'

'Not Lena? So . . . Nel? Are you saying there was something between him and Nel Abbott?'

Louise pursed her lips and turned her face from mine so I couldn't read her expression.

'Because, you know, that would be highly inappropriate. To investigate the suspicious death of someone with whom he'd had a relationship, that would be . . .'

What would that be? Unprofessional, unethical, grounds for dismissal? He wouldn't. There is no way he could have done that, no way he could have kept that from me. I would have seen something, noticed something, wouldn't I? And then I thought of how he looked the first time I saw him, stood there on the banks of the pool with Nel Abbott at his feet, head bowed as though he was praying over her. His watery eyes, his shaking hands, his absent manner, his sadness. But that was about his mother, surely?

Louise continued silently packing books into boxes.

'Listen to me,' I said, raising my voice to get her full attention. 'If you are aware that there was some sort of relationship between Sean and Nel, then—'

'I didn't say that,' she said, looking me dead in the eye. 'I didn't say anything of the sort. Sean Townsend is a good man.' She got to her feet. 'Now, I have a lot to do, Detective. I think it's probably time you left.'

Sean

THE BACK DOOR had been left open, the scene-of-crime officers said. Not just unlocked, but open. The tang of iron caught in my nostrils as I entered. Callie Buchan was already there, talking to the SOCOs; she asked me a question, but I wasn't really listening because I was straining to hear something else – an animal, whimpering.

'Shh,' I said. 'Listen.'

'They've checked the house, Sir,' Callie said. There's no one here.'

'Does he have a dog?' I asked her. She looked at me blankly. 'Is there a dog, a pet in the house? Any sign of one?'

'Nope, no sign at all, Sir. Why do you ask?'

I listened again, but the sound was gone and I was left with a sense of déjà vu: I've seen this before, I've done all this before – I've listened to a dog whimper, I've walked through a bloody kitchen into the rain.

Only it isn't raining, and there's no dog.

Callie was staring at me. 'Sir? There's something over here.' She pointed at an item on the floor, a pair

312

of kitchen scissors lying in a smear of blood. 'That's not just a nick, is it? I mean, it might not be arterial, but it doesn't look good.'

'Hospitals?'

'Nothing so far, no sign of either of them.' Her phone rang and she went outside to take the call.

I remained stock-still in the kitchen while two scene-of-crime officers worked quietly around me. I watched one of them pluck with tweezers a strand of long blonde hair which had snagged on the edge of the table. I felt a sudden wave of nausea, saliva flooding my mouth. I couldn't credit it: I've seen worse scenes than this – far worse – and remained impassive. Haven't I? Have I not walked through bloodier kitchens than this?

I touched my palm to my wrist and realized that Callie was speaking to me again, her head poked around the door frame. 'Can I have a word, Sir?' I followed her outside and while I removed the plastic covers from my shoes, she filled me in on the latest. 'Traffic have picked up Henderson's car,' she said. 'I mean, not *picked up*, but they've got his red Vauxhall on camera twice.' She looked down at her notebook. 'Thing is, it's a bit confusing because the first capture, just after three this morning, has him on the A68 going north towards Edinburgh, but then a couple of hours later, at five fifteen, he's driving south on the A1 just outside Eyemouth. So maybe he . . . dropped something off?' Got rid of something, she means. Something or someone. 'Or he's trying to confuse us?'

'Or he changed his mind about the best place to run to,' I said. 'Or he's panicking.'

She nodded. 'Running around like a headless chicken.'

I didn't like that idea, I didn't want him – or anyone else – headless. I wanted him calm. 'Was it possible to see if there was anyone else in the car, anyone in the passenger seat?' I asked her.

She shook her head, lips pursed. 'No. Of course . . .' she tailed off. Of course, that doesn't mean there isn't another person in the car. It just means that the other person isn't upright.

Again, that odd sense of having been here before, a scrap of memory which didn't feel like my own. How could it be anyone else's? It must have been part of a story, told to me by someone I don't remember. A woman lying slumped in a car seat, a sick woman, convulsing, drooling. Not much of a story – I couldn't remember the rest of it, I only knew that thinking about it turned my stomach. I pushed it aside.

'Newcastle would seem the obvious place,' Callie said. 'I mean, if he's running. Planes, trains, ferries – world's his oyster. But the odd thing is that since that five a.m. sighting, they've got nothing, so either he's stopped or he's got off the main road. He might be taking smaller roads, the coastal road even—'

'Isn't there a girlfriend?' I asked, interrupting her flow. 'A woman in Edinburgh?'

'The famous fiancée,' Callie said, eyebrows raised. 'Well, way ahead of you there. She – Tracey McBride, her name is – was picked up this morning. Uniform are bringing her down to Beckford for a chat. But, just to warn you, our Tracey claims she hasn't seen Mark Henderson for a good while. Almost a year, in fact.'

'What? I thought they'd just been on holiday to-gether?'

'That's what Henderson said when he spoke to DS Morgan, but according to Tracey, she's not seen hide nor hair of him since he called the whole thing off last autumn. She says he dumped her out of the blue, telling her he'd fallen head over heels for some other woman.'

Tracey didn't know who the woman was or what she did. 'Nor did I want to,' she told me abruptly. She was sitting in the back office of the police station, an hour later, sipping her tea. 'I was . . . I was pretty devastated, actually. One minute I'm shopping for wedding dresses and the next he's telling me he can't go through with it 'cos he's met the love of his life.' She smiled at me sadly, pushing her fingers through cropped dark hair. 'After that, I just cut him off. Deleted his number, un-friended him, the full monty. Could you please tell me, has something happened to him? No one will tell me what the hell's going on.'

I shook my head. 'I'm sorry about that, but there's not a lot I can tell you at the moment. We don't believe he's been harmed, though. We just need to find him, we need to talk to him about something. You don't know where he might go, do you? If he needed to get away? Parents, friends in the area . . . ?'

She frowned. 'This is not about that dead woman, is it? I read in the papers that there was another one a week or two back. I mean . . . he wasn't . . . *that* wasn't the woman he was seeing, was it?'

'No, no. It's nothing to do with that.'

'Oh, OK.' She looked relieved. 'I mean, she would have been a bit old for him, wouldn't she?'

'Why do you say that? Did he like younger women?'

Tracey looked confused. 'No, I mean . . . how do you mean, *younger*? That woman was, like, about forty, wasn't she? Mark's not yet thirty, so . . .'

'Right.'

'You really can't tell me what's going on?' she asked.

'Was Mark ever violent to you, did he ever lose his temper, anything like that?'

'What? God, no. Never.' She leaned back in her chair, frowning. 'Has someone accused him of something? Because he's not like that. He's selfish, no doubt about that, but he's not a bad person, not in that way.'

I walked her out to the car, where uniform were waiting to drive her home, wondering about the ways in which Mark Henderson was bad, wondering whether he'd managed to convince himself that being in love absolved him.

'You asked about where he might go,' Tracey said to me when we got to the car. 'It's difficult to say, without knowing the context, but there's one place I can think of. We – well, my dad – has a place out on the coast. Mark and I went there at weekends quite a bit. It's quite isolated, there's no one else around. Mark always said it was the perfect escape.'

'It's unoccupied, this place?'

'It's not used much. We used to leave a key out the back under a pot, but earlier this year we discovered that someone had been using it without our permission – there would be mugs left out or rubbish in the bins or whatever – so we stopped doing that.'

'When was the last time that happened? The last time someone used it without asking?'

She frowned. 'Oh, God. A while back. April, I think? Yeah, April. The Easter holidays.'

'And where exactly is this place?'

'Howick,' she said. 'It's a tiny little village, nothing much there at all. Just up the coast from Craster.'

Lena

HE APOLOGIZED WHEN he let me out of the boot. 'I'm sorry, Lena, but what would you have had me do?' I started laughing but he told me to shut up, his fist clenched, and I thought he was going to smack me again, so I did.

We were at a house by the sea – just one house, all by itself, right on the cliff, with a garden and a wall and one of those outdoor picnic tables. The house looked like it was all locked up, there was no one around. From where I was standing I couldn't see another building anywhere near us, just a track running past, not even a proper road. I couldn't hear anything either, no traffic noise, nothing like that, just the gulls and the waves on the rocks.

'No point screaming,' he said, like he'd read my mind. Then he took me by the arm and led me over to the table, and handed me a tissue to wipe my mouth.

'You'll be all right,' he said.

'Will I?' I asked, but he just looked away.

For a long time, we just sat there, side by side, with his hand still on my forearm, his grip gradually loosening as his breathing slowed. I didn't pull away. No point struggling now. Not yet. I was scared, my legs were trembling like mad under the table and I couldn't make them stop. But it actually felt like that was good, like it was helpful. I felt strong, the way I had when he found me in the house and we fought. Yeah, OK, he won, but only because I didn't go for the kill straight away, only because I wasn't sure what I was dealing with. That was only the first round. If he thought that was me beaten, he had another thing coming.

If he knew what I'd been feeling, what I'd been through, I don't think he'd be holding on to my arm. I think he'd be running for his fucking life.

I bit down hard on my lip. I could taste fresh blood on my tongue and I liked it, it felt good. I liked the metal taste, I liked the feel of blood in my mouth, something to spit at him. When the time was right. I had so many things to ask him, but I didn't know where to start so I just said, 'Why did you keep it?' I had to try really hard to keep my voice steady and not let it crack or shake or waver or show him that I was scared. He didn't say anything, so I asked again. 'Why did you keep her bracelet? Why not just throw it away? Or leave it on her wrist? Why take it?'

He let go of my arm. He didn't look at me, just stared out at the sea. 'I don't know,' he said wearily. 'Honestly, I've no idea why I took it. Insurance, I suppose. Clutching at straws. To hold something over someone else . . .' He stopped speaking suddenly and closed his eyes. I didn't understand what he was talking about, but I had a feeling, like I'd opened something up, an opportunity.

I moved very slightly away from him. Then slightly more. He opened his eyes again, but did nothing, just kept staring at the water, his face expressionless. He looked exhausted. Beaten. Like he had nothing left. I drew back on the bench. I could run. I'm really fast when I need to be. I glanced back at the track behind the house. I'd have a good chance of getting away from him if I headed straight across the track, over the stone wall and across the fields. If I did that, he wouldn't be able to follow in the car, and I'd have a chance.

I didn't do it. Even though I knew it might be the last chance I'd get, I stayed put. If it came down to it, I thought, it would be better to die knowing what happened to my mother than to live and always wonder, to never ever know. I didn't think I could bear that.

I got to my feet. He didn't move, just watched me as I rounded the table and sat down opposite him, forcing him to look at me.

'Do you know that I thought she'd left me? Mum. When they found her and they came and told me, I thought it was a choice. I thought she chose to die, because she felt guilty about what happened to Katie or because she was ashamed of that, or . . . I don't know. Just because the water had a stronger pull for her than I did.'

He said nothing.

'I believed that!' I shouted it as loud as I could and he jumped. 'I believed that she abandoned me! Do you understand what that felt like? And now it turns out she didn't. She didn't choose anything. You took her. You took her from me, just like you took Katie.'

He smiled at me. I remembered how we used to think he was handsome, and it turned my stomach. 'I didn't take Katie from you,' he said. 'Katie wasn't yours, Lena. She was mine.'

I wanted to scream at him, to scratch his face. *She wasn't yours! She wasn't! She wasn't!* I dug my nails into my hands as hard as I could, I bit my lip and tasted the blood again, and listened to him justifying himself.

'I never thought of myself as the sort of person who would fall for a girl. Never. I thought people like that were ridiculous. Sad old losers who couldn't get a woman their own age.'

I laughed. 'Exactly,' I said. 'You thought right.'

'No, no.' He shook his head. 'That's not true. It isn't. Look at me. I've never had any trouble getting women. They come on to me all the time. You shake your head now, but you've seen it. Christ, you did it yourself.'

'I did fucking not.'

'Lena—'

'Do you honestly think I wanted you? You're *deluded*. It was a game, it was—' I stopped talking. How do you even explain something like that to a man like him? How do you explain that it was nothing to do with him and everything to do with you? That – for me, in any case – it was about me and Katie and the things we could do together. The people we did them to were interchangeable. They didn't matter at all.

'Do you know what it's like when you look the way I do?' I asked him. 'I mean, I know you think you're hot or whatever, but you have no idea what it's like to be like *me*. Do you know how easy it is for me to make people do what I want, to make them uncomfortable? All I have to do is look at them a certain way, or stand near them, or stick my fingers in my mouth and suck and I can see them go red or hard or whatever. That's what I was doing to you, you retard. I was taking the piss out of you. I didn't *want* you.'

He scoffed, gave this unconvinced little laugh. 'Right, OK,' he said. 'If you say so, Lena. So what *did* you want? When you threatened to betray us, when you went shouting your mouth off so your mother could hear – what did you want?'

'I wanted . . . I wanted . . .'

I couldn't tell him what I wanted, because what I wanted was for things to go back to the way they were. I wanted us to go back to the time when Katie and I were always together, when we spent every hour of every day with each other, when we swam in the river and no one looked at us and our bodies were our own. I wanted to go back to the time before we came up with that game, before we realized what we could do. But that's only what *I* wanted. Katie didn't. Katie *liked* being looked at. For her, the game wasn't just a game, it was more. Right back at the beginning, when I first found out and we were arguing about it, she said to me, 'You don't know what it feels like, Lena. Can you imagine? To have some-one want you so much that he'll risk everything for you – like, *everything*. His job, his relationship, his *freedom*. You don't understand what that feels like.'

I could feel Henderson watching me, waiting for me to speak. I wanted to find a way to say it, to make him see that she was getting off not just on him but on her power over him. I'd have liked to be able to tell him that, to wipe that look off his face, the one that said he knew her and I didn't, not really. But I couldn't find the words just then, and in any case it wasn't the whole story because no one could deny that she did love him.

There was a pain behind my eyes, a sharp pinch that told me I was about to cry again, and I stared down at the ground because I didn't want him to see the tears in my eyes, and I saw that lying in the dirt, right between my feet, there was a nail. It was a long one, three or four inches at least. I moved my foot slightly so that I was covering the tip of it, then I pressed down to raise up the other end.

'You were just jealous, Lena,' Henderson said. 'That's the truth, isn't it? You always were. I think you were jealous of both of us, weren't you? Of me, because she chose me, and of her, because I chose her. Neither of us wanted you. And so you made us pay. You and your mother, you . . .'

I let him talk, I let him spout his deluded bullshit, and I didn't even care then that he was so wrong about everything, because all I could focus on was the tip of that nail, which I'd levered up with my foot. I slipped my hand under the table. Mark stopped talking.

'You should never have been with her,' I said. I was looking behind him, over his shoulder, trying to distract him. 'You know that. You must know that.'

'She loved me, and I loved her, completely.'

'You're an adult!' I said, keeping my eye on the space behind him, and it worked – for a second he glanced over his shoulder and I let my arm slip lower between my legs, stretching out my fingers. Cold metal in my grasp, I straightened my back, prepared myself. 'Do you really think it matters how you felt about her? You were her teacher. You're twice her fucking age. You were the one who was supposed to do the right thing.'

'She loved me,' he said again, hangdog. Pathetic.

'She was too young for you,' I said, gripping the shaft of the nail tightly in my fist. 'She was too *good* for you.'

I went for him, but I wasn't quick enough. As I sprang to my feet, I caught my hand under the table, just for a second. Mark lunged at me, grabbing my left arm, yanking it as hard as he could, pulling me halfway across the table.

'What are you doing?' He leaped to his feet, still holding on to me, and pulled me sideways, twisting my arm back behind me. I yelped with pain. 'What are you doing?' he shouted, pushing my arm higher, opening my fist with his fingers. He took the nail from my hand and shoved me down on to the table, his hand in my hair, his body on top of mine. I felt the metal spike graze against my throat, the weight of him on top of me, just like how she must have felt him when they were together. Vomit came up to my throat and I spat it out and said, 'She was too good for you! She was too good for you!' I said it again and again until he'd crushed the breath out of me.

Jules

A CLICKING SOUND. Click and hiss, click and hiss, then: 'Oh. There you are. I let myself in, hope you don't mind.'

The old woman – the one with the purple hair and the black eyeliner, the one who claims to be a psychic, the one who shuffles around town spitting and cursing at people, the one who I'd seen just the day before, arguing with Louise in front of the house – she was sitting on the window seat, swinging her swollen calves back and forth.

'I do mind!' I said loudly, trying not to show her that I'd been afraid, that I was still – stupidly, ridiculously – afraid of her. 'I bloody *do* mind. What are you doing here?' Click and hiss, click and hiss. The lighter – the silver lighter with Libby's initials engraved on it – she had it in her hand. 'That's . . . Where did you get that? That's Nel's lighter!' She shook her head. 'It is! How did you get hold of that? Have you been in this house, taking things? Have you—'

She waved a fat, gaudily bejewelled hand at me. 'Oh, calm down, will you?' She gave me a dirty brown smile.

'Sit down. Sit down, Julia.' She pointed at the armchair in front of her. 'Come and join me.'

I was so taken aback that I obliged. I crossed the room and sat down in front of her while she shifted around in her seat. 'Not very comfy this, is it? Could do with a bit more padding. Although some might say I've got enough upholstery of my own!' She chortled at her own joke.

'What do you want?' I asked her. 'Why do you have Nel's lighter?'

'Not Nel's, it's not *Nel*'s, is it? See here,' she pointed to the engraving. 'There, see? *LS*.'

'Yes, I know. LS, Libby Seeton. But it didn't actually belong to Libby, did it? I don't think they were manufacturing that particular sort of lighter in the seventeenth century.'

Nickie cackled. 'It's not Libby's! You thought LS was for Libby? No, no, no! This lighter belonged to Lauren. Lauren Townsend. Lauren used-to-be-Slater.'

'Lauren Slater?'

'That's right! Lauren Slater, also Lauren Townsend. Your detective inspector's old girl.'

'Sean's mother?' I was thinking about the boy coming up the steps, the boy on the bridge. 'The Lauren in the story is Sean Townsend's mother?'

'That's right. Jesus! You're not the sharpest, are you? And it's not a *story*, is it? Not just a story. Lauren Slater married Patrick Townsend. She had a son who she loved to bits and pieces. All hunky-dory. Only then, so the coppers would have us believe, she went and topped herself!' She leaned forward and grinned at me. 'Not very likely, is it? I said so at the time, of course, but no one listens to me.'

Was Sean really that boy? The one on the steps, the one who watched his mother fall, or didn't watch his mother fall, depending on who you believed? Was that really true, not just something you made up, Nel? Lauren was the one who had the affair, the one who drank too much, the wanton one, the bad mother. Wasn't that her story? Lauren was the one on whose page you wrote: *Beckford is not a suicide spot. Beckford is a place to get rid of troublesome women.* What is it that you were trying to tell me?

Nickie was still talking. 'See?' she said, jabbing a finger at me. 'See? This is what I mean. No one listens to me. You're sitting there and I'm right here in front of you and you're not even listening!'

'I am listening, I am. I just . . . I don't understand.'

She harrumphed. 'Well, if you'd listen you would. This lighter,' click, hiss, 'this belonged to Lauren, yes? You need to ask yourself, why's your sister got it up there with her things?'

'Up there? So you *have* been in the house! You did take it, you . . . was it *you*? Have you been in the bathroom? Did you write something on the mirror?'

'Listen to me!' She hauled herself to her feet. 'Don't worry about that, that's not important.' She took a step towards me, leaning forward, and clicked the lighter again, the flame flickering between us. She smelled of burned coffee and overblown roses. I leaned back, away from her old-woman scent.

'You know what he used this for?' she said.

'What who used it for? Sean?'

'No, you idiot.' She rolled her eyes at me and heaved herself back on to the window seat, which creaked painfully underneath her. 'Patrick! The old man. He didn't use it to light his smokes either. After his wife died, he took all her things – all her clothes and her paintings and everything she owned – and he put it out back and he burned it. Burned the lot. And this' – she clicked the lighter one final time – 'is what he used to start the fire.'

'OK,' I said, my patience wearing thin. 'But I still don't get it. Why did Nel have it? And why did you take it from her?'

'Questions, questions,' Nickie said with a smile. 'Well. As to why *I've* got it, I needed something of hers, didn't I? So's I could speak to her properly. I used to hear her voice nice and clear, but . . . you know. Sometimes voices get muted, don't they?'

'I've really no idea about that,' I said coldly.

'Oh, get you! You don't believe me? It's not like you'd ever talk to the dead, is it?' She laughed knowingly and my scalp shrivelled. 'I needed something to conjure with. Here!' She offered the lighter to me. 'You can have it back. I could've sold it, couldn't I? I could have taken all sorts and flogged them – your sister had some expensive things, didn't she, jewellery and that? But I didn't.'

'Very good of you.'

She grinned. 'On to the next question: why did your sister have that lighter? Well, I can't say for sure.'

My frustration got the better of me. 'Really?' I sneered at her. 'I thought you could talk to the spirits? I thought that was your thing?' I looked around the room. 'Is she here now? Why don't you just ask her directly?'

'It's not that easy, is it?' she said, wounded. 'I've been trying to raise her, but she's gone silent.' Could have fooled me. 'There's no need to get sniffy. All I'm trying to do is help. All I'm trying to do is tell you—'

'Well, *tell me*, then!' I snapped. 'Spit it out!'

'Keep your hair on,' she said, lower lip stuck out, chins wobbling. 'I *was* telling you, if only you'd listen. The lighter is Lauren's, and Patrick had it last. And that's what's important. I don't know why Nel had it, but her having it is the thing, see? She took it from him, perhaps, or maybe he gave it to her. In any case, it's the important thing. Lauren is the important one. All this – your Nel – it's not about poor Katie Whittaker or that silly teacher or Katie's mum or any of that. It's about Lauren, and Patrick.'

I bit my lip. 'How is this about them?'

'Well.' She shifted in her seat. 'She was writing her stories about them, wasn't she? And she got her story from Sean Townsend, because, after all, he was supposed to be a witness, wasn't he? So she thought he was telling the truth, and why wouldn't she?'

'Why wouldn't *he*? I mean, you're saying Sean lied about what happened to his mother?'

She pursed her lips. 'Have you met the old man? He's a devil, he is, and I don't mean in a good way.'

'So Sean lied about how his mother died because he's afraid of his father?'

Nickie shrugged. 'I can't say for sure. But here's what I know: the story Nel heard – the first version, the one where Lauren runs off in the night and her husband and son go chasing after her – it wasn't true. I told her as much. Because you see, my Jeannie – that's my sister – she was around at the time. She was there. That night—' Abruptly, she plunged her hand inside her coat and began fishing around. 'Thing is,' she said, 'I told your Nel our Jeannie's story and Nel wrote it down.' She pulled out a sheaf of papers. I reached for them, but Nickie snatched them back.

'Just a minute,' she said. 'You've got to understand that this' – she shook the pages at me – 'is not the whole story. Because even though I told her the whole story, she wouldn't write it all down. Stubborn woman, your sister. Part of the reason I liked her so much. So that's when we had our little disagreement.' She settled back in her seat, swinging her legs more vigorously. 'I told her about Jeannie, who was a policewoman back when Lauren died.' She coughed loudly. 'Jeannie didn't be-lieve she went in without a push, because there was all sorts of other stuff going on, you see. She knew that Lauren's old man was a devil and that he smacked her about and told stories about her meeting some fancy man up at Anne Ward's place, even though no one had ever seen hide nor hair of such a man. That was sup-posed to be the reason, see? The bloke she was doing the dirty with, he'd run off and left her and she was upset about it, so she jumped.' Nickie waved a hand at me. 'Nonsense. With a six-year-old at home? Nonsense.'

'Well, actually,' I said, 'I think you'll find that depres-sion is a complicated thing—'

'Pffft!' She silenced me with another wave of her

hand. 'There was no *fancy man*. None that anyone around here ever saw. You could ask my Jeannie about that, except for the fact that she's dead and gone. And you know who did for her, don't you?'

When at last she stopped talking, I heard the water whispering in the quiet. 'You're saying that Patrick killed his wife, and that Nel knew about it? You're saying that she wrote it down?'

Nickie tutted crossly. 'No! That's what I'm telling you. She wrote down *some* things, but not *other* things, and that's where we disagreed, because she was perfectly happy to write down the things Jeannie told me when she was still alive, but not the things Jeannie told me when she was dead. Which makes no sense at all.'

'Well . . .'

'No sense at all. But you need to listen. And if you won't listen to me,' she said, thrusting the pages towards me, 'you can listen to your sister. Because he did for them. After a fashion. Patrick Townsend did for Lauren, and he did for our Jeannie, and if I'm not mistaken, he's done for your Nel and all.'

The Drowning Pool

Lauren, again, 1983

LAUREN WALKED OUT to Anne Ward's cottage. She went there more and more often these days – it was peaceful in a way that nowhere else in Beckford seemed to be. She felt an odd sort of kinship with poor Anne. She, too, was locked into a loveless marriage with a man who couldn't stand her. Here, Lauren could swim and smoke and read and not be bothered by anyone. Usually.

One morning, there were two women out walking. She recognized them: a policewoman, Jeannie, a stout WPC with a ruddy face, and her sister, Nickie, the one who spoke to the dead. Lauren rather liked Nickie. She was funny and seemed kind. Even if she was a con artist.

Jeannie called out to her and Lauren waved in a dismissive way that she hoped would see them off. Usually she would have gone over to chat. But her face was a mess and she wasn't in the mood to explain.

She went for a swim. She was conscious of doing things one final time: one last walk, one last smoke, one last kiss *of her son's pale forehead, one last dip in the river (next-to-last). As she slipped under the water, she wondered if this was how it would be, whether she would feel anything. She wondered where all her fight had gone.*

It was Jeannie who arrived at the river first. She'd been at the station watching the storm when the call came: Patrick Townsend had been panicking and incoherent, shouting something over the radio about his wife. His wife and the Drowning Pool. When Jeannie got there, the boy was under the trees, his head on his knees. At first she thought he was asleep, but when he looked up his eyes were wide and black.

'Sean,' she said, pulling off her coat and wrapping it around him. He was blue-white and shaking, his pyjamas sodden, his bare feet caked in mud. 'What happened?'

'Mummy's in the water,' he said. 'I'm to stay here until he comes back.'

'Who? Your father? Where's your father?'

Sean disentangled one skinny arm from the coat and pointed behind her, and Jeannie saw Patrick dragging himself on to the bank, his breath coming in sobs, his face twisted with agony.

Jeannie went to him. 'Sir, I . . . The ambulance is on its way, ETA four minutes now—'

'Too late,' Patrick said, shaking his head. 'I was too late. She's gone.'

Others arrived: paramedics and uniforms and one or two senior detectives. Sean had got to his feet; with Jeannie's coat wrapped around him like a cape, he clung to his father.

'Could you take him home?' one of the other detectives said to her.

The boy began to cry. 'Please. No. I don't want to. I don't want to go.'

Patrick said, 'Jeannie, could you take him to your place? He's frightened and he doesn't want to go home.'

Patrick kneeled in the mud, holding his son, cradling his head, whispering in his ear. By the time he stood, the boy seemed calm and docile. He slipped his hand into Jeannie's, trotting along beside her without looking back.

Back at her flat, Jeannie got Sean out of his wet things. She wrapped him up in a blanket and made cheese on toast. Sean ate, quietly and carefully, leaning forward over the plate so as not to drop crumbs. When he was finished, he asked, 'Is Mum going to be all right?'

Jeannie busied herself with clearing away the plates. 'Are you warm enough, Sean?' she asked him.

'I'm OK.'

Jeannie made cups of tea and gave them two sugars each. 'Do you want to tell me what happened, Sean?' she asked, and he shook his head. 'No? How did you get down to the river? You were terribly muddy.'

'We went in the car, but I fell over on the path,' he said.

'OK. Did your dad drive you there, then? Or was it your mum?'

'We all went together,' Sean said.

'All of you?'

Sean's face crumpled. 'There was a storm when I woke up, it was very loud, and there were funny noises in the kitchen.'

'What sort of funny noises?'

'Like . . . like a dog makes, when it's sad.'

'Like a whimper?'

Sean nodded. 'But we don't have a dog because I'm not allowed. Dad says I won't look after it properly and it'll be just another thing for him to do.' He sipped his tea and wiped his eyes. 'I didn't want to be by myself because of the storm. So Dad put me in the car.'

'And your mum?'

He frowned. 'Well. She was in the river and I had to wait under the trees. I'm not supposed to talk about it.'

'What do you mean, Sean? What do you mean, not supposed to talk about it?'

He shook his head and shrugged, and didn't say another word.

Sean

HOWICK. NEAR CRASTER. Not so much history repeating itself as playing games with me. It's not far from Beckford, not much more than an hour's drive, but I never go. I don't go to the beach or the castle, I've never been to eat the famous kippers from the famous smokehouse. That was my mother's thing, my mother's wish. My father never took me, and now I never go.

When Tracey told me where the house was, where I would have to go, I felt moved. I felt guilty. I felt the way I had when I thought about my mother's promise of a birthday treat, the one I'd rejected in favour of the Tower of London. If I hadn't been so ungrateful, if I'd said I wanted to go with her to the beach, to the castle, would she have stayed? Would things have turned out differently?

That never-to-be-taken trip was one of many subjects that occupied me after my mother died, when my whole being was consumed with constructing a new world, an alternate reality in which she did not have to die. If we had taken the trip to Craster, if I had cleaned my room when I was told, if I hadn't muddied my new school satchel when I went swimming downriver, if I'd listened to my father and hadn't disobeyed him so often. Or, later, I wondered whether perhaps I *shouldn't* have listened to my father, perhaps I *should* have disobeyed him, perhaps I should have stayed up late that night instead of going to bed. Perhaps then I might have been able to persuade her not to go.

None of my alternative scenarios did the trick, and eventually, some years later, I came to understand that there was nothing I could have done. What my mother wanted was not for *me* to do something, it was for someone else to do something – or not do something: what she wanted was for the man she loved, the man she met in secret, the man with whom she'd been betraying my father, not to leave her. This man was unseen, unnamed. He was a phantom, our phantom – mine and my father's. He gave us the why, he gave us some measure of relief: *it wasn't our fault.* (It was his, or it was hers, theirs together, my traitorous mother and her lover. We couldn't have done any better, she just didn't love us enough.) He gave us a way to get up in the morning, a way to go on.

And then Nel came along.

When she first came to the house, she asked for my father. She wanted to talk to him about my mother's death. He wasn't there that day and neither was I, so she spoke to Helen, who gave her short shrift. Not only will Patrick not speak to you, Helen told her, but he won't appreciate the intrusion. Nor will Sean, nor any of us. It is private, Helen said, and it is past.

Nel ignored her and approached Dad anyway. His reaction intrigued her. He wasn't angry, as she might have expected him to be; he didn't tell her it was too painful to talk about, that he couldn't bear to go over all that again. He said there was nothing to talk about. Nothing happened. That's what he said to her. Nothing happened.

So, finally, she came to me. It was the middle of summer. I'd had a meeting at the station in Beckford and when I came out I found her leaning against my car. She was wearing a dress so long it swept the floor, leather sandals on suntanned feet, bright-blue polish on her toes. I'd seen her around before then, I'd noticed her – she was beautiful, hard not to notice. But I'd never until then seen her up close. I'd never realized how green her eyes were, how they gave her this look of otherness. Like she was not quite of this world, certainly not of this place. She was too exotic by half.

She told me what my father had said to her, that *nothing happened*, and she asked me, 'Is that how you feel, too?' I told her he didn't mean that, he didn't really mean nothing happened. He just meant that we don't talk about it, that it was behind us. We'd put it behind us.

'Well, of course you have,' she said, smiling at me. 'And I understand, but I'm working on this project, you see, a book, and maybe an exhibition, too, and I—'

'No,' I told her. 'I mean, I know what you're doing but I – we – can't be a part of all that. It's shameful.'

She drew back slightly, but her smile remained. '*Shameful*? What an odd word to use. What is it that's shameful?'

338

'It's shameful to us,' I said. 'To him.' (To us or to him, I don't remember which of these I said.)

'Oh.' The smile fell from her face then, she looked troubled, concerned. 'No. It's not . . . no. It's not shameful. I don't think anyone thinks like that any longer, do they?'

'*He* does.'

'Please,' she said, 'won't you talk to me?'

I think I must have turned away from her, because she put her hand on my arm. I looked down and I saw the silver rings on her fingers and the bracelet on her arm and the chipped blue polish on her fingers. 'Please, Mr Townsend. Sean. I've wanted to talk to you about this for such a long time.'

She was smiling again. Her way of addressing me, direct and intimate, made it impossible for me to refuse her. I knew then that I was in trouble, that *she* was trouble, the sort of trouble I'd been waiting for my whole adult life.

I agreed to tell her what I remembered about the night of my mother's death. I said I would meet her at her home, at the Mill House. I asked her to keep this meeting private, because it would upset my father, it would upset my wife. She flinched at *wife*, and smiled again, and we both knew then where it was going. The first time I went to talk to her we didn't talk at all.

So I had to go back. I kept going back to her and we kept not talking. I would spend an hour with her, or two, but when I left her it felt as though it had been days. I worried sometimes that I had drifted and lost time. I do that, occasionally. My father calls it *absenting myself*, as though it's something I do on purpose, something I can control, but it isn't. I've always done it, ever since childhood: one moment I'm there, and then I'm not. I don't mean for it to happen. Sometimes, when I've drifted away, I become aware of it, and sometimes I can bring myself back – I taught myself a long time ago: I touch the scar on my wrist. It usually works. Not always.

I didn't get around to telling her the story, not at the beginning. She pressed me, but I found her pleasingly easy to distract. I imagined that she was falling in love with me and that we would leave, she and Lena and I, we would uproot ourselves, leave the village, leave the country. I imagined that I would finally be allowed to forget. I imagined that Helen would not mourn me, that she would move on quickly to someone better suited to her steady goodness. I imagined that my father would die in his sleep.

She teased the story out of me, strand by strand, and it was clear to me that she was disappointed. It wasn't the story she wanted to hear. She wanted the myth, the horror story, she wanted the boy who watched. I realized then that her approaching my father had been the starter: I was to be the main course. I was to be the heart of her project, because that was how it had started for her, with Libby and then with me.

She coaxed things out of me that I didn't want to tell her. I knew that I should stop, but I couldn't. I knew that I was being sucked into something from which I wouldn't be able to extricate myself. I knew that I was becoming reckless. We stopped meeting at the Mill

House, because the school holidays were starting and Lena was frequently home. We went to the cottage instead, which I knew was a risk, but there were no hotel rooms to rent, not locally, and where else could we go? It never crossed my mind that I should stop seeing her; back then it seemed impossible.

My father takes his walks at dawn, so I've no idea why he was there that afternoon. But he was, and he spotted my car; he waited in the trees until Nel had left and then he beat me. He punched me to the ground, kicked me in the chest and shoulder. I curled myself up, protecting my head, the way I'd been taught. I didn't fight back, because I knew he'd stop when he'd had enough, and when he knew that I couldn't take any more.

Afterwards, he took my keys and drove me home. Helen was incandescent: first with my father, for the beating, and then with me, when he explained the reason for it. I had never seen her angry before, not like that. It was only when I witnessed her rage, cold and terrifying, that I started to imagine what she might do, how she might take her revenge. I imagined her packing her bags and leaving, I imagined her resigning from the school, the public scandal, my father's anger. That was the sort of revenge I imagined she might take. But I imagined wrong.

Lena

I GASPED. I GULPED as much air as I could and jammed my elbow into his ribs. He squirmed, but still he held me down. His hot breath in my face made me want to hurl.

'Too good for you,' I kept saying, 'she was too good for you, too good for you to touch, too good for you to fuck . . . You cost her her *life*, you piece of shit. I don't know how you do it, how you get up every day, how you go to work, how you look her mother in the eye . . .'

He scraped the nail hard against my neck and I closed my eyes and waited for it. 'You have no idea what I've suffered,' he said. 'No idea.' Then he grabbed a fistful of my hair and yanked hard, then let go suddenly so that my head slammed into the table, and I couldn't help it. I started to cry.

Mark released me and stood up. He took a few steps back and then walked around to the other side of the table so that he had a good view of me. He stood there and watched me and I wished more than anything that the earth would just open up and swallow me. Anything was better than him watching me cry. I stood up.

I was sobbing like a baby that's lost its dummy and he started saying, 'Stop it! Stop it, Lena. Don't cry like that. Don't cry like that,' and it was weird because then he was crying too, and he kept saying it, over and over, 'Stop crying, Lena, stop crying.'

I stopped. We were looking at each other, both of us with tears and snot on our faces, and he still had the nail in his hands, and he said, 'I didn't do it. What you think I did. I didn't touch your mother. I thought about it. I thought about doing all kinds of things to her, but I didn't.'

'You did,' I said. 'You have her bracelet, you—'

'She came to see me,' he said. 'After Katie died. She told me I had to come clean. For Louise's sake!' He laughed. 'As if she really gave a shit. As if she gave a shit about anyone. I know why she wanted me to say something. She felt *guilty* about putting ideas into Katie's head, she felt guilty and she wanted someone else to take the blame. She wanted to put it all on me, the selfish bitch.' I watched him turning the nail over in his hands and I pictured myself lunging at him, grabbing it and driving it into his eyeball. My mouth was dry. I licked my lips and tasted salt.

He kept talking. 'I asked her to give me some time. I told her that I would speak to Louise, I just needed to get straight what to say, how to explain it. I persuaded her.' He looked down at the nail in his hands and then back at me. 'You see, Lena, I didn't need to do anything to her. The way to deal with women like that – women like your mother – is not through violence, but through their vanity. I've known women like her before, older women, the wrong side of thirty-five, losing their looks. They want to feel wanted. You can smell the desperation a mile off. I knew what I had to do, even though it made my flesh crawl to think about it. I had to bring her onside. Charm her. Seduce her.' He paused, rubbing the back of his hand over his mouth. 'I thought maybe I'd take some pictures of her. Compromise her. Threaten to humiliate her. I thought maybe then she'd leave me alone, leave me to grieve.' He raised his chin a little. 'That was my plan. But then Helen Townsend stepped in, and I didn't have to do anything.'

He tossed the nail to one side. I watched it bounce on the grass and come to rest against the wall.

'What are you talking about?' I said. 'What do you mean?'

'I'll tell you. I will. Only . . .' He sighed. 'You know I don't want to hurt you, Lena. I've never wanted to hurt you. I had to hit you when you came at me back at the house – what else could I do? I won't do it again, though. Not unless you make me. OK?' I said nothing. 'This is what I need you to do. I need you to go back to Beckford, to tell the police that you ran away, you hitch-hiked, whatever. I don't care what you tell them – only you have to say you lied about me. You made all this up. Tell them you made it up because you were jealous, because you were mad with grief, maybe just because you're a spiteful, attention-seeking little bitch, I don't care what you tell them. OK? Just so long as you tell them you lied.'

I squinted at him. 'Why do you think I would do that? Seriously? What the fuck would make me do that?

It's too late, in any case. Josh spoke to them, I wasn't the one who—'

'Tell them Josh lied, then. Tell them you told Josh to lie. Tell Josh that he has to retract his story too. I know you can do it. And I think you will do it, too, because if you do that, not only will I not hurt you, but,' he slid his hand into the pocket of his jeans and pulled out the bracelet, 'I'll tell you what you need to know. You do this one thing for me, and I'll tell you what I know.'

I walked over to the wall. I had my back to him, and I was shaking, because I knew he could come for me, knew he could finish me off if he wanted to. But I didn't think he did want to. I could see that. He wanted to run. I nudged the nail with the toe of my shoe. The only real question was, was I going to let him?

I turned round to face him, my back to the wall. I thought about all the stupid mistakes I'd made on the way here and how I wasn't about to make another one. I played scared, I played grateful. 'Do you promise? . . . Will you let me go back to Beckford? . . . Please, Mark, do you promise?' I played relieved, I played desperate, I played contrite. I played him.

He sat down and placed the bracelet in front of him in the middle of the table.

'I found it,' he said bluntly and I started to laugh.

'You *found* it? What, like, in the river, where the police searched for *days*? Give me a fucking break.'

He sat quietly for a second and then looked at me as if he hated me more than anyone on earth. Which he probably did. 'Are you going to listen or not?'

I leaned back against the wall. 'I'm listening.'

'I went to Helen Townsend's office,' he said. 'I was looking for . . .' He looked embarrassed. 'Something of hers. Katie's. I wanted . . . something. Something I could hold . . .'

He was trying to make me feel sorry for him.

'And?' It wasn't working.

'I was looking for a key to the filing cabinet. I looked in Helen's desk drawer and I found it.'

'You found my mother's bracelet in Mrs Townsend's desk?'

He nodded. 'Don't ask me how it got there. But if she was wearing it that day, then . . .'

'Mrs Townsend,' I repeated stupidly.

'I know it makes no sense,' he said.

Only it did. Or it could. At a stretch. I would never have dreamed her capable. She's an uptight old bitch, I know that, but I would never have imagined her hurting anyone physically.

Mark was staring at me. 'There's something I'm not getting, isn't there? What did she do? To Helen? What did your mother do to her?'

I said nothing. I turned my face away from him. A cloud passed in front of the sun and I felt as cold as I had in his house that morning, cold inside and out, cold all the way through. I walked over to the table and picked up the bracelet, then slid it over my fingers and on to my wrist.

'There,' he said. 'I've told you now. I've helped you, haven't I? Now it's your turn.'

My turn. I walked back over to the wall, crouched down and picked up the nail. I turned back to face him.

'Lena,' he said, and I could tell by the way he said my name, by the way he was breathing, short and fast, that he was afraid. 'I've helped you. I—'

'You think that Katie drowned herself because she was scared I would betray her, or because she was scared that my mother would betray her – that someone would betray you both and then everyone would know, and she'd be in so much trouble, and her parents would be devastated. But you know that isn't *really* it, don't you?' He bowed his head, his hands gripping the edge of the table. 'You know that's not really the reason. The reason is that she was afraid of what might happen to you.' He kept staring at the table, he didn't move. 'She did it for you. She killed herself for you. And what have you done for her?' His shoulders were starting to shake. 'What have you done? You've lied and lied, you denied her completely, like she meant nothing to you, like she was no one to you. Don't you think she deserved better?'

With the nail in my hand, I walked over to the table. I could hear him blubbering, blubbering and saying sorry. 'I'm sorry, I'm sorry, I'm sorry,' he was saying, 'Forgive me. God forgive me.'

'Bit late for that,' I said. 'Don't you think?'

Sean

I WAS ABOUT halfway there when it started to rain, a light drizzle that suddenly turned into a downpour. Visibility was next to nothing and I had to slow to a crawl. One of the uniforms dispatched to the house in Howick rang, and I put him on speaker.

'Nothing here,' he said over a crackling line.

'Nothing?'

'No one here. There's a car – a red Vauxhall – but no sign of him.'

'Lena?'

'No sign of either of them. The house is all locked up. We're looking. We'll keep looking . . .'

The car is there, but they are not. Which means that they must be on foot somewhere, and why would they be on foot? Car broke down? If he got to the house and he found he couldn't get inside, couldn't hole up there – why not just break in? Surely that's better than *running*? Unless someone picked them up? A friend? Someone helping him? Perhaps someone might help him out of a tight spot, but we were talking about a schoolteacher, not some habitual criminal – I couldn't imagine him having the sort of friends who would get involved in a kidnapping.

And I wasn't sure if that made me feel better or worse. Because if Lena wasn't with him, we had no clue where she was. No one had seen her for almost twenty-four hours. The thought was enough to make me panic. I needed to make her safe. After all, I'd failed her mother so badly.

I'd stopped seeing Nel after the incident with my father. In fact, I did not spend another moment alone in her company until after Katie Whittaker's death, and then I had no choice. I had to question her, given her link to Katie via her daughter, given the allegations that Louise was throwing around.

I interviewed her as a witness. Which of course was unprofessional – a good deal of my conduct over the past year could fall under that description – but once I had become entangled with Nel, that seemed to be an inevitability. There was nothing I could do about it.

It felt like grief, seeing her again, because I sensed almost immediately that the Nel from before, the one who had smiled so candidly, who had grabbed hold of me, who had bewitched me, was no longer there. She hadn't disappeared so much as receded, withdrawn into another self, one I didn't know. My idle imaginings – a new life, with her and Lena, Helen left contentedly behind – seemed embarrassingly childish. The Nel that opened her door to me that day was a different woman, strange and unreachable.

Guilt spilled out of her during our interview, but

it was an amorphous, non-specific guilt. Nel was still committed to her work, she insisted that the Drowning Pool project had nothing to do with Katie's tragedy, and yet she radiated culpability, her sentences all prefaced with *I should have* or *We should have* or *I didn't realize*. But *what* she should have done, *what* she didn't realize, we didn't seem to get to. Knowing what I know now, I can only imagine that her guilt was about Henderson, that she must have known something, or suspected something, and yet done nothing.

After the interview, I left her at the Mill House and went to the cottage. I waited for her, in hope more than expectation. It was after midnight when she arrived: not entirely sober, tearful, on the edge. Afterwards, at dawn, when we were finally finished with each other, we went out to the river.

Nel was hyper, manic almost. She talked with the passion of a zealot about the truth, how she was tired of telling stories, she just wanted the truth. The truth, the whole truth, nothing but the truth. I said to her, 'You know better than that, don't you? Sometimes, with things like these, there is no truth to be found. We can't ever know what was going through Katie's mind.'

She shook her head. 'Not that, it's not just that, it's not just . . .' Her left hand gripped mine, her right tracing circles in the dirt. 'Why,' she whispered, not looking at me, 'does your father keep this place? Why does he look after it the way he does?'

'Because . . .'

'If this was the place your mother came, if this was

the place where she betrayed him, why, Sean? It makes no sense.'

'I don't know,' I said. I'd wondered the same thing myself, but I'd never asked him about it. We don't talk about that.

'And this man, this *lover*: why does no one know his name? Why did no one ever see him?'

'No one? Just because *I* didn't see him, Nel—'

'Nickie Sage told me that no one knew who this man was.'

'Nickie?' I had to laugh. 'You're talking to Nickie? You're *listening* to Nickie?'

'Why does everyone dismiss what she says?' she snapped at me. 'Because she's an old woman? Because she's ugly?'

'Because she's *crazy*.'

'Right,' she muttered to herself. 'Bitches be crazy.'

'Oh, come on, Nel! She's a fraudster! She claims to commune with the dead.'

'Yes.' Her fingers dug deeper into the soil. 'Yes, she's a con artist, but that doesn't mean everything that comes out of her mouth is a lie. You'd be surprised, Sean, at how much of what she says rings true.'

'She cold-reads, Nel. And in your case, she doesn't even need to cold-read. She knows what you want from her, she knows what you want to hear.'

She fell silent. Her fingers stopped moving and then it came from her, a whisper, a hiss. 'Why would Nickie imagine I wanted to hear that your mother was murdered?'

Lena

THERE WAS NO room for guilt. All the space was taken up with relief, grief, that weird feeling of lightness you get when you wake up from a nightmare and realize it isn't real. But that – that wasn't even true, because the nightmare was still real. Mum was no less gone. But at least she didn't choose to go. She didn't choose to leave me. Someone took her – and that was something, because it meant there was something I could do about it, for her and for me. I could do whatever it took to make sure Helen Townsend paid.

I was running along the coastal path, clasping Mum's bracelet to my wrist. I was terrified that it was going to drop off and go sliding down the cliff into the sea. I wanted to put it in my mouth for safe-keeping, like crocodiles do with their babies.

Running on the slippery path felt dangerous, because I could have fallen, but safe at the same time – you can see a really long way in either direction, so I knew there was no one behind me. Of course there was no one behind me. No one was coming.

No one was coming for me – not to get me, not to help me. And I didn't have my phone, and I had no fucking idea whether it was in Mark's house or in his car or whether he'd taken it and thrown it away, and it wasn't like I could ask him now, was it?

I'd no room for guilt. I had to focus. Who could I turn to? Who was going to help me?

I could see buildings a little way up ahead, and I started to run harder, as fast as I could. I let myself imagine that someone there would know what to do, that someone there would have all the answers.

Sean

My phone buzzed in its holder, snapping me back to the present.

'Sir?' It was Erin. 'Where are you?'

'On my way to the coast. Where are you? Did Louise have anything to say?'

There was a long pause, so long I thought she perhaps hadn't heard me.

'Did Louise have anything to say about Lena?'

'Er . . . no.' She didn't sound convinced.

'What's going on?'

'Look, I need to talk to you, but I don't want to do this on the phone . . .'

'What? Is it Lena? Tell me now, Erin, don't mess about.'

'It's not urgent. It's not Lena. It's—'

'For Christ's sake, if it's not urgent why are you ringing me?'

'I need to talk to you the second you're back in Beckford,' she said. She sounded cold and angry. 'You got that?' She cut the call.

The downpour abating, I accelerated, snaking down

narrow roads flanked by high hedges. I had that dizzied sense again, like going too fast on a rollercoaster, light-headed with adrenaline. I whipped through a narrow stone arch and down a slope, then up again as the road climbed over the brow of a hill, and there it was: a little harbour, fishing boats rising and falling on the impatient tide.

The village was quiet, presumably thanks to the awful weather. So this was Craster. The car slowed without my even registering I was braking. A few hardy walkers draped in tent-like anoraks trudged through puddles as I pulled over to park. I followed a young couple running to take refuge, and found a group of pensioners huddled over mugs of tea in the café. I showed them pictures of Lena and Mark, but they hadn't seen them. They said they'd already been asked not half an hour earlier by a copper in uniform.

As I walked back to the car, I passed the very smoke-house where my mother had promised to take me for kippers. I tried to picture her face, as I did sometimes, but I never succeeded. I think I wanted to relive her disappointment when I told her I didn't want to come here. I wanted to feel the pain, her pain then, my pain now. But the memory was too muddied.

I drove on the half-mile or so to Howick. The house was easy enough to find – it was the only one there, perched precariously on a clifftop, looking out to sea. As expected, a red Vauxhall was parked out back. Its boot was open.

As I dragged myself out of the car, my feet heavy with dread, one of the PCs came over to give me an update

– where they were looking, what they'd found. They were talking to the coastguard. 'Sea's quite rough, so if either of them was in there, they could have been washed quite some way in a short space of time,' he said. 'Of course, we don't know when they got here, or . . .' He led me over to the car and I peered into the boot. 'You can see,' he said, 'it looks as though some-one's been in there.' He pointed to the smear of blood on the carpet, another on the rear window. A strand of blonde hair was caught on the lock mechanism, just like the one found in the kitchen.

He showed me the rest of the scene: smears of blood on the garden table, on the wall, on a rusty nail. I had failed her, like I had failed my mother. No – *her* mother. I'd failed her like I'd failed her mother. I could feel myself drifting again, the sense that I was losing my grip, and then: 'Sir? We've got a call. A shopkeeper in the next village up the coast. Says he's got a girl in there, soaked through and a bit bashed up, no idea where she is, asking him to call the police.'

There was a bench outside the shop and she was sit-ting on it, her head tilted back, her eyes closed. She was draped in a dark-green jacket which was too big for her. As the car pulled up, she opened her eyes.

'Lena!' I leaped out of the car and ran towards her. 'Lena!' Her face was ghostly white, save for a smear of bright blood on her cheek. She said nothing, just shrank back on to the bench as though she didn't recognize me, as though she had no idea who I was. 'Lena, it's me. Lena. It's OK, it's me.'

Sean

I realized when her expression didn't change, when I held out my hand to her and she shrank away still further, that something was wrong. She saw me just fine – she wasn't in shock, she knew who I was. She knew who I was and she was afraid of me.

It brought something back to me sharply, a look I'd seen on her mother's face once, and on the face of the policewoman, Jeannie, when she took me home. Not just fear, but something else. Fear and incomprehension, fear and horror. It reminded me of the look I gave myself sometimes, if I ever made the mistake of catching my eye in the mirror.

Jules

AFTER NICKIE LEFT, I went upstairs to your bedroom. Your bed was stripped bare, so I went to your wardrobe and pulled out one of your coats, caramel cashmere, softer and more luxurious than anything I could dream about owning. I wrapped myself in it and still I felt colder than I had in the water. I lay on your bed for a long time, too stiff and too tired to move, I felt as though I were waiting for my bones to warm up, for my blood to circulate once more, to restart my heart. I was waiting to hear you in my head, but you were silent.

Please, Nel, I thought, *please talk to me.* I said I was sorry.

I imagined your icy riposte: *All this time, Julia. All I wanted to do was talk to you.* And: *How could you think that of me? How could you think that I would have just dismissed a rape, that I would have taunted you with it?*

I don't know, Nel. I'm sorry.

When still I couldn't hear your voice, I changed tack. Tell me about Lauren, then. Tell me about those troublesome women. Tell me about Patrick Townsend. Tell me whatever it was you were trying to tell me before. But you wouldn't say a word. I could almost feel you sulking.

My phone rang and on its bright-blue screen I saw DS Morgan's name. For a second I didn't dare pick it up. What would I do if something had happened to Lena? How could I ever atone for all the mistakes I'd made if she, too, was gone? My hand trembling, I answered. And there! My heart pumped again, pushing warm blood to my extremities. She was safe! Lena was safe. They had her. They were bringing her home.

It seemed an age, hours and hours, before I heard a car door slam outside and I was able to rouse myself, to jump up and throw off your coat and run down the stairs. Erin was already there, standing at the foot of the steps, watching while Sean helped Lena out of his car.

She was wearing a man's jacket over her shoulders and her face was pale and dirty. But she was whole. She was safe. She was fine. Only when she looked up and her eyes met mine, I saw that was a lie.

She walked gingerly, placing her feet down carefully, and I knew how that felt. Her arms were wrapped protectively around herself; when Sean reached out an arm to guide her into the house, she flinched. I thought about the man who had taken her, about his proclivities. My stomach turned and I tasted the sweetness of vodka with orange, felt hot breath on my face, the pressure of insistent fingers on soft flesh.

'Lena,' I said, and she nodded at me. I saw that what I'd taken to be dirt on her face was blood, flaking from her mouth and chin. I reached for her hand, but she only held herself tighter, so I followed her up the steps. In the hallway, we stood facing each other. She shrugged off the jacket and let it fall to the floor. I bent to reach it, but Erin got there first. She picked it up and handed it to Sean, and something passed between them – a look I couldn't read, almost like anger.

'Where is he?' I hissed at Sean. Lena was bent over at the sink, drinking water straight from the tap. 'Where is Henderson?' I had a simple, savage urge to inflict pain on him, this man who had taken on a position of trust and then abused it. I wanted to grab at him, to twist and rip clean off, to do to him what men like that deserve.

'We're looking for him,' he said. 'We have people looking for him.'

'What do you mean, *looking* for him? Wasn't she with him?'

'She was, but . . .'

Lena was still bent over the sink, gulping water.

'Did you take her to the hospital?' I asked Sean.

He shook his head. 'Not yet. Lena was very clear that she didn't want to go.'

There was something in his face I didn't like, something hidden.

'But—'

'I don't need to go to the hospital,' Lena said, straightening up and wiping her mouth. 'I'm not hurt. I'm fine.'

She was lying. I knew exactly what kind of lie she was telling because I'd told those lies myself. For the first time, I saw myself in her, not you. Her expression was one of fear and defiance; I could see that she was clutching her secret to herself like a shield. You think that the hurt will be less, the humiliation slighter, if no one else can see it.

Sean took my arm and guided me out of the room. Very quietly, he said, 'She was adamant that she come home first. We can't force her to submit to an examination if she's unwilling. But you need to take her. As soon as possible.'

'Yes, of course I will. But I still don't understand why you don't have him. Where is he? Where is Henderson?'

'He's gone,' Lena said, suddenly at my side. Her fingers brushed against mine; they felt as cold as her mother's had the last time I touched them.

'Gone where?' I asked. 'What do you mean, *gone*?'

She wouldn't look at me. 'Just gone.'

Townsend raised an eyebrow. 'We've got uniforms out looking. His car is still there, so he can't have got far.'

'Where do you think he's gone, Lena?' I asked, trying to meet her eye, but she kept turning away.

Sean shook his head, his expression rueful. 'I've tried,' he said softly. 'She doesn't want to talk. I think she's just exhausted.'

Lena's fingers closed around mine, her breath escaping in a deep sigh. 'I am. I just want to sleep. Can we do this tomorrow, Sean? I'm desperate to sleep.'

The detectives left us with reassurances they would be back; Lena would need to give a formal statement. I watched them walk out to Sean's car. When Erin got into the passenger seat, she slammed the door so hard I was surprised the window didn't shatter.

Lena called to me from the kitchen.

'I'm starving,' she said. 'Could you make spaghetti bolognese again, like you did before?' The tone of her voice, the softness in it, was new; it was as surprising as the touch of her hand.

'Of course I can,' I said. 'I'll do that now.'

'Thank you. I'm just going to go upstairs for a bit, I need to have a shower.'

I put my hand on her arm. 'Lena, no. You can't. You need to go to the hospital first.'

She shook her head. 'No, I really don't, I'm not hurt.'

'Lena.' I couldn't meet her eye as I said it. 'You need to be examined before you can shower.'

She looked momentarily confused, then she dropped her shoulders, shook her head and stepped towards me. Despite myself, I started to cry. She wrapped her arms around me. 'It's OK,' she said. 'It's OK, it's OK.' Just like you had, that night after the water. 'He didn't do anything like that. It wasn't like that. You don't understand, he wasn't some, like, evil sexual predator. He was just a sad old man.'

'Oh, thank God!' I said. 'Thank God, Lena!' We stood like that, hugging each other, for a little while until I stopped crying and she started. She sobbed like a child, her skinny body crumpling, slipping through my arms to the floor. I crouched down next to her and tried to take her hand, but it was curled tightly into a fist.

'It's going to be all right,' I told her. 'Somehow it will be. I'll take care of you.'

She looked at me, wordless; she didn't seem to be able to speak. Instead she held out her hand, her fingers unfurling to reveal the treasure inside – a little silver bracelet with an onyx clasp – and then she found her voice.

'She didn't jump,' she said, her eyes glittering. I felt the temperature in the room plummet. 'Mum didn't leave me. She didn't jump.'

Lena

I stood in the shower for a long time with the water as hot as I could stand it. I wanted to scour my skin, I wanted the whole of the past day and night and week and month washed off me. I wanted *him* washed off me, his filthy house and his fists and the stink of him, his breath, his blood.

Julia was kind to me when I got home. She wasn't faking, she was obviously glad that I was back, she was worried about me. She seemed to think that Mark had *assaulted* me, like she maybe thought he was some sort of pervert who couldn't keep his hands off teenage girls. I'll give him this: he was right about one thing – people don't understand about him and K, they never will.

(There's a tiny, twisted part of me that sort of wishes I believed in an afterlife, and that the two of them could pick up again there, and maybe things might be all right for them, and she'd be happy. As much as I hate him, I'd like to think that somehow Katie could be happy.)

When I felt clean, or at least as close to clean as I thought it was possible to get, I went to my room and sat on the window sill, because that's where I do all my best thinking. I lit a cigarette and tried to figure out what I should do. I wanted to ask Mum, I wanted to ask her so badly, but I couldn't think about that because I'd just start crying again, and what good would that be to her? I didn't know whether to tell Julia what Mark had told me. Whether I could trust her to do the right thing.

Maybe. When I told Julia that Mum didn't jump, I expected her to tell me that I was wrong or crazy or whatever, but she just accepted it. Without question. Like she knew already. Like she'd always known.

I don't even know if the shit Mark told me is true, though it would be a pretty weird thing to make up. Why point the finger at Mrs Townsend, when there are more obvious people to blame? Like Louise, for example. But maybe he feels bad enough about the Whittakers, after what he's done to them.

I don't know whether he was lying or telling the truth, but either way he deserved what I said to him, what I did. He deserved everything he got.

Jules

WHEN LENA CAME back downstairs, her face and hands scrubbed clean, she sat at the kitchen table and ate, ravenously. Afterwards, when she smiled and said thank you, I shivered, because now that I have seen it, I can't unsee it. She has her father's smile.

(What else, I wondered, does she have of his?)

'What's wrong?' Lena asked suddenly. 'You're staring at me.'

'I'm sorry,' I said, my face reddening. 'I'm just . . . I'm glad you're home. I'm glad you're safe.'

'Me too.'

I hesitated a moment before going on. 'I know you're tired, but I need to ask you, Lena, about what happened today. About the bracelet.'

She turned her face from me towards the window. 'Yeah. I know.'

'Mark had it?' She nodded again. 'And you took it from him?'

She sighed. 'He gave it to me.'

'Why did he give it to you? Why did he have it in the first place?'

'I don't know.' She turned her head back to face me, her eyes blank, shuttered. 'He told me he found it.'

'He found it? Where?' She didn't answer. 'Lena, we need to go to the police about this, we need to tell them.'

She got to her feet and took her plate over to the sink. Her back to me, she said, 'We made a deal.'

'A deal?'

'That he would give me Mum's bracelet and let me go home,' she said, 'so long as I told the police that I'd lied about him and Katie.' Her voice was incongruously light as she busied herself with the dishes.

'And he believed you would do that?' She raised her skinny shoulders to her ears. 'Lena. Tell me the truth. Do you think . . . do you believe Mark Henderson was the one who killed your mum?'

She turned around and looked at me. 'I'm telling the truth. And I don't know. He told me he took it from Mrs Townsend's office.'

'Helen Townsend?' Lena nodded. 'Sean's wife? Your head teacher? But why would she have the bracelet? I don't understand . . .'

'Neither do I,' she said quietly. 'Not really.'

I made tea and we sat together at the kitchen table, sipping our drinks in silence. I held Nel's bracelet in my hand. Lena sat loose-limbed, her head bowed, visibly sagging in front of me. I reached out and grazed her fingers with my own.

'You're exhausted,' I said. 'You should go to bed.'

She nodded, looking up at me with hooded eyes. 'Will you come up with me, please? I don't want to be by myself.'

I followed her up the stairs and into your room, not her own. She clambered on to your bed and lay her head on the pillow, patting the space next to her.

'When we first moved here,' she said, 'I couldn't sleep by myself.'

'All the noises?' I asked, lying down next to her and covering us with your coat.

She nodded. 'All the creaking and the moaning . . .'

'And all your mother's scary stories?'

'Exactly. I used to come in here and sleep next to Mum all the time.'

There was a lump in my throat, a pebble. I couldn't swallow. 'I used to do that with my mum, too.'

She fell asleep. I stayed at her side, looking down at her face, which in repose was yours *exactly*. I wanted to touch her, to stroke her hair, to do something motherly, but I didn't want to wake her, or alarm her, or do something wrong. I have no idea how to be a mother. I've never taken care of a child in my entire life. I wished that you would speak, that you would tell me what to do, what to feel. As she lay beside me, I think I did feel tenderness, but I felt it for you, and for our mother, and the second her green eyes flicked open and fixed on mine, I shivered.

'Why are you always watching me like that?' she whispered, half smiling. 'It's really weird.'

'I'm sorry,' I said, and rolled on to my back.

She slipped her fingers between mine. 'It's OK,' she said. 'Weird's OK. Weird can be good.'

We lay there, side by side, our fingers interlaced. I

listened to her breathing slow, then quicken, and then slow once again.

'You know, what I don't understand,' she whispered, 'is why you hated her so much.'

'I didn't . . .'

'She didn't understand either.'

'I know,' I said. 'I know she didn't.'

'You're crying,' she whispered, reaching over to touch my face. She brushed the tears from my cheek.

I told her. All the things I should have told you, I told them to your daughter instead. I told her how I'd let you down, how I'd believed the worst of you, how I'd allowed myself to blame you.

'But why didn't you just tell her? Why didn't you tell her what really happened?'

'It was complicated,' I said, and I felt her stiffen beside me.

'Complicated how? How complicated could it be?'

'Our mother was dying. Our parents were in a terrible way and I didn't want to do anything to make it worse.'

'But . . . but he *raped* you,' she said. 'He should have gone to prison.'

'I didn't see it that way. I was very young. I was younger than you are, and I don't just mean in years, although I was that, too. But I was naive, completely inexperienced, I was clueless. We didn't talk about consent in the way you girls do now. I thought . . .'

'You thought what he did was OK?'

'No, but I don't think I saw it for what it was. What it really was. I thought rape was something a bad man

369

did to you, a man who jumped out at you in an alley-way in the dead of night, a man who held a knife to your throat. I didn't think boys did it. Not schoolboys like Robbie, not good-looking boys, the ones who go out with the prettiest girl in town. I didn't think they did it to you in your own living room, I didn't think they talked to you about it afterwards, and asked you if you'd had a good time. I just thought I must have done something wrong, that I hadn't made it clear enough that I didn't want it.'

Lena was silent for a while, but when she spoke again her voice was higher, more insistent. 'OK, maybe you didn't want to say anything at the time, but what about later? Why didn't you explain it to her later on?'

'Because I misunderstood her,' I said. 'I misjudged her completely. I thought that she knew what had happened that night.'

'You thought that she knew and did *nothing*? How could you think that of her?'

How could I explain that? That I pieced together your words – the words you said to me that night and the words you said to me later, *Wasn't there some part of you that liked it?* – and I told myself a story about you that made sense to me, that allowed me to get on with my life without ever having to face what really happened.

'I thought that she chose to protect him,' I whispered. 'I thought she chose him over me. I couldn't blame him, because I couldn't even *think* about him. If I'd have blamed him and thought about him, I'd have made it real. So I just . . . I thought about Nel instead.'

Lena's voice grew cold. 'I don't understand you. I

don't understand people like you, who always choose to blame the woman. If there's two people doing something wrong and one of them's a girl, it's got to be her fault, right?'

'No, Lena, it's not like that, it isn't—'

'Yes, it is. It's like when someone has an affair, why does the wife always hate the other woman? Why doesn't she hate her husband? *He*'s the one who's betrayed her, *he*'s the one who swore to love her and keep her and whatever for ever and ever. Why isn't *he* the one who gets shoved off a fucking cliff?'

TUESDAY, 25 AUGUST

Erin

I LEFT THE cottage early, running upriver. I wanted to get away from Beckford, to clear my head, but though the air had been rinsed clean by rain and the sky was a perfect, pale blue, the fog in my head got darker, murkier. Nothing about this place makes sense.

By the time Sean and I left Jules and Lena at the Mill House yesterday, I'd worked myself up into a total state, and I was so pissed off at him I just came out with it, right there in the car. 'What exactly was going on with you and Nel Abbott?'

He slammed his foot on the brake so hard I thought I'd go through the windscreen. We'd stopped in the middle of the lane, but Sean didn't seem to care. 'What did you say?'

'Do you want to pull over?' I asked, checking the rear-view mirror, but he didn't. I felt like an idiot for blurting it out like that, not leading up to it, not testing the water at all.

records, he had a point. His is impeccable; I narrowly avoided getting sacked for sleeping with a younger colleague. I was sprinting now, going hell for leather down the hill, my eyes trained on the path, the gorse at the side of my vision a blur. He has an impressive arrest record, he is highly respected amongst his colleagues. He is, as Louise said, a good man. My right foot caught on a rock in the path and I went flying. I lay in the dust, fighting for breath, the wind knocked clean out of me. Sean Townsend is a good man.

There are a lot of them about. My father was a good man. He was a respected officer. Didn't stop him beating the shit out of me and my brothers when he lost his temper, but still. When my mother complained to one of his colleagues after he broke my youngest brother's nose, his colleague said, 'There's a thin blue line, love, and I'm afraid you just don't cross it.'

I hauled myself up, dusting the dirt off me. I could say nothing. I could stay on the right side of the thin blue line, I could ignore Louise's hints and intimations, I could ignore Sean's possible personal connection to Nel Abbott. But if I did that, I'd be ignoring the fact that where there is sex, there is motive. He had a motive to get rid of Nel, and his wife did, too. I thought about her face the day I spoke to her at the school, the way she spoke about Nel, about Lena. What was it she despised? Her *insistent, tiresome expression of sexual availability*?

I reached the bottom of the slope and skirted around the gorse; the cottage was just a couple of hundred yards away and I could see that there was someone outside. A figure, stout and stooped, in a dark coat. Not Patrick and not Sean. As I got closer, I realized it was the old goth, the *psychic*, mad-as-a-hatter Nickie Sage.

She was leaning against the wall of the cottage, her face puce. She looked like she might be on the verge of a heart attack.

'Mrs Sage!' I called out. 'Are you all right?'

She looked up at me, breathing heavily, and pushed her floppy velvet hat further up her brow. 'I'm fine,' she said, 'although it's been a while since I've walked this far.' She looked me up and down. 'You look like you've been playing in the muck.'

'Oh, yes,' I said, doing an ineffectual job of brushing the remaining dirt off me. 'Had a bit of a tumble.' She nodded. As she straightened up I could hear the wheeze as she breathed. 'Would you like to come in and sit down?'

'In there?' She jerked her head back towards the cottage. 'Not likely.' She took a few steps away from the front door. 'Do you know what happened in there? Do you know what Anne Ward did?'

'She murdered her husband,' I replied. 'And then she drowned herself, just out there in the river.'

Nickie shrugged, waddling off towards the river bank. I followed her. 'More of an exorcism than a murder, if you ask me. She was getting rid of whatever evil spirit had taken hold of that man. It left him, but it didn't leave that place, did it? You have trouble sleeping there?'

'Well, I . . .'

'Not surprised. Not surprised at all. I could have told you that – not that you'd have listened. The place is full of evil. Why do you think Townsend keeps it as his own, looks after it like it's his special place?'

'I've no idea,' I said. 'I thought he used it as a fishing cabin.'

'Fishing!' she exclaimed, as though she'd never heard anything quite so ridiculous in her entire life. 'Fishing!'

'Well, I have actually seen him out here fishing, so . . .'

Nickie harrumphed, dismissing the idea with a wave of her hand. We were at the water's edge. Toe to heel and heel to toe, Nickie was working her swollen, mottled feet out of her slip-on shoes. She put a toe in the water and gave a satisfied chuckle. 'The water's cold up here, isn't it? Clean.' Standing ankle-deep in the river, she asked, 'Have you been to see him? Townsend? Have you asked him about his wife?'

'You mean Helen?'

She turned to look at me, her expression contemptuous. 'Sean's wife? That Helen, with her face like a slapped arse? What's she got to do with anything? She's about as interesting as paint drying on a damp day. No, the one you should be interested in is Patrick's wife. Lauren.'

'Lauren? Lauren who died thirty years ago?'

'Yes, Lauren who died thirty years ago! You think the dead don't matter? You think the dead don't speak? You should hear the things they have to say.' She shuffled a little further into the river, bending down to soak her hands. 'This is it, this is where Annie came to wash her hands, just like this, see, only she kept going . . .'

I was losing interest. 'I need to go, Nickie, I need to

take a shower and get on with some work. It was good talking to you,' I said, turning to leave her. I was half-way back to the cottage when I heard her call out.

'You think the dead don't speak? You should listen, you might hear something. It's Lauren you're looking for, she's the one who started all this!'

I left her at the river. My plan was to get to Sean early; I thought if I showed up at his place, picked him up and drove him to the station, I'd have him captive for at least fifteen minutes. He wouldn't be able to get away from me or throw me out of the car. It was better than confronting him at the station, where there would be other people around.

It's not far from the cottage to the Townsends' place. Along the river it's probably about three miles, but there's no direct road, you have to drive all the way into the town and then back out again, so it was after eight a.m. by the time I got there. I was too late. There were no cars in the courtyard – he'd already left. The sensible thing, I knew, would be to turn the car around and head for the office, but I had Nickie's voice in my head and Louise's, too, and I thought I'd just see, on the off chance, whether Helen was around.

She wasn't. I knocked on the door a few times and there was no reply. I was heading back to my car when I thought I might as well try Patrick Townsend's place next door. No answer there either. I peered through the front window but couldn't see much, just a dark and seemingly empty room. I went back to the front door and knocked again. Nothing. But when I tried the handle, the door swung open, and that seemed as good as an invitation.

'Hello?' I called out. 'Mr Townsend? Hello?' There was no answer. I walked into the living room, a spartan space with dark wooden floors and bare walls; the only concession to decoration was a selection of framed photographs on the mantelpiece. Patrick Townsend in uniform – first army, then police – and a number of pictures of Sean as a child and then a teenager, smiling stiffly at the camera, the same pose and the same expression in each one. There was a photograph of Sean and Helen on their wedding day, too, standing in front of the church in Beckford. Sean looked young, handsome and unhappy. Helen looked much the same as she does today – a bit thinner, perhaps. She looked happier, though, smiling shyly at the camera in spite of her ugly dress.

Over on a wooden sideboard in front of the window was another set of frames, these ones containing certificates, commendations, qualifications, a monument to the achievements of father and son. There were no pictures, as far as I could see, of Sean's mother.

I left the living room and called out again. 'Mr Townsend?' My voice echoed back to me in the hallway. The whole place felt abandoned, and yet it was spotlessly clean, not a speck of dust on the skirting boards or the bannister. I walked up the stairs and on to the landing. There were two bedrooms there, side by side, as sparsely furnished as the living room downstairs, but lived in. Both of them, by the looks of things. In the main bedroom, with its large window looking down the valley to the river, were Patrick's things: polished black shoes by the wall, his suits hanging in the wardrobe. Next door, beside a neatly made single bed, was a chair with a suit jacket hanging over it, which I recognized as the one Helen wore when I interviewed her at the school. And in the wardrobe were more of her clothes, black and grey and navy and shapeless.

My phone beeped, deafeningly loud in the funeral-parlour silence of that house. I had a voicemail, a missed call. It was Jules. 'DS Morgan,' she was saying, her voice solemn, 'I need to talk to you. It's quite urgent. I'm coming in to see you. I . . . er . . . I need to talk to you alone. I'll see you at the station.'

I slipped the phone back into my pocket. I went back into Patrick's room and took another quick look around, at the books on the shelves, in the drawer next to the bed. There were photographs in there, too, old ones, of Sean and Helen together, fishing at the river near the cottage, Sean and Helen leaning proudly against a new car, Helen standing in front of the school, looking at once happy and embarrassed, Helen out in the courtyard, cradling a cat in her arms, Helen, Helen, Helen.

I heard a noise, a click, the sound of a latch lifting and then a creak of floorboards. I put the photographs back hastily and shut the drawer, then moved as quietly as I could out on to the landing. Then I froze. Helen was standing at the bottom of the stairs, looking up at me. She had a paring knife in her right hand and was gripping its blade so tightly that blood was dripping on to the floor.

379

Helen

HELEN HAD NO idea why Erin Morgan was wandering about Patrick's house as though she owned it, but for the moment she was more concerned with the blood on the floor. Patrick liked a clean house. She fetched a cloth from the kitchen and began to wipe it up, only for more to spill from the deep cut across her palm.

'I was chopping onions,' she said to the detective by way of an explanation. 'You startled me.'

This wasn't exactly true, because she'd stopped chopping onions when she'd seen the car pull up. With the knife in her hand she'd stood stock-still while Erin knocked, and then had watched her wander over to Patrick's place. She knew that he was out, so she'd assumed the detective would just leave. But then she remembered that when she'd left that morning, she hadn't locked the front door. So, knife still in hand, she walked across the courtyard to check.

'It's quite deep,' Erin said. 'You need to clean and bandage that properly.' Erin had come downstairs and was standing over Helen, watching her wipe the floor. Standing there in Patrick's house as though she had every right to be there.

'He'll be livid if he sees this,' Helen said. 'He likes a clean house. Always has.'

'And you . . . *keep house* for him, do you?'

Helen gave Erin a sharp look. 'I help out. He does most things himself, but he's getting on. And he likes things to be just so. His late wife,' she said, looking up at Erin, 'was a *slattern*. His word. An old-fashioned word. You're not allowed to say *slut* any longer, are you? It's politically incorrect.'

She stood up, facing Erin, holding the bloody cloth in front of her. The pain in her hand felt hot and bright, like a burn almost, with the same cauterizing effect. She was no longer sure who to be afraid of, or what exactly to feel guilty for, but she felt that she ought to keep Erin here, to find out what she wanted. To detain her for a while, hopefully until Patrick got back, because she was sure that he'd want to talk to her.

Helen wiped the knife handle with the cloth. 'Would you like a cup of tea, Detective?' she asked.

'Lovely,' Erin replied, her cheery smile fading as she watched Helen lock the front door and slip the key into her pocket before continuing on into the kitchen.

'Mrs Townsend—' Erin started.

'Do you take sugar?' Helen interrupted.

The way to deal with situations like this was to throw the other person off their game. Helen knew this from years of public-sector politics. Don't do what people expect you to do, it puts them on the back foot right away and, if nothing else, it buys you time. So instead of being angry, outraged that this woman had come into their home without permission, Helen was polite.

'Have you found him?' she asked Erin as she handed her the mug of tea. 'Mark Henderson? Has he turned up yet?'

'No,' Erin replied, 'not yet.'

'His car left on the cliff and no sign of him anywhere.' She sighed. 'A suicide can be an admission of guilt, can't it? It's certainly going to look that way. What a mess.' Erin nodded. She was nervous, Helen could tell, she kept glancing back at the door, fiddling around in her pocket. 'It'll be terrible for the school, for our reputation. The reputation of this entire place, tarnished again . . .'

'Is that why you disliked Nel Abbott so much?' Erin asked. 'Because she tarnished the reputation of Beckford with her work?'

Helen frowned. 'Well, it's one of the reasons. She was a bad parent, as I told you, she was disrespectful to me and to the traditions and rules of the school.'

'Was she a slut?' Erin asked.

Helen laughed in surprise. 'I beg your pardon?'

'I was just wondering if, to use your politically incorrect term, you thought Nel Abbott was a slut? I've heard she had affairs with some of the men in town . . .'

'I don't know anything about that,' Helen said, but her face was hot and she felt that she had lost the upper hand. She got to her feet, crossed over to the counter and retrieved her paring knife. Standing at the sink, she washed her blood from its blade.

'I don't profess to know anything about Nel Abbott's private life,' she said quietly. She could feel the detective's eyes on her, watching her face, her hands. She could feel her blush spread to her neck, to her chest, her body betraying her. She tried to keep her voice light. 'Though I'd hardly be surprised if she were promiscuous. She was an attention-seeker.'

She wanted this conversation to end. She wanted the detective to leave their home, she wanted Sean to be there, and Patrick. She had an urge to lay everything on the table, to confess to her own sins and demand they confess to theirs. Mistakes had been made, admittedly, but the Townsends were a good family. They were good people. They had nothing to fear. She turned to face the detective, her chin raised and with as haughty an expression as she could muster, but her hands were trembling so badly she thought she might drop the knife. Surely she had nothing to fear?

Jules

I LEFT LENA tucked up in her mother's bed in the morning, still sound asleep. I wrote her a note, saying I'd meet her at the police station at eleven for her to give her statement. There were things I needed to do first, conversations best had between adults. I had to think like a parent now, like a mother. I had to protect her, to keep her from any further harm.

I drove to the station, stopping halfway to ring Erin to warn her I'd be coming in. I wanted to make sure that it was Erin I spoke to, and I had to make sure that we could speak alone.

'Why isn't *he* the one who gets shoved off a fucking cliff?' Lena had been talking about Sean Townsend last night. It had all come out, how Sean had fallen in love with Nel and – Lena thought – Nel a bit in love with Sean. It had ended a while back – Nel had said things had 'run their course', although Lena didn't quite believe her. In any case, Helen must have found out, she must have taken revenge. Then it was my turn to be outraged: why hadn't Lena said anything before? He was in charge of the investigation into Nel's death, it was completely inappropriate.

'He loved her,' Lena said. 'Doesn't that make him a good person, that he tried to find out what happened to her?'

'But Lena, don't you see . . . ?'

'He's a good person, Julia. How could I say anything? It would have got him into trouble, and he doesn't deserve that. He's a good man.'

Erin didn't answer her phone, so I left a message and drove on to the station. I parked outside and called again, but again there was no answer, so I decided to wait for her. Half an hour went by and I decided to go in anyway. If Sean was there, I'd make an excuse, I'd pretend I thought that Lena's statement had been scheduled for nine, not eleven. I'd think of something.

As it turned out, he wasn't there. Neither of them was. The man on the desk told me DI Townsend was in Newcastle for the day, and that he wasn't entirely sure of the whereabouts of DS Morgan, but he had no doubt she'd be in any minute.

I went back to my car. I took your bracelet out of my pocket – I'd put it into a plastic bag to protect it. To protect whatever was on it. The chances of there being a fingerprint or some DNA trapped within its links were slim, but slim was something. Slim was a possibility. Slim was a shot at an answer. Nickie said you were dead because you found out something about Patrick Townsend; Lena said you were dead because you fell in love with Sean and he with you, and Helen Townsend, jealous, vengeful Helen, would not stand for that. No matter which way I turned, I saw Townsends.

Metaphorically. Literally, I saw Nickie Sage, looming large in the rear-view mirror. She was shuffling across the car park, achingly slowly, her face pink under a big floppy hat. She reached the back of my car and leaned against it, and I could hear her laboured breathing through the open window.

'Nickie.' I got out of the car. 'Are you all right?' She didn't respond. 'Nickie?' Up close, she looked like she might be on her last legs.

'I need a lift,' she gasped. 'Been on my feet for hours.'

I helped her into the car. Her clothes were soaked with sweat. 'Where on earth have you been, Nickie? What have you been doing?'

'Walking,' she wheezed. 'Up by the Wards' cottage. Listening to the river.'

'You do realize that the river runs right past your own front door, don't you?'

She shook her head. 'Not the same river. You think it's all the same, but it changes. It has a different spirit up there. Sometimes you need to travel to hear its voice.'

I turned left just before the bridge towards the square. 'Up here, yes?' She nodded, still gulping for air. 'Perhaps you should get someone to give you a lift next time you feel like travelling.'

She leaned back in the seat and closed her eyes. 'You volunteering? I didn't imagine you'd be sticking around.'

We sat in the car for a bit when we reached her flat. I didn't have the heart to make her get out and walk upstairs straight away, so instead I listened while she told me why I should stay in Beckford, why it would be good for Lena to stay by the water, why I'd never hear my sister's voice if I left.

'I don't believe in all that stuff, Nickie,' I said.

'Of course you do,' she said crossly.

'OK.' I wasn't going to argue. 'So. You were up by the Wards' cottage? That's the place where Erin Morgan is staying, right? You didn't see her, did you?'

'I did. She'd been out running around somewhere. Then she was running off somewhere else, probably to bark up the wrong tree. Banging on about Helen Townsend, when I told her it wasn't Helen she should be bothering with. No one listens to me. *Lauren*, I said, not *Helen*. But no one ever listens.'

She gave me the Townsends' address. The address and a warning: 'If the old man thinks you know something, he'll hurt you. You've got to be smart.' I didn't tell her about the bracelet, or that it was she, not Erin, who was barking up the wrong tree.

Erin

Helen kept looking up at the window, as though she was expecting someone to appear.

'You're expecting Sean back, are you?' I asked her.

She shook her head. 'No. Why would he be coming back? He's in Newcastle, talking to the brass about the Henderson mess. Surely you knew that?'

'He didn't tell me,' I said. 'It must have slipped his mind.' She raised her eyebrows in an expression of disbelief. 'He can be absent-minded, can't he?' I went on. Her eyebrows rose further still. 'I mean, not that it affects his work or anything, but sometimes—'

'Do stop talking,' she snapped.

She was impossible to read, veering from polite to exasperated, timid to aggressive; angry one minute and frightened the next. It was making me very nervous. This small, mousy, unimpressive woman sitting opposite me was frightening me because I had *no idea* what she was going to do next – offer me another cuppa or come at me with the knife.

She pushed her chair back suddenly, its feet screeching

against the tiles, got to her feet and went to the window. 'He's been gone ages,' she said quietly.

'Who has? Patrick?'

She ignored me. 'He walks in the mornings, but not usually for so long. He's not well. I . . .'

'Do you want to go and look for him?' I asked. 'I could come with you if you like.'

'He goes up to that cottage almost every day,' she said, talking as though I wasn't there, as though she couldn't hear me. 'I don't know why. That's where Sean used to take her. That's where they . . . Oh, I don't know. I don't know what to do. I'm not even sure what the right thing is any more.' She'd balled her right hand into a fist, a red bloom blossoming on her pristine white bandage.

'I was so happy when Nel Abbott died,' she said. 'We all were. It was such a relief. But short-lived. Short-lived. Because now I can't help wondering if it's caused us even more trouble.' She turned, finally, to look at me. 'Why are you here? And please don't lie, because I'm not in the mood today.' She raised her hand to her face and as she wiped her mouth, bright blood smeared over her lips.

I reached into my pocket for my phone and pulled it out. 'I think maybe it's time I left,' I said, getting slowly to my feet. 'I came here to talk to Sean, but since he's not here . . .'

'He isn't absent-minded, you know,' she said, taking a step to her left so that she stood between me and the passage to the front door. 'He has absences, but that's a different thing. No, if he didn't tell you he was going to Newcastle, that's because he doesn't trust you, and if he doesn't trust you, I'm not sure that I should. I'm only going to ask once more,' she said, 'why you are here.'

I nodded, making a conscious effort to drop my shoulders, to stay relaxed. 'As I said, I wanted to speak to Sean.'

'About?'

'About an allegation of improper conduct,' I said. 'About his relationship with Nel Abbott.'

Helen stepped towards me and I felt a sickeningly sharp kick of adrenaline to my gut. 'There will be consequences, won't there?' she said, a sad smile on her face. 'How could we have imagined that there wouldn't be?'

'Helen,' I said, 'I just need to know—'

I heard the front door slam and stepped back quickly, putting some space between us, as Patrick entered the room.

For a moment, none of us said anything. He stared at me, eyes on mine, jaw working, while he took off his jacket and slung it over the back of a chair. Then he turned his attention to Helen. He noticed her bloody hand and was immediately animated.

'What happened? Did she do something to you? Darling . . .'

Helen blushed and something in the pit of my stomach squirmed. 'It's nothing,' she said quickly. 'It's nothing. It wasn't her. My hand slipped when I was chopping onions . . .'

Patrick looked at her other hand, at the knife she still held. Gently, he took it from her. 'What's she doing here?' he asked, without looking at me.

Helen cocked her head to one side, looking from her

father-in-law to me and back again. 'She's been asking questions,' she said, 'about Nel Abbott.' She swallowed. 'About Sean. About his professional conduct.'

'I just need to clarify something, it's procedural, relating to the handling of the investigation.'

Patrick didn't seem interested. He sat down at the kitchen table without looking at me. 'Do you know,' he said to Helen, 'why they moved her up here? I asked around – I still know people, of course, and I spoke to one of my former colleagues down in London, and he told me that this fine detective here was removed from her post in the Met because she'd seduced a younger colleague. And not just any colleague, a woman! Can you imagine that?' His dry laugh segued into a hacking smoker's cough. 'Here she is, chasing down your Mr Henderson, while she's guilty of exactly the same thing. An abuse of power for her own sexual gratification. And she still has a job.' He lit a cigarette. 'And then she comes here and says she wants to talk about my son's professional conduct!'

Finally, he looked at me. 'You should have been thrown off the force altogether, but because you're a woman, because you're a *dyke*, you're allowed to get away with it. That's what they call *equality*.' He scoffed. 'Can you imagine what would happen if it were a man? If Sean got caught sleeping with one of his juniors, he'd be out on his ear.'

I balled my hands into fists to stop them shaking. 'How about if Sean was sleeping with a woman who ended up dead?' I asked. 'What d'you think would happen to him then?'

He moves quickly for an old guy. He was on his feet, chair crashing back, and his hand around my throat in what seemed like less than a second. 'Watch your mouth, you dirty bitch,' he whispered, breathing sour smoke in my face. I gave him a good hard shove in the chest and he let me go.

He stepped back, his arms by his sides, fists clenched. 'My son has done nothing wrong,' he said quietly. 'So if you make trouble for him, girlie, I'll make trouble for you. Do you understand that? You'll get it back with interest.'

'Dad,' Helen said. 'That's enough. You're scaring her.'

He turned to his daughter-in-law with a smile. 'I know, love. I mean to.' He looked back at me and smiled again. 'With some of them, it's the only thing they understand.'

Jules

I LEFT THE car on the side of the track leading to the Townsends' place. I didn't need to, there was plenty of space to park in their courtyard, but it felt right that I should. This felt like it ought to be a furtive mission, like I ought to surprise them. The fearless relic, the one who appeared the day I confronted my rapist, was back. The bracelet in my pocket, I strode into that sun-drenched courtyard, straight-backed and resolute. I had come on behalf of my sister, to make things right for her. I was determined. I was unafraid.

I was unafraid until Patrick Townsend opened the door to me, his face stained with rage, a knife in his hand.

'What do you want?' he demanded.

I took a couple of steps away from the front door. 'I . . .' He was about to slam the door in my face and I was too frightened to say what I needed to. *He did for his wife*, Nickie had told me, *and for your sister, too.* 'I was . . .'

'Jules?' a voice called out to me. 'Is that you?'

*

It was quite a scene. Helen was there, with blood on her hand and her face, and Erin, too, doing a poor job of pretending that she was in control of the situation. She greeted me with a cheery smile. 'What brings you here? We're supposed to be meeting at the station.'

'Yes, I know, I . . .'

'Spit it out,' Patrick muttered. My skin prickled with heat, breath shortening. 'You Abbotts! Christ, what a family!' His voice rose as he slammed the knife down on the kitchen table. 'I remember you, you know? Obese, weren't you, when you were younger?' He turned to speak to Helen. 'Disgusting fat thing, she was. And the parents! Pathetic.' My hands were trembling as he turned back to look at me. 'I suppose the mother had an excuse, because she was dying, but someone should have taken them in hand. You ran wild, didn't you, you and your sister? And look how well you both turned out! She was mentally unstable, and you . . . well. What are you? Simple?'

'That's quite enough, Mr Townsend,' Erin said. She took my arm. 'Come on, let's get you to the station. We need to get Lena's statement.'

'Ah yes, the girl. That one will go the same way as her mother, she's got the same dirty look about her, filthy mouth, the kind of face you want to slap—'

'You spend a lot of time thinking about doing things to my teenage niece, do you?' I said loudly. 'Do you think that's appropriate?' My anger was roused again, and Patrick wasn't ready for it. 'Well? Do you? Disgusting old man.' I turned to Erin. 'I'm actually not quite ready to leave yet,' I said. 'But I'm glad you're here, Erin,

I think it's appropriate, because the reason I came was not to speak to *him*,' I jerked my head in Patrick's direction, 'but to *her*. To you, Mrs Townsend.' My hand trembling, I fished the little plastic bag out of my pocket and placed it on the table, next to the knife. 'I wanted to ask you, when did you take this bracelet from my sister's wrist?'

Helen's eyes widened and I knew that she was guilty.

'Where did the bracelet come from, Jules?' Erin asked.

'From Lena. Who got it from Mark Henderson. Who took it from Helen. Who, I'm guessing from the guilty-as-sin look on her face, took it from my sister before she killed her.'

Patrick started laughing, a loud, fake bark of a laugh. 'She took it from Lena, who took it from Mark, who took it from Helen, who took it from the fairy on the fucking Christmas tree! Sorry, love,' he apologized to Helen, 'excuse my French, but what utter garbage.'

'It was in your office, wasn't it, Helen?' I looked at Erin. 'It'll have prints on it, DNA, won't it?'

Patrick chuckled again, but Helen looked stricken. 'No, I . . .' she said at last, her eyes flicking from me to Erin to her father-in-law. 'It was . . . No.' She took a deep breath. 'I found it,' she said. 'But I didn't know . . . I didn't know it was hers. I just . . . I kept it. I was going to hand it in to lost property.'

'You found it where, Helen?' Erin asked. 'You found it at the school?'

Helen glanced at Patrick and then back to the detective, as though considering whether the lie would hold.

'I think that I . . . yes, I did. And, er, I didn't know whose it was, so . . .'

'My sister wore that bracelet all the time,' I said. 'It has my mother's initials on it. I'm finding it a bit hard to believe you didn't realize what it was, that it was important.'

'I didn't,' Helen said, but her voice was thin and her face was reddening.

'Of course she didn't know!' Patrick shouted suddenly. 'Of course she didn't know whose it was or where it came from.' He went quickly to her side, placing his hand on her shoulder. 'Helen had the bracelet because I left it in her car. Careless of me. I was going to throw it out, I meant to, but . . . I've become rather forgetful. I've become forgetful, haven't I, darling?' Helen said nothing, she didn't move. 'I left it in the car,' he said again.

'OK,' Erin said. 'And where did *you* get it?'

He looked right at me when he answered her. 'Where do you think I got it, you moron? I ripped it off that whore's wrist before I threw her over.'

Patrick

HE HAD LOVED her a long time, but never so much as in the moment when she flew to his defence.

'That is not what happened!' Helen sprang to her feet. 'That is not . . . Don't! Don't you take the blame for this, Dad, that is *not* what happened. You didn't . . . you didn't even . . .'

Patrick smiled at her, reaching out a hand. She took it and he pulled her closer. She was soft, but not weak, her modesty, her unashamed plainness more stirring than any facile beauty. It moved him now – he felt his blood rising, the pump of his weakened old heart.

No one spoke. The sister was crying silently, mouthing words without any sound. The detective watched him, watched Helen, something knowing in her face.

'Are you . . . ?' She shook her head, lost for words. 'Mr Townsend, I . . .'

'Come on, then!' He felt suddenly irritable, desperate to get away from the woman's evident distress. 'For Christ's sake, you're a police officer, do what you have to do.'

Erin took a deep breath and stepped towards him. 'Patrick Townsend, I am arresting you on suspicion of the murder of Danielle Abbott. You do not have to say anything—'

'Yes, yes, yes, all right,' he said wearily. 'I know, I know all that. God. Women like you, you don't ever know when to stop talking.' Then he turned to Helen. 'But you, darling, you do. You know when to speak and when to be quiet. You tell the truth, my girl.'

She started to cry, and he wanted more than anything to be beside her, in the room upstairs, just one last time, before he was taken away from her. He kissed her forehead then, and before he followed the detective out of the door, bid her goodbye.

Patrick had never been one for mysticism, for gut feelings or hunches, but if he was honest, he'd felt this coming: the reckoning. The endgame. He'd felt it long before they'd dragged Nel Abbott's cold corpse out of the water, only he'd dismissed it as a symptom of age. His mind had been playing a lot of tricks lately, boosting the colour and the sound in his old memories, blurring the edges of his new ones. He knew it was the start of it, the long goodbye, that he would be eaten from the inside out, core to husk. He could be grateful, at least, that he still had time to tie up the loose ends, to seize control. It was, he realized now, the only way to salvage something of the life they'd built, though he knew that not everyone could be spared.

When they sat him in the interview room at Beckford station, he thought at first that the humiliation was more than he could bear, but bear it he did. What made it easier, he found, was the surprising sensation of relief. He wanted to tell his story. If it was going to come out, then he should be the one to tell it, while he still had time, while his mind was still his own. More than just relief, there was pride. All his life, there had been a part of him that had wanted to tell what had happened the night Lauren died, but he hadn't been able to. He had held back, out of love for his son.

He spoke in short, simple sentences. He was very clear. He expressed his intention to make a full confession to the murders of Lauren Slater in 1983 and Danielle Abbott in 2015.

Lauren was easier, of course. It was a straightforward tale. They had argued at the house. She had attacked him, and he had defended himself, and in the course of that defence she had been seriously wounded, too grievously to save. So, in an effort to spare his son the truth, and – he admitted – to spare himself a prison sentence, he drove her to the river, carried her body to the top of the cliff, and threw her, lifeless now, into the water.

DS Morgan listened politely, but she stopped him there. 'Was your son with you at this time, Mr Townsend?' she asked.

'He didn't see anything,' Patrick replied. 'He was too little, and too frightened, to understand what was happening. He didn't see his mother get hurt, and he didn't see her fall.'

'He didn't watch you throw her from the cliff?'

It took every ounce of his strength not to leap across

the table and smack her. 'He didn't see *anything*. I had to put him in the car because I couldn't leave a six-year-old alone in the house during a thunderstorm. If you had children, you would understand that. He didn't see anything. He was confused, and so I told him . . . a version of the truth that would make sense to him. That he could make sense of.'

'A version of the truth?'

'I told him a story – that's what you do with children, with things they won't be able to understand. I told him a story he could live with, one which would make his life liveable. Don't you see that?' Try as he might, he couldn't stop his voice from rising. 'I wasn't going to leave him alone, was I? His mother was gone, and if I went to prison, what would have happened to him then? What sort of life would he have had? He would have been put in care. I've seen what happens to kids who grow up in care, there's not one of them that doesn't come out damaged and perverted. I have protected him,' Patrick said, pride swelling his chest, 'all his life.'

The story of Nel Abbott was, inevitably, less easy to recount. When he discovered that she had been speaking to Nickie Sage and taking her allegations about Lauren seriously, he became concerned. Not that she would go to the police, no. She wasn't interested in justice or anything like that, she was only interested in sensationalizing her worthless art. What concerned him was that she might say something upsetting to Sean. Once again, he was protecting his son. 'It's what fathers do,' he pointed out. 'Though you might not be

aware of that. I'm told yours was a boozer.' He smiled at
Erin Morgan, watching her flinch as that punch landed.
'I'm told he had a temper.'

He said that he arranged to meet Nel Abbott late one
evening to speak about the allegations.

'And she went to meet you at the cliff?' DS Morgan
was incredulous.

Patrick smiled. 'You never met her. You have no idea
of the extent of her vanity, her self-importance. All
I had to do was suggest to her that I would take her
through exactly what happened between Lauren and
me. I would show her how the terrible events of that
night unfolded, right there, on the spot where they took
place. I would tell her the story as it had never been told
before, she would be the first to hear it. Then, once I had
her up there, it was easy. She'd been drinking, she was
unsteady on her feet.'

'And the bracelet?'

Patrick shifted in his seat and forced himself to look
DS Morgan directly in the eye. 'There was a bit of a
struggle, and I grabbed her arm as she was trying to
pull away from me. Her bracelet came off her wrist.'

'You ripped it off – that's what you told me earlier,
isn't it?' She looked down at her notes. 'You "ripped it
off that whore's wrist"?'

Patrick nodded. 'Yes. I was angry, I'll admit. I was
angry that she had been carrying on with my son,
threatening his marriage. She seduced him. Even the
strongest and most moral of men can find themselves
in thrall to a woman who offers herself in that way . . .'

'In what way?'

Patrick ground his teeth. 'Offering a sort of sexual abandon he might not find at home. It's sad, I know. It happens. I was angry about it. My son's marriage is very strong.' Patrick saw DS Morgan's eyebrows shoot up, and again, he had to steel himself. 'I was angry about that. I ripped the bracelet from her wrist. I pushed her.'

PART FOUR

SEPTEMBER

Lena

I THOUGHT I wouldn't want to leave, but I can't look at the river every day, cross it on my way to school. I don't even want to swim in it any more. It's too cold now, in any case. We're going to London tomorrow, I'm almost all packed.

The house will be rented out. I didn't want that. I didn't want people living in our rooms and filling up our spaces, but Jules said that if we didn't we might get squatters, or things might start to fall apart and there would be no one there to pick up the pieces, and I didn't like that idea either. So I agreed.

It'll still be mine. Mum left it to me, so when I'm eighteen (or twenty-one, or something like that) it'll be mine properly. And I will live here again. I know I will. I'll come back when it doesn't hurt so much and I don't see her everywhere I look.

I'm scared about going to London, but I feel better about it than I did. Jules (not Julia) is really odd, she's always going to be odd, she's fucked up. But I'm a bit weird and fucked up too, so maybe we'll be fine. There are things I like about her. She cooks and fusses around me, she tells me off for smoking, she makes me tell her where I'm going and when I'll be back. Like other people's mums do.

In any case, I'm glad it'll just be the two of us, no husband and I'm guessing no boyfriends or anything like that, and at least when I go to my new school no one will know who I am or anything about me. You can remake yourself, Jules said, which I thought was a bit off because, like, what's wrong with me? But I know what she meant. I cut all my hair off and I look different now, and when I go to the new school in London, I won't be the pretty girl that no one likes, I'll just be ordinary.

Josh

LENA CAME OVER to say goodbye. She's cut all her hair off. She's still pretty, but not as pretty as she used to be. I said I liked it more when it was longer and she laughed and said it'll grow back. She said, it'll be long again next time you see me, and that made me feel better because at least she thinks that we'll see each other again, which I wasn't sure about, because she'll be in London now and we're going to Devon, which is not exactly close by. But she said it wasn't that far, only five hours or something, and in a few years she would have her driver's licence and she'd come and get me and see what trouble we could get into.

We sat in my room for a bit. It was kind of awkward because we didn't know what to say to each other. I asked if she'd had any more news and she sort of looked blank and I said, about Mr Henderson, and she shook her head. She didn't seem to want to talk about it. There's been lots of rumours – people at school are saying that she killed him and pushed him into the sea. I think it's rubbish, but even if it isn't, I wouldn't blame her.

I know it would have made Katie really unhappy for something to happen to Mr Henderson, but she doesn't know, does she? There's no such thing as an afterlife. All that matters are the people who are left, and I think that things have improved. Mum and Dad aren't happy, but they're getting better, they're different than they were. Relieved, maybe? Like they don't have to wonder any more, about why. They've got something they can point to and say, there, that's why. *Something to hold on to*, someone said, and I can see that, although for me I don't think any of it will ever make any sense.

Louise

THE SUITCASES WERE in the car and the boxes were labelled and just before noon they would hand over the keys. Josh and Alec were doing a quick tour of Beckford, saying their goodbyes, but Louise had stayed behind.

Some days were better than others.

Louise had stayed to say goodbye to the house where her daughter had lived, the only home she'd ever known. She had to bid farewell to the height chart in the cupboard under the stairs, to the stone step in the garden where Katie had fallen and cut her knee, where for the first time Louise had had to face that her child wouldn't be perfect, she would be blemished, scarred. She had to say goodbye to her bedroom, where she and her daughter had sat and chatted while Katie blow-dried her hair and applied her lipstick and said that she was going to Lena's later and would it be all right if she stayed the night? How many times, she wondered, had that been a lie?

(The thing that kept her awake at night – one of the things – was that day by the river when she'd been so touched, so moved, to see tears in Mark Henderson's eyes when he offered his condolences.)

Lena had come to say goodbye and had brought with her Nel's manuscript, the pictures, the notes, a USB with all the computer files. 'Do what you want with it,' she said. 'Burn it if you like. I don't want to look at any of it again.' Louise was glad that Lena had come, and gladder still that she would never have to see her again. 'Can you forgive me, do you think?' Lena asked. 'Will you ever?' And Louise said that she already had, which was a lie, spoken out of kindness.

Kindness was her new project. She hoped it might be gentler on the soul than anger. And in any case, while she knew that she could never forgive Lena – for her dissembling, for her secret-keeping, for simply *existing* where her own daughter did not – she couldn't hate her either. Because if anything was clear, anything at all, if anything in this horror was without doubt, it was Lena's love for Katie.

DECEMBER

Nickie

NICKIE'S BAGS WERE PACKED.

Things were quieter in the town. It was always like that with winter coming, but lots of people had moved on, too. Patrick Townsend was rotting in his cell (ha!) and his son had run away to find some peace. Good luck to him with that. The Mill House was empty, Lena Abbott and her aunt off to London. The Whittakers had left, too – the house was on the market for less than a week, it seemed, before some people with a Range Rover and three children and a dog turned up.

Things were quieter in her head, too. Jeannie wasn't talking as loudly as she used to, and when she did, it was more of a chat, less of a tirade. These days, Nickie found she spent less time sitting at the window looking out and more time in bed. She felt very tired and her legs ached more than ever.

In the morning, she was going to Spain, for two weeks in the sunshine. Rest and recreation, that was what she needed. The money came as a surprise: ten thousand pounds from Nel Abbott's estate, left to one Nicola Sage of Marsh Street, Beckford. Whoever would have thought it? But then perhaps Nickie shouldn't have been surprised, because Nel was really the only one who'd ever listened. Poor soul! Much good it did her.

Erin

I WENT BACK just before Christmas. I can't really say why, except that I'd dreamed about the river almost every night, and I thought a trip to Beckford might exorcize the demon.

I left the car by the church and walked north from the pool, up the cliff, past a few bunches of flowers dying in cellophane. I walked all the way to the cottage. It was hunched and miserable, with its curtains drawn and red paint splashed on the door. I tried the handle, but it was locked, so I turned and crunched down over the frosted grass to the river, which was pale blue and silent, mist rising off it like a ghost. My breath hung white in the air in front of me, my ears ached with the cold. Should have worn a hat.

I came to the river because there was nowhere else to go, and no one to talk to. The person I really wanted to speak to was Sean, but I couldn't find him. I was told he'd moved to a place called Pity Me in County Durham – it sounds made up, but it isn't. The town is there, but he wasn't. The address I was given turned out to be an empty house with a TO LET sign outside. I even contacted HMP Frankland, which is where Patrick will see out the rest of his days, but they said the old man hadn't had a single visitor since his arrival.

I wanted to ask Sean for the truth. I thought he might tell me, now he's no longer with the police. I thought he might be able to explain how he'd lived the life he did and whether, when he was supposedly investigating Nel's death, he'd known about his father all along. It wouldn't be such a stretch. He'd been protecting his father all his life, after all.

The river itself offered no answers. When, a month back, a fisherman dug a mobile phone out of the mud in which his wellington boots were planted, I had hope. But Nel Abbott's phone told us nothing we hadn't already gleaned from her phone records. If there were damning photographs, images that would explain all that was left unexplained, we had no way of accessing them – the phone wouldn't even turn on, it was dead, its insides clogged and corroded by silt and water.

After Sean left, there was a mountain of paperwork to get through, an inquiry, questions asked and left unanswered over what Sean knew and when, and why the fuck the whole thing had been handled as badly as it had. And not just Nel's case, but Henderson's, too: how was it that he was able to disappear without trace from under our noses?

As for me, I just went over and over that last interview with Patrick, the story he told. Nel's bracelet torn from her wrist, Patrick grabbing her arm. The struggle they'd had up there on the cliff before he pushed her. But there had been no bruises in the places where he said he had grabbed her, no marks on her wrist where he'd torn off that bracelet, no signs of any struggle whatsoever. And the clasp on the bracelet was unbroken.

I did point all of this out at the time, but after everything that had happened, after Patrick's confession and Sean's resignation and all the general arse-covering and buck-passing, no one was really in the mood to listen.

I sat by the river and I felt as I'd been feeling for a while: that all this, Nel's story and Lauren's and Katie's too, it was all incomplete, unfinished. I never really saw all there was to see.

Helen

HELEN HAD AN aunt who lived outside Pity Me, just north of Durham. She had a farm, and Helen could remember visiting one summer, feeding donkeys with bits of carrot and picking blackberries in the hedgerows. The aunt was no longer there; Helen wasn't sure about the farm. The town was shabbier and poorer than she'd remembered and there were no donkeys to be seen, but it was small and anonymous and no one paid her any mind.

She'd found herself a job for which she was overqualified, and a small ground-floor flat with a patio at the back. It got the sun in the afternoon. When they first got to the town, they rented a house, but that only lasted a matter of weeks and then she woke up one morning and Sean was gone, so she gave the keys back to the landlord and started looking again.

She hadn't tried to call him. She knew he wasn't coming back. Their family was broken, it was always going to break without Patrick, he was the glue that held them together.

Her heart, too, was shattered in ways she didn't like to think about. She hadn't been to visit Patrick. She knew she shouldn't even feel sorry for him – he had admitted killing his wife, murdering Nel Abbott in cold blood.

Not cold blood, no. That's not right. Helen understood that Patrick saw things in very black and white terms, and that he believed, genuinely believed, that Nel Abbott was a threat to their family, to their togetherness. She was. And so he acted. He did it for Sean, and he did it for her. That's not so cold-blooded, is it?

But every night she had the same nightmare: Patrick holding her tabby under the water. In the dream, his eyes were sealed shut but the cat's were open, and when the struggling animal twisted its head around towards her, she saw that its eyes were bright green, just like Nel Abbott's.

She slept badly, and she was lonely. A few days previously she had driven twenty miles to the nearest garden centre to purchase a rosemary bush. And later that day she was driving to the animal-rescue centre over in Chester-le-Street, to select a suitable cat.

JANUARY

Jules

IT'S AN ODD thing, to sit across the breakfast table every
morning from fifteen-year-old you. She has your same
bad table manners, and rolls her eyes as hard as you did
when this is pointed out. She sits at the table with her
feet tucked up underneath her on the chair, bony knees
sticking out to either side, exactly the way that you used
to do. She adopts the same dreamlike expression when
she is lost in music, or thought. She doesn't listen. She
is wilful and annoying. She sings, constantly and tune-
lessly, just like Mum did. She has our father's laugh. She
kisses me on the cheek every morning before she goes
to school.

I cannot make up to you the things I did wrong – my
refusal to listen to you, my eagerness to think the worst
of you, my failure to help you when you were desperate, my failure to even try to love you. Because there is
nothing I can do for you, my atonement will have to
be an act of motherhood. Many acts of motherhood. I

could not be a sister to you, but I will try to be a mother to your child.

In my tiny, ordered Stoke Newington flat, she wreaks havoc on a daily basis. It takes an enormous effort of will not to become anxious and panicked by the chaos. But I'm trying. I remember the fearless version of myself who surfaced the day I confronted Lena's father; I would like that woman to return. I would like to have more of that woman in me, more of you in me, more of Lena. (When Sean Townsend dropped me home on the day of your funeral, he told me I was like you, and I denied it, I said I was the anti-Nel. I used to be proud of that. Not any more.)

I try to take pleasure in the life I have with your daughter, since she's the only family I have, or will ever have now. I take pleasure in her, and comfort in this: the man who killed you will die in jail, not too long from now. He is paying for what he did to his wife, and to his son, and to you.

Patrick

PATRICK NO LONGER dreamed of his wife. Nowadays, he had a different dream, in which that day at the house played out differently. Instead of confessing to the detective, he took the paring knife from the table and put it into her heart, and when he was done with her he started on Nel Abbott's sister. The excitement of it built and built until, finally sated, he pulled the knife from the sister's chest and looked up, and there was Helen, watching, tears coursing down her cheeks and blood dripping from her hands.

'Dad, don't,' she said. 'You're scaring her.'

When he woke, it was always Helen's face he thought of, her stricken expression when he told them what he'd done. He was grateful that he did not have to witness Sean's reaction. By the time his son returned to Beckford that evening, Patrick's confession had been made in full. Sean came to visit him once, on remand. Patrick doubted he would come again, which broke his heart, because everything he had done, the stories he had told and the life he had constructed, it had all been for Sean.

Sean

I AM NOT what I think I am.

I was not who I thought I was.

When things started to fracture, when I started to frac-ture, with Nel saying things she shouldn't have said, I held the world together by repeating: *Things are the way they are, the way they've always been. They cannot be different.*

I was the child of a suicided mother and a good man. When I was the child of a suicided mother and a good man, I became a police officer; I married a decent and responsible woman and lived a decent and responsible life. It was simple, and it was clear.

There were doubts, of course. My father told me that after my mother died, I didn't speak for three days. But I had a memory – what I thought was a memory – of speaking to kind, sweet Jeannie Sage. She drove me back to her house that night, didn't she? Didn't we sit, eating cheese on toast? Didn't I tell her how we'd gone to the river in the car together. *Together?* she asked me. *All three of you?* I thought it best not to speak at all then, because I didn't want to get things wrong.

I thought I remembered all three of us being in the car, but my father told me that was a nightmare.

In the nightmare, it wasn't the storm that woke me, it was my father shouting. My mother, too, they were saying ugly things to one another. Her: *failure, brute*; him: *slut, whore, not fit to be a mother*. I heard a sharp sound, a slap. And then some other noises. And then no noise at all.

Just the rain, the storm.

Then a chair scraping across the floor, the back door opening. In the nightmare, I crept down the stairs and stood outside the kitchen, holding my breath. I heard my father's voice again, lower, muttering. Something else: a dog, whimpering. But we didn't have a dog. (In the nightmare, I wondered if my parents were arguing because my mother had brought a stray dog home. It was the sort of thing she'd do.)

In the nightmare, when I realized I was alone in the house, I ran outside, and both my parents were there, they were getting into the car. They were leaving me, abandoning me. I panicked, I ran screaming to the car and clambered into the back seat. My father dragged me out, yelling and cursing. I clung to the door handle, I kicked and spat and bit my father's hand.

In the nightmare, there were three of us in the car: my father driving, me in the back, and my mother in the passenger seat, not sitting up properly but slumped against the door. When we rounded a sharp bend, she moved, her head lolling over to the right so that I could see her, I could see the blood on her head and on the side of her face. I could see that she was trying to speak, but I couldn't understand what she was saying, her words sounded strange as though she were talking in a language I didn't understand. Her face looked strange, too, lopsided, her mouth twisted, her eyes were white as they rolled back into her head. Her tongue lolled from her mouth like a dog's; pink, frothy saliva oozed from the side of her mouth. In the nightmare, she reached for me and touched my hand and I was terrified, I cowered back in my seat and clung to the door, trying to get as far away from her as I could.

My father said, Your mother reaching for you, that was a nightmare, Sean. That wasn't real. It's like that time you said you could remember having kippers at Craster with your mum and me, but you were only three months old then. You said you remembered the smokehouse, but it was only because you'd seen a picture. It was like that.

That made sense. It didn't feel right, but at least it made sense.

When I was twelve, I remembered something else: I remembered the storm, running out into the rain, but this time, my father wasn't getting into the car, he was putting my mother into it. Helping her into the passenger seat. That came to me very clearly, it didn't seem to be part of the nightmare, the quality of the memory seemed different. In it, I was afraid, but it was a different sort of terror, less visceral than the one I felt when my mother reached for me. It troubled me, that memory, so I asked Dad about it.

He dislocated my shoulder knocking me against the wall, but it was what happened afterwards that stuck. He said he needed to teach me a lesson, so he took a filleting knife and cut cleanly across my wrist. It was a warning. 'This is so you remember,' he said. 'So you never forget. If you do, it'll be different next time. I'll cut the other way.' He placed the tip of the blade on my right wrist, at the base of my palm, and dragged its point slowly towards my elbow. 'Like that. I don't want to discuss this again, Sean. You know that. We've talked about it quite enough. We don't mention your mother. What she did was shameful.'

He told me about the seventh circle of hell, where suicides are turned to thorny bushes and fed upon by Harpies. I asked him what a Harpy was and he said, your mother was one. It was confusing: was she the thorny bush, or was she the Harpy? I thought of the nightmare, of her in the car, reaching out to me, her mouth open and bloody drool dripping from her lips. I didn't want her to feed upon me.

When my wrist healed, I found the scar very sensitive and quite useful. Whenever I found myself drifting, I would touch it, and most times, it brought me back to myself.

There was always a fault line there, in me, between my understanding of what I knew had happened, what I knew myself to be and my father to be, and the strange, slippery sense of wrongness. Like dinosaurs not being in the Bible, it was something that made no sense and yet I knew it had to be. It had to be, because I had been told these things were true, both Adam and Eve *and* brontosaurus. Over the years there were occasional shifts, and I felt the tremor of earth above the fault line, but the quake didn't come until I met Nel.

Not at the beginning. At the beginning it was about her, about us together. She accepted, with some disappointment, the story I told her, the story I knew to be true. But after Katie died, Nel changed. Katie's death made her different. She started talking to Nickie Sage more and more, and she no longer believed what I'd told her. Nickie's story fitted so much better with Nel's view of the Drowning Pool, the place she had conjured up, a place of persecuted women, outsiders and misfits fallen foul of patriarchal edicts, and my father was the embodiment of all that. She told me that she believed my father had killed my mother and the fault line widened; everything shifted, and the more it shifted, the more odd visions returned to me, as nightmares at first and then as memories.

She'll bring you low, my father said when he found out about Nel and me. She did more than that. She unmade me. If I listened to her, if I believed her story, I was no longer the tragic son of a suicided mother and a decent family man, I was the son of a monster. More than that, worse than that: I was the boy who watched his mother die and said nothing. I was the boy, the teenager, the man who protected her killer, lived with her killer, and loved him.

I found that man a difficult man to be.

The night she died, we met at the cottage, as we had before. I lost myself. She wanted so much for me to get to the truth, she said it would release me from myself, from a life I didn't want. But she was thinking of herself, too, of the things she had discovered and what it would mean for her, her work, her life, her place. That, more than anything: her place was no longer a suicide spot. It was a place to get rid of troublesome women.

We walked back towards the town together. We'd done it often before – since my father had discovered us at the cottage, I no longer parked the car outside, I left it in town instead. She was dizzy with drink and sex and renewed purpose. You need to remember it, she told me. You need to stand there and look at it and remember it, Sean. The way it happened. Now. At night.

It was raining, I told her. When she died, it was raining. It wasn't clear like tonight. We should wait for the rain.

She didn't want to wait.

We stood at the top of the cliff looking down. I didn't see it from here, Nel, I said. I wasn't here. I was in the trees below, I couldn't see anything. She was on the edge of the cliff, her back to me.

Did she cry out? she asked me. When she fell, did you hear anything?

I closed my eyes and I saw her in the car, reaching out for me, and I wanted to get away from her. I shrank back, but she kept coming at me and I tried to push her away. With my hands in the small of Nel's back, I pushed her away.

Acknowledgements

The source of this particular river is not all that easy to find, but my first thanks must go to Lizzy Kremer and Harriet Moore, providers of strange ideas and strong opinions, challenging reading lists and inexhaustible support.

Finding the source was one thing, following the river's course quite another: thank you to my exceptional editors, Sarah Adams and Sarah McGrath, for helping me find my way. Thank you also to Frankie Gray, Kate Samano and Danya Kukafka for all their editorial support.

Thank you to Alison Barrow, without whose friendship and advice I might never have made it through the past couple of years.

For their support and encouragement, reading recommendations and brilliant ideas, thank you to Simon Lipskar, Larry Finlay, Geoff Kloske, Kristin Cochrane, Amy Black, Bill Scott-Kerr, Liz Hohenadel, Jynne Martin, Tracey Turriff, Kate Stark, Lydia Hirt and Mary Stone.

For their striking and beautiful jacket designs, thank you to Richard Ogle, Jaya Miceli and Helen Yentus.

Thank you to Alice Howe, Emma Jamison, Emily Randle, Camilla Dubini and Margaux Vialleron for all their work to ensure this book can be read in dozens of different languages.

Thank you to Markus Dohle, Madeleine McIntosh and Tom Weldon.

For professional insights, thank you to James Ellson, formerly of Greater Manchester Police, and Professor Sharon Cowan of the Edinburgh Law School – needless to say that any legal or procedural errors are entirely of my own making.

Thanks to the Rooke sisters of Windsor Close for a lifetime of friendship and inspiration.

Thanks to Mr Rigsby for all his advice and constructive criticism.

Thank you to Ben Maiden for keeping me grounded.

Thank you to my parents, Glynne and Tony, and to my brother Richard.

Thank you to each and every one of my long-suffering friends.

And thank you to Simon Davis, for everything.

A Q&A with the author, Paula Hawkins

How would you introduce *Into the Water* to your readers, and what do you hope readers will find within it?
Into the Water is a psychological suspense novel centred on the fractured relationship between two sisters, Nel and Jules. When Nel dies unexpectedly, Jules finds herself trying to figure out not just what has happened to her elder sister, but what has happened between the two of them to leave them so estranged. This is a book of many mysteries. It is about searching for answers, for meaning.

Fans of *The Girl on the Train* will be curious to see the similarities or differences between that book and this one. Do you see a through-line?
They are both novels of psychological suspense, both are focused primarily on women, their relationships to each other and to society around them. The unreliability of memory plays a part in both books, although it occurs in a very different, more fundamental way in *Into the Water*.

Once again, the story is narrated from multiple points of view, although this time I have many more characters' perspectives, and six different first-person narratives. Necessarily, these narratives are unreliable: all first-person narration is unreliable. Everybody lies, exaggerates, obfuscates to a greater or lesser degree.

Memory is clearly a subject that interests you. Tell us a little more about this fascination.

We trust our memories implicitly – how could we not? They allow us to make sense of the worlds we live in, they inform who we are and how we relate to people. And yet, they aren't trustworthy. All of us mis-remember things, often things from childhood, sometimes events from later in life. All of us are capable of altering our own stories through the telling of them. In many cases, misremembered stories are minor, trivial. But I wanted to ask: what if someone mis-remembered something crucial, something fundamental to their identity, to the wholeness of their life? What might happen to them when they discovered that what they thought was solid was built on shifting sands?

Into the Water, like The Girl on the Train, is narrated from multiple perspectives. What do you like about this storytelling approach?

I enjoy the insight that shifts in perspective can give; the way that viewing one event through the eyes of different characters changes our understanding of that event, giving us a fuller picture of what happened, or raising doubts in our minds, not just about the event itself but about the motivations of the characters telling us the story.

I like the immediacy of first-person narration, but it can be limiting; multiple first-person perspectives allow the reader to immerse herself in the characters' psychologies, to more fully understand their motiva-tions and their weaknesses.

You write about childhood in this book, something that is new in your work, with a focus on the vastly divergent ways that members of the same family can remember the same events. What inspired this decision?

The stories we tell about ourselves and our families are definitive; they inform the people we become. So it fascinates me the way members of the same family can tell such different stories about living in the same home, with the same people. In this book I wanted to explore the way children regard adult relationships, adult actions and decisions, and the way they limit their interpretations of these things along lines of what will make sense to them – sometimes with great perspicacity, sometimes with comical, or disastrous, misunderstanding.

Into the Water **is set in a tiny rural town – very different from the suburban London setting for** *The Girl on the Train*. **What inspired this imaginary town of Beckford?**

I should say first of all that the Beckford of the book does not exist. It is an entirely fictional town, placed in a mostly non-fictional landscape. I wanted to write about a small community, because I was interested in what living in a small town does to people: it can foster a great sense of solidarity, of neighbourhood, but it can also be quite suffocating to live somewhere where everyone knows everyone else. I wondered whether this might encourage a culture of secrecy, whether it might drive some members – particularly the young – to seek ways in which to rebel, to break out of their designated roles.

The reader can suspect all the characters in *Into the Water*, because they all seem to have a dark side, and this ensures a brilliantly twisty read. Do you think we do all have a dark side?
I think that people are capable of extraordinary things – good and bad – given the right (or wrong) circumstances. Subject to exceptional pressures, we might all behave in ways we could not conceive of in our ordinary, day-to-day existence.

A Guide for Reading Groups

Family relationships, particularly the bond between sisters, feature heavily in *Into the Water*. How do you think Lena is affected by Nel and Jules's estrangement? How does it influence her friendship with Katie?

Jules and Nel's estrangement hinges on a misremembering of an event in their past. Are there any childhood or teenage memories you have that are no longer as clear when you look back now? How has this novel made you view your past, and the way it reflects upon your present?

Within the novel there are several inappropriate relationships – for example, Katie and Mark; Sean and Nel; Helen and Patrick. How does the depiction of the relationships between these characters affect your interpretation of their behaviour and actions?

'Beckford is not a suicide spot. Beckford is a place to get rid of troublesome women.' Discuss the gender dynamic in *Into the Water*. How much power does each of the women in the novel hold? What are the different types of power they hold?

Into the Water contains several different voices and perspectives. How did this structure affect your reading of the novel?

How do the epigraphs relate to the novel? Does one speak to you more than another? If so, why?

The structure of the novel means that we get tremendous insight into our suspects throughout. Who did you originally think was responsible for Nel's death? Did your opinion change as the plot developed?

Was there a particular character you identified with? Was there a particular moment you found moving, surprising, or terrifying?

Many of the characters in the novel are grieving – some from more recent, raw losses and others from historic ones. How sympathetic were you to these characters? Was there a character you felt more sympathy for than another? Does their grief excuse their behaviour?

Nickie Sage represents the legacy of witches that haunts the novel. Do you believe she sees things others cannot? Do you agree with the way she behaves?

Paula Hawkins worked as a journalist for fifteen years before turning her hand to fiction. Born and brought up in Zimbabwe, Paula moved to London in 1989 and has lived there ever since. Her first thriller, *The Girl on the Train*, has been a global phenomenon, selling almost 20 million copies worldwide. Published in over forty languages, it has been a No.1 bestseller around the world and was a No.1 box-office-hit film starring Emily Blunt.

Into the Water is her second stand-alone thriller.

#intothewater

EVERY DAY THE SAME. UNTIL TODAY.

Rachel catches the same commuter train every
morning. She knows it will wait at the same signal
each time, overlooking a row of back gardens. She's
even started to feel like she knows the people who
live in one of the houses. Their life – as she sees
it – is perfect. If only Rachel could be that happy.

And then she sees something shocking, and
in one moment everything changes.

Now Rachel has a chance to become a part
of the lives she's only watched from afar.

Now they'll see: she's much more than
just the girl on the train . . .

dead good

For everyone who finds a crime story irresistible.

Discover the very best **crime and thriller books** and get tailored recommendations to help you choose what to read next.

Read **exclusive interviews with top authors** or join our **live web chats** and speak to them directly.

And it's not just about books. We'll be bringing you **specially commissioned features** on everything criminal, from **TV and film** to **true crime stories**.

We also love a good competition. Our **monthly contest** offers you the chance to win the latest thrilling fiction, plus there are DVD box sets and devices to be won.

Sign up for our free fortnightly newsletter at www.deadgoodbooks.co.uk/signup

Join the conversation on: